BOOKS BY CORRINE JACKSON

If I Lie

The Sense Thieves series

Touched

Pushed

Pushed

CORRINE JACKSON

KENSINGTON PUBLISHING CORP.

www.kensingtonbooks.com

KTEEN BOOKS are published by

Kensington Publishing Corp.
119 West 40th Street
New York, NY 10018

All Kensington titles, imprints, and distributed lines are available at special quantity discounts for bulk purchases for sales promotions, premiums, fund-raising, educational, or institutional use.

Special book excerpts or customized printings can also be created to fit specific needs. For details, write or phone the office of the Kensington special sales manager: Kensington Publishing Corp., 119 West 40th Street, New York, NY 10018, attn: Special Sales Department; phone 1-800-221-2647.

KENSINGTON and the KTeen logo are Reg. U.S. Pat. & TM Off.

ISBN-13: 978-0-7582-7334-5
ISBN-10: 0-7582-7334-7

First Trade Paperback Printing: December 2013

10 9 8 7 6 5 4 3 2 1

Printed in the United States of America

First electronic edition: December 2013

ISBN-13: 978-0-7582-9155-4
ISBN-10: 0-7582-9155-8

To my dear friend, Kari—

"Writing" at Starbucks, daily sanity checks, asthma-inducing laughter—
these are the things a lifelong friend is made of.

Love,
Me

ACKNOWLEDGMENTS

To my agent, Laura Bradford, thank you for loving this series and kindly talking me down from the ledge of a deadline meltdown, tears and all. It helps to know that you'll be there when I freak out.

I was lucky enough to work with two editors on this book. Megan Records, thank you for enthusiastically climbing aboard when my plot jumped rails. My wide-eyed terror turned to outright laughter at your love of a certain character that would not stay where I'd assigned him. And to Martin Biro, you took over mid-series, and you made the transition seamless. I will forever be grateful for that and your dedication ever since. The team at KTeen has been amazing to work with, especially Vida Engstrand, Craig Bentley, Arthur Maisel, Alicia Condon, Colleen Andrews, and Alexandra Nicolajsen.

I wrote this book in my final semester at Spalding University's MFA program with the encouragement of my faculty mentor, Mary Yukari Waters, who had a way of seeing my plot holes before I fell in them. I was also lucky enough to workshop the first chapters in Italy with faculty mentor Lesléa Newman and fellow students Emily Smith, Lisa McShane, Cheri Thomas, Crystal Gold, Leah Henderson, and Kathie Wrightson.

Some readers proved invaluable in giving me feedback on various drafts. To Kari Young, Jay Lehmann, Stephanie Kuehn, and Karen Langford, you are the best critique group bar none. And to my beta readers, Gina Rosati, Kari Young, Debra Driza, and Jennifer Shaw Wolf, your notes and comments made a world of difference.

Lots of love to the Class of 2k12, Bookanistas, Apocalypsies, and YA Rebels groups for seeing me through a crazy year.

And last, but never least, Kym, my smart, generous sister, you manage my launch parties like Martha Stewart so I can fret about reading and having the right Sharpie. Steve, you always nag me for my next book, and that is the BEST compliment. Mom, you flyer parking lots like a pro. To all of my family, thank you for the love, support, and story fodder. I love you more than SpaghettiOs and llamas, though not necessarily in that order.

From Track 2 on Remy O'Malley's iPod:

Protectors found the key to immortality. If they killed a Healer, they absorbed her energy and became immortal. Her energy cured them of any possible sickness, including the greatest disease—aging. See, the war was never really about money. Oh yeah, the Protectors were greedy, too, but what they wanted was eternal youth.

But nothing comes for free. The Protectors got their immortality all right, but it cost them. When they stole a Healer's energy, they got more than they counted on. The surge of energy shorted out their systems, and the Protectors lost the use of most of their senses. Touch, taste, smell—all gone in the blink of an eye.

Can you imagine living forever and never being able to feel another person's touch?

It's ironic, isn't it? The Protectors are in a living hell of their own making, and the Healers are the only ones who can cure them.

Since the Protectors discovered what they'd done, they've been hunting the few Healers that remain. Those Healers caught have a single fate: death. It's your energy, see? It's like radiation for cancer patients: a full dose kills what makes them human while a small dose is therapeutic. It makes them feel alive again. They take their time to draw it out, keep a Healer like a pet to feel a little at a time, until the Healer is all used up. Dead. The sensations never last long, though, so they are always on the hunt for another Healer to feed on.

But some time ago, we made a discovery of our own. It's another reason why I kept you hidden all these years. Because of what you can do. You're not like other Healers.

Oh Remy, you have the power to make them mortal again.

It's what they want more than anything, and they'll kill you to get it. If you think they've found you, run. Because if they catch you . . . Don't. Get. Caught.

Now, the third track will tell you how to find your grandfather. I should've taken you to him long ago, but I couldn't . . . I ignored my instincts and we ended up . . . You're better than I am, kid.

Trust your instincts.

CHAPTER ONE

*G*abe Blackwell never saw me coming.

In the tick of a hummingbird's wings, I had launched myself at his back, taking him down in a tangle of arms and legs. Our bodies hit the blue mat in the middle of the Blackwells' gym with a thud that shivered from my teeth to my backbone.

Gabe's breath hissed out when Asher, leaning against a rack of weights, laughed at his older brother's defeat at the hands of a gangly girl half his size. I took advantage of Gabe's distraction to wrap an arm around his neck, putting the whole of my weight into pinning him. My height rivaled his, with me close to six feet and him just over, but he had a good sixty pounds of muscle on me. Unwilling to loosen my hold for even a second, I considered biting him in retribution for the thousand times he'd insulted me. And then I wondered if I might have given away my abnormal speed. I really hoped not.

"What is it you're always yelling at me?" I pretended to think about it, enjoying my little victory over my boyfriend's brother. With his sculpted features, Gabe never lacked for company, and he never let anyone forget it. I savored any opportunity I had to take his ego down a notch. "Oh right. I remember now. Never turn your back on the enemy, Protector."

Gabe cursed and cut my amusement short when his muscles tightened and gathered under me. He might look twenty to my eighteen, but Gabe had lived more than a century, and his experience with our powers surpassed mine. Too late, I tried to strengthen my grip. The thought had scarcely occurred to me when I found my face planted in the mat with his knee bending my spine like a bow.

"I also told you to concentrate instead of getting cocky." The cheer in Gabe's proper British voice grated on my nerves. "Now, be a good little mortal, and say it."

His humiliating version of saying "uncle," he meant. Ten minutes ago I'd bet him that I could take him down in a fair fight, and he'd agreed with terms of his own if I lost.

"Come on, Healer. Say it. Tell me I'm the greatest Protector who ever lived."

His knee pressed harder, as he settled in with more of his weight. Grunting, I tested my range of motion and felt an electric storm of agony gathering inside my body. Powerful energy, but not enough to turn the tables. *Almost there, you smug jackass.*

"All right." Defeat colored my tone, and my body went limp. "You win. I'll say it."

I could picture the smirk on his carved, handsome face, and I used the anger to steel myself against the coming pain. In an explosion of movement, my body jerked backward, forcing his knee to dig in that little bit more I needed. A disk popped in my spine and slid sideways. The tempest exploded out of me, firing my pain into Gabe. Another *pop* and he collapsed with a *thump* next to me, his back now screwed up, too. Poetic justice. In the quiet that followed, I pressed my cheek into the cushioned mat and studied my nemesis, curled up in the fetal position next to me.

My voice came out weaker than I intended when I declared, "I am the greatest Protector who ever lived."

Asher choked on a laugh and came to kneel at my side. With his dark chocolate hair falling forward to cover the two-inch white scar cutting through one eyebrow, he looked like a less perfect, leaner version of Gabe. The concern in his dark green eyes almost made up for the pain. He hated watching Gabe pound me in these training sessions, but he'd tried training me himself and it had been a disaster. We'd been too afraid of hurting each other to take it seriously, and we both knew the training was necessary. I could choose to ignore the danger in the world I'd fallen into these last months, or I could do my damnedest to be prepared for the day the other Protectors—the ones who were not like these two—found me. Was there really a choice when it came to protecting my new family? My dad, stepmom, and sister needed me to be ready.

"You okay?" Asher asked, looping a wayward strand of blond hair behind my ear.

Are you kidding? I shut Gabe up for once. I'm friggin' brilliant. Except I think I need a chiropractor.

Asher smiled at my triumphant thoughts, more at ease with hearing my voice in his head than any person should be. Our bonding had its ups and downs. "Want my help?" he asked.

He meant to allow me to use his Protector energy to heal myself.

I shook my head. "Let me take care of Gabe first."

Asher nodded and eased me closer to his brother.

"Would either of you care to explain what happened?" Gabe said in a tight voice.

He lay unmoving, his spine out of alignment in an injury that mirrored mine. Unused to the return of their sense of touch after a century of feeling nothing, all the

Blackwells suffered when my power reminded them what it felt like to be human. Of course, Gabe rarely let me get close enough to use my ability on him, and I couldn't really blame him. The two times I'd slipped through his defenses during training had resulted in my breaking his arm and dislocating his shoulder. And now this.

I didn't particularly like Gabe, but pain humanized him. It tightened the corners of his green eyes, making him look vulnerable. For once, he reminded me of Asher, instead of his usual distant self. I fought the instinct to comfort him, knowing he would tear me apart before admitting to a weakness.

"Isn't it obvious?" I answered, setting aside my pain. "I took you down. I wiped the floor with you. It was a WWF Smackdown, and I won. Twice."

"Like hell you did."

He breathed through his nose when I ran a hand over his spine. I couldn't loan him my energy like the Protectors could do for Healers, but I could use my own to reorganize his insides. Gabe didn't like my touch, or the sensations it brought with it, but he put up with it at times like these. Taking pity on him, I adjusted my ability to the workings of his immortal body. The racing heart, the sleek, oiled machinery that ran hotter and faster than any human's; these things had to be accounted for when I sent my energy unwinding into his body. The *hum* of my power charged the air, and green sparks crackled where my fingers touched him.

"Twice," I crowed, and Gabe groaned when his back snapped into realignment.

I patted him on the shoulder because the friendly gesture would annoy him, and then collapsed on my stomach, shivering with the near hypothermia that always set in after a difficult healing. A warm hand stroked down my spine, and a little of Asher's familiar power seeped into me.

Closing my eyes, I borrowed his energy to imagine my spine realigned and perfect. I winced when the slipped disk nestled back into place with a sickening *crunch*. Sighing, I rested a moment, enjoying the heat of his skin through my shirt. This was how Protectors and Healers were meant to work together. Before the War. Before the Protectors had nearly hunted the Healers into extinction.

A few moments later, I let Asher haul me to my feet. Both of my arms slipped around his waist to press closer to him, and his fingers caught the belt loops of my jeans to keep me there. He smelled of everything I loved—the woods, the sea, and him.

Gabe rose to his feet with easy grace and stared at us with open disgust. He couldn't figure out how I'd overpowered him, even for a brief moment. In our months of training, I'd never been able to match his speed or strength. Despite my height, I had no curves and most seven-year-old boys had more muscles than me.

My only defense against Gabe had been my ability to transfer my injuries to him, but I couldn't control that power and it only worked after he'd hurt me, and only if I could catch him. Odds had been against me 99.9 percent of the time, which meant a lot of bruises for me and scarcely a scratch on him.

But things had changed a month ago when my stepfather had arrived in Blackwell Falls, Maine. He'd kidnapped me from my new home and nearly tortured me to death. Dean had shot my half sister, Lucy, so he could see how my powers worked when I healed her. Asher had almost died, too, when he stepped in front of a bullet meant for me. To save us both, I had hijacked Asher's energy, using it to stop Dean. My stepfather had died that night, though only Lucy, the Blackwells, and I knew that.

I'd thought that I would die, too, when I'd healed Asher and returned his powers. Two days later I'd woken up in the hospital and discovered instead that some of his abilities had remained in my body. A tiny detail I'd hidden from Gabe with every intention of getting a little petty revenge for all the times he'd mocked and threatened me.

"Show him, Remy," Asher said, his accent falling somewhere between American and British.

I frowned into his T-shirt, the soft blue cotton warm from his skin. "Do I have to? I like him so much better when he's not acting like he's a god."

His voice hinted at a smile. "I know, *mo cridhe,* but it's time to come clean."

If we were together for fifty years, I'd never tire of Asher calling me "my heart" in Gaelic.

"Then I'll never stop saying it," he said, answering my thought. "Stop stalling, and show him."

Sighing, I stepped back from Asher and turned to face Gabe. "Remember when Asher was dying, and he forced his power on me?"

Asher winced at my description. He'd meant to allow me enough time to save myself from Dean, to heal my injuries. None of us had known that the immortality went both ways, or that I could become like them.

Gabe waited in watchful silence.

"Even though I returned his power when I healed him, it changed me."

"Changed you how, Remy?" His low tone reminded me how dangerous Protectors could be. His rare use of my name sent the bad kind of shiver down my spine.

I sucked in a breath and let it out in a rush. "Like this."

A heartbeat later, I'd done two laps around Gabe in a time that would have shamed an Olympic sprinter. The breeze of my movement still ruffled his wavy brown hair long after I'd returned to Asher's side. To any stranger, Gabe's stony expression remained inscrutable, but the tic in his left eye said there would be hell to pay for hiding this new ability from him.

Too calmly, he said, "This happened in May, and it's now June. It's been weeks. Neither of you thought to mention this?"

Asher took a not-so-subtle step in front of me, and I glared at his back. *Don't do that. I don't need you to protect me from your brother.* I considered slugging him when he ignored my thought, but that mental image had no effect on him, either.

"It didn't matter before," Asher said. "Remy's been too weak to train until she recovered from her injuries. She's better, so we're telling you now."

I tried to shove Asher to the side, but even with my increased strength, he proved immobile. Rolling my eyes, I moved to race around him. He heard my intention and grasped the waist of my shirt in his fist to keep me at his side.

Contrary to what you may think, you Neanderthal, this behavior stopped being attractive the first time you were eighteen.

Asher shrugged in response, and I scowled.

"Enough," Gabe commanded, irritated. He hated it when his brother and I communicated silently, leaving him out of the conversation because he couldn't hear my thoughts, too.

Giving up on the tug-of-war with my shirt, I told Gabe, "It was my idea. I wanted to try out my new powers in a fight with you. Learn my limits. And it worked. I learned something."

"What's that?" Gabe asked.

His curiosity sparked, temporarily overcoming his anger as I'd known it would. There had never been another like me with half-Healer, half-Protector blood that we knew about. Every time we thought we knew the limits of my powers, I surprised us all by breaking one of Gabe's bones from across the room during training or causing all of the Blackwells to smell roses when they had traded their senses of touch, taste, and smell to become immortal long ago.

"You've been going easy on me all this time, you big softy," I said. Gabe looked pissed at my accusation, and I laughed, adding in a singsong voice, "Come on, admit it. You *like* me."

Hate would have been a better description of the expression on his face. Healers and Protectors were natural enemies. At best, Gabe put up with me because he loved his brother almost as fiercely as I did. We'd settled on an uneasy truce based on that fact alone. Yet, I could never forget that if not for Asher, Gabe might have killed me the first time our paths crossed. Or worse, I could have ended up bonded to him, the eldest brother, instead of Asher in the natural order of things between our bloodlines.

The idea of Gabe reading my thoughts and using his energy to heal my injuries, freaked me out. I loved Asher, and I'd only just grown used to our connection and the way he could read my mind, fighting it every step of the way since we'd met when I moved to Blackwell Falls to live with my dad three months ago.

Gabe knew the relief I felt bonding to his younger brother instead of him, and whatever he thought about it, he never said. He criticized and bullied me, and I retaliated by teasing him and shoving back. And Asher stood between us, ready to keep us from doing too much damage to each other in the process.

Gabe raised one dark eyebrow at my taunt. "I like you about as much as you like me, I suspect."

I grinned. "Too true."

If I believed Gabe had a sense of humor, I might have thought the corner of his mouth twitched up in amusement. Thank goodness that was impossible. I couldn't handle Gabe if he started cracking jokes. Swinging back toward Asher, I punched his arm, hurting my hand more than I hurt him.

"What was that for?"

"You could have told me that Gabe was holding back all this time." Even with my increased power, he'd taken me down with ease. No way had he been using his full strength in our training before now. Which meant I had more to worry about with the Protectors than I'd realized.

Asher shrugged again. "To what end? Would you rather I have let him break your neck to demonstrate our superior strength?" Before I could punch him again, he grabbed my hand and massaged the bruised knuckle, raising it to his lips. "I happen to like you the way you are, and I'd prefer not finding out what would happen if Gabe harmed you beyond repair."

Though he kept his tone light, the tension in his shoulders hinted at his true feelings. Despite his loyalty to his family and loved ones, he would fight anyone who hurt me. He'd proven that when Gabe threatened me long ago in a wayward attempt to protect their sister, Lottie.

Sighing, I curved my hand to his square jaw. His messy hair had grown past the collar of his shirt and begged my fingers to run through it.

Asher's full lips curved, and he opened my palm to press a kiss in it. "You're doing it again."

Doing what?

Leaning down, he whispered in my ear, "Thinking about how irresistible you find me."

Gabe snorted when he heard Asher. Damned superpower hearing. It was one ability that I hadn't kept when I'd returned Asher's powers.

"Could we get back to the matter at hand? I have things

to do, if the two of you could unglue yourselves from each other."

Asher and I separated with reluctance. Seeing the way Gabe's body tensed, I realized the constant *hum* of my Healer power was hurting him again. Slowly, I raised my mental defenses to protect the Blackwells, blocking Asher from my mind in the process. Caving to the inevitable, I described in detail the increased strength and speed that had been added to my repertoire of healing and sometimes causing injuries. Not immortal like the Protectors or defenseless like the Healers, but something else.

Gabe shot Asher a meaningful look when I finished, and Asher nodded, rubbing his forehead as if a headache had formed there.

Before I could question them, two female voices sounded in the hall outside the gym. Lottie and Lucy were arguing from the sound of it.

"You can't go in there!"

Despite her protest, Lottie had already given up the fight or my petite, powerless sister would have found herself deposited in the forest outside the Blackwells' Victorian-style manor in five seconds flat. Lucy proved me right by shoving past her. My sister had not forgiven Lottie for threatening to reveal my existence to the type of Protectors who would have killed me. Neither had Asher, for that matter, and sometimes I felt bad for Lottie. She didn't want anything to do with me, or the pain I caused her with my proximity. I couldn't really blame her for that.

My half sister and I couldn't have looked more different. Where I had my mother's wavy, dirty-blond hair and our father's height, blue eyes, and tanned skin, Lucy had my stepmother's short red curls, petite frame, brown eyes, and pale skin. Her head skimmed my shoulder when we stood next to each other.

Our upbringings had been polar opposites, too. While Dean had started beating me at eleven, Lucy had been protected and safe, ignorant of Protectors and Healers. I'd wanted to hate her when my father moved me here from New York City, but my sister had made that impossible, accepting me even when she found out what I was. She'd even helped me hide the truth from our friends and parents to protect me.

"Seriously, Lottie, get the hell out of my way," Lucy said.

She strode to Asher and me, ignoring Lottie and Gabe, who terrified her still. The only Blackwell she liked was Asher, and that was because of how I felt about him.

"Hey, Asher," she said. "Sorry to barge in on you."

"Not a problem. You're always welcome here," he said, acting like my sister showed up at his house every day.

"Remy, you finally got a response to the ad today," Lucy said. "I thought you'd want to read it right away."

She held out a sheet of paper, and my hand shook when I took it from her and traced the return e-mail address. My mother had told me that if I ever wanted to reach my grandfather, I should put a death notice for my grandmother in the *New York Times*. The contact information for a false funeral home would be the key to reaching out to the sender. She'd promised that my grandfather had taught her that code before she left home at eighteen and would respond, but I hadn't really believed her. She'd lied so often. I'd run the obituary twice, and Lucy had been helping me wade through the e-mail we'd received at the anonymous e-mail address we'd set up.

"Is it from him?"

Asher's quiet question prodded me to read the e-mail. I wasn't sure what I'd expected, but the tears that came to my eyes surprised me. Stunned, I looked up to find Asher and Lucy staring at me with varying degrees of anxiety. Gabe watched from a distance with his usual blank expression.

"Remy?" Lucy asked, rubbing my arm. "What did he say? Does he want to meet you?"

"Not exactly," I said.

Asher's relief was palpable. He'd supported my decision to find my grandfather, but not without worry. For good reason. My mother had told me how my grandfather had watched Protectors kill my grandmother, a powerful Healer. I'd inherited my abilities from her, and the Protectors had stolen her energy, trading it for a moment of sensation. The death of a Healer in exchange for immortality, but at the cost of their ability to feel, taste, and smell. The death of a Healer to feel human again for five minutes before the sensation faded, and it was on to the next Healer. Who knew how my grandfather would react when he found out I loved a Protector? That I was half-Protector?

Lucy sympathized with me. "I'm sorry, sis. He doesn't deserve you."

Asher's eyes met mine over Lucy's shoulder when she hugged me. Even though he couldn't hear my thoughts through my mental defenses, he knew me. Knew I hadn't said everything. His hand slipped into mine, his heat warming my chilled skin. The familiar touch sent my defenses crashing to the ground, and he knew the truth as if he'd read the e-mail.

"No," I repeated. "He doesn't want to meet me. He wants me to come live with him."

CHAPTER TWO

"*L*ike hell," Asher said.

Looking around the room, I could see that Lucy and Gabe agreed with him. They acted like they supported my decision to contact my grandfather, but when confronted with the reality of the meeting happening, they all wanted me to forget he existed.

The paper crumpled in my hand, as Asher proceeded to outline all the reasons why I should not contact my grandfather again—we had no way of knowing if my grandfather could be trusted outside my mother's word, and she hadn't exactly been the most trustworthy person.

Not only had she allowed my stepfather to beat the hell out of me while she drank herself into a stupor, she'd forced me to witness her own beatings. And when I was old enough to heal both of our injuries, she'd hidden what she'd known about me being a Healer, leaving me alone and terrified by my ability. It was only after she died that I'd discovered what she'd known when I found the recordings she'd left on my iPod. Too little, too late.

And my grandfather had no idea she'd passed away.

Nobody gave me the chance to explain that the e-mail had been written to my mother. It had never occurred to me that he'd mistake me for her, thinking she'd placed the ad, but it should have. On top of everything, I would have to tell him his daughter had died at the hands of my step-father. I opened my mouth to tell everyone this, but then Lucy started in with all the reasons I should ignore my grandfather's e-mail.

My phone rang, and I gladly answered it when my friend Brandon's name popped up on the screen.

"Hey, Brand. What's up?"

"You haven't forgotten Crimson Chaos is playing to-night?"

Brandon's band often played at the Underground. We spoke for a few minutes, and I promised to see him later that night.

Irritated and hurt, I told the others, "I have to go."

"Remy?"

Asher sounded worried, but I just wanted to be alone.

"I'll see you later."

Lucy and I left the Blackwells and went home to get ready. The e-mail was tucked into one of the boots in my closet for safekeeping, though I knew my dad and step-mother would never snoop through my belongings. They had no idea what I was, and I couldn't take the chance they'd discover the truth because I left a letter lying around for them to find.

A crowd of teenagers had already packed into the Un-derground by the time Lucy and I arrived. From the small stage, Brandon's band churned out a raw, aching sound that brought everyone to their feet. Bodies crashed into each other on the fingernail-sized dance floor, bouncing off each other in a sweaty mess. With graduation only a few days away, the seniors celebrated the end of the school year in a feverish frenzy, and the lowerclassmen couldn't help but join in.

I hadn't told anyone yet, but I'd been accepted into two of the three premed programs I'd applied to. It wasn't like my dad not to press me for my post–high school plans, but I'd moved to Blackwell Falls in March and we'd only known each other a short time. I think Ben assumed I'd missed my chance to apply for the fall semester. He didn't know that I'd mailed off my applications months ago. Long before I had to question if college even mattered when every day brought the Protectors closer to my doorstep.

Wanting to forget everything for five minutes, I snaked my way through the crowd with Lucy, until we found a spot next to Greg and Susan on the dance floor. They had their arms around each other, more lost in each other than the music. Lucy and I grinned, delighted that our friends had gone from "just friends" to full-fledged couple. The pretty brunette had crushed on Greg forever before he'd realized he felt the same way about her.

Marina Gilbert, the lead singer of Brandon's band, jumped up and down with the microphone in her hand. Her short blue hair stood on end, and her eyes looked glazed as if she'd been drinking. What her voice lacked, the rest of the band made up for. Brandon hammered out a solo on his guitar, the lights playing over his pierced ears and the tattooed vines inked on his biceps. Like Lucy and Asher, Brandon had made me feel at home in this ocean-side town, even going so far as to teach me to swim so I would be comfortable near the water. Watching him hit his groove, I screamed like a groupie, along with the others.

Hearing my shout, Brandon looked up and grinned when he spotted me. I pressed a button on my phone to light up the screen and waved it over my head like an impromptu lighter. Brandon threw back his head in a laugh.

A body bumped into mine, and strong arms slid around my waist. Asher leaned down to yell over the music, "I should have listened to you. Forgive me for being a jerk?"

The words tickled my ear, and I leaned back into his

embrace, letting him support my weight. The warmth spread wherever we touched, and I thought, *Of course* and *I love you* and *Kiss me.*

My feet left the ground, and I found myself anchored to Asher's side, as he carried me off the dance floor. He pushed his way through the crowd, and his size demanded that people part. I laughed at his urgency and waved to my amused friends. Then we were outside on the club's secluded patio, and he caught my laugh with his mouth. Asher's hands grasped my hips and pulled me on my tiptoes so my mouth came flush with his. Full lips pressed into mine, and I sank into the heat, my fingers arrowing through his hair.

Against my eyelids, a fireworks show exploded. I was lost in Asher, and it didn't register right away that the green sparks were real. We pulled away at the same time, our disappointed sighs mingling. We'd forgotten to put our mental walls up. A side effect of my powers, the green sparks meant my body had set to curing his immortality, a little at a time. Not painful to either of us in these short spurts, but definitely capable of freaking out the innocent bystander who discovered us lighting up the night.

He rested his forehead against mine, a slight grimace curving his mouth down. This had happened before. For some reason—perhaps because of my mixed blood—I affected Asher like no other Healer ever had. He regained the use of his human senses the more time we spent together, the more frequently we touched. And he lost his immortality the more time my body had to heal him. The last time I'd cured him entirely, I'd nearly killed him when my Protector instincts had kicked in and I'd stolen his energy. Returning his immortality had nearly killed me. Kissing like this without our guard up was stupid and reckless and breathtaking.

Longing to diffuse the tension, I said the first thing I could think of. "Oops?"

It worked. His tense body relaxed and he laughed, the sound rumbling through his chest and my body where we touched.

"You are far too tempting for your own good. And mine, come to think of it." His lips returned to nuzzle the corner of my mouth. "I'm adding a new rule. No thinking 'kiss me' in the middle of a crowded dance floor."

I let my head fall back so he could trail kisses from my jaw to my neck. "Uh-uh. No adding more rules. We hardly touch as it is."

We had a multitude of rules restricting when and how we were allowed to touch. One of us had to stay guarded when we kissed, which left both of us frustrated. These little forbidden tastes of what it would be like to lose control only made things harder.

Asher's hand slipped from my hip to the middle of my back. His fingers tangled in the long hair at my back, wrapping the waving length around his palm. "Mmm. We always seem to be surrounded by people. This is the first time we've been alone in days."

I tipped my head to meet his gaze. "We'd better make it worth it then."

"You're right." The teasing light that entered his green eyes should have clued me in. His hand grasped mine, and he whirled me away from him in a dizzying spin. "Dance with me, Remy."

I know what you're doing, but I'll let you get away with it. This time. He meant to distract us, to distract me from what we couldn't have.

We'd never danced together before. Asher had grown up in Victorian England, and I expected his moves to be old-fashioned, especially when you added in the messy, grinding beat of the music drifting from inside the club. Of course, Asher surprised me. The boy could seriously move his hips. Breathless and laughing, I let him spin me about the patio, tugging me close and digging into the rhythm. When the music stopped, we swayed together, not wanting the moment to end, and Asher tucked my head into the curve of his neck.

The slamming of the patio door jarred us back to reality.

We stepped apart, glancing about. Marina stumbled onto the patio with Brandon on her heels. Unsteady on her feet, she tripped and had to catch herself on a nearby table.

"Damn it, Rina. You completely screwed up the vocals on that entire last set."

Brandon sounded furious, as he reached out to steady her. I'd heard rumors that the band was having problems, but he hadn't mentioned anything.

"Piss off, Brandon. I don't need you in my face."

Marina's words slurred, and I wondered how much she'd had to drink tonight. The club didn't serve alcohol, but that didn't mean everyone didn't find a way to get it.

"You're drunk!" Brandon yelled at her. "Son of a bitch, Rina. Do you know what a cliché you are? You're out."

"You think I care?" she screamed. She stepped forward and raised a fist to hit him. She started when instead she found her wrist clasped in Asher's hand. She began to sob into his shirt, her rage fading as fast as it had appeared.

I wanted to help. I really did. But something stopped me. The mascara caked beneath her eyes and tracking down her cheeks. The sloppy movements. The uncontrolled outburst of emotion. Marina reminded me of my mother on a binge, and I froze, watching her thin shoulders heave.

After a minute, her crying subsided into a silence filled with the echoes of my past. If I could have shed my skin and run away, people would have found nothing but my pink shell on the patio floor. Brandon sighed and stepped toward Asher. He looped an arm over Marina's shoulder and tried to peel her away. Her body slackened, and Asher caught her before she hit the concrete.

"Rina!"

Brandon helped lower her to the ground. I knew better than both of them what had happened. The signs had been there when she stood on stage and when she stepped onto the patio. Red face. Dilated pupils. Dizziness. And now unconsciousness. She wasn't just drunk. She'd taken something.

I didn't remember moving, but I was at her side, reaching for her when Asher knocked my hand away.

"Don't even think about it, Remy."

"What the hell, man?" Brandon saw Asher's violent move, but didn't understand the panic behind it. His shoulders squared, and I thought he might shove Asher.

"Brandon." I placed a hand on his arm to get his attention. He glared at Asher, but finally turned to face me when I yelled his name again. "Brandon, what did Marina take?"

He shook his head, confused. "I don't—I don't know. She's not breathing."

"She's OD'ing," I explained. "Asher, you need to get help."

"Like hell."

I couldn't read his mind, but his obstinate expression said he'd guessed I would try to heal Marina the second he walked away. He would stop me if I tried to touch her again.

"What is your problem?" Brandon looked ready to punch Asher, and suddenly I was fed up with both of them.

"Stop it!" I shouted. *Asher, so help me, if you make me watch this girl die, I will never forgive you.*

I knew he'd heard me when his expression turned bleak. "I can't," he whispered.

It's not up to you. I decide. You're no better than Dean if you try to control who I heal.

He reeled back as if I'd slapped him. He knew Dean had planned to use my ability to make a profit once he'd figured out what I was, and Asher knew that I'd hated my stepfather.

"Brandon, go get the manager. Now." My eyes never left Asher's when I ordered Brandon to leave. I wasn't stupid. If this could be done without a witness, it would be best for all of us.

Something in my tone sent Brandon scrambling to his feet. He ran inside, presumably to find an adult. The second he left I told Asher, "Tell me you know CPR. If this goes wrong, I might need you to use it."

He nodded with a grimace. Before he could change his mind, I laid a hand in the middle of Marina's chest. My energy *hummed* as I scanned her body. Her breathing had stopped, and I couldn't find a heartbeat. I didn't know what to do about the drug in her system; I didn't even know what drug she'd taken, though I suspected some kind of stimulant. Maybe coke.

Hoping it was enough to treat the worst symptom, I went to work. Marina's body jerked in the air when I sent a pulse of electricity through her to jump-start her heart. She gasped, her eyelids fluttering. Blue sparks lit the air where I touched her, and I glanced up at Asher.

Ready?

He nodded again, his eyes wide with fear as he waited for me to let go of Marina. The second I did, her injuries would settle in my body, become mine. Energy traded for injury. My powers forever a balancing act. One that might leave me teetering, too damaged to heal myself.

Terrified, I let go and collapsed into Asher's waiting arms.

My heart raced, a horse clomping to the finish line. Flat on my back, I sensed Asher's hands on my chest, pressing. And then nothing.

A bubble surrounded me, insulating me.

From a distant place, I registered two things. First, chaos had erupted outside the bubble in the smattering of voices talking nearby. I thought I heard Asher, Brandon, and Lucy arguing. Words like *hospital, drugs,* and *CPR* were thrown about before I stopped paying attention so I could focus on revelation number two.

I felt *awesome*. Floating and vibrant. So alive my heart could beat its way out of my chest. So alive my lungs wanted to expand to take in an entire ocean.

Waving a hand in front of my face, I saw a trail of golden sparks. Cheerful sparks. Sparklers. I waved my hand again faster, to make the sparks fly and dance.

"Remy, cut it out. People are going to see." My sister's worried face appeared next to me where I lay on the ground, shivering for some reason. She grabbed my hand out of the air.

"Lucy!" I squealed and threw my arms around her, knocking her sideways. "Have I told you how much I love you? My sister. Little sister. Little, little sis."

"Sh. Yes, I know how much you love me."

It didn't sound like she believed me. She had to know how I felt about her. "No, I mean, I didn't love you at first, but that's 'cause I didn't know you. I swear I've loved you as long as I've known you. I would die for you! Cross my heart and . . ." I stopped, confused by the slur in my voice. "I don't remember the rest."

I tried to stand and tipped sideways. Glancing around, I

recognized the patio at the Underground, but I couldn't remember how we'd ended up out here. Or why Asher would block Brandon when he tried to step out of the club. They were definitely arguing. Something was wrong. "Luce, what's the matter with me?"

"You are high, love." An arm fell across around my shoulders, and I glanced up into both of Asher's solemn gazes. One of him stole my breath, but two of him stole my willpower. I steadied myself with a hand at his waist. Thin cotton shifting between my skin and his. Golden skin and golden sparks.

"Uh-oh." I giggled, popping like a cork in a loud hiccup. My head threatened to ditch my boneless neck and glide away.

Asher's hand caught mine in a tight grasp, grounding me as Brandon slammed onto the patio without his interference.

"An ambulance is on the way. Rina, are you okay?" He knelt down, and I recognized the lead singer of his band lying on the ground. She looked as confused as I felt, her blue hair standing on end and black tears tracking down her hollow cheeks.

Brandon sounded scared, and I wanted to reassure him. But what about? Right. Blue hair. Cocaine. Shivering. I'd healed Marina, hadn't I? "Brand, don't worry. I made her all bet—"

The world spun like a brilliant, glittering carousel as Asher spun me toward him. My breath escaped in a loud *oomph*, and I found myself upside down, staring at a gorgeous backside. Asher had tossed me over his shoulder.

"Hey! Put me down. I lost Lucy, and I need to tell her something." Pushing against Asher's back, I spied my upside-down sister staring at me with horror. That seemed hysterical, and I giggled again. "There you are, Luce. Did you see me zap Rina? I totally rule. But don't tell Brandon, okay?"

"Don't tell me what? Is she okay?" Brandon's deep voice sounded suspicious. I blamed Asher, though I wasn't sure why.

Lucy choked. "Um, Asher. I think we should get home now. Remy doesn't seem to feel well."

"What?" I asked, outraged at her lie. "I feel great. I am the greatest Prote—"

"Time to go!"

Asher interrupted me, and I glared at his back. Lucy slapped a hand over my mouth when I opened it to argue with him. I grabbed hold of Asher's shirt when he started to move. The world spun again, and this time it wasn't funny. My stomach swished on spin cycle, and I closed my eyes to escape.

"Oh, just hell."

My mouth had been invaded by fluffy bunnies. Awful, cottony bunnies with their stupid cotton tails. They'd robbed my mouth of any moisture and left a horrid taste behind. Like soured, rancid carrots. I resolved to hate bunnies.

"Remy?"

Lucy's voice came out of the darkness beside me. Sitting up, I could make out her pale face and the familiar shapes of my dresser and sitting chair. We were in my bedroom, and I had no memory of getting there.

"You okay?"

Her soft whisper clanged in my head like a church bell, and I clasped my head to keep it attached to my ravaged body. "Oh, please, please don't shout. For the love of all that's holy, don't shout."

"I'll take that to mean you're not feeling so good." She

placed one cool hand on my forehead, and I moaned in relief. My head ached, my chest ached. Generally, everything ached.

"What the hell happened to me, Luce?"

"You don't remember?" My sister sounded amazed. And amused. Oh, just hell.

I shook my head. "The last thing I remember is Asher picking me up after I nearly told the whole world what I could do. Is there more?"

"Well . . ."

I groaned. I could tell she was enjoying herself when she continued.

"You are a terrible drunk, Remy. Asher and I got you out of there before you could tell Brandon how much you rocked and how badass you are as a Healer. We stuffed you in my car, and then you slobbered all over Asher for a very long, very uncomfortable ride home."

My next groan reverberated through my skull. "Did Mom and Dad see?"

"No. Lucky for you, they weren't home yet, or you would've been grounded for the rest of your life. Asher had to carry you in."

How stupid could I be? Take away my inhibitions, and I turned into a slobbering freak. Horrified, I closed my eyes. I wasn't sure if I was going to be able to look Asher in the face in the morning. As gone as I'd been, there was no way I'd been controlling my thoughts around him. What had he heard? And why would anyone seek this out for fun? My stomach scooted a little further up my throat, intent on escape.

"What else?" I asked.

"That's about it. Except for the singing."

She took no pity on me and laughed when I smothered my face with a pillow. Tugging the pillow away, she lounged next to me and grinned. "I didn't know Asher could blush until you started singing this really awful song you said you'd heard Dean sing when he was drunk. It was about a man from Nantucket and . . ." She hummed a few bars.

"You can stop. I know exactly which song you're talking about."

I hadn't realized I'd memorized the words to that particular ditty. Dirtier than any song I'd ever heard, it did not bear repeating, especially from my sister's mouth. I winced, imagining Asher's face as he heard me belting it at the top of my lungs. Lucy snickered, obviously picturing the same thing, and I couldn't help smiling. The humiliation was worth it a hundred times over to hear her laugh like that again. Since Dean had hurt her, she hadn't smiled often and I'd hated him for stealing that from her.

"How did you persuade Asher to leave?" He would have wanted to care for me himself.

"It wasn't easy. He was pretty upset. I don't think he was too happy about you helping Marina."

I sighed. "I know. He tried to stop me."

Lucy sat up, leaning over me, and I could feel her stare in the dark. "He's right, stupid. You have to be more careful. You can't heal anyone, anywhere."

The accusation set my teeth on edge, coming on top of Asher's interference at the club. "I couldn't sit there and do nothing. Should I have let her die?"

My sister tensed beside me. "She was dying?" she asked in a small voice.

I could have hit myself. Lucy didn't know about the drugs. She hadn't seen Asher giving me CPR. And he must have, given how sore my chest felt. If she'd seen him, she would have known how close things had been. She'd only been thinking of the questions my "drunken" actions might have caused.

"Are you kidding me?" she said. "After everything our

family has been through, you were going to throw it all away for some girl who doesn't care if she lives or dies?"

Lucy shook with anger. I put out a hand to touch her arm, but she shoved me away. Rising to her feet, she padded to the door to the bathroom that connected our rooms.

"You know, you can be really selfish sometimes. Don't you ever think about what it will do to us if you can't heal yourself one of these days?"

"Lucy, you don't understand—"

"Understand what? That you choose strangers over the people who love you? I have no problem grasping the obvious. You really don't get it."

She closed the bathroom door with a *click*. I wanted to scream that she wasn't being fair. My powers didn't work like that. I didn't shout, though, because I couldn't erase the memory of the hurt I'd seen on her face before the door closed.

And I couldn't deny that I'd put it there.

CHAPTER THREE

*W*earing the darkest sunglasses I owned and a grimace, I hit Clover Café as soon as it opened. A ceiling fan swirled with lazy abandon, but the room stewed in a rare early summer heat. An iced café mocha with a double shot of espresso went a long way toward soothing my raw nerves, and I sucked on the straw with more desperation than relief. The view of the bay offered comfort.

When Ben had moved me here, I'd only thought of escaping. Somehow, though, the town had crept inside me. Bordered by forests, Blackwell Falls hugged the Atlantic Ocean. Out in the harbor, sailboats and working fishing boats dotted the waters. Above the town, houses dotted the cliffs with the Blackwell mansion being the most prominent.

Once upon a time, I'd thought Asher's home with its rose gardens and fancy turrets a hotel. He'd laughed when I told him so. The house had been owned by him, his brother, and Lottie since they founded the town in the late 1800s and opened the paper mill that still puffed smoke in the distance. Everyone thought the town hall painting of Mayor Gabriel Blackwell was a long-dead Blackwell ancestor, which amused Asher's family.

The Blackwells only stuck around in town for a decade or so at a time. When it would become obvious that they never aged, they moved on and willed their property to their distant "cousins." Those "cousins" eventually returned with twenty-year-old Gabe acting as guardian to his younger siblings. The ploy worked, because who in their right mind would believe the family were immortals?

I sighed. Today, the view failed to soothe me.

Lucy hadn't said two words to me this morning. She'd never given me the cold shoulder before, even when she'd disapproved of me dating Asher with his playboy reputation or when she'd discovered the secrets I'd been keeping from her. It killed me to hurt her.

And yet . . . The way everyone kept telling me when and where I could use my powers grated on my nerves. I hadn't chosen to be a Healer, nor could I change my blood. Not to please any of them. Not to save myself. When my powers developed, I'd been terrified and so alone. My only solace had been the good I might be able to do with them. A legacy from my grandmother, though I hadn't known that until recently.

If someone hurt, I healed them. It was the one solid thing I knew about myself. Help where I could. Heal who I could. No questions, no judgments. I didn't understand why that concept was so hard to grasp. Lucy and Asher acted like I deliberately chose to hurt them when I used my powers.

"Feeling better?"

Brandon stood beside my table, his brown spikes more mussed than usual and flattened on one side of his head as if he'd slept on them. Somehow he always reminded me of growing up in Brooklyn. His edgy appearance had linked me to him from the get-go, as if he were a string connecting me to the few good things I remembered about my old home. That didn't mean I could share my secrets with him. For his sake or mine.

Shoving my oversized purse off the spare chair at my table, I made room for him to join me and resumed fanning myself with a plastic menu when he sat across from me. I tried to remember what I'd said and done in front of him. I had a hazy memory of Asher blocking him from me after I'd come to, so it was a safe bet that he didn't know anything. "I'm fine now. I'm not sure what happened last night."

Instead of coffee, he sipped on his usual herbal green tea and studied me with calm eyes. It amused me that he looked like a rebel and acted like a do-gooder.

"Really. I have a guess."

My internal sirens blared. Brandon enjoyed teasing me. About my husky voice, my bad eating habits, and my music tastes. He'd made an art form of doing whatever it took to get a laugh out of me. Most of the time by hitting on me in some outrageous manner, despite my boyfriend sitting two feet away. This Brandon was different. This was Serious Brandon.

"What's to guess? I had a bug. It passed." I waved a hand in casual dismissal, but his direct gaze never left my face.

"You didn't have a bug. I know the signs of someone who's high. I'm not stupid, Remy."

Did he know what I could do? Months ago, I'd healed Brandon when he'd nearly drowned at the community pool while giving me swimming lessons. He'd hit his head on the siding, knocking himself unconscious, and I'd healed his head injury with him none the wiser. It had been my fault he'd fallen in the pool in the first place. An accident, yes, but proof that everyone in my life lived in constant danger. Asher, Lucy, Asher's family. They had all been harmed in some way by my secrets. I couldn't do that to Brandon again.

"You know my history. You know I wouldn't touch

anything." Dean's drunken binges and cruel fists had seen to that.

"I know."

His quiet tone scared me, and I wiped my sweaty hand on my skirt under the table. "What are you saying, Brand?"

He took another sip of his tea, his brown eyes solemn. "I'm saying, I know what I saw."

"And what did you see?"

"Marina. Dying of a drug overdose. And then not. You—sober. And then not."

"So, I got buzzed by osmosis? That's insane." I laughed, but it sounded forced even to my ears.

He sat forward in a rush, touching my arm with gentle fingers. My energy *hummed,* and I scanned him out of habit. Healthy. "Remy, tell me what's going on. Trust me."

Asher had said the same thing once. I'd given in to the impulse, and he'd nearly died trying to protect me, despite being a Protector. Powerless, Brandon wouldn't stand a chance.

Surging to my feet, I shoved his hand away and snapped, "Geez, Brand. I felt sick. I left. The end." Avoiding his eyes, I reached for my bag.

"You know I care about you, right?"

His worried tone made me look up, and I softened my words.

"Of course, I know. But there's nothing to tell. I swear."

The lie came off my tongue easier than I cared to admit. One day I wouldn't be able to keep the gnarled words from strangling me. With a smile meant to reassure, I dropped a light kiss on Brandon's cheek and walked out of the café.

I didn't want to go home.

Parked outside our house, I studied the white New

England–style cottage. Hot sunlight set the bits of sea glass hanging in the windows aglow. My stepmother, Laura, loved to collect the glass when she walked on the beach that curved below at the edge of the marina. I loved our house. I loved the woods that cradled it, and the sea grass that bowed to the salty air when it blew through the sand. No concrete in sight, but this place felt more real to me than the city I'd grown up in.

Ben and Laura would be in the living room watching TV, or Laura would be in the back garden while Ben caught up on work he'd brought home from his shipbuilding office. If I walked in the house, they would drop whatever they were doing to hug me and ask me about my day. I soaked up their attention, my craving for it unending after so many years of starvation. Today, though, they would wonder why Lucy was mad at me, and I didn't want to lie.

Clambering out of my red Mustang, I paced myself until I reached the entrance to Townsend Park's labyrinth at the edge of our backyard. Standing still, I listened for a sign that the park sat empty of bird-watchers and kids who liked to play in its maze. I heard nothing but the tittering of birds and leaves bristling in the wind.

Excited now, I shook my hair out and dropped all pretense of human speed. I couldn't stop the laugh that escaped when my feet raced over the uneven path, my body bending around curves a moment before I slammed into this tree or tripped over that fallen log. The lingering headache disappeared. Too soon, I stood in the circular clearing at the center of the labyrinth, my hair swirling at my waist as my body came to a sudden rest.

"It's exhilarating, isn't it?"

Asher sat on one of the stone benches, the sun splashing over his skin. He had a way of guessing my next move and had obviously been waiting for me. His ability to peek into my mind didn't hurt. He smiled, and an answering smile curved my mouth.

"I never get tired of it," I admitted. "The speed. It's freeing somehow."

Striding toward him, I planted myself on his lap, and his arms surrounded me.

"How are you feeling?"

"Better now that the bells have stopped ringing in my skull. My powers have been slow to kick in this morning."

I traced the white scar slashing through one of his eyebrows to the top of his cheekbone in a light touch, and he turned his face into my palm. More rugged than his brother, the sharp angles and square, shadowed jaw were pure Asher.

"Mad at me?"

"No. Why?"

He grimaced. "Usually you think of how handsome Gabe is when you're mad at me."

I wrapped one hand behind his neck, letting his heat sink into me. His internal body temperature ran hotter than any human's, as if it burned through energy faster to keep his heart beating at its abnormal pace. "That's because he's the one image sure to get you out of my head when I need a little privacy. If you'd been paying attention, though, you would have noticed that my thoughts today were not on Gabe at all."

"No?"

His voice sounded hoarse when I began trailing nibbles along his jaw. "Hmm . . ." I said between kisses. "Listen closely."

I pulled away a few inches so I could meet his dark green gaze. We stared at each other, and I let my thoughts spin free and land on Asher. The way his skin felt against mine. The way his muscles shifted under the hand I rested at his back. How the whiskers on his chin rasped against my fingertips.

"Asher?"

"Yeah?"

"We're not on a crowded dance floor." *I love you.*

I expected him to pick up where we'd left off last night. A kiss that would take my breath away. He surprised me by dropping his head to the curve of my neck, his breath tickling my neck as he inhaled.

"Lemons," he growled.

I pushed him away so I could see his face. The smug satisfaction in his grin told me what he hadn't.

"You smell me?" I asked.

At his nod, I shrieked and threw my arms around his neck. He let himself tumble back into the grass, cushioning my landing with his body. His laugh rumbled under my ear, and I rested my chin on his chest to see how his face lit up. His ability to *feel* my touch had never gone away, even when I'd made him an immortal again. His sense of smell and taste, though, had disappeared. We'd both wondered if they would ever return. Now, it seemed time and proximity to me had begun to work their magic for a second time.

Which meant he could become mortal once more.

I didn't realize I frowned until Asher reached out to smooth the wrinkles on my forehead.

"Don't worry about me. I'm okay."

"For how long, though?" I asked.

An image of Asher dying from a bullet wound filled my mind. He'd been more mortal than Protector when Dean had shot him. An injury that should have had no lingering impact had nearly killed him.

He tugged on the end of my hair to get my attention. "We knew this might happen again if we stayed together. We made a choice."

I sighed. "I know. I just can't stand the idea that you might be hurt. Or worse."

"Then you know how I feel watching you heal injuries that could kill you."

A fight tangled in his words. The peaceful moment disappeared, and I shoved away from him to sit up, propping myself on one arm.

"Not you, too," I said, irritated. "I've already had it out with Lucy and Brandon."

He tensed, and a fire snapped in his eyes. "Brandon?"

"He doesn't know anything for sure," I rushed to reassure him. "But he saw and heard enough to be suspicious. We'll have to be careful for a while."

Asher swore in French before switching back to English. "Damn it, Remy! This is exactly what I was afraid of. It only takes one person knowing for the whole thing to come down on our heads."

"Are you pissed because I healed Marina or because Brandon saw something?"

"Both," Asher snapped.

He sounded so petulant, I couldn't help it: I laughed. My reaction was all wrong, and I knew it. I understood his anger. My actions had put us in danger. There was nothing funny about any part of this situation. And yet . . . He glared at me, and any effort I'd made to sober up dissolved in flames. Between giggles, I said, "I'm sorry. Oh, Asher, I'm sorry."

He watched me with a bemused expression. "I knew you would snap one day, but I thought it would take longer."

"Hey, watch it! That's just mean."

Asher reached over and pulled on my supporting arm until I fell against him again. "Me? You're the one with the whacked sense of humor. What is so funny?"

"Nothing, I guess. That's the problem, isn't it?" Actions

and reactions. Consequences. "We're always waiting for hell to come raining down on our heads."

"If the other Protectors find out about you, hell will seem like a pleasant vacation."

Torture and death awaited the Healer captured by Protectors. They would do anything to feel human again, and I could be their rechargeable battery. And if they found out about my unique ability to heal their immortality, death wouldn't come fast enough. Most Protectors didn't want to be mortal again.

Asher's heart beat steady and fast under my palm. "You can't ask me not to use my powers. It's who I am."

"Remy, look at me." He shook me slightly until I looked up. "I don't want to change you. I love you. But I want a lifetime with you. I'm asking you to be more careful. Think before you react. Please, promise me."

I nodded. He shook me again, and I laughed. "Okay, okay. I promise. I'll be more careful."

We lay together again, his deep breaths lifting me, and I exhaled with him, pressing him into the ground. I wished we could stay like that forever with the sun warming my skin from above, and his fingers trailing liquid heat in lazy circles down my spine.

Then he said, "About that song last night . . ."

I groaned, my forehead thumping his chest, and his laugh rumbled through me.

Chapter Four

I hated lying to Asher about my plans, but I knew what I had to do.

Something in my mother's recordings had stuck in my mind. She'd said I had the power to make the Protectors mortal again. It's why she'd kept me hidden from them. But how had she known that? Because if I was the first, how could she have guessed the extent of my power? Someone, somewhere had to know something.

If Asher could become human again, I needed to understand the extent of my Healer powers. I couldn't stop using my ability, and no matter how careful I was, I wouldn't be able to keep it a secret forever. My mother had understood that. It was why she'd provided me with the clues to find my grandfather. She'd known she wouldn't be around to help me, and that someday I would need to go to the Healers, even if it meant hiding my Protector half from them.

My mother had chosen Dean over me a thousand times. A thousand times he'd hurt her, and I had picked up the pieces by healing her injuries and hiding my own. The cigarette burns and the broken bones had threatened to break me—but the old scars strengthened me now, coiling steel around my spine.

I could never forget Dean shooting Lucy, or the way his

face had twisted with pleasure when he held me hostage, torturing me to see how my powers worked. The way he'd looked at the end with terror in his eyes as he fell from the cliff at the Edge of the World, with every injury he'd inflicted on me transferred to him, lived in my nightmares. Dean's body would never be found and my injuries had healed, but the memories had burrowed so deep that my guts were now made entirely of scar tissue.

I would never be a victim again. My friends and family would not be victims because of me. My grandfather might be able to help. At least my mother had told me to go to him if things turned dangerous. Maybe he knew another way I could keep my family safe from the Protectors. At the very least, I could learn more about Healers. Gabe had been so sure they would want to use me or see me dead if they knew the extent of my powers. My mother thought the same. Time to find out, and stop living in status quo. Status quo was too easy and could leave everyone unprepared when the danger landed on our doorstep.

So when I left Asher in Townsend Park and returned home, I wrote my grandfather a long e-mail. My mother's people had set up codes and ways to communicate to each other long ago, and the rules had been ingrained into her as a child. She'd been taught how to reach her parents through the personal ads if she was separated from them during a Protector attack. I couldn't imagine a childhood that would have required such precautions. I'd doubted her when she said he would respond. After all, she'd run away from him and his anger. Why would he still have been checking the ads? Yet, the proof was in his response. And now I was glad that she'd passed this information on to me in her final recording.

I used what I'd learned as I explained who I was and that I had inherited my grandmother's healing powers. It took me hours to figure out how to tell him about my mother's death. He'd blamed her for my grandmother's death. My mother had blamed herself, too. She'd told the wrong person about my grandmother's abilities, and the Protectors had found her. My grandfather had watched his wife get tortured to death. And now he'd lost his only child.

In the end, I couldn't think of a way to cushion the news, so I wrote about it matter-of-factly, hoping he wouldn't be offended by my bluntness. I had enough strikes against me, considering that I was half-Protector.

I just hoped he never found out about my mixed blood.

Ben woke me by waving a chipped ceramic mug of coffee under my nose. I opened one eye, and my dad grinned, his salt-and-pepper black hair tumbling over his forehead. "I waited as long as I could. Laura told me to let you sleep."

Graduation day. Yay. I sat up to take the mug. Our fingers brushed, and I sensed the irregular beat of his heart. I'd given up trying to heal it a month ago. Every time I did, it simply returned. My father didn't know it, but he had Protector blood running through his veins and it affected the internal workings of his body. From what I knew about his parents, they'd passed away when he was pretty young. Like my mother, my father didn't have any powers. They skipped generations, and both he and my mother had been part of the generation sans power. Lucky me.

I moved over to make room for Ben, and he sat next to me with his back against the headboard, and his long denim-covered legs crossed at the ankle. I tipped my head to lean against his arm, as I sipped my coffee.

"Morning, Dad."

He turned to mush, the way he did every time I called him Dad. The experience was still so new to both of us.

We were strangely alike despite our years apart, right down to the way we looked and certain expressions we shared. My height mimicked his tall stature, and I shared the warm brown shade of his skin. My mother's contributions—the dirty blond shade of my hair, the haphazard freckles sprinkled across my skin, and fragile bone structure—reminded everyone that I'd been a latecomer to the O'Malley household.

"Hey, kid. How're you doing this morning?" he asked.

He'd been worried about me since March when he'd arrived at the hospital in New York and found me broken from the latest confrontation with Dean. It was as if Ben had seventeen years of worry to make up for in a few short months. I didn't mind. His worry felt like a balm on the wounds caused by his abandonment and my mother's betrayal. Ben hadn't known what he'd abandoned me to, but sometimes that didn't make a damn bit of difference when the old feelings of betrayal nipped at me.

For now, inhaling the scent of wood shavings that always clung to Ben, I studied his bare feet and loved that he sat beside me and worried about me. "Ask me again when I wake up," I grumbled.

A long moment of companionable silence passed, and then Laura's voice trailed up the stairs. "Ben O'Malley, you'd better not be up there waking that girl up!"

He studied me from the corner of navy blue eyes. I stared back at him from eyes like his, until we both laughed.

"You're in trouble now."

"Only if you tell on me," he said. "You ready for today?"

"You mean the whole cap and gown thing? Not my best look, but I think I can pull it off with Lucy's help."

"Smart-ass. I mean, the whole cap and gown thing without your mom there."

He nudged me with his foot when I didn't respond

right away. I tried to find the right words. My feelings for my mother were a crazy mixture of love and hate and sorrow. Sometimes there weren't words, so I shrugged.

"It's enough that you guys will be there."

Ben didn't push for more. "Everything okay with Asher and Lucy? Things have seemed a little tense between all of you the last couple of days."

I shrugged again. "High school stuff. Nothing we won't get over in a few days."

It hurt that I couldn't tell the truth. That Lucy was still mad at me for putting myself at risk. That my lie of omission had strained things with Asher. I'd been blocking him from my mind constantly for the last couple of days so he wouldn't learn about the e-mail I'd written my grandfather. The constant tension had affected both of us.

"I love you, kiddo. I'll get out of your hair so you can get ready."

Ben dropped a kiss on my forehead when I glanced up, and I smiled. He rose, and I followed, stumbling to my feet and over to my dresser.

"Remy?" He stood at my bedroom door with his hand on the doorknob. "I'm proud of you. You know that, right?"

Warmth flooded through me to hear him say it. He turned to leave, and suddenly I wanted to come clean about one thing. It was the least I could do.

"Dad? You never asked what my plans were. After school, I mean."

He nodded, his hesitation palpable. "I didn't want to push. I thought you might want to take some time off after everything that's happened this year."

"Well, I didn't want to say anything when I didn't know if I would be sticking around, but I applied to a few colleges last year. Premed. I didn't mention it because I didn't get any scholarship money. I feel stupid for even applying when I knew I couldn't afford to go, but I got into Columbia. I—"

Ben cut off my air when he picked me up and crushed my ribs in a bear hug. His shout threatened to deafen me, but I couldn't stop grinning at him.

He looked at me with awe when he set me down. "We'll figure out the tuition. Damn, my kid's going to be a doctor."

Lucy appeared in the doorway to our shared bathroom in her pajamas at the same time my stepmother burst in from the hall with her short red curls swinging.

"What happened?" Lucy grumbled.

Laura thumped my father in the back with the dish towel she had in one hand. "Ben, I told you to let her sleep in."

He turned to face both of them with an arm thrown over my shoulder. "Listen to this. Tell them, Remy." Before I could do more than open my mouth, he blurted out, "Our daughter got admitted into Columbia University's premed program."

Laura's shout was louder than Ben's, as she rushed to embrace me. I watched Lucy over her shoulder and saw her struggling to resist the pull of family when she wanted to stay mad at me. I knew the feeling because I'd tried for weeks to not care about any of them when Ben first brought me here, and I'd failed.

Lucy wasn't any stronger than me. A small smile curved her stubborn mouth when her eyes met mine. I held out an arm, and she settled next to me in our small circle.

Only I heard her whisper, "You're still a jerk, but I love you."

It was tougher than I thought to get through graduation. My eighteenth birthday had been a quiet enough event a few weeks ago, but then we'd been caught up in the aftermath of Dean's attack. I'd been so busy worrying about my grandfather and the consequences of the e-mail I'd written him that I hadn't thought about how graduation would affect me.

The ceremony itself passed in a blur of red gowns and ended when matching red caps flew in the air. My family sat in the crowd behind me, along with Asher's brother and sister. My father had guessed what I hadn't. The absence of my mother hovered over me like the fog that sometimes crept in to hug the coastline.

Asher sat beside me in a matching gown, and I knew he sensed my sadness despite my raised defenses. He gave me a frustrated glance, and I guessed I had to confess the truth. I'd intended to wait for my grandfather's response to my e-mail to confess. If he didn't write, I had no need to upset anyone. I couldn't keep blocking Asher, though, not when he looked so hurt.

While others celebrated around us, I hugged him. *Let's enjoy today. We'll talk later, okay?*

He nodded.

My father appeared at my side with a bouquet of roses and pulled me away. Laura planned to cook my favorite meal of baked mac and cheese to celebrate, and I invited Asher to join us that evening. He agreed before his own family arrived to pull him away. I put aside thoughts of him and savored my father's excitement as he told anyone who listened about Columbia U.

Later, at home, I stripped off my cap and gown as I entered the house. Telling my family I wanted to change, I raced up the stairs. As I did a thousand times a day, I checked my e-mail.

My grandfather's e-mail address popped up, and I clicked on the e-mail, my heart beating faster. There was an attachment, and I opened that first. An airline e-ticket. He'd sent me an airplane ticket to San Francisco.

Dear Remy,

I am so very grieved to hear about my daughter. Your mother meant the world to me, and I have never forgiven myself for the way I treated her. I wish that we'd had the chance to meet again so I could apologize. My only consolation is that I've discovered I have a granddaughter. There is much we need to discuss. So much that I have to tell you. You are in danger, as is whoever you are living with. I've attached this ticket in hopes you will come to me, as your mother could not. Please do not delay—it's time to heal the wounds of the past.

Your grandfather,
François Marche

That last line I recognized from my mother's recordings—a code designed to tell me two things. I could go to my grandfather safely, and I should do it as quickly as possible. I looked at the ticket again. The flight would leave JFK in less than a week. My mother had insisted I keep my father a secret from my grandfather, unsure how he would react to Ben having Protector blood, so I'd led him to believe I'd lived with friends in Brooklyn since she'd died. More lies.

I'd known I would have to leave Blackwell Falls at some point, but I hadn't expected that time to come so soon. How would I tell my family? How would I tell Asher? They would fight me.

But if going would keep them all safe, I had to go.

Really the only question was, how would I survive without them?

I ripped the Band-Aid off right away.

I heard Ben, Laura, and Lucy in the kitchen when I thudded downstairs, my leaden feet heavy with dread.

Lucy and Ben sat at the kitchen table chatting, while Laura stood at the stove stirring pasta for homemade macaroni and cheese.

"I need to talk to you," I said.

They all turned to face me, and I almost lost my nerve.

Ben's brows rose. "That sounds serious."

"It is. After Mom died, I found my grandfather's information in some of her paperwork." I ignored Lucy's suspicious stare and continued. "I e-mailed him to let him know what happened to her. He wrote back, and he wants me to come for a visit."

Laura's mouth pinched in concern. "Do you want to go?"

I nodded. "I've never met him, and I'd really like to."

"No."

I'd thought the argument would come from Ben, but Lucy protested first.

"There's more," I added quickly. I couldn't give her a chance to fight me on this. "He sent me a ticket. I leave on Friday."

Ben frowned. "This Friday? Why so soon?"

"I guess he's anxious after missing out on seeing my mom. Doesn't want to waste time getting to know me and all that."

"And you?" Ben asked.

"I start college in the fall. The timing is right."

Ben tapped his fingers on the table thoughtfully, and Lucy turned on him. "You can't let her go."

"Lucy, she's eighteen. I can't exactly stop her." He looked like he wanted to, though.

My sister stood up. "I can't believe you're going to let her go out on her own with Dean still out there." She tossed me a smug look.

Oh, low blow. I glared at her.

"All the more reason for me to take some time away

from here on a different coast. Dean won't follow me across the country." *Or anywhere, ever again.*

Lucy scowled, and Laura put a hand on her arm. "How long do you think you'll be gone?" my stepmother asked.

I shrugged and met her concerned gaze. "A month maybe."

My family reacted to that in silence. We'd been together such a short time, and it felt like I'd just suggested tearing us apart. My resolve started to crumble, and I gritted my teeth, reminding myself that I had to do this to keep them safe.

Ben sighed. "I can't say I'm happy about it, Remy, but if it's what you want . . ."

Lucy jerked away from Laura and glared at me as she stormed out of the room. Her bedroom door slammed a minute later, making her opinion of my going clear.

With a grimace, I settled at the table with Ben to work out the details. Twenty minutes later, the doorbell rang. I went to open the door for Asher and found Lucy had beaten me to it. Arms crossed, she smirked at me, and I knew in an instant that she'd tattled on me.

And I'd never seen Asher look so pissed.

CHAPTER FIVE

"*You* are *so* in trouble."

Lucy ignored my warning and flounced out of the room. She'd never behaved so childishly in the time I'd known her, and I stared after her in shock. With another glance at Asher's furious expression, I yelled to my parents, "I'm taking a walk with Asher in the park. Be back in a bit."

Without a word, he turned on his heel and headed to the entrance to Townsend Park. At the edge of the labyrinth, he took off running in a blur of furious energy, and I followed him with more caution, lacking his Protector hearing and sight. There were no lights in the woods, but a couple of streetlights managed to penetrate the clearing at the center of the maze with a timid glow.

Asher had his hands in his coat pockets and waited for me to appear. He had his guard up, as if he worried that his anger would affect his control.

"Are you going to yell at me?" I asked. We'd fought before, but this rage was new.

"No," he bit off. "You'll get defensive, and then we'll argue about the wrong thing."

Ouch. I winced because he was probably right. I didn't deal with people yelling at me with any kind of grace. When pushed, I kicked back like a mule.

"I'm sorry, Asher." I held up both hands in entreaty. "I planned to tell you tonight, but then that e-mail came from my grandfather. Lucy shouldn't have said anything to you."

"She's worried about you. And she's right to. Why, Remy?"

I sighed and leaned against a tree trunk. "Why am I going or why didn't I tell you I wrote him?"

Asher sped across the clearing and braced himself on the tree trunk with his hands planted above my shoulders. His face rested mere inches from mine, and I saw the hurt beneath the anger.

"Why didn't you tell me? All that talk of how we're in this together, but you leave me out of the biggest decisions."

I wanted to look away, but I couldn't. "You're right. I'm sorry. I was afraid you would try to talk me out of it."

"Damn right I would have. You have no idea what you'll be walking into, and I can't be there to protect you without bringing a bunch of Protectors down on your relatives."

"I have to do this." His jaw clenched, and I curled a hand around his wrist. "I need to find out what he knows about my powers. I can't risk hurting someone. Not my family. Not you."

"We've been doing fine."

My brows rose. "Fine? Dean is dead. Brandon nearly drowned because of me. Lucy was shot because of me. You nearly died. I—"

Asher touched a finger to my lips. "Enough. Please."

I paused, listening to an owl hoot nearby. Asher hated to be reminded about what had almost happened, but I couldn't let him forget it. I sighed, wishing I could make him understand.

"I do understand," he said, hearing my thought. "That doesn't mean I agree."

"What would you have me do? Stay here and wait for your friends to come for me and my family?"

The last time his Protector friends had come to town, he'd done everything he could to keep me off their radar. But that time he'd known they were coming in advance. What if they decided to surprise the Blackwells? Friendship with Asher wouldn't mean much if they knew what I could do.

He stepped back, forcing me to drop my hand. "That's not fair. You know you come first."

"You come first for me, too. I'm doing this to keep us all safe. I want a future, Asher. I don't know how to make that happen the way things are. Please don't fight me on this."

Asher walked away. I couldn't read his expression in the bad light, and he didn't speak for a long time.

Finally he said, "You're going to go no matter what I say."

"Asher . . ."

My voice tapered off. The truth sounded awful when he said it like that. He'd been disappointed and frustrated before, and he'd even been angry. I'd never known him to sound so bitter, though. Despite the heat, I shivered. I wanted to hug him, but I could see he needed some distance. I didn't know what to do.

Asher tilted his head, hearing something I couldn't. In a quiet voice, he said, "We should go. Your dad just sent Lucy to find us."

I trailed after him when he headed back toward my house. Lucy didn't look so triumphant when she saw Asher and me emerge from the woods with a good five feet between us. She shot me a quizzical look that I ignored.

At dinner, Asher hardly spoke. My parents noticed the odd tension in the room, obviously gathering that Asher and I had argued. They did their best to keep the conversation going, while I shoved my food around my plate and Asher gave polite answers to their questions about his plans after high school, which included a photography school in New York City near Columbia U. An answer that surprised me since we hadn't even spoken of the future yet.

The longer the stilted conversation staggered on, the more miserable I felt.

Later, when I walked Asher to the door, he didn't kiss me good night, and I felt like crying, watching him walk away.

The days following graduation didn't get any better. The weight of everyone's expectations bore down, crushing me. Part of me wished I could get on the plane sooner than Friday.

Brandon thought I had lied about Marina but couldn't pinpoint how. He tried more than once to get me to confide in him, and my evasions irritated him. Lucy hated me for going. My parents watched me with sad expressions that added to my guilt. And Asher . . .

He avoided me. My calls went to voice mail. When I phoned his house, Lottie made excuses for why he couldn't come to the phone.

Gabe wasn't so pleasant when I called for the twentieth time.

"You're wrong to go," he said bluntly after I gave him my flight information for Asher.

"I know you and Asher think so," I said.

Silence met that statement, and I imagined Gabe's furious face. Honestly, all he cared about was keeping his family safe. He should have been on my side in this argument.

"Don't you think I should learn everything I can about my ability?" I argued. "I don't want Asher to constantly have to protect me. And if there's some way to help all of you . . . to make you mortal, don't you want that?"

"The last time you tried to make one of us mortal, you nearly became one of us. Do you think we hate you enough to wish that upon you?"

I didn't know what Gabe or Lottie desired, but I knew what Asher would want. Me, safe and out of harm's way. But I'd learned that you had to be willing to risk something to get what you wanted.

"I'm going," I insisted to Gabe.

"You're going to get yourself killed."

"You almost sound like you care, Protector."

Gabe hung up on me then, as if to show me how wrong I was.

The day before my plane left, Ben took me to the Seaside Café for breakfast. He stared out the window at the view of the bay, while we sipped our coffee. My father didn't want me to go. I could almost feel his yearning for me to stay, along with a good dose of worry and sadness.

Dana, our regular server, poured me a third cup of coffee, and Ben watched me dump sugar and creamer into the mug.

"You need to take better care of yourself," he observed, throwing an arm along the back of the maroon vinyl booth. "Go easy on the caffeine."

I stuck my tongue out at him.

He laughed. "I'm serious. You're going to be on your own." He sobered again. "Are you sure you can't postpone this trip for a while? It seems too soon after everything that's happened this year."

"Dad, stop worrying. I'm going to be fine. You know I can take care of myself."

His expression soured. The guilt ate at him still and would for a long time. I'd learned to take care of myself because nobody—including him—had been there to help me. I touched his hand to reassure him, healing his skipping heart again. The abnormal beat always returned, but I couldn't help myself.

"It's only for a few weeks and then I'll be back."

He grasped my hand, and his mouth tipped up in a small smile. "Promise? Blackwell Falls isn't going to be the same without you."

"Oh, I can think of a few people who won't miss me."

I hadn't seen Asher in four days. Would he let me leave without even saying good-bye? The thought tormented me every night, making for some sleepless nights. I needed to know he'd be there for me so I could get through this, but he wouldn't even return a stupid text message.

Ben seemed to read my mind. "Things okay with you and Asher? I haven't seen much of him since graduation."

My dad didn't sound unhappy about that. He liked Asher, but sometimes I got the sense that he wished we hadn't gotten so serious so soon after my mother died.

I crumpled my napkin in my lap. "I'm not really sure. He's mad that I decided to go without talking to him first."

Ben frowned. "It's your decision, isn't it? You don't need his permission."

I could see where he was going with that train of thought from a mile away. "Relax, Dad. He's not trying to control me. Give me some credit."

He held up both hands in a placating gesture. "Sorry. Why's he angry then?"

"We'd kind of made other plans, and I blew them out of the water. I think maybe I would've felt the same way in his shoes."

"You tried talking to him?"

"Repeatedly. He doesn't want to see me."

Ben gestured to Dana to get the check. "Give him some time. He'll cave."

Bemused, I shook my head at my father. Earlier this year, I never could have imagined a world in which I'd be discussing my boyfriend with my father. Or that I would have a boyfriend.

"What?" Ben said, noticing my stare.

"You. Me. This." I gestured between us. "I'm just . . ." I pursed my lips trying to find the words. "Having family. It's cool. Unexpected but cool."

My father's expression softened. "Not all family is the same. I hope you're not disappointed when you meet your grandfather."

Curious, I asked, "What do you know about him?"

"Not much. Your mom rarely mentioned him. Something happened between them, and Anna blamed herself for it. I always wondered if that was the whole story, though."

"Yeah, she mentioned something like that once."

In the recording she'd left me, she'd told me how she'd been the one to reveal her mom's location to the Protectors. My grandfather had blamed her when they killed her mother. My mom had run away soon after.

"Are you sure you want to do this alone? I could take some time off work and go with you. Act as a buffer for you and your grandfather."

I grinned, touched by the offer. "I think I can handle an old man. I've handled you, haven't I?"

"Brat."

After Ben paid our bill, we walked to my car, the red Mustang he'd bought me and taught me to drive.

He threw an arm around my shoulder. "I'm going to miss you, Remy. I feel like I've just begun to know you."

I brushed the sawdust from his shoulder. My father built ships for a living, and he always seemed to have wood shavings somewhere on his body, even before he went to work for the day.

"I'll be back before you know it."

He chucked me under the chin. "I'm going to hold you to that."

I hoped I was telling the truth. I would miss my family fiercely. If I could tell my father the truth about everything, I wouldn't have to do this alone. That would be selfish, though. My mother had told me to keep Ben a secret. She'd sacrificed everything to keep his Protector blood from my grandfather.

I shivered, wondering what she'd known about the Healers that could have driven her to give up my father when she loved him more than anything. And I hoped I wouldn't be forced to make a similar choice when it came to Asher.

That night, I woke to find Lucy curled up in my bed with her back to me. She sniffled, and I thought maybe that was the sound that had wakened me. Since Dean had shot her, she sometimes slipped into my room in the middle of the night, though she always left before morning. She didn't know I knew about these nights or her bad dreams.

Only a year younger than I, she looked small and fragile lying there. Dean had introduced her to a nightmarish world, and I'd been the one to introduce her to my stepfather by coming to Blackwell Falls. I hated it that I hadn't been able to shield her from a world with Dean, Protectors, and Healers.

She muffled another sob, and I couldn't take it anymore. I smoothed a hand over her hair and she jumped before settling again.

"Don't go, Remy."

Her voice sounded small in the dark. Nothing had swayed me from my course, but her words nearly did it. As if she sensed my weakening defenses, she rolled over to face me. Moonlight reflected off the sheen of tears on her cheeks, and I reached over to swipe them away.

I didn't answer, and she whispered, "Please."

My deep breath sounded shaky. "If it was just me, I'd stay. But what if my grandfather knows something that could make Asher mortal? I don't want to give up on a life with him. I have to do something. Lucy, I love him."

I started to cry, too, and somehow that had the effect of calming Lucy. She gripped my fingers tightly, and we listened to the silence in the house, a peace that had been shredded not too long ago when Dean attacked us. That night had been made of blood, tears, and pain. I thought maybe Lucy was remembering that night, too.

"Shit," she said in a more normal tone, startling a laugh out of me. "I want to stay mad at you, but then you go and pull the 'Lucy, I love him' card. Totally unfair."

"Sorry," I said, sniffing.

She shoved my shoulder. "No, you're not. Aren't you scared?"

"Terrified," I whispered. It was true.

I hadn't realized how much so until she asked me. I would be on my own again.

"Good," she answered in a more firm tone. "You'll be on your guard."

Asher didn't come to say good-bye.

Ben and Laura both insisted on taking me to the airport. Luckily, neither of them thought to check my ticket or they'd have seen that I'd had to book a connecting flight to New York, using my meager savings. I didn't want to have to explain why I didn't want my grandfather to know where I lived and with whom.

Lucy stayed home, and I was glad that was one good-bye I could have in private. We both cried, and it struck me that we were all acting as if I wasn't coming back. I hoped that wasn't a bad omen of things to come.

At the airport, I hugged my parents and listened to their

warnings and last words of advice. *Don't talk to strangers* headlined the list, along with orders to call home often.

"I promise to yell 'Stranger, danger' if anyone I don't know comes near me," I said, straight-faced.

My father grinned over Laura's head and pretended to cuff me in the chin. "That's my kid." He turned to my stepmother. "I told you the sarcasm would eventually come. The sweet daughter thing couldn't last forever."

Laura smirked at him. "That apple didn't fall far."

If she only knew.

Finally, I made my way through security and left them behind with a wave as I headed to my gate. As I sat in a plastic chair better designed for torture than waiting, I couldn't decide if I felt angry or hurt that Asher had blown me off. Was this a permanent good-bye? His way of breaking up with me? What a coward. Okay, whatever. Rage won out over hurt at last, and the anger felt good.

Trailing after a family of four, I made my way on to the plane when they called for boarding. After I stowed my bag, I slipped into a window seat and closed my eyes so I wouldn't have to talk to anyone. Someone jostled my seat when they took the one on the aisle, but they didn't try to speak to me to my great relief. Long minutes later, the plane took off and we were under way.

That was when the anger died and it hit me. Asher had really let me go.

What if I'd screwed everything up? My body curved toward the window to hide that I was falling apart on a plane full of strangers. I wished I'd never rediscovered tears. They didn't make me feel a damn bit better. Nothing would if Asher had stopped loving me.

"Never."

I swung around, and Asher smiled from two seats away.

CHAPTER SIX

"*D*on't you know me at all by now?" Asher said.

Joy and surprise rioted within me, and he didn't need to touch me to hear my thoughts. Asher unclipped his seat belt and shoved the armrests up. With nothing between us, he slid across the seats and pulled me close. The soft cotton of his shirt rubbed against my nose when I hugged him.

I tilted my head back to see his expression. "What are you doing here, Asher? I'm so glad you're here, but I don't understand."

He dropped a lazy kiss on my forehead. "It's simple. I'm coming with you."

Asher's face tightened into a fierce expression when I started to speak. He pulled away, leaving a few inches of space between us, and I immediately missed his warmth.

"Don't argue," he continued. "You made the decision to go without me, and I'm trying to make the best of it. But don't you dare tell me to stay behind while you risk your life for all of us."

A flight attendant stopped in the narrow aisle beside us, and Asher calmly ordered a water for himself and a coffee with extra cream and sugar for me. The man moved on, and Asher spoke again as if he hadn't been interrupted.

"You're pissed. I get that. I can live with you being mad at me, Remy, but I won't live without you."

He faked being relaxed as he faced the front of the plane, but his body betrayed him. His fisted hands rested on his legs. Someday his jaw would snap from the way he ground his teeth when upset. For once, I wished that I could read his thoughts so I could understand what was going on inside him. But in this way, I was like any other human.

"Asher?"

Green eyes met mine and flashed in defiance.

"I don't want to do this alone." I pulled one of his fists into my lap and smoothed the tension away, until his palm flattened on my thigh. "As soon as I boarded the plane, I wished you were here. I should have talked to you, and I'm sorry."

He turned his hand over and wound his fingers through mine. "You act like you're not afraid of anything. That terrifies me, Remy."

I'm sure my smile looked sheepish. "If I were any more afraid, I'd be curled up in a ball and rocking in a corner. I don't think you fully get what those years with my mother did to me."

I focused on our hands to avoid his gaze. Anna and the time before I arrived in Blackwell Falls were two of my least favorite topics. Asher knew a lot of what happened—how could he not with all the time he spent in my head?—but that was different from me talking about my feelings.

"I spent years healing her injuries. Every time Dean hurt her, I cleaned up his mess." I squeezed my eyes shut. "She begged me to keep it a secret. I told myself that asking for help wouldn't make a difference. No matter what I did, she would just go back to Dean. But I should have told, Asher. I should have told someone. Maybe she would be alive now if I had."

"You don't know that."

"Don't I? You know what the sick part was? I felt like I helped Dean. Maybe if someone had seen her injuries they would have stepped in. But I always covered up the evidence. It's like I was his accomplice. All the while, I kept hoping for a miracle. Wishing someone would save us."

Asher didn't jump in to disagree, even though I sensed how much he wanted to. I didn't need him to argue with me. I needed him to understand.

I continued. "You said they would come for me. Gabe and Lottie said it. I believe you. No more sitting back and waiting for a miracle. I won't risk my family or you. Can you understand that?"

The flight attendant chose that moment to return with our drinks, and Asher and I had to separate to put our tray tables down. I waited impatiently for the man to go. He left and still Asher remained mute. I didn't know what else I could say and turned to gaze out the window. The cloud-filled view didn't offer any answers. And the coffee tasted like crap. This day kept getting better.

"Okay."

Asher seemed to have reached a decision.

"Okay?" I asked hopefully.

"Okay, we do this. We meet your grandfather and get our answers. No more waiting. But at the first sign of danger, we're out of there. No arguments. I'll pick you up and carry you out if I have to."

I threw my arms around his neck and tugged his head down so I could kiss his cheek. "You won't have to. I don't want to die. Or have to explain to Gabe why his brother has a broken back from carrying me across the country."

Asher laughed, and I knew we would be okay. We could do this. Together.

★   ★   ★

The rest of the flight passed quickly as we planned.

My mother had wanted me to keep my Protector blood a secret. No way could I show up at my grandfather's with my Protector boyfriend. As it turned out, Asher hadn't ignored me the past few days to torture me. He'd been busy finding a place to live in San Francisco so he could be near me.

"Why didn't you tell me?" I asked.

"You would have tried to talk me out of coming."

I thought about that for a moment and nodded. "You're right. I'm glad you didn't call."

When I reached for my coffee, he beat me to it, swapping his cup of water for mine. He grimaced. "Please don't drink that. It's awful."

I realized he'd been "tasting" my coffee since we'd been touching while I drank. Another side effect of my powers. Heads turned when I laughed.

"You actually thought about how bad it tasted and then took another sip."

He shook his head at me, mystified, and I giggled again. He didn't love coffee the way I did, even when it tasted good.

"I need the caffeine boost. I didn't sleep much last night."

"I'll keep you awake," he said.

I raised my brows at him, and he flushed, his cheeks turning pink.

"I didn't mean that the way it sounded."

"Damn," I muttered, to tease him.

He got that look in his eyes, the one that said I'd thrown down a challenge he would accept all too willingly. For two seconds I thought about the sparks that might fly where people could see them, and then my mind shut down because Asher's lips touched mine.

I thought, *I love you*, and he smiled.
We didn't speak for a long time after that.

I took the escalator alone with Asher trailing a good twenty feet behind me. My grandfather would meet me at baggage claim, and Asher and I had decided that he and my grandfather shouldn't meet until we knew more. We'd kissed good-bye at the gate, and it had been difficult to let him go.

A group of people waited at the bottom of the escalator, a few holding up signs. Nerves had my hands shaking, and I rubbed my damp palms against my jeans. Would I know my grandfather? Would I recognize him, or somehow feel a pang of kinship because we had the same blood running in our veins?

I studied the crowd, but no one person stood out. Then, a man with a tuft of white hair shoved his way to the front. Larger than any man I'd ever seen, he was at least six and a half feet tall. The span of shoulders would easily force him to turn sideways to pass through doorways. I imagined if his skin were green, he could pass for an aging Hulk. He had the presence to go with his appearance, too. It wasn't just his size that made people get out of his way. The man had a commanding air about him that demanded it.

Without a doubt, this scowling man was François Marche, my grandfather.

He took one look at me and his scowl melted into a huge grin that transformed his entire face from slightly menacing to mischievous overgrown child. My foot had scarcely left the escalator step when he took one ginormous step toward me and swooped me into his arms.

The air pushed out of me in a *whoosh*, and my grandfather immediately loosened his grip, allowing me to step back. I tossed a quick look over my shoulder in time to see

Asher settling back into a casual stance. For a moment, he'd mistaken my grandfather's aggressive greeting for an attack and gone into Protector mode.

"I hope you are Remy, or I'm going to be very embarrassed."

My grandfather rested a hand on my back and steered me away from the escalator so other people could pass. His gravelly voice suited him, and the warmth in it helped me to relax a little.

I smiled. "I'm Remy."

"Well, then," he answered. He clicked his tongue and held out his arms, indicating I should spin. "Let me have a look at you."

I spun about. "Will I do?"

He folded his arms, pretending to think about it, but I could see his eyes twinkling with hidden laughter.

"Too skinny by far. Sadly, that won't change while you're under my roof. I'm a lousy cook. But I guess you'll do."

I waited, tapping my foot impatiently. He cocked one eyebrow at me, and I made a spinning motion in the air with my finger.

"I do believe you take after your mother," my grandfather muttered, but he spun about like I had a moment ago. "Will I do?" he asked.

I shrugged. "Aside from your appalling lack of skill in the kitchen? I suppose we can eat out."

We stood there, grinning at each other like idiots.

And I realized that I liked my grandfather a great deal.

My grandfather had to be in his sixties but, except for the shocking cloud of white hair, you never could have guessed it. He refused to let me help with my bags, lifting them with ease. I hadn't known a lot of old people, but when I thought of them, I guess I expected them to be crabby. François Marche laughed a lot, and he had a booming laugh that made me smile in response.

The short drive from the airport to the city passed quickly and with none of the awkward small talk I'd expected. He fired questions at me, as if he were filled with an insatiable curiosity to know me. He wanted to know about the "friends" I'd been living with in New York since my mother died. I had practiced my lies with Asher, so I was prepared with a story.

In between my made-up answers, he pointed out the sights we passed. The Bay Bridge that led to Oakland. The city hall that looked like it had escaped from postcards of Paris with its gold detailing. The red-orange Golden Gate Bridge that stood as the gateway to the ocean.

I'd seen pictures of San Francisco, but it surpassed my expectations. Gray-blue water peeked over the horizon between buildings, and my grandfather's truck climbed hill after hill only to dip down the other sides. The city seemed made of extreme peaks and valleys with no flat surfaces anywhere to be found.

I'd lived in New York City most of my life, but where that city supported the steel and concrete industries, San Francisco had somehow managed to allow nature to keep a foothold amidst the buildings. When we passed through the "gate" into the Presidio, I eyed the cannon sitting at the entrance.

"It's just for looks," my grandfather said. "The Presidio used to be a military base before they decommissioned it and turned it into a national park. Now all the soldiers' living quarters have been turned into private homes or offices."

"You live in here?" I asked. Eucalyptus and pine trees covered the nearby hills, towering over neat rows of white clapboard homes.

"Yep. It's like getting to live in a forest, but with all the perks of the city in screaming distance."

We drove for a few minutes along twisting roads until we arrived at one of those two-story white clapboard homes with the redbrick-tiled roof.

My grandfather parked the truck at the curb. "Home sweet home. Come on."

He hauled my bags out of the truck bed like they were feather-filled, and I followed him up the concrete steps and onto the porch. Light filled the house. That was my first impression when he opened the front door. Warm wood floors glowed around the edges of woven rugs. A brown leather couch, built for a giant, took up most of the living room. Few pictures hung on the wall, and the place fairly shouted that a man lived alone in it.

My grandfather disappeared up the stairs and reappeared moments later sans my luggage.

"I'm guessing you'll be hungry, then?" he said.

I nodded solemnly. "I am a growing teenager, after all."

"Ha! If you grow any taller, you'll be looking down at me from the clouds."

I made a face at him, surprised by how comfortable I felt with his sarcasm. *Takes one to know one,* I guessed.

"Whatever you say, Paul Bunyan."

That comparison tickled him, and he grinned. In the kitchen, I sat at the table, watching him make us sandwiches stacked at least three inches high.

"How long have you lived here?" I asked. The kitchen, with its sparkling counters and serious lack of appliances, supported his claim that he couldn't cook.

"Oh, a few years. I've moved around a bit over the years, but I really like it here." Pulling out a block of cheese, he set to slicing it. "There are hiking trails all over the par—"

Mid–sentence, he cut off and cursed. Blood dripped from his finger as he rushed to the sink to turn on the tap. The water turned pink when he put his finger into the stream of water. He'd cut himself.

I took a deep breath and walked over to him. *Now or never,* I thought.

"May I?" I asked, holding out my hand.

He hesitated a moment before shutting off the tap and placing his palm in mine. I didn't have to touch the cut to heal him. The *humming* inside me grew in intensity when I opened up my senses. I imagined the edges of the sliced skin tugging together and mending. My grandfather sucked in a breath when the cut healed as he watched.

I bent my head so I wouldn't see his expression, scared he feared me even though this gift had been passed down from my grandmother. Gentle blue sparks lit the air when I dropped his hand. The pain sliced swift and sharp when the skin of my finger split open. The water turned on again, and I hoped he missed my wince as he shifted to wash the last of the blood off his finger.

The way Asher and my mother had explained it to me, other Healers didn't absorb the injuries they healed. That special talent was a side effect of my Protector blood. A side effect I wasn't ready to reveal to my grandfather yet. While he finished at the sink, I made a quick excuse and rushed off to find a bathroom.

As soon as the door closed behind me, I turned on the faucet to wash away the blood from my cut finger. I scowled at my reflection. Ten minutes. I'd been here a whole ten minutes before using my ability. Asher would be pissed.

Sighing, I set to minimize the damage by healing my finger. No hint of the injury remained when I returned to the kitchen, other than the usual cold that set in after a healing. The chair legs scraped across the floor when I sat

at the small dining table and waited for my grandfather to
join me. All of the camaraderie had been sucked out of the
air and had been replaced by the awkwardness I'd expected.

My grandfather's shoulders curved forward in sadness
or exhaustion, and he looked a little closer to his age. He
carried two plates to the table and set one in front of me
before sitting across from me. The table's scarred wood
surface shook when he planted his elbows on it and
steepled his hands under his chin. Where I had my father's
blue eyes, my grandfather had obviously passed his brown
eyes to my mother. She had never looked at me this directly, though, with a gaze that made me want to squirm.

"I'd kind of hoped you were mistaken when you wrote
me about your abilities, Remy," he said finally.

"You thought I lied?" I asked, offended.

He shook his head. "No. I was just an old man wishing
his granddaughter wouldn't have to deal with this curse
that tore our family apart. Go on and eat up."

I tried, but my appetite had disappeared. I hadn't expected him to jump for joy at me being a Healer, but I
didn't know what to make of his disappointment.

Eventually, my grandfather gave up the pretense of eating, too. He pushed his plate away and gave another
weighty sigh. One huge hand rubbed his face.

"So then, maybe it's time you tell me what happened to
my Anna."

CHAPTER SEVEN

*O*f course, he began with that question first.

"My mother . . ." I started. I bit my lip. I didn't have a lot of good things to say about Anna. How much did he want to know? Would it be better to lie?

He seemed to sense my turmoil. "You don't have to worry about my feelings, Remy. I'm old, but the ticker works just fine."

He gave me the ghost of a smile, and I decided to take him at his word. I launched into our story, starting with my earliest memories. We'd been poor, but things hadn't always been terrible. My mother had worked a lot in those years, but when we'd been together, I'd known she loved me. I moved on to the year Dean moved in with us and the years that followed their marriage.

My grandfather's face tensed when I described the abuse Dean had subjected us to. It felt weird to be telling a stranger the horrible details, but somehow it seemed like my grandfather needed to know what had happened to us. I thought maybe my mother had told me about him so that I could be here with her father, confessing this. Anna had blamed herself for my grandmother's death, and Dean had been her punishment and penance. Except she'd taken me down the rabbit hole with her.

I left out the parts of the story where I'd taken on Anna's

injuries time and again. It was bad enough that Dean had beaten me, too. I told him how my mother had pretended not to know about me being a Healer, and that I'd found out what I was from a recording she'd made in the days before she died.

At some point, I asked my grandfather if he had any coffee and he got up to make a pot. We moved to the living room, and I wrapped my cold fingers around the mug to warm them. It had grown dark out, and I curled up in a corner of the couch, tucking my feet beneath me.

My grandfather sat on the other end of the couch, his face lit a warm amber shade by the floor lamp perched over his head. He leaned forward, resting his elbows on his thighs, with a coffee mug hanging forgotten in his hands.

"Are you sorry I told you?" I asked when the silence became unbearable.

His mouth curved in a quick, sad smile. "Not a bit. It's just a very sad story to hear, Remy. I'm sorry my anger drove your mother to that."

"You blamed her then?"

"At first," he admitted. "It was terrible, Remy. Watching your grandmother sacrifice herself to save me."

I didn't have to rely on my imagination to understand how awful it had been. Dean had forced Asher and me into the same situation.

He continued. "I loved your grandmother more than life itself. When she died like that, I . . . well, I grieved hard. I needed someone to blame and for a time, that person was your mother. By the time I realized the only people at fault were the Protectors, it was too late. Your mother had gone. Those bastards stole everything."

He practically spat out the word *Protectors,* and I dropped my gaze to my coffee, studying the dregs of the grounds. I'd been right to hide my father from him. Franc vibrated with rage even now, two decades later.

"Hey," he said. He tugged on the toe of my sock to get my attention. "It's okay. You're safe here."

He'd mistaken my upset expression for that of fear of the Protectors discovering me in San Francisco.

"What makes you so sure?" I asked, curious. He sounded certain.

Setting his mug on the coffee table, he relaxed back into the couch cushions. I swear he took up the space of two people and would make Asher and Gabe look small in comparison. I wasn't sure I would ever get used to Franc's size.

"You're not the only Healer around here," he said.

I sat up in shock. "There are more of us? You know where they are?"

He nodded. "Of course. With the Protectors hunting them into near extinction, the Healers needed a place to feel safe. Rather than running and hiding, we've banded together. Joined forces, if you will."

I frowned. "What do you mean? Wouldn't a group of Healers draw more attention?"

"You didn't know about us, did you?"

"No, but I'm not exactly in the know. I've been isolated for a long time."

"Not anymore, Remy. You have a family now."

For an instant, I felt guilty for not telling him about my father, stepmother, and sister. But what choice did I have? The lying thing sucked, but the protecting thing was in my blood.

"What was my mom like before?" I asked to change the subject.

My grandfather warmed to the question and launched into a dozen happy stories about the scrapes my mother had gotten into as a child. Obviously, he'd loved her a great deal. He'd doted on her, and they'd been close until she hit her teen years. I laughed along with him as he described teaching my mother to ride a bike, but I couldn't help thinking how sad their life sounded. They'd always been on the run, moving from place to place, and never really letting anyone know them. My grandparents had held on to each other, but what about my mother? Never able to have friends or a boyfriend. Never able to share her life with anyone for fear she'd spill her family secrets. I thought her life must have been very lonely, even if she had been my grandfather's golden child until that day she told someone their secret.

Despite the kick of caffeine the coffee offered, my eyes began to droop eventually, and my grandfather showed me to my room. My suitcase rested on the bed, and I remembered what I had brought along with me.

"Fran—" I stopped and frowned. "You know I just realized I have no idea what to call you. Grandpa seems weird."

"How about Franc with an option for 'hey, old man' when I begin to lose my hearing?"

"Franc, it is." His face split in one of those huge, gentle grins, and I smiled back.

"Can I ask you something?" He nodded. "When Mom left, you were angry with her. Why were you still checking for the ad? How did you know she'd write you one day?"

Franc swallowed and his eyes watered. "I didn't know. I hoped. I checked the ads every week, and I hoped she would one day reach out to me. I prayed she had forgiven me. And when she didn't contact me, I prayed it was because she'd found a happier life away from the Healers and Protectors."

And even though he'd prayed, he'd still hoped she would one day write him. What would our lives have been like if she had? We might have lived on the run, but at least there wouldn't have been a Dean.

I reached into my bag and pulled out the disk I'd recorded the night before. "You know that recording I told you about? The one my mother made before she died? I made a copy if you want it. I thought maybe you'd want to hear her voice again."

I'd edited out the parts that revealed I might be different from other Healers, but he didn't have to know that. My grandfather's smile had slipped, and I hesitated before holding out the disk to him.

"I should warn you that there's not much on here that's happy. My mother was . . . not a sunshiny person."

Franc took the disk with an expression I couldn't read. With a soft good night, he left, leaving the door open a crack. I wondered if he would ever listen to it. Sometimes I wished I'd never heard it, and I'd lived with her through a lot of what she described.

After changing into my pajamas, I texted Asher with an update. He answered right away, as if he'd been waiting to hear from me. I hated it that I couldn't call him, but I didn't want my grandfather to wonder whom I spoke to. Soon, we said good night, and I closed my eyes, hoping tomorrow would be easier.

I woke to my mother's voice.

She sounded muffled, as if she spoke from a distance. I sat straight up in bed, shoving my hair out of my face. It took a moment to realize her words were familiar. I could practically recite them because I'd listened to the recording so many times. She was describing her parents and what it had been like growing up on the road with them.

We lived quietly, moving around a lot, and they did odd jobs. Mom was a housekeeper, and Dad a handyman. They tried to make things as normal as possible for me, but it was necessary for us to stay "off the grid," according to Dad. I didn't mind as a child. We never had much, but it was enough.

Quietly, I climbed out of bed and tiptoed into the hall. A light shone downstairs in the living room. I wished I could spare my grandfather what she would say next. My mother went on to describe the day he'd shown up at her school and pulled her out of class. He'd been covered in blood and had just watched his wife die. He'd taken my mother on the run to hide her from the Protectors, but not before she'd seen her house burning down in the distance.

My father did what Mom would've wanted him to. He saved me and made sure we stayed hidden.

I teetered at the top of the landing, wondering if I should reveal myself, but something stopped me. I hadn't wanted anyone to see me when I'd first listened to this recording.

But he never looked at me the same way. I think he hated me.

The recording continued, but I couldn't hear her words anymore. They were drowned out by my grandfather's sobs. The wrenching sound haunted me long after I'd tiptoed back to my room.

My mother had blamed herself for her mother's death. I blamed myself for my mother's death. And now my grandfather blamed himself, too.

It seemed blame was an endless thing with enough to go around for everyone.

Chapter Eight

*T*he next morning at breakfast, my grandfather did not mention the recording, and I didn't bring it up. Instead, he'd reverted back to the jovial man who'd greeted me at the airport. Last night might have been my imagination except for the dark circles under his eyes.

"What would you like to do today, Remy?"

He'd mentioned showing me around the city, and much as I wanted to do that, I had come here for a reason.

"Do you think we could meet the other Healers you mentioned? I've never met anyone like me."

I didn't have to fake my curiosity. I'd grown up learning to use my powers by trial and error. My mother hadn't given me any insights until that damned recording, when it had been too late to help me. Even she hadn't really known how my Protector side had affected my Healer abilities.

My grandfather smiled. "I was hoping you'd say that. There are a lot of people eager to meet you."

After cleaning up the kitchen, we hopped in his truck. I could have sworn I saw Asher in the rearview mirror for just a second. He'd promised to check in on me. We'd made plans for me to sneak out that night so I could see him, and I counted the hours until then. I had so much to tell him that wouldn't fit in a text.

A short time later, we left the hilly city behind and drove south on Highway 1. This time, I grilled my grandfather, focusing my interrogation on the Healers.

"You said they've joined forces. What does that mean?" I asked.

"Well, the Healers used to live by a creed where they traveled alone and changed their name often. The better to stay lost. After what happened to your grandmother, though, I realized that wasn't working. Living apart made us easier pickings for the Protectors. I thought it was time we came up with a better plan."

I noticed that my grandfather used "we" when he talked about the Healers. He wasn't like them and didn't have their blood running through his veins. Marriage to my grandmother had obviously been his induction into their ranks if he considered himself one of them.

"But how did you even find each other? If you'd all gone into hiding, where did you even begin?"

"Easy. You're family, all descended from the same bloodlines. Did you forget that? Just like your mother knew how to find me, Healers long ago established ways to find each other. A way to exchange news or keep each other informed about known Protectors entering an area. I used the old ways to find Healers who had tired of running for their lives."

"And they what? Live on a compound with electric fences and 'Keep out, Protectors' signs?"

My grandfather laughed, shaking his head. "Geez, you take after your mother." He snorted, giving me a sideways glance. "No, we don't live on a compound. Most of the Healers have made a home here in Pacifica."

We pulled off the highway at a town that looked a little worn around the edges with buildings that had seen better days. Wedged between the shore and the hills, something about the area reminded me of movies set in the sixties. The houses were an eclectic mix of bungalows and ranch-style homes. Unlike San Francisco with its tall buildings, these structures squatted low to the earth. Despite how tired everything looked, the view of the beach made up for it as we closed in on the coast.

In Blackwell Falls, the water only worked itself into waves when a solid storm hit us. Here the velvet blue ocean frothed and slammed the beach over and over again. An alive, wild thing, it stood up in eight-foot waves, daring the humans to come play. I sat forward in my seat, straining against the seat belt to get a better glimpse of the horizon.

"That's Rockaway Beach," my grandfather said, noticing my eagerness. "I'll have Erin take you down for a closer look, if you like."

"Erin?" I asked.

"One of the younger Healers. She's about your age. You'll like her. I thought maybe you'd like to spend time with someone other than an old man."

We arrived at one of the bungalows lining the shore. This one was white with worn clapboard siding that needed a paint job. I hopped out of the truck and followed my grandfather to the front door. A girl opened the door at my grandfather's knock and hugged him. When she noticed me, she turned slightly pink and dropped her gaze to the floor. Blond with brown eyes, she resembled my mother more than I did. It occurred to me that this girl could be a distant relative.

"Erin, this is my granddaughter, Remy."

I waved at the shy girl. "Hey."

Her lips slipped into a quick smile and she gestured for us to enter. "They're all here, Franc. Mom couldn't keep them away."

They who?

I didn't have long to ponder that, as a wall of noise hit

me. Inside the house, people of every age packed the living room and connected dining room. They sat on every
surface, including the arms of chairs and sofas and the
floor, or stood against the walls where they could find
space. All conversation stopped and at least fifty people
turned to stare at me.

What had I been thinking listening to my mother's advice? No way could I defend myself against this many people if they wanted to hurt me.

I didn't know I'd stopped moving, until my grandfather
laid a hand on my shoulder. He bent at the knees to meet
my eyes, which I'm sure had fixed wide in terror.

"Hey, kiddo. Nothing to worry about here. We're all
friends."

*Chill out, Remy, and try to act like you're not dating the en-
emy.* I took a deep breath and nodded.

"I think maybe we overwhelmed her, Franc," a slim
blond woman said as she stepped forward. She held out a
hand to me. "Hi, Remy. I'm Dorthea Angelini. You met
my daughter, Erin, at the door."

I shook her hand and she introduced me to the others
in the room. I didn't catch a lot of the names—there were
too many to remember. What I did notice were the other
teens in the room, at least five of them around my age.
Only two were female, including Erin. And the room
held way more men than women overall.

I stepped close to my grandfather and whispered, "I
thought only women were Healers?"

He frowned. "Your mother really did leave some gaps
in your education. The men here are not Healers. Like
me, they are the husbands, brothers, and sons of Healers.
There are only eight Healers here, plus you."

*Eight? After years of searching for them, he'd only been able
to find eight Healers? What chance did I have of surviving?*

He pointed to Erin and the other teen girl, Delia, plus

a younger girl who looked to be about six or seven. Chrissy, the child, slipped behind Delia when I glanced their way. Delia glared at me, her birdlike features sharpening in distaste like I'd invaded her nest. From there, my grandfather pointed out five other women, ranging from their early twenties to one woman who looked to be about thirty-five. If I took the room's stats to heart, Healers did not grow old. Or reach their forties.

Depressed and more than a little shaken, I nodded hello, and Dorthea ushered me to a seat on the couch, shooing away a boy about my age who sat there. Handsome in a blond surfer kind of way, the boy shot me a cocky grin before getting up. I thought he might be Dorthea's son, Alcais. These people had a thing for French names that I couldn't keep straight.

I sat and that seemed to be all the group needed to launch into action. One after another, they shot questions at me like my grandfather had the day before. Most of their questions centered on what I knew about the Protectors. They seemed to assume that my powers worked exactly like theirs and didn't bother to ask questions about that. No, they wanted to know if I'd ever been discovered or attacked.

I couldn't say yes without talking about Asher and the Blackwells, so I lied. Varying degrees of disappointment and relief lit the faces of the people around me. I pictured myself as a soldier being questioned for intel, and I didn't think reality was too far off. These people lived by keeping the Protectors unaware of their existence.

"How do you know I wasn't followed?" I asked. It had suddenly occurred to me that they should have been more concerned about that. "What if my coming here had been a trick?"

From a huge armchair, my grandfather spoke in a serious tone. "I didn't go to the airport on my own, Remy."

My pulse skipped. He gestured to Alcais and a couple of the larger men. "They followed us to ensure you arrived alone. I'm sorry, but we had to make sure."

What if Asher and I hadn't separated at the gate? What if he hadn't hung back? We'd come closer than we imagined to being discovered.

"What would you have done if I was followed?" I asked, trying to keep the tremor out of my voice.

"Taken care of it. Nothing for you to concern yourself about," he said with a placating smile.

That seemed to be a going theme. I lowered my eyes to my lap to hide my expression. I felt like I'd just been patted on the head and told not to worry my silly self. I'd been surviving out there on my own, and I didn't need anyone patronizing me. Still, I'd come here to listen and learn, not cause friction. So I bit my tongue, and the questions continued. Some of the group faded away into other rooms when I revealed how little I knew about Protectors.

Erin approached me, obviously prodded by her mother, and asked, "Delia, Alcais, and I thought maybe you'd want to go for a walk."

I jumped up, happy to get away from the curious stares, even if this hadn't been Erin's idea. "Sure. That would be great."

Outside on the sidewalk, we fell into pairs. Alcais and Delia walked slightly ahead, and I kept pace with Erin. Alcais had a swagger to his step that would put Gabe's to shame. No lack of confidence there. Delia matched him in sarcasm, tossing her dark hair and shooting him sidelong gazes. I listened to their banter for a while, trying to figure them out. They acted like a couple, but they didn't touch.

"Sorry about them," Erin said so softly the wind almost carried the words away.

I moved closer to her, straining to hear her. Something gentle in her manner made me like her. Where the others in my grandfather's group seemed on edge and pushy, Erin had held back her thoughts, her gaze trained on the floor more often than not.

She gestured toward Alcais and Delia. "My brother's always flirting with her, even though he's not interested. It drives Delia nuts."

I smiled. "I get that."

"You seemed surprised when Franc said there only eight of us at the house."

She'd been paying closer attention to me than I'd thought.

"I was," I admitted. "Franc mentioned a community of Healers, and I guess I thought there would be more of us."

Alcais laughed sharply. He'd heard my comment and walked backward to taunt me. "There are more of us. You didn't seriously think that was the whole group?"

Delia jerked his elbow to steer him around a crack in the sidewalk, and he didn't bother to thank her.

He continued without pause. "There are eighty-three Healers altogether, and we're growing more every year. Franc doesn't like too many of us to gather in one place, though. That way we're not all wiped out at once if the Protectors attack."

To hear military-like strategy tossed out by another teen sent a chill down my back. I'd grown up knowing Dean could kill me on any given day. I should be used to talk of death, but somehow, knowing Asher's people were the ones doing the killing changed things. I hated this. All of it. I wanted a world where my only concerns were college and parties and kissing my boyfriend. Fat chance.

We reached the retainer wall separating the bike path from the sand ten feet below. Alcais jumped up on the cement barrier and began to walk along the edge.

Delia scowled at him. "I'm not going to heal you again if you fall, Al."

He grinned down at her and gave me a sly glance. "Maybe Remy will do it this time."

She shot a pissed-off look at me, and I held up both hands, unwilling to be drawn into their reindeer games. "Hey, I don't heal people who come to harm through sheer stupidity. You're on your own."

Erin smothered a laugh behind me, and I guessed most of the girls around here sucked up to Alcais and his pretty boy looks. They could have him. I had Asher waiting for me.

I hitched myself up so I could sit on the wall, turning so I could dangle my legs over the other side, facing the ocean. The waves formed in rows of tight curls and rolled in. A mother chased her little boy at the water's edge, and his giggle drifted in the air. A cool breeze touched my face, whipping my hair back, and I closed my eyes. I heard Erin sit beside me, and I tried to tune out Alcais and Delia when they began sniping at each other again.

Finally, I turned to Erin. "Do they ever stop?"

She grinned. "Only when they sleep."

"Do you have a sleeping potion? Maybe a pill?"

"I heard that," Alcais called out cheerfully.

I ignored him and attempted to draw Erin out. She told me about how my grandfather had helped to establish the group of Healers here. He'd helped the first ones find homes, and then he'd put protocols in place to ensure the Protectors couldn't find them. They did this by going on the offense. The men in the group scouted and made sure they knew where the Protectors were at all times.

"They don't exactly hide," Delia cut in when I questioned how that was possible. "Why would they?"

"The hunter doesn't really need to hide from his prey, does he? Not when he has all the power," Alcais added, his face tightening in a harsh expression as he dropped down on my other side. "Protectors take what they want whenever they're hungry."

A shrill scream pierced the air, interrupting my next question.

We turned toward the sound. A wave had swept to shore and caught the boy I'd noticed playing with his mother earlier. I jumped into action, and I wasn't alone. Alcais, Delia, and Erin launched off the wall and took the steps to the beach alongside me, and I had to remind myself to move at a normal non-Protector pace. Other Healers couldn't move like me.

By the time we reached them, the mother had pulled the boy from the water. He wasn't breathing.

I almost touched his hand, but something stopped me. Just a pause while I considered what would happen if I revealed how different my abilities were, and these people saw me "drowning." The moment passed when I saw the boy's face. He was four or five, and his lips had turned blue. The mother had started CPR, but she was doing it all wrong. If she kept at it, she would break his ribs. I started forward again, but Delia beat me to them, kneeling at the boy's side with her hand hovering over him.

She shared a quick glance with Alcais and Erin, and those two moved in unison. Alcais told the crying mother that Delia had trained as a lifeguard and knew CPR. He and Erin somehow managed to wrench the woman away from her son and placed themselves as a shield between prying eyes and Delia.

She placed both hands on the boy's chest and closed her eyes. As if she really was attempting to do CPR, she pressed into his chest, but I could see it was all for show. The ruse would work for those approaching in the distance, but from where I stood, I saw how light her touch was.

I'd never seen another Healer in action. I guess I had imagined it as something remarkable, but in reality not much happened. No *humming* buzzed through the air like when I healed someone. Nothing that I could sense, anyway.

Not more than ten seconds had passed, though, and I saw why Alcais and Erin had bothered to remove the mother. Hot pink sparks lit where Delia's hands rested on the boy's chest. A moment later, he gasped and began choking and spitting out the gallon of water he'd inhaled while in the ocean.

Delia had healed him, but she didn't show any signs of having absorbed his injuries. Jealousy nipped at me. What would it be like to heal someone and not have to take on whatever had injured them or made them sick? These people didn't know how lucky they were.

Alcais and Erin parted to let the mother at her son when Delia rose to her feet. The crying woman rolled him to his side as he coughed. Erin's eyes widened when I glanced her way, and she gestured for us to go.

Now, she mouthed.

I noticed Alcais and Delia had already taken off, retreating back to the sidewalk above the beach.

"Shouldn't we stay?" I asked Erin in confusion when we followed them. "Won't it look suspicious that Delia saved that boy's life and then disappeared?"

"It will look more suspicious when they find out that Delia was never a lifeguard," Erin muttered.

I blinked. "Oh."

Nobody paid any mind to us as we left. A few onlookers had already made their way over to the mother and her child in our wake. By the time it occurred to any of them to ask who had saved the boy, we would have disappeared from the beach.

As we walked back to Erin's house, raw emotion played

across the faces of the others. Delia gripped Alcais's hand, and he clasped hers tightly in return. Erin's mouth had turned down in a grimace. Fear, I realized. They were terrified they'd be discovered. These Healers weren't so different from me, after all. They might band together, but they still hid their abilities from the world.

What would the world be like if we could openly use our powers? If every injury or illness wouldn't debilitate these Healers like it could for me, we could help so many. Save so many.

But it would never happen. Someone would always try to control us.

"You okay?" Erin asked. And she touched my arm.

A surge of hunger swept through me, and a dark, starving thing inside me yearned to tear at her as if she were the last bit of food on earth. Erin's lips moved, but I couldn't hear her words. I locked on the energy flowing under her skin where her fingers rested on my forearm, and a rushing sound drowned out all noise. My *humming*, I guessed. It had grown in intensity, and I swayed as the electricity vibrated inside me. Electricity that craved Erin's energy. I wanted to take it. I could take it, and I doubted she'd be able to stop me. *Mine, mine, mine* whispered through me. Erin turned to speak to someone in the distance. That dark thing unwound inside me and began to reach for her.

She dropped her hand, and I staggered. I had to lock my knees to stay standing. The electricity buzzing inside me didn't disappear with her touch. The hair on my arms stood straight up. Caught between pushing and pulling energy, I felt like a live wire that could not be grounded. Sweat popped up over my forehead.

"Remy?" I turned at the sound of my name. Erin had walked ahead to join Alcais and Delia. Her brow wrinkled in concern. I must have looked awful because she asked, "You okay?"

"Yes," I said, but it came out shaky. In a more steady voice, I said, "I'm fine. Be there in a minute, okay?"

She paused a moment, and then walked away, shrugging when Delia asked her something. They disappeared down the driveway. Alone, I bent forward, bracing my palms on my thighs. I inhaled deep, calming breaths. To my ears, I sounded like a woman in labor.

Two questions formed as I stood there, trying not to freak out. What the hell had just happened to me? And how could I stop it from ever happening again?

Because some instinct told me that I could have killed Erin if she'd touched me any longer.

CHAPTER NINE

*M*y grandfather and I had said very little on the way back to the city.

I'd returned to the house in time to hear Delia and the others explaining what had happened on the beach. My grandfather had watched me the whole while, and I guessed maybe he wanted to see what my reaction had been to seeing another Healer in action. I'd kept my thoughts to myself while Delia's mother berated her for healing the boy in the open.

If I hadn't been so traumatized by what had happened with Erin, I would have smiled at hearing another—even the scowling Delia—get the same lecture I'd heard time and again from Asher and Lucy. Apparently, these Healers had some of the same struggles I did. As it was, I'd kept my mouth shut and hoped no one noticed how freaked out I must have looked.

Back at my grandfather's house, he stopped me on the staircase when I would have headed straight to my room. I worried he might have guessed what had happened with Erin. Maybe she'd picked up on something and told him. What if—

"What Delia did . . . you know she took a great risk, right?" he asked.

I rolled my shoulders, forcing myself to relax. This was

about the boy. Perhaps Erin or one of the others had mentioned that I'd been reaching for him. I'd been raised away from this community, away from their rules and guidelines. I could expose them if I wasn't careful. Delia had taken a risk, and suddenly, I was grateful that she'd beat me to it. In a way, she had saved me from discovery.

I nodded at my grandfather.

He patted my hand where it rested on the banister. "We have to be careful, Remy. It's not just one life at risk when a Healer uses her powers. Every life in our community is at stake."

After saying good night, he left me on the stairs. Guilt pinched me like a pair of too tight shoes because I had every intention of sneaking out to meet my Protector boyfriend that night.

Sinking down on the bed, I scraped my hair away from my face. Then, I picked up my mobile phone.

Gabe answered on the third ring with an irritated, "What?"

I smiled despite myself. I could always count on Asher's brother to be a jerk. "I'm sorry. Did I interrupt you with one of your Sororitoys?"

That was the name my friends and I had given the string of college girls he dated. Gabe had broken a lot of hearts in Blackwell Falls, and elsewhere in the world, considering how long he'd been alive.

"What do you want, Healer?" he asked, a scowl in his voice.

I hesitated. "Never mind," I said. "I shouldn't have called." Why had I called Gabe? Maybe I should have waited and talked to Asher first. Except . . . sometimes Asher didn't tell me everything. Gabe didn't have Asher's instinct to protect me; he had no problem telling me the ugly truth.

I started to hang up anyway, but Gabe's voice stopped me. "Remy, what do you need?"

He used my name so rarely that I spoke without thinking. "Something happened today, Gabe. I'm seriously freaking out."

"You don't freak out," he said. "It's one of the few things I like about you."

I opened my mouth to answer and then snapped it closed again. A compliment from Gabe?

"Spit it out."

I almost made a snide comment, but I bit it back. Too much was at stake to let Gabe get to me. "A Healer touched me today, and I had this uncontrollable urge to attack her."

That shut him up.

"You're freaking out, aren't you?" I asked.

He snorted, and I launched into a description of what had happened.

"Have you heard of anything like this before?" I asked, desperate for some kind of answer.

His sigh sounded loud. "You're not going to like it. Have you talked to Asher about this?"

"Tonight."

"Let him explain it to you then. And tell my brother to stay safe."

"Damn it, Gabe. Please . . ."

Too late. The bastard had hung up on me.

Later, long after my grandfather had gone to his room, I put on a coat and tied my hair back into a ponytail. Then, I tiptoed down the stairs and out the back door. I'd texted Asher to meet me in the forest at the edge of the yard. I strolled toward the forest like I was taking a walk in case anyone watched the house.

As soon as I entered the tree line, an arm snagged my waist. I didn't have to have Asher's heightened senses, but I would know his touch blindfolded. His hands slid up my back to my shoulder blades, and he exerted enough pressure to tip me off balance and into him. I didn't mind. For the first time since I'd gotten off the plane yesterday, I felt safe.

"I missed you," he said.

Even that whisper sounded loud in the silence. I pulled away and held a finger to my lips. I gestured for us to go deeper into the forest. He kept up with me when I began to run at a breakneck pace. I stopped in a small clearing when the pine trees crowded together too closely to run safely and the house had disappeared behind us.

The clearing reminded me of the one in Townsend Park, except here the menthol scent of eucalyptus overpowered everything.

"I think we're okay now," I said, wrapping my arms around myself.

Asher had gone watchful, studying the area with sight and hearing far better than mine.

"Do you think someone is on to us?"

I shook my head, pacing nervously. "No, but we have to be careful. They're more prepared than we thought. They had people watching me at the airport. They're always on guard for Protectors."

Asher leaned against a tree trunk, his hand tucked in his coat pockets. "Want to tell me what happened to freak you out?"

I'm sure I looked like a crazy person when I threw back my head and laughed. One side of his mouth tilted up in a small smile as he waited for me to sober up.

"Gabe said that I don't freak out," I said wryly.

Asher's eyebrow shot up. "You spoke to Gabe?"

I nodded. For the second time that night I explained what had happened when Erin touched me. Asher dropped his relaxed pose and pushed away from the tree. His hands tightened into fists, and I thought maybe he was angry.

Like Gabe, he said nothing for a while after I finished. I

could tell he wanted to speak, but couldn't get the words out. The longer that went on, the more I worried.

"WHAT?" I finally blurted out. "What do you know that I don't? Asher, I was terrified. I thought I was going to attack that girl. What's happening to me?"

I covered my face with my hands. I didn't hear Asher approach, but I fought him when he tried to pull my hands away. It did no good. He simply tugged them down. His thumbs brushed the inside of my wrists, and I doubted he was even aware he did it. Despite everything, my pulse jumped.

Asher bent at the knees, so he could look me in the eye. "Everything's okay. What happened to you is perfectly normal. For a Protector."

My mouth dropped open, and he tapped my chin with our joined hands.

"Remember how I told you that our parents train us from a young age to keep our guard up around Healers? There was a reason for that. One you know too well now."

"That hunger . . . You mean you feel that all the time?"

"No. Just around Healers. And you."

I groaned and pulled away from him. I paced away with my hands on my hips. He let me go, obviously concluding that I needed space to process this one. He'd warned me so many times that he was a danger to me, that he had to control himself around me. Having only felt the pull of my power around him, I'd had no idea what he meant. The way my body had craved Erin's energy . . . Hurting her had been more than a possibility. How stupid and naïve I had been! How had he been fighting that hunger whenever we touched? Asher was far stronger than I'd guessed.

"Well . . ." I said.

"Well," he repeated.

"Every time I think I know what we're up against, I get a good slap across the face."

"We can't seem to get a break, huh?"

His hair fell across his forehead, and my fingers itched to touch it. Instead, I tucked my hands in my pockets.

Shifting my weight from foot to foot, I asked, "You really get that overload of hunger and energy whenever we touch?" He nodded. "How can you stand it?"

His eyes trailed over me, and I felt a blush start at my toes and work its way up, even though I never blushed.

"Totally worth it," he said in a deep voice.

My mouth dried up, and I swallowed, pretty sure I could be running a fever.

"Hey, Remy?"

"Yeah?"

"Are you ever going to kiss me? I missed you."

If I had doubted that he would feel the same way about me, knowing this new challenge we faced, the need in his voice set me straight. I took two running steps and then launched myself at him. He caught me easily, holding me against him with my feet hanging in the air and our noses touching. This close, I could see the green of his eyes.

I put my guard up. Then I pressed my lips to Asher's, and I forgot all about Healers and Protectors.

Much later, we came up for air long enough for me to tell him what had happened in the last two days. Asher had cleared the pine needles and leaves from a spot on the ground. I curled up between his outstretched legs, bracing myself against his chest while he leaned against a tree.

"I'm sorry you had to be the one to tell him about Anna," Asher said, after I told him about hearing my grandfather cry while listening to my mother's recordings.

I shrugged. "The last couple of days have been weird. He's formed a community of Healers here, Asher. There are a lot of them."

His arms tensed around me. "That's not possible. We'd know. The Protectors would know if that were true."

I twisted about to face him, sitting on my heels. "I'm telling you it is possible. I met some of them. Today I even watched a girl my age heal a child who nearly drowned."

I described what had happened with Delia and the boy, and Asher listened thoughtfully.

"You said I was different from them, but I didn't understand how much." I shook my head. "Delia healed that little boy and walked away without a mark on her. I could never do that."

I sounded jealous. I could hear it in my voice. Since that afternoon, when I wasn't reliving the nightmare with Erin, I'd been replaying the moment Delia had used her powers. My mother had described a Protector as an absorber of energy and a Healer as a conduit for energy, controlling it and using it to heal people. Basically, Protectors absorbed energy while Healers pushed it.

As for me? I'd become some screwed-up mix of the two—pushing energy to heal, but absorbing the injuries and illnesses after. And now, like Protectors, apparently I could steal Healer energy. I would have to constantly be on my guard around them.

I thought about what had happened with my grandfather the day before at dinner and how I'd healed his cut finger.

"Already? That happened fast," Asher said, reading my mind.

We'd known I'd be forced to use my ability sooner or later, if for no other reason than to prove that I had one. Now more than ever, I guessed my grandfather would not have shared all he had so quickly without some type of demonstration from me. As he'd said, they had too much at stake here.

"We kind of lucked out there," I said in a solemn tone. "At least it was a small injury that I could hide."

I'd been able to prove myself and not reveal the nasty side effect of my ability that other Healers didn't share. The side effect that had left me bruised, scraped, sick, and with broken bones from things that had never happened to me.

Asher gave me a small, sad smile. "I wouldn't exactly call it lucky that you were hurt," he said.

He reached for the hand that had bled the night before and brushed his lips across my knuckles. I shivered as he placed my hand on his shoulder. Freed from mine, his fingers trailed down my bare forearm to the sensitive skin of my inner elbow. Goose bumps popped up wherever he touched me.

"You know what I mean." My voice sounded breathy.

"I do," he admitted.

Those magic fingers continued up my arm, brushed over my shoulders, and then skimmed my ribs on their way to my waist. I locked my gaze on Asher's. They gleamed with a hint of desperation.

"Asher?" I asked, uncertain.

I'd had my guard lowered to share my thoughts. But kissing was something else. He should have his walls up, a fact he was choosing to ignore for some reason.

"Kiss me," he said.

I started to raise my walls, all too happy to comply, but his fingers distracted me as they slipped under the hem of my T-shirt and flattened against the bare skin of my back. He pulled, knocking me off balance and into his arms. One hand left my back, and I immediately missed the warmth. But then his fingers were in my hair, working on the rubber band that held it back. Another tug and my hair fell across my shoulders. Asher leaned forward, burying his face in it.

"Kiss me," he whispered again.

He wanted me to kiss him without our barriers up. I understood that, but I didn't know why. I could hurt him. I had before. My body didn't just cure his immortality. It stole it. He could end up dead. It wasn't right to take chances with his life. Not like this.

I shook my head. "No."

His eyebrows shot up in surprise, and my mouth quirked. I'm not sure it flattered me that my boyfriend thought I would say yes to his every request.

Asher's sudden laugh sounded loud, and he didn't loosen his grip when I moved my hands to his chest to push away.

"We'd still be back in Blackwell Falls if you always said yes to me," he said, clear amusement lightening his mood a degree.

I pushed against him again, but to no avail. Damned super strength. "It's completely unfair that you can read my mind, but I can't read yours," I grumbled. "Let me go."

His hold finally loosened and I sat up. His innocent expression looked so put on I didn't trust it.

"What's wrong with you? You're always telling me how dangerous it is for both of us to have our guard down."

"Maybe I just don't feel like being in control right now."

I stared at him for a moment in silence. He gazed back in defiance.

"No, that's not it," I said emphatically.

It was one thing for Asher to lose control in the heat of the moment. That had happened to both of us more than once. This was something different. To suggest we knowingly take a chance went against everything we'd agreed to. He was holding something back. This felt like the days when he knew about my Healer blood, while I had tried to figure out what the hell he was. Today had been stressful enough.

Asher raised his mental guard. He ran a hand through his hair, messing it up in his frustration. "I'm sorry. I'm acting like an ass."

"No argument here. Care to explain why?"

"I'm tired. I hate being away from you. And I really hoped . . ." He rubbed a hand over his face. "I can't believe I let myself hope they'd have a cure."

The missing puzzle piece slotted into place. He'd wanted my grandfather to be able to help us. As much as Asher had protested my coming here, he'd hoped the other Healers might know a way to solve our problems. We didn't like to talk about it, but the possibility existed that I could become immortal, while he became human. We would never be in the same place for long with each of us constantly changing. I'd hardly admitted it to myself, but sometimes I worried that the return of Asher's touch meant my ability to feel anything might disappear.

Healing always came at a cost for me.

The whole situation was so screwed up, no wonder we didn't talk about it. I didn't see a solution in sight, but I'd hoped my grandfather might have answers, too. It seemed I wasn't the only one freaking out. Some selfish part of me felt glad that I wasn't the only one acting irrationally.

"Asher, lower your guard."

"No, you're right. That was a reckless idea. I don't know what the hell I was thinking."

"You weren't thinking. You were feeling," I said, moving closer to him. *Trust me. Lower your guard,* I repeated in my thoughts. *And close your eyes.*

He did as I asked.

"Promise me you'll stand still," I whispered.

He nodded after a slight hesitation. His heartbeat spiked when I laid a palm on his chest. His skin radiated heat, and

I wanted to curl into it, but I took a deep breath. One of us had to be in control, so I raised my mental walls, knowing that when I felt this much, Asher could see through them. I opened my mind and let my imagination go, as I closed my eyes, too.

I pictured myself touching him the way I wished I could without fear of repercussions. I pushed the coat off of his shoulders, letting it fall to the ground. My jacket and his T-shirt followed, leaving miles of skin and muscle for me to explore. I inhaled the scent of the woods mixed with that of Asher. In my mind, I placed one of his hands on my shoulder, bare except for the thin strap of a tank top. Then, mimicking what he'd done to me earlier, I trailed my fingers down his forearm, into the crook of his elbow, up his arm, and very lightly down his side.

Asher's real-life chest moved under my hand, as he sucked in a deep breath and I smiled. And then the mental version of me grazed her lips across Asher's cheek to his mouth, sharing a breath with him. The kiss the imaginary me laid on him could have burned down the forest.

"Remy," Asher said.

He sounded tortured, and I let the images fade from my mind, worried he hadn't liked what I'd pictured. Back in the reality of the forest, we opened our eyes. My hand still rested against the *thump, thump, thump* of his heart.

"You're not the only one who's frustrated," I said.

His expression looked pained. "We should go. Now."

He didn't wait for my response, merely clasped my hand and took off running. Even with my new speed, I struggled to keep up with him. I didn't get his urgency, but he didn't listen when I asked him to slow down. We arrived near my grandfather's property, and Asher sidestepped me when I would have hugged him good-bye. Instead, he gave me a light push toward the house. My ego took a bruising, too.

"I love you. Text me when you're inside, okay?"

I scowled and didn't move. "Seriously? That's all you're going to say?"

Maybe it had only happened in my mind, but the moment we had shared in the forest had been intense.

Asher inhaled a deep, calming breath and looked toward the sky. "You really don't get how you affect me, do you?" He tipped my chin up with one of his knuckles. "You have to go now because I need to find a cold ocean to jump in. Can I make it any clearer?"

I clapped a hand over my mouth to stifle a laugh when I grasped what he was trying to tell me. Heat crawled up my neck, and I turned to go in a hurry. Just before I stepped out of the forest, Asher whispered my name.

"One day we won't have to worry about mental walls. It's going to be better than we can imagine."

He slipped through an opening in the trees and disappeared. Left alone with the thought of something better, I shivered and wished for it with all my might.

CHAPTER TEN

*M*y days settled into a rhythm. Not comfortable exactly, but I didn't have too many complaints. Sometimes my grandfather played tour guide and showed me
around San Francisco. Most days, we drove out to Pacifica, and I absorbed what I could about the Healers. Asher
had warned me to keep my guard up at all times, and after that first day, I agreed. I would never forgive myself if
I hurt any of them. To be on the safe side, I also made a
point of avoiding any accidental touches, sidestepping
shaking hands with Healers even to the point of rudeness.
I'd rather they think me rude, though, than chance feeling
what I had with Erin.

In the evenings, I slipped away to call my family. I told
my grandfather that I was calling my friends back in
Brooklyn, and I told my father that my grandfather was
out when Ben asked to speak to him. I lied to my grandfather about my family in Blackwell Falls, and I lied to my
family about how I spent my time with my grandfather.
Someone should have given me a sash with THE WORLD'S
GREATEST FIBBER written across it in caps. I'm fairly certain Lucy would have been happy to make it by hand. She
avoided me like I had the chicken pox. Most of my up-
dates about her came from Laura and Brandon. Gabe, on
the other hand, had taken to sending me imperative texts.

I could almost hear his arrogant tone when I read TAKE CARE OF MY BRTHR or REMEMBER YR TRAINING. I usually ignored his texts or texted back PISS OFF because I knew it would irritate him.

The only person I didn't lie to was Asher. Our time together came in stolen moments every few nights when I could sneak away. We feared that if we met more often, my grandfather would become suspicious. Plus, since our first night in the forest, Asher and I had spent more minutes in pent-up, awkward silence than talking. What conversation we had revolved around what I was learning about the other Healers in Pacifica.

A couple of weeks after I arrived, my grandfather left me at Erin's house while he ran errands. Alcais and Delia had gone off together somewhere, so I spent a rare moment alone with Erin. As had become our habit, we strolled to the beach, stopping at a small café along the way to pick up a hot cocoa for her and a mocha for me.

I swiped a finger through the whipped cream and wrinkled my nose. "This is so wrong to be drinking hot coffee in July. We should be in the middle of a heat wave that's melting our shoes into the concrete."

Erin smiled. "That's the Bay Area for you. Summer doesn't get here until September. Too bad you'll be gone by then. Franc said you live with friends in Brooklyn?"

"Yes," I lied. "Ever since my mother died."

"I'm sorry," she responded simply.

I nodded and sipped my drink. "Can I ask you something? What does it feel like? When you heal people?"

Her head tipped to the side, and her hair spilled over her shoulder. "Don't you know? You've experienced it yourself."

"So it's the same for everyone then?" I asked.

She blew on her cocoa. "Sure. Why wouldn't it be? Someone is hurt or sick. We gather our energy and touch a person to heal him or her. There are sparks, and it's a done deal. Nothing to it."

"Don't you ever get cold after?"

Asher said it looked like I had hypothermia, especially after healings that required more energy. My lips turned blue, and shivers racked my body until I could warm myself again. Delia hadn't suffered any of this from what I'd seen.

Erin gave me a curious look, tucking her hair behind one ear. "No. Do you?"

I shrugged, not answering the question. I thought about the differences between our mothers. Erin spoke about her abilities with such ease. She'd grown up accepting that they were a part of her and not something to be hated or feared. Her mother had been the opposite of mine.

"You're lucky, Erin. To have all these people around to teach you. I didn't have that."

We reached the breaker wall, and she held my drink while I hitched myself up onto the ledge. Then I held her drink while she did the same. I wore gloves, but I still maneuvered carefully to avoid our fingers touching. We studied the waves, and I could sense how badly she wanted to question me. It didn't take long.

"Your mother really didn't tell you anything?"

"No. I think she hoped that if she pretended my abilities didn't exist, they would go away." That was the truth. She'd admitted as much on the recordings. "She didn't want me to be part of this life. Constantly in danger." I turned to Erin. "How do you do it? Living with the threat of the Protectors hanging over you all the time?"

Erin's forehead wrinkled as she thought about the question. "It's not like I know anything different. Besides, we go about our lives like everyone else does. Just more quietly and with a bit more caution."

"Really?" I asked, genuinely bewildered. "What about dating? Or kissing boys?"

Erin's skin turned blotchy as color climbed her neck to reach her cheeks. "I can't speak from personal experience, but being a Healer hasn't exactly stopped Delia from getting around."

My brows rose at that, and Erin seemed to realize what she'd said. She slapped a hand over her mouth.

"I didn't mean that."

She collapsed into giggles when I said, "Sure, you didn't," drawing the words out.

"Okay, maybe I did mean it." It took her a moment to get serious again when I lost it at her admission. When she sobered, she said, "I think you have the wrong idea about what it means to be one of us. Being a Healer isn't a punishment, Remy. It's a gift."

She really believed that. Sincerity practically oozed out of her. But then she didn't have a Protector side throwing her powers out of whack.

My doubt must have been obvious because she laughed. "I'm serious. Listen, your grandfather changed everything for us. He realized we'd been going about things all wrong. Separating. Hiding. A lot of people died alone and without help. Franc believes it's safer to hide in plain sight. A few of us have been caught, but it's not like before. We lead our lives in the open, and nobody suspects anything."

It sounded good in theory, but . . . "What about using your powers? I mean, isn't healing people what usually gets our kind caught?"

She bumped my shoulder with hers and didn't seem to notice when I moved away quickly. "That's the one part of our lives we keep hidden."

I frowned. I didn't understand how that was possible for a group this size. I'd almost been busted a dozen times.

The sparks and "now you seem 'em, now you don't" injuries were always a dead giveaway. At the very least, the person you healed would notice. How many people could you heal before someone blabbed?

The only thing that had saved me from discovery had been my isolation. Before I'd arrived in Blackwell Falls, I'd healed myself or my mother after Dean had beat the crap out of us. There had been occasional brushes with strangers that I couldn't help, and every once in a while, there had been someone hurt or sick that I'd healed because some decent part of me demanded that I had to. Somehow I'd always managed to slip away, though, before their minds could accept what they'd seen. I'd gotten too good at blending into walls to hide what a freak I was and to hide what damage Dean had done to us. Shame could be a powerful thing. Asher had changed everything by seeing the real me the very first day we'd met.

Before I could ask Erin more questions, she waved at someone in the distance. I followed her gaze to see Alcais and Delia approaching and had to smother my disappointment. The pair tended to steer the conversation with their bickering.

Erin gave me a sweet smile as her brother and friend reached us. "You should ask your grandfather to show you our library."

I sat up straight. "Library?"

"Sure. We all have to spend time in there at some point. There's a book that might answer your questions about our kind. How our abilities work, how to avoid Protectors, that kind of thing."

"You're kidding me. Someone wrote a book about that?"

"Books. It's a library, after all. It would be a crappy library if it only had one book." She kicked off the wall

with her foot, waving at Delia and Alcais. "You know, if
the story we've heard is true, soon we won't have to
worry about Protectors anyway."

I froze, but she didn't seem to notice. "What story?"

Delia overheard Erin's last comment as she joined us
and rolled her eyes. "I can't believe you're repeating that
shit."

"It's just a story, Delia," Erin protested weakly. "I didn't
say I believed it."

Alcais stole Erin's cocoa and sipped it. "Oh, back off,
Delia. Let her have her fun."

"What story?" I repeated.

Erin hesitated a moment and then shot Delia a defiant
look before she spoke. "It's no big deal. Some people say
they've heard of a story the Protectors tell each other.
They say one day there will be a different kind of Healer
who can cure their immortality."

The contents of my stomach flipped over. I fought to
speak around the lump that had formed in my throat.
"Why? I mean, why would they think there would be a
Healer who could do that?"

Did they know the Healer in that story would have
Protector blood? *Please, no.*

Alcais scoffed at my question. "Who knows? It doesn't
matter anyway. One day we're going to figure out a way
to kill them, immortal or not. It's only a matter of time before we outnumber them."

Delia hissed and exchanged a harsh glance with Alcais.
He grinned unrepentantly and launched into a tale about
a time he'd surfed during a storm. Of course, the storm
was practically a monsoon the way he told it, and the
waves had been at least twenty feet high in his estimation.
Delia sniped at him for exaggerating, and their usual bickering started.

They should have saved their efforts to distract me. No way would I forget what they'd said. They had a library. A library with books that could hold the key to my future with Asher. These Healers had secrets, but secrets could be uncovered.

CHAPTER ELEVEN

*M*y grandfather had been right about his cooking skills. He even sucked at breakfast, which should have been the easiest meal to make. Who couldn't scramble some eggs and pop bread in the toaster? My grandfather, apparently.

After the first couple of mornings of me politely trying to eat the burnt toast and runny eggs he'd prepared, he'd taken pity on me. We now walked to a nearby diner in the Presidio to eat each morning. My coffee addiction amused him. He loved to watch the whole process of me adding cream and sugar to my cup.

"How's your coffee-flavored milk?" he asked.

I'd gotten surprisingly comfortable with him. We spoke the same language: smart-ass.

"Better than your weak tea. Real men drink coffee, Franc."

"What about the British?"

I waved a hand. "They're the exception, obviously. What's your excuse?"

"Good taste?" he suggested.

I snorted. "Your shirt would argue otherwise."

My grandfather laughed, knowing his shirt—another red-and-black checked button-up flannel à la lumberjack—looked perfectly fine. After finishing our meal, we stood, gathering our wrappers and plates to drop them into the recycling and compost bins.

We started the uphill walk to his house, our breath puffing into white clouds that blended with the gray skies. Every one of his giant steps equaled three of mine, but he slowed his pace so I could keep up. I screwed my courage up to ask him the question that had been weighing on me.

"Hey, Franc, Erin mentioned that you had a library with books about Healers?" At his nod, I took a chance. "I feel like I have these huge gaps in my education. There are all these things I should know, but I'm clueless because Mom didn't want me to know about this world. Do you think maybe I could borrow some books?"

"Sure. I'll get you a book to browse next time we're in Pacifica."

I exhaled the breath I'd been holding. It wasn't access to the library like I wanted, but it was a start. Another question had been bugging me, but I wondered if I'd gained enough for the day. Except I could feel my time here running out, and the pressure of what I didn't know crushed me more every day. *In for a penny, in for a pound,* I thought.

"Something has been bothering me. Alcais mentioned something in passing about the Healers outnumbering the Protectors. What did he mean? I thought there weren't many of us left."

My grandfather's lips tightened for second, as if in anger, but the emotion disappeared. "Have you ever wondered where you get your abilities from?"

I hadn't really. I'd had too many other things to wonder about.

"Something to do with our very special double X chromosomes?" I guessed.

"We think it's something to do with your brain chemistry. As far as we can tell, your brain waves are different. Every human has kinetic energy that enables us to move

and think. We all have electricity in our bodies. But somehow Healers are able to control their energy. As you already know, you can manipulate that energy to heal
others."

I'm sure I looked confused. "What does this have to do
with increasing our numbers?"

He smiled. "If we can isolate what makes you a Healer,
maybe we can replicate it."

I stumbled a little before catching myself. Replicate?
This sounded too freaky to me.

"You're going to make Healers?" I asked.

"Not just Healers, Remy. Male Healers. Why shouldn't
men have this ability, too? Think of everyone we could
help if there were more of us."

He finally noticed that I no longer walked beside him.
Shocked, I stared at him when he turned about.

He frowned a little as if disappointed with my reaction.
"You look upset."

I bit my lip, trying to find the right words to explain
what I felt. "Not upset, exactly. More like weirded out.
What you're talking about sounds like a midnight sci-fi
flick. Brain waves? Replicate?" I shook my head at a loss.

He tapped a finger to his mouth. "When you look at it
that way, I guess you're right. I'm sorry I sprang it on you
that way. But think about it from our perspective. Healers
are being hunted into extinction. We need to come up
with some way to protect our people. How do we do that
when our enemy is immortal? When they gain power
from murdering us?" He held his hands out, palms up.
"We're trying to survive here."

I couldn't process what he'd said, even though I could
see the reasons behind it. After a long moment, my grandfather and I continued walking, both of us lost in our
thoughts. Asher hadn't wanted to come near me in the beginning because of the danger he represented to me. A

danger I understood better after what had happened with Erin. But for Asher, his hunger had another dimension since he'd lost his senses. He'd worried he'd give in to his desire to feel human again, at the expense of my life. And maybe if I'd been like other Healers he would have.

As soon as the thought occurred, I felt sick. Asher would never hurt me. I knew that to the very core of me. To think it had been a possibility was a betrayal to him. He'd met other Healers, and he'd never harmed them. He'd only killed by accident when he'd tried to protect his sister from the Healer threatening her. A Healer who'd already gotten his brother killed.

At one time, the Healers had been the bad guys. Even my mother had admitted to that. Eighty years ago, their abuse of the Protectors had led to the War that had nearly wiped out the Healers. Even if the Healers increased their numbers, did they really stand a chance?

Eventually, I broke the awkward silence. "How close do you think you are to figuring out how to make lots of little mutant Healers?"

I tried to keep my tone light to bring us back to comfortable footing. I'm not sure I fooled my grandfather, though. Caution colored the edges of his words when he answered me.

"We have some scientists in our group who have been working on it for a long time. They could have the answer any day. In the meantime, we'll do what's necessary to keep our people safe. Every Healer is valuable."

His ginormous hand rested on my shoulder to comfort me. I started to let myself believe that he could accept my Protector side if I ever revealed it to him. Maybe my value as a Healer would outweigh the side of me that he hated.

I didn't know for sure, but I could feel hope uncurl inside me.

★   ★   ★

Some nights Asher and I raced through the forest and down to Fort Point at the base of the Golden Gate Bridge. He listened to my stories with wariness whenever I could escape to meet him. Since he couldn't follow me to Pacifica without raising suspicion, he often stayed in the city. I laughed when he admitted that he'd taken to surfing at Fort Point. The water temperature hovered around the high fifties in the summer and most of the surfers wore full body wet suits, including booties, to fight off the cold. I hadn't yet been able to sneak down to the water during the day to watch him, but I loved the idea of him skimming the waves, all elegance and easy balance as he dodged the rocks scattered across the shoreline.

The day after my discussion with Franc, I mentioned to Asher that the Healers were looking for a way to increase their numbers, but he didn't seem concerned. His eyes did light up when I told him that my grandfather thought they'd isolated what made our powers work and I guessed at the reason why. If they'd figured out what made us tick, maybe they could figure out how to reverse the process that made the Protectors immortal.

"They've heard the stories about me, Asher," I confessed. "I don't think they believe they're true, but they have heard rumors about how a Healer could end Protector immortality."

He frowned. "Remy, be careful. If they suspect anything . . . If you think they even have a clue as to what you are, promise me you'll get out of there." He tucked my hair my ear. "I know you like your grandfather, but remember, we can't trust anyone."

I didn't agree. Every day, I was coming closer to believing that I could trust my grandfather with the truth about me. Franc wanted a family as bad as I always had. I could see it in the way he watched me with a mix of tenderness and affection. If he knew the full truth about me, maybe we could get to a cure for Asher that much sooner. At least, maybe Franc could help Asher and me figure out a way to be together without hurting each other.

I didn't argue with Asher, though. He looked too upset, and I didn't want to make things worse. In the end, I promised to keep my secret awhile longer.

"What's the worst thing you've ever healed, Remy?" Alcais asked the next day.

He'd been playing darts alone at Delia's house, while Delia, Erin, and I sat around a small card table. Franc had given me an untitled book that was really more of a diary that some Healer had kept long ago. So far, the author—a Healer named Maria—hadn't revealed anything I didn't already know. She spent most of her time listing the names of people she'd healed and how much money she'd made on each occasion. She'd even created a chart that listed what each type of injury or illness was worth. The more energy the healing required, the more Maria charged. The mercenary quality to her writings turned my stomach, but I kept at it, hoping she would eventually offer up something of value.

As I flipped through the pages, Erin and I chatted, while Delia stole glances at an indifferent Alcais. After he asked his question, he lined up a second dart and then let it fly at the dartboard Delia's father had nailed to one wall of her family's garage. Pausing before he sent a third arrow after it, he threw me another of his sly looks.

I had a feeling his question was another type of dart. For some reason, he'd been picking at me all day, asking me ridiculous questions. How many times had I cured the flu? Did I ever bump into strangers whose illness I couldn't cure? Had I ever healed an STD? Despite his sister's protests, he'd kept after me until I wanted to hit him.

I'd noticed an indifference in Alcais that I didn't like. He took chances he shouldn't. A lot of boys his age did, really, as if they'd sprouted stupidity hormones at puberty that they somehow mistook for courage. Unlike other boys, Alcais took his carelessness to a new level, using his sister and Delia as safety nets for whatever pranks he pulled. What did it matter if he burned his hand waving it through a candle for fun? Delia could fix him right up. And then there was the day he'd jumped off the pier for kicks. He'd broken his collarbone and come out of the water laughing like a freaking idiot. Erin healed him that time.

As far as Alcais was concerned, someone would always heal him, so what did it matter how recklessly he acted? At first, I didn't understand why my grandfather or Alcais's parents let him get away with it. Weren't these people all about hiding their abilities so the Protectors didn't find them? Then I realized that the adults had no idea what he was up to. Delia and Erin never told on him and, since they didn't absorb his injuries, what did it matter if they had to fix him?

Except it did matter. These full-blooded Healers might not absorb injuries like I did, but using their powers exhausted them. When Erin had fixed Alcais's broken collarbone, her skin had grayed and her eyes had taken on a sunken quality as if her life force drained out of her. I had to swallow my anger when Alcais took her sacrifice for granted, just as he did Delia's when she healed his burned hand.

Both girls had claimed to feel fine the next day, but I still didn't like Alcais. So most of the time, I dodged his pointed questions with sarcasm. When he asked about the worst injury or illness I'd healed, though, Erin and Delia's heads lifted in curiosity and I felt pressured to answer.

I couldn't very well tell them that I'd healed my sister, Lucy, when my stepfather had shot her. They didn't know

Lucy existed, and I wanted to keep it that way. And then there were the times I'd healed Gabe and Asher . . . Right. Like I could explain how I'd healed Protectors.

I faked a calm I didn't feel and flipped a page in my book. "I healed someone with cancer once."

The person had been a teacher at my school in Brooklyn. I wished I could say I'd meant to heal the woman, but it had been an accident. I'd only had my ability for a couple of years, and I hadn't known how to shield myself all the time then. Sometimes my powers kicked in if I bumped into someone, and there was no stopping it. The cancer thing had sucked. I'd been in pain for weeks before I'd been able to heal myself completely.

A sudden quiet in the garage alerted me that I'd answered the question wrong. I looked up from another of Maria's charts to find all three of them staring at me with disbelief.

Delia muttered, "Bullshit," under her breath.

"What?" I asked, confused.

Erin leaned forward in her chair. "Remy, that's impossible. Only the older, more powerful Healers can do that."

"What do you mean?" I asked.

"We can only heal smaller things. Like mending broken bones, or helping that boy to breathe on the beach. Cancer, heart problems, third-degree burns, more life-threatening injuries can kill us. We just don't have the ability to handle the energy they require. That takes more experience."

Damn, damn, damn. Asher had mentioned that my powers worked differently. He hadn't told me that I was healing things beyond what I should be able to at my age. Then again, I'm not sure I'd ever mentioned to him that I'd healed someone with cancer.

I shrugged again, wishing I could eat my words, but it was too late to take them back. "I don't know what to tell you. A woman had stomach cancer. I healed it. Nobody told me there was an age requirement."

I turned back to my book with studied nonchalance, while my heart beat way too fast inside my chest.

Alcais jolted the table when he jerked out the chair beside me, turning it backward so he could straddle it. He crossed his arms over the back, and then planted his chin on them. A dart dangled from his fingers, and he let it swing lazily.

"Come on, then," he demanded. "Let's hear it. Tell us all about how you did what nobody our age can do when you've had zero training from your mother or another Healer."

If his jeering tone was anything to go by, he expected me to back down and admit to lying. Something about his attitude ate at me, and I slammed my book closed on the table, giving up all pretense of reading. I slouched in my seat, acting like I didn't have a care in the world.

"It wasn't exactly a big deal," I drawled, meeting his direct stare. Hoping it would get me off the hook I'd managed to get myself stuck on, I admitted, "It was actually kind of an accident."

I confessed how I'd bumped into the teacher and my abilities had taken over. On the recording she'd left me, my mother had mentioned that my grandmother used to wear gloves to avoid that very thing, so I knew it wasn't a side effect of my Protector side. I left out how the pain I'd taken on had made me want to shriek and how I'd worried I wouldn't recover. If my mother had noticed at the time, she'd never said a word.

I finished my story, and they all continued to stare at me. Erin looked like she might believe me, but Delia flat-out wanted to call me a liar. I could see it in the disdain she levied my way. Alcais appeared thoughtful for a moment, and then his muscles tightened. He reached toward me aggressively with the dart he still held, aiming to stab through the hand I had resting on the table.

If I hadn't been staring at him, I might not have been able to dodge him. My hours of training with Gabe and Asher kicked in, and I used Alcais's momentum against him, jerking him toward me by the arm he'd stretched out to hurt me. Caught off balance, his chair rocked forward. I let him go, and he tipped over. Alcais hit the floor with a loud crash, and I jumped to my feet, moving out of his reach.

Breathing hard, I watched Alcais roll over. My grandfather and Delia's mother saved him from a swift kick between the legs when they came running through the door to the house. Mouth agape, my grandfather skidded to a stop when he saw me standing over a pissed-off Alcais.

"Remy? Alcais? What the hell is going on here?"

Erin spoke up when I remained quiet. "Alcais was messing with her. She was just giving him back what he was asking for."

I shot her a grateful glance.

My grandfather seemed to accept her answer and glared at her brother. "What have I told you, Alcais? You need to grow up and stop acting like an eight-year-old picking on the girl he likes at the playground."

Trying to put a dart through my hand was not the same as pulling on my braid at recess. I didn't try to explain this to my grandfather, though, because he already looked mad enough to put his fist through a wall.

"Get up," he spat at Alcais. "Come with me."

I expected (hoped?) Alcais was about to be on the receiving end of a long, tedious lecture. Before he could follow my grandfather into the house, I whispered, "You *ever* try anything like that again, and I swear I'll make you regret it."

Unease flickered over Alcais's features. Then he recovered and grinned at me. "Promises, promises. I just wanted to see what you were capable of."

"Don't test me, Alcais. I know how to fight back."

After he left, we put the table to rights and took our seats again. Erin sat quietly for all of two seconds before she started howling with laughter. Delia scowled at her, but that only made her laugh harder.

She wiped the tears from her eyes. "I'm sorry, Delia. I swear. But I've been wanting to knock my brother on his ass for years." Erin turned to me with a wide grin. "If I pay you, will you do it again? Pretty please?"

Delia stomped away into the house, probably to comfort Alcais. Despite the anger still simmering under my skin, I laughed with Erin.

But even as I settled back into my book, I told myself that this had been a good reminder to watch my back. You never knew when someone would try to stab something in it.

CHAPTER TWELVE

*W*hatever my grandfather said to Alcais, he acted subdued for the rest of the day. He didn't join Erin and me when we made our usual trek to the beach. I couldn't help feeling gleeful. Even Erin relaxed, laughing more than she did when Alcais and Delia hung out with us.

I liked Erin, a fact that made me feel guilty for keeping things from her. She'd been nothing but kind and generous to me. I think she liked me, too, especially when I refused to take Alcais's crap. She didn't stand up for herself often enough, and I wished I could help her change that. In a way, she reminded me of a shyer version of Lucy.

The time came to return to her house, and our feet dragged the closer we got.

"How do you like that book Franc gave you?"

I grimaced. "Let's just say Maria was one mercenary chick."

She grinned. "Oh Maria. She did like her tables. My mom used to say Maria's diary was a love letter to gold."

"You're so lucky," I told her. "To grow up able to talk about your abilities with your parents. Sometimes I wish my mother hadn't been so scared to tell me the truth."

Maybe my abilities wouldn't have scared me so much if

my mother had told me what to expect. The pain might have been more manageable if she'd been there to comfort me.

"Hey, Remy, would it be okay if I offered you some advice?" Erin asked.

Her house had just come into view, but something in her tone gave me pause. I paused on the sidewalk, careful not to let our shoulders touch.

"Be careful, okay? Things aren't always what they seem."

"You mean what happened with Alcais earlier?"

She glanced toward her house, wrapping her arms around her waist as if to warm herself even though the sun shone bright and hot today. "Just take care who you trust."

With that cryptic comment, she continued walking, refusing to say anything more. I trailed after her more thoughtfully. Alcais was so far from being trustworthy that I wondered if she really could be talking about him. Or maybe she meant to be careful around Delia, who probably shared everything with Alcais. Frustrated, I wished I could question her, but she wore a tight, closed-off expression.

Besides, we'd reached her driveway and my grandfather called my name from the front stoop.

"Remy, you ready to get going back to the city?"

Erin hurried past me into the house. My gaze followed her a moment before I answered my grandfather.

"Sure. I'm ready whenev—"

The sound of squealing brakes and screeching tires ripped through the late afternoon air. I spun about on my heel and watched in horror as a girl on a bicycle rode directly into the path of a white pickup truck. The truck's driver tried to swerve and miss the girl, but it was too late. The right corner of the bumper struck her. She cartwheeled through the air on impact, while the truck's tires flattened the bicycle. The girl hit the ground, lying half on the sidewalk and half in the gutter with her leg bent at an awkward angle. She didn't move.

I ran, and my grandfather was at my heels. The driver had already climbed out his truck as I fell to my knees by the girl. I gasped, recognizing her. It was Chrissy, the youngest of the Healers. Blood trickled down her pale cheek from a gash on her forehead.

"I'm sorry, Franc. I didn't see her," the driver said to my grandfather. I vaguely remembered him from the night I'd arrived in Pacifica.

Chrissy's eyes were closed, but when I laid a hand on her cheek I knew she still lived. That voracious hunger I'd felt with Erin clawed at me, but I clamped tight on it. Letting the energy rise in me, I scanned the little girl. Two broken bones—right femur and left elbow. The cut on her forehead looked worse than it was. She wouldn't even have a concussion. I breathed a quick sigh of relief, and the metallic scent of the girl's blood filled my nostrils. I could handle these injuries.

Then the voices penetrated the *humming* of my energy. My grandfather hovered behind me, not quite touching me. "She's okay. A few broken bones and scrapes, but nothing life-threatening."

"Remy, step back. We need to move her before we draw too much attention."

Glancing around, I noticed a neighbor coming out of her house, probably to investigate the noise. My grandfather whispered something to the driver, and he took off to speak to the neighbor. I didn't ask why they wanted to avoid an ambulance and the hospital. The attention could hurt everyone in this community.

Franc lifted Chrissy's sleight body in his arms and strode toward Erin's house. I trailed after him into the living room, where he set Chrissy on the couch with gentle hands. I knelt by her side. I realized I was the most experienced Healer in the room, and they seemed to realize it, too.

"Can you heal her?" my grandfather asked.

My eyes met Erin's worried gaze, and it occurred to me that I shouldn't do this. Shouldn't expose what happened to me after a healing. Then I met Alcais's mocking stare and knew that not healing the girl would cause problems, too. These people would wonder why I hesitated.

I wavered, unsure what to do.

Chrissy groaned in pain, drawing my attention. She'd come to and started to cry, huge tears leaking from the corners of her eyes to mix with the blood and dirt smeared on her cheeks.

The crying decided me, and my insides settled into some semblance of calm. *Heal who I can when I can. Okay, let's do this.*

I held her hand and concentrated on pushing my energy toward her, seeking out the injuries one by one. The monster inside me rose again, wanting to steal Chrissy's energy, but I controlled it. Her internal workings felt different from mine and Asher's, but I couldn't stop to figure out how. Then it hit me. For the first time in my life, I was healing another Healer. I started with the head wound and then moved on to the broken bones, imagining them healed and good as new. Chrissy roused under my hands, her eyes huge with confusion and no longer clouded with pain.

Time to face the music.

Sparks flashed as I released her hand after one last squeeze. *The sparks are purple,* I thought. *Like my grandmother's.*

My bones snapped and the skin on my forehead ripped open. I bit back a scream, drawing blood as my teeth sank into my lip. Gasping and breathing through my nose, I rolled onto my back on the carpet, trying to calm myself as the room erupted in chaotic shouts.

Now you've gone and done it, I thought.

A hand pressed a cloth to my forehead. Somebody had given my grandfather a kitchen towel to use as a compress.

"Remy?"

Franc sounded scared, his deep voice rumbling like summer thunder. I wanted to smile to reassure him, but someone—Chrissy?—jarred my broken leg and the pain nearly sent my teeth through my tongue.

"God, what's happened to you?" my grandfather asked.

He reached for me, but his hand hovered a few inches above my skin like he couldn't bring himself to touch me. *Fantastic,* I thought. *Once again I prove I'm a freak. Get ahold of yourself, damn it.*

"I'll be fine," I said through gritted teeth. "Just give me a minute."

I closed my eyes against the curious stares of Delia, Alcais, Erin, my grandfather, and the driver, who had joined us. I blocked everyone out to concentrate on healing my injuries. It would have been so much easier with Asher there to lend me some of his energy. Healing Chrissy had nearly depleted me. I scraped the remnants of my powers together and took on the broken bones. Slowly, slowly, I felt the breaks mending. The throbbing pain began to ease off. I didn't even bother to try healing my head. The injury wasn't that serious, and I had no juice left.

I lay there, catching my breath and shivering from my version of Healer Hypothermia. To be truthful, though, I hid, not wanting to see the suspicious expressions on the faces of my grandfather's people. Or worse, the fear that must now be in my grandfather's eyes. They knew I was different from the other Healers. There would be no going back.

A warm hand traced the skin on my arm. The hunger crawled up inside me, and my eyes flew open. Immediately, I threw up walls to control the monster that scratched and clawed against my defenses. Where the monster was easier to control with Chrissy, it fought harder to get at Erin, as if sensing that she was more powerful. She knelt beside me on her living room carpet, her face tensed as she gave me an asking glance. It took me a moment to grasp what she wanted to do. She wanted to heal the head injury that I couldn't.

I gave her a hesitant nod, feeling somewhat in control. Her brow knit in concentration, and heat zapped into me where she touched me. It arrowed straight toward the wound on my head. It didn't hurt, but it didn't exactly feel good, either. The closest sensation I could compare it to was getting zapped by static electricity, but only if you multiplied that experience times ten. Was this what healing felt like to the people I healed?

The cut on my head closed, and her touch fell away. The monster inside me receded, and I wanted to cry with relief. The shivering resumed, and I tried to imagine a way to explain all of this.

My grandfather tugged my chin toward him, his crazy white eyebrows practically meeting in a stern scowl. He pitched his voice so only I could hear his accusation.

"You've been keeping secrets, granddaughter."

I was getting blood on the carpet, I realized. And somebody must have lit up their phone to get so many Healers to Erin's house so quickly.

Irritated by the growing crowd, Erin's mom suggested we move to the kitchen. My grandfather couldn't decide between carrying me and trusting I could reach the room under my own steam. The result was him getting in my way every two steps and a constant stream of "Are you okay?" in my ear. Another shiver racked my body, and he dropped an arm across my shoulders, fitting me to his side.

My head spun. What would I say? How could I explain

this? I certainly couldn't say I had Protector blood that caused me to absorb everything I healed. My thoughts collapsed into an unhelpful repetition of *damn, damn, damn* that offered no answers.

In the kitchen, he pushed me into a seat at the small table. He wet a towel and swiped it across my forehead. Of course, it came away bloody. He almost ignored me while he cleaned my face, a difficult feat considering he was touching me and dismissing me all at once. Several people lingered in the doorway to the living room, chief among them Erin and Alcais's mother.

Chrissy's parents arrived. Her mother unleashed her fury on the driver who'd hit her daughter, and the crowd shifted their attention to that drama. The driver insisted it had been an accident, and eventually Chrissy's parents decided to take her home. My grandfather had already asked a few of the men to help the apologetic driver move his damaged truck, and they'd prepared a story in case nosy neighbors asked any questions. Still, a crowd remained.

"Um, Franc?" I whispered.

He followed the direction of my stare, and said, "Dorthea, do you mind keeping everyone out for a few minutes?"

She nodded and shooed everyone away. They only went as far as the living room from the sound of it, giving us only the semblance of privacy. The word *prophecy* floated back to us, and I sighed. First, the Protectors thought that I was the one mentioned in that stupid rumor, and now these people would, too.

My grandfather threw the red-stained towel into the sink. I shoved my wet hair away from my face and waited for the explosion I could feel coming. He leaned his hips against the kitchen counter, crossed his arms over his chest, and leveled a suspicious stare at me.

"Well?" he said at last. "Care to explain what I just saw?"

Why was I always having to defend myself to everyone? I hadn't freaking asked for these abilities. I could feel my chin lift in defiance, as I saw all the progress I'd made with him going up in huge, fiery flames.

"Chrissy got hit by a car. I healed her."

Franc's jaw tightened. "Your damned bones snapped. I watched your head split open. Just like Chrissy's."

He stalked toward me and placed both hands on the table. Other girls might have been intimidated, but I'd grown up with Dean, the Master of Fear. Irritation swelled at my grandfather's tactics, and I forced myself to stay seated. I decided to play dumb and raised my eyebrows.

"Doesn't that happen to any of your other Healers?" I asked in false surprise.

I didn't fool him. His features sharpened, and the corners of his mouth turned down in disappointment.

"You are just like your mother," he accused. "Keeping secrets."

That hurt, but I refused to let him see how much. It wasn't like he knew my mother in her last years.

"I thought her problem was telling secrets," I answered, my voice dripping with sarcasm.

He shrank away from me, standing straight as he sucked in a breath. I thought he might want to hit me for that comment, and some broken thing inside me calmed because his reaction was an all-too-familiar one that I knew how to deal with. He opened his mouth to speak or maybe to yell. A voice from the living room interrupted him.

Dorthea, Erin's mom, clutched her mobile phone in one hand, and terror had bleached her face white.

"Franc, we have a problem. It's the Protectors. They're here."

CHAPTER THIRTEEN

I'd never seen so many people frozen in place at once.

Within ten minutes, more than thirty people had packed into Erin's house. I kept looking about for the threat with questions tripping over each other in my mind. Where were the Protectors? Could it be Asher? Had he followed me here and been discovered?

It took several minutes of watching everyone and listening to their quiet conversations before I understood that by here, Dorthea meant Pacifica and not her front yard.

If I had thought about how Healers would react to an impending Protector invasion, I would have guessed that these people would jump into action to protect one of their own.

Instead, I watched in confusion as they did the opposite. They sat around and talked about what the woman's fate might be. Many of them made a beeline straight for my grandfather, their faces bright with fear. It had been eight months since a Healer went missing, and they wanted his assurance that they were safe. For the first time, I grasped his true place in this society of Healers. Not just as an old wise man, but as their leader. They wanted Franc to tell them all what to do next.

From what I could gather from my eavesdropping, a

Healer had given herself away. A nurse at a local hospital, she'd used her ability to heal someone who hadn't kept her secret. That was what the group speculated anyway. None of them seemed quite sure how the Healer had been discovered. What they did know for certain was that a Protector—one they'd kept under watch for the last couple of months—had been spotted entering her home about an hour ago.

I set aside the fact that Protectors lived nearby and that the Healers tracked their movements. My grandfather had forgotten about me in the midst of the confusion, and I slipped away from him, making my way over to Erin. She had curled up in a chair with her knees pulled to her chest.

"Why aren't they moving to save that woman?" I whispered, crouching beside her.

Her eyes rounded in shock. "Save her? Remy, we can't go anywhere near her. Not now."

I rocked back on my heels. "You're kidding me, right?"

She shook her head slowly. "Risk one and we risk all. Yvette knows that. She would never expect us to try to save her."

"I thought she was a friend?"

Anger raised my voice, and Erin shifted uncomfortably. I couldn't believe they were all going to sit around and let a woman be killed. Not when there was still a possibility that she could be saved. My mother had said that Protectors would sometimes keep Healers around for a while, preferring to use us to feel something again, if only for a short time. Some Protectors outright killed us for an immediate fix, but most wanted to string it out.

"Pipe down, newbie," Alcais said in a low voice.

He slipped onto the arm of the chair next to Erin, laying a hand on her shoulder. For once, Delia wasn't glued to his side.

"What if there are a group of them waiting for us?" he

continued. "We don't rush into things. That's how we get killed. You may not like it, but it's our way."

Abashed, I rubbed my hands together. Asher always accused me of rushing into situations without thinking through the consequences. If only he knew that these Healers agreed with him.

A few minutes later, my grandfather entered the room, and all conversation stopped.

"We've received word that the Protector is a known loner," he announced. "Now that we know he's acting alone, a few of us are going to move in to see if we can help Yvette."

He called out to several men in the group, and one of the older Healers. As he followed them to the door, I stood and he seemed to finally remember I existed.

He hesitated and then said decisively, "Remy, come with me."

His command surprised Alcais and Erin, but I didn't question his motive. I wanted to be there, to see how they dealt with Protectors. I trailed after him to his truck and climbed into the passenger side.

The sun had set while we'd waited for news at Erin's house. We drove in tense silence for a time. When my grandfather did speak, his voice sounded sharp, brooking no argument.

"You'll do exactly as I say when we get there. Until we have the Protector contained, you'll stay in the truck. You don't go anywhere near the house until I tell you to. Do you understand?"

I nodded. His obvious fear penetrated my defenses. My hands shook a little, and I clasped them around my knee.

We turned onto a street I'd never been on. We'd driven inland, away from the water, and my grandfather parked at a curb between streetlights. With a terse reminder to stay put, he jumped out of the truck. His long strides ate up the sidewalk as he backtracked a block to meet up with the other men. I didn't see the Healer with them.

I couldn't hear what they said from so far away, but a couple of men drew something from under their jackets. Guns, I realized, when the light glinted off the metal. They had guns. The weapons wouldn't kill an immortal Protector, but they could slow him down. Moving quickly, the men split up and approached the house, disappearing from my sight.

What if my grandfather gets hurt?

I might have been upset with him, but I liked him. I'd even grown to care about him. Until tonight, he'd been nothing but sweet and welcoming to me. I shivered, wanting to do something, anything to help them.

Outside the truck, the darkness threatened as my imagination created monsters where none existed. I wished I'd remembered my purse with my phone, but in the rush to leave, I'd forgotten it at Erin's house. Asher would have known what to do if I could have reached him. After he finished yelling at me for healing someone so publicly.

It felt like an hour had passed before my grandfather reappeared on the street, although it was probably only ten minutes in reality. He raised an arm, gesturing for me to join him. I jumped out of the truck and jogged toward him.

My heart sank when I got close enough to see his grim expression in the dim light.

"We were too late," he said, confirming my suspicions. "Come with me. I think you need to see this."

His hand grasped my elbow in a gentle hold, and he guided me into the house. My pulse picked up, and I heard my breath coming faster when we entered through the front door. Only one of my grandfather's men lingered in the living room. If he had a gun, he'd already tucked it away out of sight. The corners of his mouth were turned down, and his eyes glistened like he cried as he gazed on something in the next room that I couldn't see.

My grandfather stopped in the entryway. "Remy, the Protectors are killers. I don't think your mother prepared you for just how dangerous they are. This may not be right, but I'm not sure how else to show you. You need to know."

Know what?

I didn't fight my grandfather when he steered me around the couch and gestured for me to enter the kitchen before him. His body felt like a brick wall, though, when I recoiled into him a moment later.

My gasp hissed loudly through the room as I saw what my grandfather's man had been staring at. Who he'd been staring at. Stretched out upon the black-and-white tiled floor, the woman lay in a widening pool of crimson blood.

She'd been tortured. Small red gashes banded her arms and bare legs where she'd been cut, probably to coerce her into using her powers. Blood matted her brunette hair, dyeing it a reddish-black. The Protector who'd killed her hadn't intended to keep her around. He'd brutally weakened her and taken her energy. And for what? To smell, taste, and touch after decades of no sensation. In a screwed-up kind of irony, a Protector had done inhumane things in order to feel human again.

Yvette had not given in easily. She'd fought against her murderer. That much was clear from the bruising that covered her face. I'd been on the receiving end of injuries like that before, and I could guess how much pain she'd been in. Her unseeing eyes stared into mine in accusation. As if she knew I had Protector blood, knew that I loved a Protector.

My stomach heaved, and I barely reached the front yard before I fell to my knees and threw up on the neatly manicured lawn.

My grandfather waited behind me when I stood, wiping the back of my hand across my mouth. His expression wasn't unkind. I didn't know I was crying until he swiped a finger across my wet cheek. Franc opened his arms, and I gladly went into them. He didn't seem to mind when I soaked the front of his shirt with tears.

I hadn't known Yvette, but I cried for her.

If this was what Protectors did to people, I was ashamed to be even half of one.

We left the woman as we'd found her.

During our drive back to the city, my grandfather explained that one of the men was a cop—and the husband of the Healer who'd accompanied us in case there had been any chance of saving Yvette. The man would take care of Yvette's body.

Franc's people did what they had to in order to stay hidden, and I guessed they wouldn't leave the Healer's body there to draw suspicion. Especially if questions about her killer could draw the attention of other Protectors. I didn't respond to my grandfather's explanation. I worried I would throw up again if I discovered exactly how that man would dispose of her body.

At my grandfather's house, we migrated to the kitchen in unison and he made us tea. I didn't drink tea, but somehow it was the right drink, and I think the process of boiling the water and steeping the tea bags offered comfort to my grandfather.

He set a mug in front of me on the table, and I wrapped my freezing hands around it to warm them. Suddenly, exhaustion set in. Healing Chrissy and then myself had drained me. What energy I'd had left had been stolen by seeing that woman dead.

My grandfather sat across from me, and he looked older than when I'd first met him. His white hair, crazy at the best of times, stood up all over his head, and his movements dragged, his limbs weighted by responsibility and sadness.

He sighed in a deep gust of breath and pushed his mug away. "I'm sorry I forced that on you. I think maybe I made a mistake. Can you forgive me?"

"Why did you take me there?" I asked.

The question had bothered me all the way back to the city. I remembered how surprised Erin and Alcais had been when he ordered me to go with him. I don't think they had ever been along on a "rescue," if that was what you could have called tonight.

My grandfather crossed his arms, resting his elbows on the table. "It was what happened when you healed Chrissy." He gave me a direct look that made me want to flinch. "Secrets get people killed, especially if they're revealed at the wrong time and in front of the wrong people. Yvette died tonight because she healed the wrong person. Did you know that?"

"I heard some of the others whispering," I admitted. "They said she was a nurse."

He nodded. "Yes. Our kind tend to gravitate toward the healing professions."

I got that. I wanted to be a doctor, after all.

"It's not always a good thing," he continued. "It makes us easier to find, especially if one knows what to look for. Word of a miraculous healing tends to get out. We have to be careful."

Wasn't Asher always saying the same thing to me? I ran a finger around the rim of my mug, catching the condensation. The thought of Asher made me shift in my seat uncomfortably. He hadn't tortured Elizabeth, the Healer he'd accidentally killed. Yet, seeing that woman—Yvette—dead had made things very real to me. Someone had died for him to become immortal.

My grandfather misinterpreted my discomfort. "I'm sorry I was so angry with you earlier tonight. I should have told you that it scared the shit out of me to see you hurt, and instead I yelled at you."

I shrugged. "It's okay."

"No, it's not. You just took me by surprise. I've never seen anything like it. What happened, Remy? Why did it happen?"

I tried to figure out a way to explain it without giving too much away.

"I don't know why, but my ability works differently. When I heal people, I take on their injury. I always have."

His forehead furrowed as he thought about that. One brow lifted, and his eyes flicked to the sink. I guessed what he would say before his mouth opened to ask the question.

My words came out in a rush. "Yes, my finger was cut after I healed you. I took care of it in the bathroom while you finished making lunch. And please don't yell at me."

His lips pressed into a thin line, while he suppressed his urge to bellow. I waited for him to work out the rest of it. He would know that I'd taken on my mother's injuries all those years Dean had beat her. It didn't take long.

Pure horror crossed his face, but all he said was, "Your mother?"

I nodded.

He swallowed. "For how long?"

"Since my powers showed up when I was twelve."

His chair flew into the wall when he shoved to his feet. I nearly stood in a panic, bad memories of Dean's abuse rising in my throat. Before I could do more than sit up straight, my grandfather had left the room. I frowned after him. A moment later, he stalked back into the kitchen. He stared at me and then left again without saying a word. He did this three more times as I watched in confusion.

It took a while for him to calm down. He set his chair to rights, every movement precise. After resuming his seat, he spoke, but he sounded choked up.

"Your mother was wrong to put you through that. I hope you don't think all of us are like that. Using gifts like yours in that way."

Alcais popped into my mind, and I wondered if Franc knew how he used Delia and Erin. With my grandfather sounding so upset, though, I could only nod.

"Did your mother know why your abilities are different?"

I met Franc's gaze with a direct one of my own, as I lied through my teeth. "She didn't say. I didn't know I was different until I got here."

He accepted my answer to my great relief and grilled me about how my abilities worked. I didn't see any point in lying about that. I'd wanted his help understanding the limitations of what I could do so that maybe I could find a way to have a future with Asher, or at least a way to not get myself killed by healing the wrong person. I described how I healed a person and what it felt like when I took on whatever I'd healed. He asked me a thousand questions about the process and what happened afterward. He'd noticed how I'd healed myself after taking Chrissy's injuries, but left the cut on my head.

We'd finished our second cup of tea before I'd sated his curiosity. And that's when he hit me with a request that left me reeling.

"I want to test you. You know that some in our group are working to understand how Healers get their power. The differences in your abilities may help them in their research. We can begin tomorrow."

He sounded excited, and I hated to disappoint him, but no way in hell could I let him test me. Gabe had confirmed that my blood matched that of the Protectors. One blood test and the Healers would know exactly how different I was.

"No. I don't want to be tested."

My answer surprised my grandfather. Obviously, he hadn't considered that I would refuse him and that irritated me. I should be the one to decide what happened to my body. I refused to be poked and prodded like someone's lab rat. I told him as much.

"I don't consider you a lab rat, Remy," he protested.

"I'm sorry, Franc. I'm not going to change my mind on this."

He blew out a frustrated breath, but he let the subject drop. I had a feeling it wouldn't be for long.

Later, he hugged me before I headed up the stairs to my room. "You haven't had it easy, have you?" he asked. "Just know you can always trust me. I won't hurt you."

I would die of guilt for withholding the truth from him.

In my room, I pulled my mobile phone from my purse and discovered that Asher had sent me several text messages. We'd planned to meet that night. I sent him a text telling him I planned to go to bed early. Then I slipped out of my clothes and under the covers.

I'd lied to Asher.

The dirty truth was that I couldn't face him while the image of Yvette's mutilated body burned fresh in my mind. He'd hear my thoughts and know that I was horrified that he was a Protector.

CHAPTER FOURTEEN

$\mathscr{T}$he next morning I told my grandfather I didn't want to go to Pacifica. Last night burned fresh in my mind, and I couldn't handle seeing the looks the others would give me. By now, they would all know that my abilities differed from theirs. A freak even among my own kind.

My grandfather offered to stay home to keep me company, but the phone had been ringing off the hook all morning. People wanted assurances that they were safe, that Yvette had been the only one discovered. They wanted to know what was being done to find the Protector who had killed her. I told him to go to Pacifica without me, and he looked so relieved that I knew I'd said the right thing.

I spent the morning calling my family back in Blackwell Falls. Lucy answered the phone on the first ring. As soon as I heard her voice, an urge to cry nearly overwhelmed me.

"Hey, Luce, it's me."

"Remy! How are things going with Gramps?"

Bad. Terrible. Someone died.

I forced a lightness into my voice. "He has me darning his socks, but other than that things are good."

"What's wrong?" she demanded.

I should have known that I couldn't fool her. My sister

had a way of knowing when I lied to her. I heard a door slam shut on her end, and I closed my eyes, imagining her in her pink and purple bedroom. My dad and stepmom would be downstairs. Laura loved the kitchen, a place my mother had only liked to escape to when Dean was around. Laura might be cooking something that would make the entire house smell wonderful. Maybe Dad would be working at the dining room table—something he did to be near us, rather than locked away in his office. My stomach cramped.

My voice sounded even, though. "Nothing, really, other than a little homesickness. I miss you."

"Then come home," she whispered.

"Soon. I promise." I changed the subject before she could break me down and force the truth out of me. "How are things? How's Tim?"

Asking about her boyfriend did the trick of distracting her. She spent the next twenty minutes going on about a fight they'd had the day before. I happily listened to her complaints, wishing I could see her face. Afterward, my parents came on the line, and we chatted about my visit. I described all the sights I'd visited the days my grandfather and I had played tourist. It seemed an eon ago. Eventually we said our good-byes and hung up.

After talking to my family, the house felt emptier than before. I wandered from room to room. The house consisted of three small bedrooms, two bathrooms, a living room, a small dining room, the kitchen, and an attached garage with laundry room. As I studied the photos in each room on the first floor, it occurred to me that none of them were of my mother. Not even childhood ones. Had they been lost in the fire that had consumed my grandmother? Or maybe my grandfather kept them in his room.

I climbed the stairs and hesitated in front of my grand-

father's domain. I dared to open the bedroom door, calling myself a trespassing traitor as I stepped over the threshold.

I'm not sure what I expected to find. My grandfather
was a neat man, and his room reflected that. The bed had
been made, and his clothes all put away. Even the carpet
had recently been vacuumed and neat horizontal lines
marked the carpet.

His closet and dresser stood closed, and I couldn't bring
myself to go through his things. I hovered in the middle
of the room, unsure what to do. The phone rang on his
nightstand, and I almost jumped through the roof. I backed
out of the room and practically galloped back downstairs
as if I'd been caught snooping. In the living room, an answering machine clicked on. A moment later it clicked off
again when the caller decided not to leave a message.

The silence threatened to close in on me, and I couldn't
take it anymore. My grandfather had asked me to stay close
to the house. I considered the forest within that realm, and
I headed in that direction as soon as I'd locked the front
door behind me.

Sunshine shone through the trees. For once, fog didn't
coat their tops, and only a few puffs of cotton-white
clouds drifted through the blue sky. Off in the distance I
could hear hikers making their way along a Presidio trail,
their shouts to each other echoing off the hills. My grandfather had mentioned the trails were popular, and I could
see why. Even though I couldn't let loose and run the way
I longed to, I already felt calmer.

I was glad I showed caution when a man ran past me
with his labradoodle. The dog's tongue hung out of the
side of his mouth, lapping up the wind and dripping slob-
ber with each step. He looked like a cartoon character, all
clumsy limbs and happy smiles.

I decided to follow the man and dog to see where the

trail led. I guessed we went about a mile, winding up through the woods and through an open meadow before we came upon a set of steps built into the hillside. The staircase dropped us into a parking lot filled with cars and two tour buses. The man continued to the left, running toward the street, but I turned to the right to follow the tourists.

I gasped when I saw the view of the bay laid out in front of me. I had arrived at an overlook, replete with benches for taking in the sights. People lined up to take pictures with their backs to the blue water, framed on either side by the forest of the Presidio. It reminded me of home so much I had to get closer.

A concrete ledge enclosed the overlook, and I sank down on it, setting my chin on my knees. Just like at home, sailboats dotted the water, their sails billowing out as they crisscrossed the bay. More than anything at that moment, I longed to go home. An actual ache sprouted inside me.

After a while, the tourists loaded back into their buses, and only a few people remained lounging on the benches a ways from me. The air shifted, and someone sat down beside me. *Asher.* I wasn't sure I was ready to see him. In silence, we sat side by side like that for long minutes not touching. I tried to figure out how to tell him about everything that had happened.

I shifted to face him, bringing my leg up to rest my cheek on my knee. The wind played havoc with his hair and it stood on end.

"Hey."

"Hey," he answered. "I missed you last night."

At the mention of last night, a dozen images crowded into my mind. Me, healing Chrissy. The alarm going up about a Protector coming to town. Yvette dead. Asher reached for me right when the last memory popped up. I yanked away, but not before he had a glimpse of my thoughts.

Shock rounded his eyes. "What happened?"

I shook my head, staring at his throat because I couldn't quite meet his gaze.

"Remy?"

He reached out to touch me, and I jerked back again. I didn't want him to see what I'd thought, how I'd compared him to that other Protector. I didn't want him to know how the thought still lingered today.

His hand hovered, frozen in midair, and confusion clouded his features. "You're scaring me, *mo cridhe*. What happened last night?"

"A woman died, Asher. Another Healer."

My voice sounded hollow to my ears.

"How?" he asked in a low voice.

"A Protector."

Asher cursed. At least I think he did. He'd switched to French, his favorite language to swear in. He threw a sideways glance at the other people hanging about, but none had come close enough to overhear us.

"Were you in danger?" he asked.

"No. She was a nurse at the hospital. She healed someone and word got out. Whoever the Protector was, he didn't know there were others. At least my grandfather doesn't think he knows." I pictured Yvette again, and my eyes burned. "It was awful. What he did to her. He—"

I cut off, shaking my head when words failed me. To get it over with, I pictured Yvette as she'd lain on the floor, unseeing and bloodied. I tapped his hand, allowing him to see the image in a quick flash before I pulled away again.

"You're afraid of me."

I hadn't been fast enough, and Asher had seen more than I wanted him to. He sounded destroyed, his voice cut up and rough. I hated myself for doing that to him, but I couldn't hug him or hold his hand in comfort. He'd know I'd dreamed of him killing Elizabeth over and over again last night. Except in my dreams, Elizabeth had looked like Yvette.

So I denied what he'd said. "No. You're wrong."

He laughed, but there was no humor in it. "I really wish I was."

"It's not fear," I protested. "Not of you, at least. I just had never imagined how awful it would be. You told me, but I didn't understand."

"How could you?" he asked.

"He tortured her, Asher. He cut her to weaken her so he could take what he wanted. How does someone be-come a monster like that?"

"A monster like me, you mean?" he asked bitterly.

"No! I know you're not like that."

Before I could stop him, he picked up my hand. His fingers cradled mine gently, not holding them hostage. I tried to think of us as we'd been in the forest, happy and full of hope. If he was testing me, I failed. Whatever he saw in my mind, a terrible sadness settled over him. He set my hand on my leg with the same gentle touch and then rose to his feet beside me.

"Come on," he said. "We should get back to your grandfather's."

The silent hike back was agonizing. Where before the scenery had entranced me, now I walked blindly, trying to think of a way to fix this. I'd never hated our bond so much as I did at that moment because it allowed him to see what I wanted to hide.

At the edge of the forest near my grandfather's house, we stopped, and I turned toward Asher. I would have hugged him, but he stood apart from me, his hands in his pockets and his expression remote. I wrapped my arms around myself instead and wished I could take back the last hour.

"Please don't go," I begged. "Not like this."

His smile didn't reach his eyes. "I swear I'll be nearby if you need me, but I think maybe it will be easier for you to figure out how you feel about this if I'm not around."

He meant about him, but I already knew how I felt about him. I loved him. Why couldn't I stop picturing Yvette, though? Why couldn't I stop imagining how Elizabeth had died?

A truck engine roared in the distance. My grandfather had arrived home.

Wind whipped a strand of my hair out of my ponytail, and Asher caught it, tucking it behind my ear. He didn't touch my skin, I noticed with a twinge of pain.

"Be careful, okay?"

A door slammed, and I turned my head toward the house when my grandfather called my name. A light breeze caressed my face, and I spun about in a panic.

Asher had gone.

My grandfather stood at the counter when I entered through the kitchen door.

"Hey," I said.

I hoped he wouldn't want to talk. All I wanted to do was go to my room and hide under the covers. I didn't want to have to pretend I didn't feel tired and scared and sad.

"Who was that?" my grandfather asked, nodding his head toward the kitchen window that faced the forest.

I grabbed a bottle of water out of the fridge, giving myself time to think. What had he seen? I closed the fridge door and dropped into one of the kitchen chairs, slouching as if I didn't have a care in the world.

"Just a boy I met when I went hiking."

Asher and I hadn't hugged or kissed. In fact, we'd done nothing to make my grandfather think I knew Asher that well. I hoped the mention of hiking would distract him. If he got busy yelling at me for going off on my own, maybe he'd forget about Asher.

I continued. "I was going stir-crazy in the house, so I went up to that overlook that's near here. Inspiration Point, I think the sign said."

I tossed back a sip of water while my grandfather eyed me.

"And you met him there?" he asked.

I shrugged and ducked my head like I was embarrassed. "Honestly, I got a little turned around on the trail. He was nice enough to walk me here."

Did he believe me? My knuckles turned white with my tense grip on the water bottle. I relaxed my fingers before I spilled liquid everywhere.

"I'm sorry," I added. "I know you said to stay close."

My grandfather rested his hips against the counter, crossing his arms over his chest.

He gave me a stern look. "You need to be more cautious."

"I will. I promise," I said in a rush. "I'm going to shower before dinner."

I jumped up and practically ran out of the kitchen. But not before I saw my grandfather turn to gaze out the window with a thoughtful expression.

CHAPTER FIFTEEN

*A*fter Yvette's death, people treated me differently in Pacifica, and I found myself wishing the weekend would arrive because that would mean I would be on a plane back home to Blackwell Falls.

The way I healed injuries scared some of Franc's people and fascinated others. And if the looks were anything to judge by, my refusal to be tested had pissed off many of them. My feelings didn't seem to matter in the scheme of things when studying me could advance their research.

My grandfather had warned me that some people were angry. He'd asked them to leave me alone, but I alternated between feeling like a bug under a microscope or one burned under a magnifying glass. Before when I'd visited Erin's house, we'd been left to our own devices. We'd tended to wander off to the beach to hang out without adult eyes watching our every move.

With Yvette's death still fresh, our hangouts had been restricted to Erin's or Delia's. This would have been fine, but suddenly whichever house I was at suffered an influx of Healers and their families passing through. Not one of them defied my grandfather's order to leave me be, but that didn't stop the looks or the whispers that followed me everywhere.

If my grandfather would have let me, I'd have stayed at

his house. But after seeing me with Asher, he'd begun watching my every move, refusing to leave me alone. I hadn't seen Asher in three days. If not for his nightly text to check in, I'd have been freaking out.

Asher refused to talk about us, and that told me how much I'd hurt him, albeit unintentionally. It wasn't like I could always control my thoughts, but somehow that made it worse. He knew I'd doubted him so strongly that I couldn't hide those fears from him.

As if I didn't feel bad enough, at Erin's house, her mother left any room I entered. I couldn't tell if Dorthea thought me the Antichrist or just something to be avoided, like gum someone had spat out on the sidewalk. Delia would have followed her lead, except that Alcais wouldn't leave my side.

The bastard had decided he wanted to experiment on me. Yesterday he'd tried hurting himself to force me to heal him. He'd sliced his hand open with a pocket knife. I'd refused to play along and he'd had to run to Delia or Erin to heal himself.

The next day I arrived at Erin's house, and Delia greeted me with a scowl. Franc had foisted me on her and her friends, and she hated me for it. I followed her into the garage in time to hear Erin shriek in pain. Alcais stood over his sister, holding her flattened palm over a burning candle. She struggled against her brother, but he didn't relent. Instead, his eyes met mine in a dark challenge, and he smiled.

At last, he let her go, and she shrank away from him, crying. The scent of burnt flesh wafted toward me, and with it came memories of Dean holding lit cigarettes to my skin. I had a particularly nasty scar under my arm from where he'd hurt me over and over. I considered it a reminder that some people were evil through and through.

Alcais had hurt Erin because of me. He knew Delia

couldn't heal anything but surface burns, and probably suspected I might be able to. If I'd had Asher's strength, I would have sent him flying into the wall. I didn't, though. I only had my abilities. My very special abilities.

I dropped my purse on the card table where we'd hung out days before, reading and laughing. Then I knelt before Erin and gave her a reassuring smile.

"Let me help you."

Her brown eyes shuttered in pain, but she shook her head. For a second, I thought she didn't want to be healed by a freak like me, but she said, "No. I don't want you to be hurt, too."

I felt like crap for doubting her, and more determined than ever to heal her. "Trust me, okay? I've been through worse. Please."

Alcais shoved her shoulder, ignoring her cry. "Just give her your hand already."

"You're an ass, Alcais," Delia said from behind me.

She actually sounded pissed at him for once, and I wanted to cheer because she'd found a backbone. My gaze didn't veer from Erin. I gave her another smile and she finally relented. Huge tears slid down her cheek as she placed her hand in mine.

Little did they know that I had experience healing burns. Dean had often ground his cigarettes into my skin when the mood struck him, and I'd once healed Asher's burned hand when he'd saved me from falling into a fire. I could heal Erin, but it would be a bitch when I absorbed the injury. Plus there was the fact that I had to let my guard down and touch her in order to do it.

Gritting my teeth, I rested a hand on hers, dropped my guard, and waited. The monster inside me instantly reared its head, but I shoved it down, determined not to give in. It almost hurt to deny myself Erin's energy, but I stayed in control.

I let the *humming* begin and scanned Erin. Like Chrissy, her internal workings differed from that of a normal human's and from Asher's. I hadn't really had time to study Chrissy with everyone watching me, and I couldn't take the time to study Erin now.

Erin gasped, and I focused on her injury. Quickly, I pictured the damage to her flesh and the nerves beneath it. I imagined the flesh perfect and pink once more, and it shifted under my hand, mending as my energy worked on her.

When I'd healed her, I looked up and said, "Don't panic, okay?"

She nodded, her eyes huge as purple sparks lit the air. I let my hand fall from hers. And then I stopped thinking as my flesh charred and my nerves roared in pain. I wanted to howl, but more than that I wanted to teach Alcais a lesson. I made myself get up.

"Hey, Alcais," I said through gritted teeth. "You wanted to know how my powers work? That's why you hurt Erin, right?"

He nodded, and a hint of anxiety flickered over his face. I held out my burned hand, palm down so he couldn't see the burns.

"See for yourself."

He hesitated a moment before curiosity overcame him. He took a step closer. As soon as he was within reach, I latched on to him with my good hand. The scary red sparks had always come before when I was in danger. I'd never called them to me with such a minor injury. I wasn't even sure if I could, but in that moment, with Erin still crying and my hand blistered and raw, I wanted to hurt Alcais.

I thought it wouldn't work, but suddenly the energy rose in me. It scorched my insides like a flash fire, and the red sparks arced between me and Alcais where we touched. He screamed and fell to the floor, writhing from the same injury I had, and I let him go.

Crouching beside him, I whispered, "I'm not going to heal you, Alcais. You deserve that for hurting Erin. For using her and Delia the way you do. You better hope I never catch you hurting either one of them again. And if you so much as get a hangnail that you expect them to heal, I will make you regret it. Got it?"

He nodded fast and furious like a bobblehead doll. I didn't find it funny, though. My hand hurt like hell. Standing again, I faced Delia and Erin. I'd scared them as bad as Alcais. Tough luck. I didn't regret what I'd done. I'd watched Dean abuse my mom all those years, unable to do more than heal her afterward. I wouldn't stand by and watch another sadistic bastard hurt someone.

Raising my chin, I grabbed my purse with my good hand and stormed out of the garage.

Erin found me in the guest bathroom.

I needed a bit of time to recharge before I could heal myself. In the meantime, I'd climbed up on the sink to rest my back against the vanity mirror while I let cold water run over my palm. Leaving the door ajar, Erin crossed the small room to sit on the toilet, giving me a wide berth. I threw up my defenses, uncertain if I could protect her from myself at this point.

I sighed. "I'm not sorry. Your brother is a creep."

"A complete psycho," she agreed.

I gave her an uncertain look. She didn't sound afraid.

After a moment, I blurted out, "You need to take vitamins. Your immune system is weak."

Her brows shot up. "How do you know?"

"Same as you, I expect. I touch someone and I sense what injuries or illnesses they have."

"Remy, our powers don't work to that degree. I can't see when someone is getting a cold. I can tell when they already have a cold."

I closed my eyes. "That's super. I'm a cold detector."

She laughed. "Isn't that a good thing?"

I squinted at her to see if she was kidding. "Sometimes. Mostly, it sucks. I'm more of a vacuum than a cold detector if you get my drift," I said, referring to how I absorbed what I healed.

"I thought you were more of a badass weapon myself," she observed in a wry tone.

I couldn't figure her out. She rose and grabbed a towel from a rack when I shut off the water. I took it from her to dry my hand, and we both examined the damage.

"I wish I could heal you, but burns this bad are beyond me," she said. "I didn't say thank you earlier, did I? Thank you."

Her hug shocked me. Before I could figure out how to respond, my grandfather shoved his way into the room. *Uh-oh,* I thought. *Someone told.*

I had to give him credit. He fussed over my hand instead of climbing up my back for hurting Alcais.

"Franc, I'm seriously okay," I finally protested when he kept on.

"I'm going to kill Alcais," he said. "You okay, Erin?"

Erin smiled. "Yep. Thanks to Remy. And no need to kill Alcais. Remy took care of him."

My grandfather scowled. "I heard."

Delia told, then. Alcais wouldn't have admitted I'd bested him, especially after I'd done it for torturing his sister.

I jumped off the bathroom counter, cradling my hand against my belly. "Can we go, Franc? I'm tired."

On the way home, I concentrated on healing my hand.

When that fun task was out of the way, I shivered and stared out the window, making it clear I didn't want to talk. My grandfather didn't push me.

It had occurred to me as I sat in the bathroom with my injured hand that maybe I'd made a mistake in coming to California. What had I gained? Some knowledge, yes, but nothing that would help Asher and me. I hadn't even gained access to the Healers' library. In fact, the damage this trip had done outweighed the good. I was in danger of losing Asher, and I was lying to my family at home. And now I'd exposed my abilities to these Healers who wanted to experiment on me.

The saving graces were my newfound relationships with my grandfather and Erin. I didn't regret meeting them, but what would it cost me? Beyond my burned hand?

My grandfather parked the truck in front of his house and turned off the engine. He made no move to get out, and I waited.

"I think I get why you've been keeping the extent of what you can do hidden."

I could only see a bit of his expression in the light slanting into the car from the street. I'd expected blustering and anger, and when that didn't happen I couldn't tell what he thought about this latest discovery.

He tapped his fingers on the steering wheel. "What you can do . . . It must be terrifying. When did you know you could hurt people, too?"

My reflection appeared pale in the side-view mirror. "When Dean tried to strangle me a few months ago."

My grandfather swore under his breath. "It's too bad the man disappeared. I'd like to kill him."

I said nothing.

"Listen, Remy. I don't want you to go back to New York this weekend. I think you should move here permanently."

I swung about to stare at him. It had occurred to me that this might come up, but as the weeks passed, he'd never brought it up. I wasn't prepared to deal with it now. My grandfather put his arm across the back of the seat and held up a hand when I opened my mouth to protest.

"I know you have friends you can stay with back there, but you should be with family. People who understand what you are. Unlike your friends, we can help you if you're ever in danger."

"Franc, I appreciate the offer, but . . ." *But I have family back in Blackwell Falls. A family I've only just discovered. And a boyfriend I love.*

"You've been lucky, kid. So damned lucky I think you must have a fairy godmother sprinkling dust on you. You don't know how to spot a Protector much less how to evade them if they find you."

I could tell a Protector from a single touch, plus their energy felt different. My training with Gabe had helped me grow stronger in that area, and I could defend myself to an extent with the abilities I'd picked up when I'd stolen Asher's energy. I couldn't very well explain any of that to my grandfather, though.

He dropped his voice. "Don't forget that the Protectors are always going to be hunting you. You put your friends' lives at stake when you stay with them. To the enemy, they are merely collateral to be used against you."

I hated that he was right. My family and Asher's could get killed because of me. I yanked on the door handle and shoved the truck door open, jumping to the ground before my grandfather could stop me.

His shout followed me into the house.

"Think about it, Remy. You belong with us!"

I wasn't so sure. All I knew was that this trip had clouded everything. I no longer knew where I belonged.

★   ★   ★

My stubborn streak had been handed down from my grandfather. All during dinner, he hounded me, listing all the reasons I should stay with him in California. I'd be safer. I'd be with my own kind. I'd have family. Others would be safer if I weren't there to draw Protector attention. He even talked about how great the schools were in San Francisco, and how he'd be there to help me through college. But while he spoke, I couldn't help wondering if maybe he was more interested in how I differed from other Healers. How did I factor into his plans for a new Healer race?

He hadn't given me a hard time for hurting Alcais. In fact, he hadn't asked me two questions about it, except to understand how the ability to transfer injuries worked. If my father had heard that I'd used violence on another, he'd have reamed me but good. He would have expected better of me. Why hadn't my grandfather yelled at me? Why had he let me off without a warning? I tried to convince myself that he thought Alcais deserved it, but the pieces didn't add up.

Franc left me alone when I locked myself in my room.

I waited until I heard him go to bed, and then I raced out the kitchen door, running for the forest. I needed to see Asher. I'd texted him to meet me up at Inspiration Point, and I hoped he would be there. Too much was happening too fast. My world had shifted in some way, and I wished I could go back to the way it had been before.

I hurried along the trail, moving too fast in the dark, but I couldn't slow down. Climbing the stairs to Inspiration Point took forever, and the whole way I worried Asher wouldn't be waiting at the top.

One thing had become crystal clear to me today. When my grandfather asked me to move here permanently, everything in me had rejected the idea. A big part of the reason was my family, but my gut reaction had more to do with Asher.

I loved him. End of story. He would never hurt me. Alcais, for all his connections to my grandfather and this community, was a psychopath in the making. He had tortured his sister out of idle curiosity, and in my eyes that made him no better than the Protector who had hurt Yvette. My boyfriend, on the other hand, had stepped in front of a bullet to save me. He'd put his hand in a blazing fire to help me when I'd been little more than a stranger to him. How could I have forgotten who he was?

I needed to apologize. The shame of my betrayal threatened to choke me, and I prayed I hadn't screwed up things between us beyond all repair.

The hillside steps stretched on forever, but I finally reached the top. Holding my breath, I faced the overlook, and then exhaled in a gust because Asher was sitting on a bench with his back to me. In a flash, I circled around the bench.

Too late, I saw his eyes widen in panic when they focused on me. He shifted, fighting against whatever bound his hands behind his back, and the lamplight reflected off something shiny covering his mouth. Duct tape.

My mind took ages to comprehend the scene, but when it did I skidded to a stop. Someone had gagged Asher and tied him to the bench. He tried to scream at me, to warn me. His terror-filled eyes were the last thing I saw before my head lit up in an explosion of lights.

Chapter Sixteen

"*R*emy, please wake up."

The sound penetrated the dense black void.

"Wake up!"

Louder now, the voice acted like a flashlight shining in my eyes. Pain ricocheted around my skull, and I wanted to punch the screaming person in the face for amplifying the hurt.

"Please, *mo cridhe,*" the male voice pleaded.

Asher, I thought. That was Asher's voice. For him, I could try to push the blackness away. I breathed through my nose. When I could handle the throbbing, I slowly opened my eyes.

More blackness.

"That's it, love. You can do it."

His voice drifted toward me out of the shadows to my right. I couldn't see him, but I thought he wasn't too far away. I was lying on my back, and I rolled my head in his direction, regretting the move almost immediately when the pounding in my head increased in intensity.

Memories came back to me in a rush. Asher tied to the bench. Someone hitting me over the head. *It had to be Protectors,* I thought. Who else could get to Asher with all his speed and strength? What did they have planned for us? Did they know about me? About what I could do? That I was part Healer? My head pounded more with each question, and I pressed on my forehead to make it stop.

"Asher, where are we?"

"I don't know. They blindfolded me to bring me here. I can't really move around much. Can you sit up?"

I levered my elbows under me to raise myself up. I only got so far before I collapsed back again. Something dripped down my neck, and I thought it might be blood. I could swear they'd hit me with a brick.

"Try to sit up again, Remy."

I wondered how he knew I'd already attempted it once until I remembered he could probably make out my outline in the dark with his Protector eyesight. After a minute of pumping myself up, I tried and managed a crouching position.

Half-dragging and half-scooting across the floor, I pulled myself toward the spot where I'd heard Asher's voice. I bumped into something. His leg?

"Are you okay?" he asked.

The concern in his voice almost made me fall apart. I cleared my throat to push the tears back.

"My neck hurts from where they hit me, but otherwise I'm okay. What about you?"

His chest moved under my fingers when I finally found him in the dark.

"I'm fine. I wasn't the one they were after. I was just the bait."

Well, that answered one of my questions. They knew I was a Healer at the very least. And if I knew Asher, he was beating himself up for getting used as bait. I ran my hands up his chest to his shoulders and then up his arms, which were stretched above his head. They had handcuffed his wrists to some kind of hook burrowed into the cold concrete wall. He had to feel cramped in that position.

"Can you break those?" I asked.

His muscles bunched as he pulled against the wall, but the cuffs didn't give.

"I've been trying for the last hour. No go. These aren't normal cuffs. I could break those. These are made of a stronger metal."

"Don't tell me. It's Adamantium," I said lightly.

"Thousand points for the X-Men reference," he said, some of the frustration easing from his tone as I'd meant it to. "I'd love you even more if you could feel your way around to see if there's anything we could use to get free. I only saw the room a second before they closed the door."

I traced my way back to his face, his day's growth of whiskers rasping against my skin. "Do you? Still love me, I mean?" I asked in a small voice.

I felt like such a silly idiot for even asking at a time like this. But hey, if we were going to die, I wanted to know. He strained against his bonds as if he wanted to hold me. He couldn't, so I wrapped my arms around him, laying my cheek against his heart.

"Always," he whispered, rubbing his jaw against my hair. "You?"

"To infinity." *I'm sorry I doubted you.*

I tipped my head to drop a kiss on his lips. I missed in the dark and ended up kissing the tip of his nose. Immediately, I corrected my error and he strained his neck to meet me halfway. The kiss lasted only a second, but I felt all the wildly spinning pieces in me fall back into place. Everything clicked, and my world made sense again.

My needy impulse in check, I got down to the business of escape.

"Can you help me heal myself?" I asked. "I want to explore, but my brain feels like it's doing a mad tango around my skull."

Without a word, he sent his energy into me and I grabbed hold of it, using it to close the open wound on my neck. It took longer than I liked to take care of the swelling. I hated concussions. A small throb remained when I backed away from Asher, but the pain had become manageable.

"Thanks," I said, rising to my feet.

Using one hand to feel my way along the wall, I put the other out to avoid running into any objects. I remembered I'd had my mobile phone and patted my pockets. No luck. They'd taken it.

"How did they find us, Asher?" I asked.

"I'm not sure. I must've done something to give myself away."

I paused. "Wait. That makes no sense. If they used you as bait to get to me, then it had to be me who screwed up." I thought about it a moment, before a lightbulb went off. "Yvette. I was at Yvette's after a Protector killed her. They were watching her house. That has to be it."

"Who's Yvette?"

Asher had seen glimpses of what happened in my thoughts, but I'd never explained that night. As I walked the four corners of the room, I told him everything that had happened in the last few days, from the car accident and discovering Yvette to hurting Alcais.

"Someone knows about your grandfather's community," Asher said when I finished. "I bet they killed Yvette to draw the rest of you out."

He didn't bring up how I'd compared what those other Protectors had done to Yvette to what Asher had done to Elizabeth, and I was grateful. I didn't want to rehash that now.

"But why come after me?" I asked. "Why not go after the rest of the Healers?"

"I don't know, love. Maybe they've figured out that you're different. Could one of the other Healers have betrayed you?"

I balked at that. "No way. They would never work with the Protectors. You don't know how scared they are. Nobody would dare break one of my grandfather's sacred rules."

Asher didn't argue. Instead, he asked, "Any luck finding a way out?"

I guessed the room had to be eight feet by ten feet. At the door, I twisted the knob, but either it locked from the outside or our captors had something wedged against it. Either way, it didn't budge.

"I hate to tell you this, but we are trapped."

I slid down the wall until I sat beside him on the ground. I dropped my head on his shoulder.

Asher sighed. "I guessed as much."

Neither of us said anything for a long moment. What was there to say? We'd covered this territory so many times. I had a good idea what the Protectors would do with me, so why go there and scare myself more? I wanted to climb into the denial boat and take a trip down the "let's pretend everything's okay" river. If I was going to die tonight, I didn't want my last moments with Asher to be full of thoughts of the torture ahead of me. Unbidden, a few examples of what might be coming flickered through my mind.

"Please, Remy," Asher choked out.

It hit me that I'd had my walls down, and he'd been hearing my unpleasant thoughts.

"I'm sorry," I whispered.

"You're going to make it out of this. I swear it."

He sounded so sure, but I couldn't see how that could be true. I didn't want to argue, though. No, I wanted something else. If these guys were only after me, then most likely they'd let Asher go once they finished with me. That thought comforted me.

"Asher, do something for me? I don't want my dad to

know what happened to me. Or Lucy." He started to protest, his entire body jerking, but I kept going to get the words out. "Tell them I decided to live with my grandfather permanently. Tell them I ran away. Whatever you say, don't tell them the truth about how I di—"

"Don't you dare say it," Asher said fiercely. "You're not going to die!"

"Sh . . ."

Finding his face in the dark, I shifted until I could kiss him. He surprised me by kissing me back with more raw emotion than I'd ever felt from him. I couldn't read his thoughts, but I sensed his rage at his inability to save me mixing with grief and love. I touched his face, and my fingers brushed wet skin.

Whatever happened when the Protectors opened the door to our prison, odds were against me making it home alive. And Asher knew it, too. Every day he'd been with me, I'd been making him mortal again. Every day he'd begun to feel more, smell more, taste more. What if I could heal him all the way? We'd never tried because of the danger to me, but if I was going to go out, I wanted it to be on my own terms, doing something I wanted to do. Making Asher mortal again . . . that was something we'd both dreamed of. Maybe it was time to take a chance.

I tried to kiss him again, thinking to put my plan in action, but he turned his head away.

"No way in hell are we giving up now," he said. "Not after everything we've been through. You will not give up your life for me. Got that?"

I imagined I could see his green eyes glaring at me. Frustrated, I dropped my hands into my lap. "Sometimes I really hate your ability to read my mind."

"I'm not sorry. I'm glad I have a way to see what crazy plan your mind is coming up with."

"Okay, what are we going to do? Just sit around and wait for them to come back for me?"

"I have an idea, but you're not going to like it," he said.

"What?" I asked.

Beside me, I felt him shift until he knelt. He seemed to be getting himself situated to get better leverage, but to do what? He'd already tried to break the cuffs without success. I heard him take a deep breath, like I did when I knew I was about to do something that would hurt like the devil. Then I heard a rush of movement and the chains rattling, followed by his muffled groan. A second later he fell forward to the ground, and metal clanked against the brick wall.

He'd freed himself somehow. I reached for him, but he shouted, "No, damn it! Don't touch me!"

My hand hovered over him, frozen in place. At first, I thought he sounded angry, and it took a moment for me to realize pain had sharpened his voice. Asher didn't want me to touch him and take on whatever he'd done to free himself. *Come to think of it, how had he freed himself?*

I traced a hand along the wall until I found the cuffs. They were intact, still locked. He hadn't broken the cuffs, which meant . . .

"You idiot!" I shouted, pissed. He'd broken his hands in order to get them out of the cuffs. "What were you thinking?"

"Not so fun when the shoe's on the other foot, huh?" he teased, gasping.

He'd been forced to watch me hurt myself in order to free myself from Gabe many a time. For the first time, I appreciated how much it sucked being on the other side of that.

I started to reach for Asher again, intending to heal him, but he rolled away from me. "Asher!"

"Remy, if you try to heal me, so help me, I'll . . ."

"You'll do what? Spank me? Give me a break."

"Damn it, think! If you heal me, you're going to take on my injuries. Even if I help you heal yourself, you're going to be weak. Too weak to fight them off when they come for you. This way, we can both fight."

I used the wall to brace myself so I could stand. I could sense him doing the same across the room.

"How the hell are you going to fight if your hands are useless?"

"Babe, I could kick your ass a dozen times over with my hands tied behind my back."

The smirk in his voice made me want to slap him. Instead, I crossed my arms over my chest and taunted him. "Too bad you'll be taking on Protectors instead of puny little me then."

I started to say more, but suddenly Asher stood beside me, tension vibrating through his body.

"They're coming," he whispered. "Get ready to run if you get the chance. And don't look back. Promise me."

I would never leave him behind. I didn't get the chance to argue, though, because something clicked, like a lock turning over, and then someone opened the door. I threw up an arm to shield my eyes from the blinding light that entered our prison from the outer room.

By the time I dropped my arm, Asher had shoved me behind him. I peeked around him to see two men standing in the doorway. They were total opposites of each other. One had black hair, olive skin, and stood over six feet tall. The other had pale skin, hair so blond it was almost white, and was a few inches shorter than me. The one thing both men had in common was the grace of their movements, an economy of motion that the Blackwell family all had, too. I guessed it was a Protector trait, seeing these two strangers.

"How'd you get out of the cuffs?" the black-haired one

said to Asher. He must have noticed Asher's injured hands because he laughed. "Shit, Mark. He broke his wrists to get free. He must really like her."

"Or else he wants her for himself." The man called Mark entered the room. He called to me in a mocking tone. "You know what he is, dontcha?"

Asher practically growled at the man, and I rested a hand on his back.

"I know exactly who he is," I told him. "And what you are."

Mark smiled. "You think you know about your boyfriend there, but I think he's been holding out on you. Maybe it's time we show you what he is."

He made a move forward that Asher countered with one of his own. Mark's brows shot up as if Asher's defense of me surprised him. Both Protectors scowled at my boyfriend. They obviously thought Asher had kept his Protector side hidden from me.

"Now, I realize you don't want to share her, boy, but you're going to have to get over that. Finders, keepers, and all that."

Both men moved forward and again Asher countered their movements. "You can't have her."

The taller man who'd spoken first considered Asher for a long moment, crossing his arms as he leaned a hip against the doorjamb.

"You know, he said you had some kind of attachment to the Healer. We didn't believe him, of course, but I'm thinking he was right."

He? Someone had told these men about Asher and me. Who?

The man must have seen the shock on my face. He laughed. "You didn't think it was an accident that we found you?" He shook his head. "No, we knew exactly where you would be. He even told us how to get to you." He tipped his head toward Asher. "I'd never have figured on using one of us to catch a Healer, but I guess weirder things have happened."

He shrugged and straightened. Every movement calm and casual, he pulled a gun from behind his back. He kept the muzzle pointed at the ground as he spoke almost kindly to Asher. "There's no way you can take both of us, man. Let us have her, and we'll let you go. You can walk yourself right out of here and find yourself another girlfriend. Maybe one less fragile."

His smirk almost caused Asher to lose control. I could feel him trembling under my hand. The thing was, the Protector was right. I wouldn't make it out of here, and what was the point of both of us dying?

Please, Asher. Just go. Save yourself.

"No!" he shouted.

He faced the men, but I knew Asher spoke to me, as well.

The black-haired stranger sighed. "I thought you might say that," he said.

The gun flashed when he fired off three rounds in a blast of noise that threatened to blow my eardrums. Asher could have dodged the shots, but he stepped into them instead. A human shield, his entire body jerked backward into mine with the force of the bullets. We hit the hard concrete floor, with my body cradling his and the back of my head bouncing off the ground in a blitzkrieg of pain. My ears rang, and the smell of iron burned my nose. Sounds swirled around me, but it felt like listening to a conversation while underwater.

Stunned, I waited a moment for my eyes to stop seeing flashes of light and readjust. When they did, I realized Asher lay on me, unmoving. Asher, who'd become more mortal every day we'd spent together.

"Asher?"

He didn't respond.

"Asher?" I yelled louder.

Nothing. I opened my senses, scanning him. I'd only begun when someone shoved his body off of me and pulled me to my feet. Acting on pure instinct, I fought back the way Gabe had taught me and my fist connected with a jaw.

The man couldn't feel it, but the motion forced the arms holding me to fall away. Immediately, I dropped back to my knees beside Asher. I laid a hand on his chest, where blood had already soaked his dark blue shirt a deep scarlet.

I couldn't hear a heartbeat.

"No, no, no . . ."

Frantic, I sent my senses spiraling out again to scan him. The keening noise distracted me, until I realized it was me screaming. I choked off the strangled cries.

I can heal him. I can heal him. I can . . .

"Oh no, you don't." Arms cinched around my waist, yanking me backward into a chest. They squeezed tighter when I began to fight, digging into my ribs and cutting off my air supply. Mark whispered in my ear. "Save all that energy for us, darlin'. We have big plans for you."

"No," I tried to say, but nothing came out.

They didn't know. Asher might not be able to heal himself. Not from an injury this bad and not when I'd gone and made him more mortal than immortal.

I kicked my legs as hard as I could, and Mark grunted when my boots connected with his shins. His grip tightened. Cut off from oxygen, my vision blurred, bright dots popping everywhere I looked. I strained toward Asher. Blood pooled all around his unmoving body. With the last of my strength, I tried to gather my energy, to use my power against the Protector.

The black-haired man stood over Asher. Unsmiling, he pointed the gun at Asher's head.

"He never said we had to keep this one alive," he said.

I went nuts, scratching the arms holding me and tearing at the skin I could reach. The arms around my ribs became steel bands.

Everything went black, but the gunshot echoed on and on, until even that slipped away.

CHAPTER SEVENTEEN

*O*h *God. Asher.*

The Protectors had chained me to a wall and left me alone. I could sit on the floor, but they'd locked my arms together above my head like Asher's had been. They'd long ago gone numb, and ached when I fought against the cuffs. I couldn't free myself, no matter how I struggled. I turned my attention to the room, but the lighting was too bad to see much. With no windows or light, I couldn't tell how long I'd been out, or even what time of day it was. Was I in the same room?

"Asher?" I whispered, my voice husky from screaming.

No answer. I stretched out my legs to see if I could feel him on the floor nearby. I wasn't sure I wanted to find him. If Asher lived, the Protectors would never leave him with me. They knew I'd try to heal him.

Twisting against the chains, I flattened out, lengthening my body to extend my reach. Something wet soaked through the ankle of my jeans when I swept it across the floor, but otherwise I touched only air. I sighed with relief, hoping they'd taken Asher away to help him.

Did they know he wasn't like them anymore? That he could no longer heal himself in the same way?

I wiped my damp face on my coat. Pressing my back

into the cold wall, I pulled my knees in, wanting to curl into a ball.

Asher's survived worse, I reminded myself. *And he was still a Protector.* He could still be alive. Those men might have shot him to get out of the way, but maybe they didn't want him dead, if for no other reason than he was a Protector, too. I tried to hold on to that thought, while my mind replayed that damned gunshot and Asher's unmoving body until I wanted to scream.

The door opened, and I jumped, setting the chains to rattle like a damned ghost. The light blinded me for a moment, but when my eyes adjusted I saw the black-haired man. I was in the same room as before.

"Where's Asher?" I asked, swallowing. "Did you get him to a hospital?"

Bewilderment and curiosity flickered over the man's cold features. "Why would you care? He kills your kind for sport."

I ignored that. "Please. Is he okay? He's not like you. He might not be able to heal himself. I can hel—"

He waved a hand, and the onyx stone set in his silver ring glinted in the light. "You should be less worried about him and more worried about yourself."

He crouched down beside me, bracing his hands on either side of the wall behind me. His knuckles brushed my bare neck, and I recoiled, trying to melt into the bricks to get away from him. He smiled, and I smelled peppermint on his breath.

"Remy, we're going to have so much fun. I can tell you're special. I bet that's why your boyfriend was so happy to die for you."

I heard one word and one word only. *Die. He died. Asher died.* A sob started in my chest and tried to claw its way out of my throat. I couldn't catch my breath, as the

weight of my grief crushed my chest. In the light, I saw
that blood soaked the floor where Asher had been and
stained the leg of my pants.

Noooooooo!!!!

The wild shrieking erupted from me, and I couldn't
stop it. Didn't want to stop it.

The black-haired Protector brushed my hair away from
my forehead, almost as if to comfort me. My stomach
roiled at his touch, and I wanted to kill him.

I twisted away from him and kicked out with both legs.
The move didn't even knock him off balance. Something
dark and cold flickered in his brown eyes, and that was my
only warning. His energy came at me with a force that
nearly rolled my eyes into the back of my head.

I gritted my teeth and reinforced my mental walls. His
energy crashed on me like stormy waves hitting a breaker
wall. I'd never felt anything like it. Gabe and Asher had
tested me, but they'd never unleashed the full force of their
power on me. Another Healer would have had no way to
block them. Healers had no walls to keep the Protectors
from stealing what they wanted. Only Protectors had
mental defenses. I'd never been so grateful for my Protector blood.

"What the hell?" the man whispered.

The surge of his power rolled at me like a tsunami about
to overtake everything in its path. My defenses shook
and shivered under the onslaught, but I refused to cave to
this man who'd murdered Asher. Protectors killed to feel
something, but I would die before I gave him what he
wanted. Sheer willpower kept me together, and sweat
sprouted on my forehead. One salty drop trickled down
my cheek to the corner of my mouth, but I ignored it. I
lifted my chin and imagined my walls made of impenetra-
ble titanium.

The Protector's right eye twitched, and the flow of his

energy halted as he stood. He staggered back, weaving like a drunk person.

"What are you?" he asked at last.

"What you want from me . . . you'll never get it," I answered. "Go ahead and kill me, but I swear you'll never feel anything because of me."

Dean had told me once that he could read my defiance in my eyes, and he'd tried and failed to break me for years. I hoped this Protector could see that same defiance and know how much I wanted him dead.

Abruptly, he stalked out, leaving me alone in the pitch-black room once more. If he thought to scare me, it worked. Without my sense of sight, my imagination played messed-up games with me. My jeans stiffened as Asher's blood dried, and I wondered how long they'd left him lying on the floor, dying, while I had been right next to him unable to save him. What good were these abilities if people died because of me? My mother. Asher. Like a nasty burr, sorrow had spikes that hooked into my flesh.

Asher.

I wasn't sure what I begged for, except for everything that had happened to be a lie. I yearned for him to pop up out of another room and tell me this had all been a test. One I'd failed, sure, but a test all the same, meant to show me how unprepared I was for the Protectors to overtake me. This couldn't be happening.

I had known the Protectors would try to take my energy, to get some kind of high from it to feel human, but I hadn't understood how it would happen. Once, before I knew what he was, Asher had threatened me, trying to make me afraid so I would stay away from him. I remembered the burning pain of it and how I'd thought him a kind of energy thief. My strength had faded as I'd felt his growing. And that had only been a small taste of what he could do. After that, I'd learned that I could block him, though he'd never done anything like that to me again. No, that ability came from my non-Healer side. All Protectors had them. Asher had explained to me that Protectors had once-upon-a-time trained their kids to use their mental walls to protect Healers back when they were all allies, to keep their energy from mingling with a Healer's during a healing. I was the first Healer he'd come across who had similar defenses, and we'd only figured out why once we'd learned I was part-Protector, too.

Now these men knew I could block them. Would they make that leap in logic and grasp what I was? What would they do to me? The minutes pushed into each other. As time stretched on, it became harder to convince myself that Asher had done this to test me. He would never hurt me like that, not even to teach me a lesson. The last of my pitiful hope blew away when the door opened, and my two captors returned.

I nearly broke down again. Asher really was gone. He wasn't coming to save me or fix this. They'd killed him.

The Protectors approached me with barely contained zeal, and I remembered what had been done to Yvette in their quest for sensation.

Then I heard Gabe and Asher telling me to be patient. These men didn't know that I could inflict my injuries on them. If I waited, they would choose their own punishment and I would avenge what they did to Asher.

That was the thought I held on to when the torture began.

An eon of pain had passed while they'd held me prisoner. I thought it had been two days, but I couldn't be sure.

The man named Mark slapped me awake for the umpteenth time. As soon as my eyes opened, he pressed a knife to my bare arm. At some point, they'd taken my coat and left me in just my tank top and jeans. The more skin they could reach, the better. The black-haired man—Xavier, I'd learned—had left while I'd been unconscious. I'd heard him talking to someone on the phone, but he never slipped up and said their name during these check-ins.

Mark leaned down until I could see my reflection in his irises. "I really need you to pay attention, darlin'." The jerk berated me in a charming voice. "I know you're groggy, but we don't have time for these games."

The ceiling beyond him had twenty-two panels. When the pain had threatened to crush me, I'd spent long minutes counting them. Every movement made my head pound, and I saw spots if I turned it too sharply. Suffocation could do that to you. That had been the last experiment they'd conducted in their ongoing campaign to break me.

Mark didn't like my continued silence. While they'd tortured me, they'd asked me a litany of questions. *Did I know Asher was a Protector? How was I different? What could I do? Did I know others like me? Did I know other Protectors?* I'd clamped my jaw shut, refusing to answer them, and they carried on tormenting me.

Now, the pressure of the knife increased until the blade sliced through my skin. It amazed me how cold the metal could feel and then how hot the pain burned in comparison. This was what they had done to that other Healer, Yvette. These Protectors thought the cuts and the suffocation and all the rest would weaken me until they could steal everything from me. Like Dean had, they thought they could control me with pain. Stupid men.

Losing Asher had scraped everything out of me, except for the all-consuming need to wipe these men off the face of the earth. So far, an opportunity hadn't presented itself, but the moment would come. I just had to wait long enough to gather my powers again, a difficult thing to do when they kept at me so relentlessly. Why wouldn't they just kill me already?

I imagined I heard Asher's voice. *Easy, Remy. Be smart. You can get out of this.* He might only live in my imagination, but I listened. I would never give in to these bastards. I would rather die fighting.

Mark cut me again, and I flinched, but my walls held strong. *Amateur,* my inner voice mocked. Dean had done far worse damage. I could withstand this, but it was wearing me out. Time to change tactics, even if it meant using up my energy stores temporarily.

I smiled. As Mark sliced into my thigh, I healed the cuts on my arms. His head jerked up when he noticed the wounds disappearing. I didn't care. I *wanted* him to see what I could do. To know that I had power and would never use it to help him. I imagined Asher screaming at me to stop taunting these men. But Asher had died and left me on my own.

"What's it like to be this close to a Healer and know you'll never taste her power?" I taunted.

Mark cursed and lifted the knife away from me.

I pretended to think, then shook my head like I'd just remembered. "Oh right. You can't *feel* anything."

Mark jerked his arm back like he would plant his fist in my face.

Do it, you bastard, I thought. *And I'll heal that, too, while you watch like a salivating dog.*

His scowl darkened before he spun on his heel. The door almost tore from its hinges when he slammed it closed behind him.

Alone again, I whimpered.

Oh Asher. I need you.

★ ★ ★

The next time the door opened and I heard people enter, I didn't acknowledge them with so much as an eye blink in their direction. Why bother? Soon they would kill me and this would all be over. I was chained to a wall, and I couldn't see a way out of this.

"I told you once that the only good Healer is a dead Healer."

The familiar silky voice had me twisting toward the door. Gabe.

He stood in the doorway, looking as perfect and untouchable as ever. The shock of his presence surprised a relieved sob out me. Asher would be avenged. Mark and Xavier would die. Gabe had always told me that his family came first. He'd promised to kill anyone who put them in danger, including me.

I waited, soaking up that face that looked so much like Asher's.

"Hey, Remy," Gabe said softly, crossing the room to crouch beside me.

I stared at him. Why wasn't he attacking the men? What did he have planned? His face gave nothing away, beyond disgust when his eyes flicked to the dried blood on my jeans. His brother's blood.

Something wasn't right. My brain waded through molasses, trying to make sense of what it was seeing. Gabe had entered the room *with* the Protectors. They were not threatened by his appearance. He wasn't here to help me, or even to avenge Asher.

Our capture had made no sense. Someone had told the Protectors where to find us. That person had also known that Asher could be used as bait to catch me. Who else could have known these things other than the one person we'd trusted enough to confide in? Gabe had never liked me. He'd tolerated me for a time. Then, like Lottie, Gabe had betrayed me to the Protectors. Worse, he'd betrayed

Asher. He'd been the one on the phone, the person giving information to Xavier.

Asher had died because of his brother.

Rage snapped and snarled inside me. I wanted to tear Gabe apart with my hands. Better yet, I wanted to pull him apart with my powers. If I'd been free, I would have killed him. The metal restraints chaining me to the wall bit into my wrists when I launched myself at Gabe. I screamed in frustration when I couldn't reach him, and Asher's brother watched me with the same distant expression he'd worn the first time we met.

"How could you?" I asked. "He loved you. Do you know how they killed him? They shot him and left him to bleed to death on the floor. Does it give you pleasure knowing he died feeling all of that?"

Gabe didn't answer. He waited for me to stop fighting before he leaned closer, his beautiful face cold. I didn't think. I spat in his face. Gabe's stillness sent a chill through me when he stared at me with my saliva dripping down his cheek. After a long moment, he reached for me. I shrank back, but he only lifted my tank top, using the hem to wipe the spit from his face.

"Not nearly as much pleasure as I'm going to get from watching you die, Healer," he said loudly.

I strained forward. "I'm going to kill you, Gabe."

One dark eyebrow lifted.

I continued. "It's going to be painful, and I swear to you I'm going to make you feel every bit of it."

His lips curved in a half smile. "Before or after I break you? Healers are such fragile things."

He trailed his fingers from my shoulder to my arm. Before I could unleash my power on him, he grasped my forearm and twisted it like he'd done in our training sessions. Except, where before he tempered his strength to keep from harming me, now he exerted pressure until something broke. Sudden pain burned through me, and I screamed. I heard the men laugh.

A shadow passed over Gabe's face. An emotion I couldn't read.

Then I stopped caring how he hurt me.

CHAPTER EIGHTEEN

"*R*emy? Wake up."

I ached like my soul had been scraped out of my body with a dull razor blade. With consciousness, memory returned. *Asher. Oh God. Your brother. I'm so sorry.* A sob caught in my throat, and I folded in on myself, pulling my knees into my chest. The voice kept talking, and I waited for the blow that would soon come.

Someone had loosened the tension on the chains at my wrists, and I lay on the stone floor instead of leaning against the wall. I tried to cradle my broken right forearm against my ribs and flinched at the new agony the movement set off. Once Gabe had broken my arm, he'd stepped back and let the other two Protectors take over. Bruises and cuts covered my body from their fists. They'd taken turns hitting me while Gabe watched, his jaw working like he'd been clenching his teeth.

"Remy?" the voice said again.

A body hovered inches above me blocking the light. I threw up my uninjured left hand to protect myself before I realized who lingered there. Gabe. Gabe, who'd trained me while his brother watched. Gabe, who had snapped my arm while the others laughed at my screams. And Asher . . . Gabe might as well have murdered his brother himself. He'd set all of this in motion by giving us over to these people. What had I done to make him hate me so much?

Asher's brother whispered my name again and then grunted when my left fist connected with his cheekbone.

"You bastard!"

Clambering to my knees, I threw myself against him. Stronger and bigger than me, Gabe clasped my wrists to hold me off. Pain streaked from my broken forearm to the rest of my body, and I almost threw up. If not for him holding me up, I would have fallen.

"I hate you," I said, moaning.

"Remy, you have to be quiet."

Like hell. I threw back my head and screamed.

"Damn it! I'm trying to help you!"

He clamped a hand to my mouth, and I glared at him. It didn't matter. I could hear movement from somewhere in the building. It wouldn't be long before they arrived to check on us. Gabe had shut us in the room, probably so he could steal my energy without having to share me with the others. If he thought he could overpower me on his own, he'd screwed up.

It seemed like he'd come to the same conclusion. He threw a nervous glance toward the door. I took advantage of his distraction to gather my energy and hoped the *humming* of it would hurt him. In the past, he'd spent enough time with me to feel at least that again.

Gabe didn't back away or cower when I lowered my walls. Instead, he crowded me, gripping the front of my shirt in one fist and leaning close enough for his nose to almost touch mine.

"Don't do it," he warned. "I didn't want to hurt you, but they had to believe I was like them or they wouldn't have let me near you. I don't have time to explain everything, but please stop fighting me. I'm trying to get you out of here, and you'll need your energy."

I frowned at the urgency in Gabe's low voice. The *hum* of my energy waned a second, but then I regrouped, remembering how he'd snapped my arm without blinking. It had to be a trick.

"Think! I knew you could use your injuries against them."

"Liar," I accused. "You told them where to find Asher and me. You were the only one who knew, Gabe."

"Was I?" he asked, shaking me slightly. "Asher didn't call to check in, and I followed the GPS on his phone to this place. I lied my way in."

A small, niggling doubt wouldn't shut the hell up. Hadn't the Protectors found the Healers before despite my grandfather's precautions? Hadn't they found Yvette? They could have been watching us all along. Every time I went into the forest, I'd drawn them to Asher.

No! I thought. *Don't be stupid. You can't trust Gabe. He's threatened you before.* Gabe had been the one to betray us. Hadn't he? This had to be another trick. Except that he'd also tried to help me in the past. When Asher had struggled with training me, afraid of hurting me, Gabe had stepped in to do it in his place. Then, later he'd helped Asher protect my family.

In the next room, someone tried to open the door to my prison. The man shouted when he found it locked. The door shivered when he threw his weight against it. Gabe's grip on me loosened, and I focused on him. He almost looked . . . hurt that I doubted him. Which made less than zero sense because Gabe had never cared what I thought about anything.

"Whatever I've done, you know I would never hurt my brother," Gabe pleaded. "Please tell me you know that, Remy. At least give me that."

I searched his face, wanting to believe him.

Before I could respond, someone struck the door with enough force to splinter the wood. In seconds, the Protectors had ripped it off its hinges and tossed it aside. Xavier entered the room first, his gun pointed at Gabe's back. I hated that damned gun.

Gabe's expression hardened, all emotion shutting off until he once again wore a polite mask. I'd never seen anything like it, the way he seemed to flick off a light inside.

In a single, elegant move, he eased me to the ground and then rose to face the men with me behind him. Almost like he intended to shield me from harm, the way Asher would have. That couldn't be right. I shook my head to clear it. Gabe had hurt me. He wasn't like Asher at all.

"What the hell are you doing, Gabriel?" Xavier asked. "I told you not to come in here alone."

Gabe shrugged. "I didn't think I needed help to break a Healer."

Healer. Gabe always called me Healer, as if to distance himself from what I was. Earlier he had called me Remy, though, as he tried to wake me. Another memory prodded me. When Gabe had first arrived, he'd said something. A phrase he'd used before. I frowned, trying to remember. Then it hit me.

I told you once that the only good Healer is a dead Healer.

The night Dean died, Gabe had said those exact words to me to provoke me into saving myself and Asher. It had worked that night.

Oh God. Gabe had been trying to give me a signal, and I'd been too caught up in losing Asher to notice. Exhausted, I shifted to ease the ache in my muscles. Gabe shadowed the movement, confusing me. Why was he blocking me? And then I realized. The Protectors didn't know yet that I was unchained. I froze in place, but it was too late.

"You freed her," Xavier said. He patted his pocket, and then growled, "You stole the keys."

"I told you not to trust him," Mark growled, shoving forward.

Gabe crossed his arms, relaxed and arrogant as usual. "I don't need to chain a Healer to the wall in order to control her."

The implied insult hit its mark, and Xavier had to throw an arm out to stop Mark from attacking Gabe.

"Or maybe," Xavier said thoughtfully, "you're like your brother."

"I think I've proven that I'm nothing like my brother." Gabe said. "I'm not a slave to a Healer."

"And yet . . ." Xavier gestured toward me. "You're trying to save the girl."

Gabe laughed. I wondered if the men could tell it was forced. If I believed what my instincts were telling me, then Gabe would try to save me. Out of pity or loyalty to his brother, he would put himself between me and the Protectors. And I would watch him get hurt, too. Protectors shouldn't die from bullet wounds, but . . . I'd trained with Gabe for months. Who knew how mortal he'd become around me? He'd never said anything, but then, he wouldn't.

I imagined Gabe dying in the same spot Asher had and knew it would kill me. I wouldn't come back from that. As it was, I already felt severed from myself. I would not chance letting another Blackwell die for me. A new calm settled over me.

"You're wrong, you know," I said. I continued, ignoring the warning look Gabe sent over his shoulder. "Asher loved me. He was honest and courageous and would do anything for those he cared about. Gabe is nothing like his brother. "

I injected as much venom as I could into my perusal of Gabe. He actually flinched, and part of me wanted to tell him I was sorry. Sorry for doubting him and for getting him into this mess. He wouldn't be in this situation if Asher hadn't followed me to San Francisco. If I did nothing else before these men killed me, I would fix this.

Using the wall for support, I rose to my feet, groaning at the pain but glad for it because it would be our way out of here. The weaker and more pathetic I seemed, the better.

"Gabe always wanted my power for himself, and he hated me for choosing Asher." I sounded fierce as I faced Xavier. "I would rather kill myself than let Gabe have any piece of me."

Xavier's mouth twitched in a smug smile.

"You win," I told him. "We all know I'm not getting out of here. If I'm going to die, I choose you. I swear I won't fight you. Just don't let him touch me again."

My movements slow and creaking, I limped toward Xavier. Dropping my mental walls, I controlled my energy, letting it unfurl inside me. It was the first time I'd had my walls down since meeting these Protectors. The *hum* of it hurt Protectors, even when they could feel nothing else. That sensation was how Asher had known I was different when we'd met.

Now, with my defenses crashing down, Mark and Xavier sensed my energy for the first time. Mark recoiled, bringing a hand to his head. Xavier's gun hand faltered and the muzzle dropped, pointing at the floor as he frowned at Gabe. They understood something was off, but they didn't know what.

I spared a glance at Gabe. He felt my energy, too, but unlike the others, he had no doubt where it came from. He had that tense look about him, the one that signaled he was about to jump into action. He'd guessed what I intended to do, but I didn't know if he planned to stop me or help me.

Xavier's glance bounced between Gabe and me, and then remained on me. His eyes flashed with a darkening realization. I had seconds to act and I used them, hoping Gabe would be on my side.

Using every last bit of my strength, I launched forward with the speed of the Protectors. I wasn't fast enough to surprise them entirely. Xavier managed to lift his gun and fire off a shot off just as I reached him. I recoiled backward when the bullet hit me with the force of a baseball bat to the belly. A bat that had been lit on fire.

I fell to my knees, absorbing the pain. Using it. Luckily, Mark and Xavier stood close enough together that I could reach over and touch an ankle of each man. The right grip made my eyes water as pain shot up my side from my broken arm. I'd never tried to take out two people at once, let alone two Protectors. What if I failed? I imagined my power striking out of me like lightning and lashing each man. Behind me I sensed movement, but Gabe didn't interfere. Red sparks lit the room.

Bones snapped as arms broke, and Xavier dropped the gun. Cuts opened on their skin, the blood seeping through their clothes to mirror mine, and matching bruises formed on their skin. Wet stains spread across their stomachs like dark red ink blots.

These two Protectors had felt nothing for a century, except the snatches of feeling they'd stolen when they'd taken the lives of Healers. I fiercely wished that they could have felt the pain of the injuries I'd inflicted on them, but I knew it was hopeless when they didn't even drop to the ground. I hadn't spent enough time with them for them to begin to feel mortal like I had with the Blackwells.

My hands fell away from them, not out of choice, but

because I was too weak to hold on when they jerked away from me. Like an autumn leaf falling to the ground, I dropped, landing hard on the cold concrete. I touched my stomach, and my fingers came away bloody. Xavier had shot me.

Shivers racked my body like I'd gone swimming in an icy lake. I struggled to stay aware, but I could feel myself losing the battle. From a distance, I heard the sickening crunch of skin and bones giving way to fists. Gabe had taken up where I left off.

My teeth chattered, and I slid toward sleep. Every limb weighed a ton, and I melted into the concrete. The abyss called to me, and the agony of my wounds began to fade as I stepped into the mist where I no longer felt anything. I welcomed the anesthesia.

Then arms lifted me. Someone carried me, and I shook off the drowsiness enough to wonder if I should be afraid, though I couldn't recall why. I opened my eyes a slit and familiar green eyes stared down at me.

"Asher," I whispered, and I sounded sleepy and happy. "I knew you would come. I knew you couldn't be dead."

He stumbled, and I thought he choked on a cry. The air changed, becoming hotter and brighter as if the sun had come out. I squeezed my eyes closed against the light. With the return of warmth, though, the numbness seeped out of me. The tremors began, jarring every wound and setting off expanding rings of agony. I shuddered against Asher. In the distance, a loud blast sounded, and I remembered he'd been shot. He'd been shot, but now he was carrying me.

"How did you heal yourself?" I asked, confused.

He didn't answer, but he began to sing to me in a language I didn't know. I didn't understand the words, but the rhythm gave me something other than the pain to concentrate on. Desperate to feel his skin, I tucked one hand inside the collar of his shirt, curving my fingers around his neck until I could feel his heartbeat. The abnormally fast *thump, thump* of his pulse comforted me.

"Please don't leave me again," I begged. "It's too much. I don't know what to do without you."

Asher cradled me closer to his chest, his heat seeping into my body. He dropped a kiss against the inside of my raised wrist. Blood smeared across his neck where I touched him. Too much blood. I would not be able to heal this.

"I love you," I told him.

"Shh, Remy," he said. "You'll be okay. I promise."

Something about his voice bothered me, but I chose to ignore it. I had to believe we would be okay.

CHAPTER NINETEEN

$\mathcal{W}$e walked forever.

I floated in and out of the ether, but every time I drifted back, Asher's green eyes watched over me. He never tired, and it reminded me of that other time he'd carried me. He'd almost died, and I'd thought I would die in his place when I took his injuries. It seemed like one or the other of us was always on the verge of death. We swirled in a mad waltz with the Grim Reaper, balancing on our toes to keep from falling.

A dark gray haze coated the world, and Asher looked fuzzier than before. I blinked, but that only made it more difficult to keep my eyes open. It didn't seem right to give in to unconsciousness. It occurred to me that I was losing too much blood, but I couldn't open my mouth to tell Asher. I couldn't fight the desire to close my eyes anymore.

"Remy?"

I'm not sure how much time had passed before he abruptly stopped and shook me. Someone had replaced my insides with dust and left me a bloodless human sandbag. The beat of my heart slowed and stuttered.

Asher whispered to me, but the words no longer made sense. He laid me on the ground, and his hands pressed into my chest.

CPR. I was dying. Asher would want me to heal myself.

I tried. Really, I did. But I was so tired, and the *humming* wouldn't start. *Let me sleep.*

"Damn you, Healer! Fight! Don't you dare give up!"

The furious cursing wouldn't stop. It badgered and prodded, screaming at me to heal myself.

"You can do this. Come on!"

I dug deep for a spark of energy and forced it straight to my heart. My entire body jerked into an arch and then slammed into the ground. It was like launching back into myself, and the reentry brought with it such a fiery storm of pain that I screamed. Then I did my best to make the bleeding stop.

"That's it, Remy. You did good. I'm here."

Arms encircled me, cradling me against a chest once more. If I could have fought him, I would have. The hold was tender, but not Asher's. Reentry brought more than physical pain; it also brought me back to reality. He'd called me "Healer." I didn't need to open my eyes to see the truth of who held me, but I made myself to do it anyway.

Green eyes studied me with concern. Gabe's green eyes.

I shuddered and hated him for making me come back to this hell.

If Gabe had a choice between saving his brother or me from our prison, he would always choose his brother. Gabe held me now, and that could only mean one thing. Asher really had died.

Gabe took me to a motel. He left me propped against a wall in an alley, while he went inside to secure a room. I'm not sure how he got away without questions, covered in bruises, dirt, and blood as he was, but Asher had always said that money could move mountains. God knew the Blackwells had a lot of it.

Asher.

He'd died in that damned prison. What had been the point of my coming to San Francisco? I'd been trying to save us, but I'd gotten him killed instead. The Protectors had made it clear they were after me, not Asher.

I'd screwed up and lost the one person who mattered the most.

I should have died in that prison.

Gabe returned with a room key in his hand, took one look at the tears streaming down my face, and picked me up again without a word. Somehow he managed to work the key in the lock and get me into the room without having to set me down. He carried me straight into the bathroom and set me down on the toilet.

Standing over me, he examined me with a grimace. The look was one reserved for a task that you hated, like cleaning the hair out of a drain or taking out the trash.

He reached for me, and I shoved his hands away with my good arm.

"Go away, Gabe."

One of his dark eyebrows peaked. "You know who I am?"

"Yes," I answered bitterly.

"Good. That will make this much easier."

He didn't give me the chance to protest again. He gripped the hem of my tank top in both hands and yanked it up and over my head. Covering myself didn't even enter my mind. Biting my lip bloody to hold in the screams pretty much took up all my strength as bits of the material that had stuck to my stomach wound loosened. The skin tore open again, and blood trickled down my belly and my back where the bullet had exited.

Gabe sucked in a deep breath and cursed.

I cursed right back at him, until he smacked a hand down over my mouth.

"Remy, shut up. We have to get this wound taken care of. I can't take you to a hospital because they'll be looking for you. So you and I are going to do this together. Got it?"

I didn't want Gabe touching me. I could tell I didn't have the ability to heal myself—I'd shorted out my powers and it would be hours or days before they returned. It didn't matter, though. I didn't deserve to be healed.

Gabe sighed. "Fine. You just sit there, and I'll take care of it. But you should know, I'm tired and pissed off. Fight me once, and I'll make you sorry."

The threat in his voice sounded real enough that I sat very still. For a long moment. As soon as his hand lifted from my mouth, I shoved him again and ran, aiming for the door to the next room.

I'd gone a single step before I collapsed on the floor in a huddle, too weak to go any farther. I moaned. Gabe crossed his arms and stood over me, looking patient and arrogant all at once.

"Finished?" he asked.

It hit me how ridiculous I must look lying on the bathroom floor in my bra and jeans. I hated Gabe at that moment more than I'd ever hated anyone in my life. He bent and picked me up. After propping me against the wall, he stripped off my jeans so I stood before him in just my underwear. Then he spread a clean towel on the linoleum floor and laid me on top of it. He set to work on my injuries.

I decided the best way to deal with the situation was to pretend he didn't exist. He pressed a towel to my stomach to stop the blood flow. That red-stained towel landed on the floor with a *splat* and was replaced by another.

At one point, he disappeared into the other room and made a call. I didn't move when he answered a knock on the door a short time later. What was the point? Blood loss had made me too weak to fight, and I would never make it past him. The reason for his call became clear when he returned to the bathroom with a first aid kit and more clean towels.

Using alcohol wipes, Gabe cleaned the cuts that Xavier and Mark had taken their time giving me. I hissed and sank my nails into his forearm when he dug around in the bullet hole to clean it, and he didn't react, even though I'd drawn blood. His touch remained impersonal, almost like a doctor working on a patient, but that didn't take the sting of humiliation away. Laid out before him almost naked, I felt unbearably vulnerable. As I used to with Dean, I retreated into my oldest defense. I cut myself off from my emotions, refusing to cry in front of Gabe.

Once he'd bandaged the worst of my injuries, Gabe sat me up and knelt beside me, wiping his bloody hands on a hand towel. A sudden wave of dizziness hit me, and I glued my gaze to the wall, straining to stay upright.

Unable to stand the strained silence anymore, I said, "Are you finished?"

Out of the corner of my eye, I saw him shake his head. "Why aren't you healing yourself?" he asked.

The blunt question startled me into looking at him. I swayed, and he pushed me upright again, guiding me to lean against the wall.

"Your arm is broken—"

"Whose fault is that?" I broke in.

He acted like I hadn't said anything. "I've managed to dig out the bullet. We're lucky it missed any vital organs. But it keeps bleeding."

To prove his point, he tugged on the fresh towel he'd pressed to my stomach a short time ago. Fresh blood coated it. Well, that explained the light-headedness. How much had I lost? I started to explain that I couldn't heal myself, even if I wanted to. My powers had shorted out. He didn't give me a chance, though.

"You have to stop it," he demanded, putting the towel back. "Heal yourself."

The order infuriated me. For the last two days, every decision had been stolen from me. I'd been beaten and tortured. Toyed with by the bastards who'd killed Asher. And I'd been able to do nothing but take it. No more.

"No," I whispered to Gabe. "Maybe I don't want to live."

"That's bullshit. Help me heal you, Remy."

He meant use his energy to heal myself. Asher had helped me that way a hundred times, but I couldn't bear the thought of my energy mixing with Gabe's like that. His touch and the way he resembled Asher hurt badly enough.

"No!"

Gabe didn't listen. He started talking and wouldn't stop. He badgered me. When that didn't work, he ordered me to heal myself. His voice droned on. Fed up, I shut down. I sat in a motel bathroom with Gabe, but I had retreated inside myself. I wasn't anyone's property to be ordered about. I'd rather be dead. Without Asher, that seemed a real possibility.

At last, the words stopped. I watched Gabe give up, his shoulders sagging in defeat. He leaned against the opposite wall. His feet almost touched my bare ones. Resting his elbows on his knees, he cradled his head in his hands. He swiped his fingers across his face, and I realized with surprise that he was crying. Gabe, the big bad Protector, was crying. I hadn't known he was capable of sorrow.

"He knew he might die for you. Asher knew it might

happen, but he loved you enough to chance it." Gabe's deep voice echoed in the bathroom, and he spoke in a halting tone. "My brother died trying to save you. Are you such a coward that you'd throw that back in his face?"

That accusation battered me worse than every wound on my body. I crushed a fist to my mouth to hold in the sob that tried to escape.

"I can't," I pleaded with Gabe. "Not without him."

"You can. You're making a choice, Remy. A wrong choice that dishonors my brother." He rose up on his knees again before me, but didn't touch me when I shrank away from him. "And what about your family? You think these people won't go after them?"

I hadn't thought of my family. It hadn't even occurred to me to think of them. God, I was so selfish. All I could see was the sharp knife of my grief. What if they got to my father or Laura or Lucy? But wouldn't it be better if I just disappeared? Everywhere I went, I brought death. If I was gone, maybe my family stood a better chance.

As if he could hear the teetering of my thoughts, Gabe touched my knee. "Think, Remy. You have to be smart. I want to get the people who did this to my family, but I need your help. Please help me."

His words, so like Asher's, peeled a layer of my anger away. "You'll die, too, Gabe. If I help you, you'll end up dead. I can't . . ." I broke off and took a deep breath. "I can't be responsible for another person dying. Please don't ask me . . ."

Gabe's touch fell away from me when he stood and took a step back. His voice sounded cold and bitter. "Then I was right all along. You never deserved my brother, Healer."

He left the bathroom, shutting the door behind him with a quiet *click* instead of slamming it. I almost wished he had slammed it. Anger was so much easier to deal with than disappointment. Sliding to the floor, I curled into a ball, wishing I'd died in that prison instead of Asher.

Gabe was right.

Asher deserved better than for me to give up. The longer I lay on that stupid bathroom floor, the more a singular solution began to take shape.

Revenge. Even with everything Dean had done to my mother and me, I'd only wanted to get away from him and the pain he'd caused. I hadn't fantasized about hurting him the way he'd hurt me. Yet, the image of Asher getting shot point-blank had burned itself into my skull, and with Gabe's words, a fire had started in my belly.

I wanted those men dead. They deserved to die.

The only thing I could do for Asher now was hunt down whoever had betrayed us in the first place. Gabe had stayed loyal to his brother, so who had told those men how to find us? It couldn't have been chance that they kidnapped us at Inspiration Point. They'd waited for us and used Asher as bait to catch me. They knew I had a connection to Asher. The Protectors had to be watching my grandfather's people closely, which meant that others were in danger. My grandfather must be sick with worry, and I'd hardly spared him a thought. I had to warn his people, help them if I could. And if I died doing so, what would it matter? At least, I would be dying for something instead of giving up on the floor of some lousy motel.

Eventually, I pulled myself up. Every muscle protested, reminding me of how bad my injuries were, and I grasped the sink when the world shifted and spun. I would never be able to heal myself alone in this condition.

I opened the bathroom door and nearly tripped over a sleeping Gabe. He'd stretched himself out on the floor next to the bathroom door, either to listen for my cries or to stop me from leaving if I tried to run. I hadn't noticed it before, but he looked like hell.

Even sprawled out, he looked more wound up and tense than relaxed. Dark circles ringed his eyes. A purple bruise colored his forehead near the hairline, and I imagined he had bruises elsewhere. Too bad I wouldn't be able to heal him anytime soon.

I nudged him with my foot, afraid I would pass out if I leaned down to wake him.

"Gabe," I said.

He woke completely, shaking off sleep and shooting to his feet from one second to the next. When he grasped there was no threat, he relaxed from his fighting stance and sent me a curious glance.

I inhaled and exhaled through my nose. "Let's get this over with, okay?"

I didn't have to explain what I meant to him, and I was grateful. I knew I sounded bitchy, but I couldn't help that. Gabe responded by guiding me to the bed and helping me to sit. Then he tugged a chair over and sank down into it. Unsure how to go about this without Asher's guidance, I waited for Gabe to direct me. He held up his hand until I rested mine in it.

"Ready?" he asked.

"Are you sure you can do this, Gabe?" I asked hesitantly. "Asher said my energy isn't like other Healers. Won't you be tempted to steal it?"

"I can handle it."

"But what if I can't?" I asked. "Sometimes I start healing Protectors and can't stop. It happened with Asher. I could hurt you."

"Don't worry about me, okay? Stop stalling."

I was stalling. The intimacy that came with using his energy to heal myself scared me. I hated the idea of letting my guard down with him. Training was one thing, but this . . . it was like exposing myself. Putting my trust in him entirely. I wished I saw another way, but I couldn't think of anything except going to the hospital. Where Protectors could be waiting for me. *Never going to happen.*

"Okay, I'm ready," I said, closing my eyes.

Gabe didn't want to give me a chance to change my mind, and he immediately let his energy loose. It swept over me, dark and dangerous and unlike Asher's. Everything in me wanted to reject it and fight him off.

I tensed and Gabe must have felt it because he said, "Relax, Remy. I swear I won't hurt you. You can let your guard down."

I didn't relax, but I dropped my mental walls, the whole while expecting him to attack me despite his words. It didn't happen. In fact, Gabe seemed more in control of his ability than Asher had. Gabe's energy didn't swirl in the air for me to grab; he directed it exactly where he wanted it to go—my injuries. I tried to pretend that it was Asher helping me.

The heat of his energy flow scorched my insides, and I used it to heal the worst of my injuries first. I imagined the stomach wound closing, the blood clotting, and the tissues and muscles pulling back together. When that was finished, I moved on to my broken arm and dislocated shoulder. By the time I'd taken care of those injuries, I was weakening. The bruises and cuts covering me would remain. I was too exhausted, too wasted from concentrating so hard to do anymore.

Sighing, I let go of Gabe's hand and opened my eyes in time to see red sparks tripping from my skin to his. Gabe's face had turned a sick shade of gray and glowed with a sheen of sweat. His mouth had tightened into a grimace, and his brow lowered as if he was fighting off a tremendous amount of pain. I cringed, scared he might be losing a battle for control.

"Are you okay?" I asked.

"Yes," he answered after a long moment.

He didn't sound okay. He sounded fierce.

"I hurt you, didn't I? I'm sor—"

"I'm fine," he cut in, his accent sharp. He stood, putting his back to me. "Why don't you try to get some sleep, and we'll figure things out in the morning?"

Unable to see his expression, I had to take his words at face value. Glancing down at myself, I remembered I wore only my underwear. Maybe I should have been embarrassed, but I shrugged. What did it matter? Gabe hated me, and I didn't like him. It wasn't like he was sneaking peeks between cussing me out and cleaning my injuries. Besides, between the cuts and bruises, I looked more like roadkill than someone's dream poster girl. Still, when he threw a clean T-shirt to me, I gladly pulled it over my head. Apparently, he'd had more than a first aid kit delivered to our room. Money working miracles again.

I burrowed under the covers and pretended to fall asleep. Gabe shut off the light, and I heard him take the chair by the bed. For a long time, I listened to his breathing, the steady in and out of his inhalations and exhalations. Like using his energy, it felt too intimate to be stuck in this tiny space with him, sharing the same air. I wanted to be alone. I bit down on my knuckle.

Soon his breathing slowed into a pattern, and I thought he slept. That was when I let the tears fall. I turned my face into the scratchy pillowcase to cover the sounds. I'd mistaken Gabe for Asher and fooled myself into thinking Asher had survived that prison. These wounds would not be patched. I would not heal.

The bed shifted, and I choked on a cry. Gabe lay down on top of the covers. He pulled me into his side, covers and all, and pressed my face to his shirt. I started to fight him, wanting his touch least of all. He reminded me too much of Asher with his damned green eyes.

Then my fingers brushed Gabe's cheek. Tears. Gabe cried for his brother, too. That deflated my anger like nothing else could have, and I stopped fighting him. There was nothing romantic in his hold. We both grieved for Asher, and sometimes it hurt a little less to cry with someone else. Even if it was in the dark and you didn't really like the person who held you.

CHAPTER TWENTY

$\mathscr{L}$ight barely penetrated the heavy curtains when I woke in the morning. Gabe had spared me the awkwardness of waking up beside him. The water ran in the bathroom, and I jumped up to get dressed. I groaned at the aches that move caused. I'd healed the worst of my injuries, but my body had taken a tremendous amount of abuse in the last couple of days.

My jeans, torn and ruined, had been folded and left on the dresser. I held them up, disgusted by how stiff the dried blood had made them. If anyone saw me wearing them and looking the way I did, there would be questions. Besides, I would go crazy if I had to walk around wearing Asher's blood.

The water shut off while I tried to figure out what to do about my clothing, and then it was too late because Gabe opened the bathroom door, rubbing a towel to his head. His wet hair stood up in spikes all over his head, and he had yet to put on a shirt with his jeans. Standing there in just a T-shirt, again the forced closeness of the situation struck me. I backed up and sank into the room's only chair, clutching the jeans to my chest.

Gabe noticed me and stopped in the doorway. "You're up."

"What are we going to do, Gabe?" I asked, sounding lost.

I was talking about losing Asher. Gabe paced forward and took the jeans from me.

"One step at a time, Remy. First, let's see what we can do about these." He gestured to my face and legs. "We can't go anywhere with you looking like that."

I thought he meant the way I was dressed, but when I looked down I gasped. The bruises and cuts had swelled into ugly, multicolored blots that marked much of my exposed skin.

Gabe sat on the bed across from me and dumped his towel and my jeans on the floor. "Are you feeling up to healing yourself?"

He waited patiently while I tested my strength. In truth, I could heal myself, but it would use up the little energy I'd stored up overnight. I still wasn't at 100 percent. Gabe seemed to read my response in my expression.

"Let me help you, Remy."

I shook my head.

Gabe exhaled in frustration. "You're a damned mule! Fine. Have at it."

He crossed his arms over his chest, and for the first time I noticed the discoloration covering his ribs. Those marks had been caused by fists when he'd been trying to rescue me. I wondered if Mark and Xavier had survived and hoped not.

I swallowed and tugged the hem of my T-shirt over my thighs. I hated this. I didn't want to be here with Asher's brother. I didn't want to owe him anything or depend on him.

Gabe sighed. "Please, don't cry. I'm sorry I yelled at you." He rubbed his face. "Can you see it from my side? We can't stay here. We need to get moving, but if we go anywhere with you looking like that, it'll draw attention to us. Attention we don't need. Let me help you."

I chewed on my lip, undecided.

Gabe pounded a fist on his thigh and stared at the ceiling in disgust. "I can't believe I'm begging a Healer to let me help heal her."

That kind of comment was exactly the Gabe I knew. The Gabe who'd held me last night while I cried was someone I wanted to forget. The arrogant, irritable Gabe in front of me was someone I could deal with.

"Okay," I said. "But on one condition."

"What?" he snarled.

"I heal you first." He started to balk and I sliced a hand through the air. "I'm not going to have you walking around with an injury because of me. I heal you, and then you help me take care of my injuries. That's the deal."

Gabe rolled his shoulders back, and he appeared bigger and more intimidating. He'd used the tactic before to get me to do what he wanted. I'd thought him a predator then. Something along the lines of a shark.

I snorted. "That won't work. You can't make me heal myself."

The silence stretched on.

"You're either a masochist or a martyr," Gabe accused. "Do you like it when you take on other people's injuries? Does it make you feel important?"

I nearly punched him. Of course, that was what he wanted. Me, so angry I'd refuse to heal him. Rather than give in to my anger, I smiled. Then, I clasped Gabe's hand. He wasn't expecting it, and I held on when he jerked away in reaction. I dropped my walls and sent my energy unwinding toward him, only to find he had his guard up.

"Come on, Gabe," I said. "You're wasting time."

If anything, his scowl grew darker, but he did what I

wanted and dropped his defenses. I watched him closely as I scanned him. Like last night, he squeezed his eyes shut and gritted his teeth, but he remained in control. I hurried to take care of his injuries, and moments later the bruising stippling his side disappeared. Green sparks lit the air, and I sucked in a breath as my side began to ache. *Stupid, macho jerk*. If I'd made him mortal at all, he'd been in pain and hiding it.

I started to drop my hand, but Gabe grasped it.

"Now you," he said. He did not sound happy.

I prepared myself for the way his energy would come at me, aggressive and sure like Gabe. It still made me shudder in distaste when I felt it. I set to work on my injuries. I'd never healed myself so quickly. Gabe was more powerful than Asher. His energy would have overwhelmed me if he wasn't in such perfect control of it. The bruises and cuts disappeared, and with them, the constant edge of pain faded. I'd become so used to it in the last few days that its retreat made me sigh in relief. *Good as new, except for my heart*. More green sparks lit the air when I pulled away from Gabe.

"Thank you," I said simply.

Gabe stared at me with an expression I couldn't interpret. Then he rose and picked up my jeans. "Why don't you take a shower, and I'll see what I can do about finding you some clothes?"

I stood and escaped to the bathroom. We hadn't talked about what he had planned, but I thought I wasn't going to like it.

Gabe sat on the opposite side of the booth at the tiny café in Oakland. He sipped coffee without any expression, and I wondered if he'd ever tasted it. Asher didn't like coffee in any form. *Hadn't* liked it.

Earlier I'd stepped out of the shower to find a pair of

sweats and another T-shirt folded on the closed lid of the toilet. Worn and soft, they belonged to a stranger, but they smelled like laundry detergent. I hadn't asked where he'd found them, or the clean clothes he wore, but I'd guessed that they belonged to the same person. The sweats would have fallen off my hips if I hadn't cinched the tie at the waist. We'd checked out of the motel and stopped at a Walgreens. Gabe had run in and bought me a pair of flip-flops so I wouldn't have to go barefoot. Then we'd walked to this café. Mostly, we'd eaten in silence, each of us lost in our separate thoughts.

I didn't know what to do next. I wanted to kill the men who'd murdered Asher, but I didn't know the first thing about how to find them or go about it. It would take time, but what was I supposed to do in the meantime? Twiddle my thumbs and wait for the Protectors to find me before I had a plan? Right. I needed to warn Franc. And then maybe I should go home and give myself time to regroup.

"You can't go back to Blackwell Falls."

I dropped my fork. "Excuse me?" I asked.

"I know how your mind works, Healer." Gabe swirled a bit of sugar through a water ring on the stained tabletop. "You're thinking about running home to Daddy."

The way he put it made me sound like a coward. Okay, I had been thinking about going home, but I couldn't see another option that didn't involve me dying a slow death at the hands of Protectors or hiding in a cave in a desert somewhere.

"So what?" I sounded belligerent and I didn't care.

"So you'll get your family killed."

I felt like he'd struck me. He hadn't ended his statement with *"too,"* but we were both thinking it. I couldn't even argue because I agreed with him. Asher had died because of me. I should never have come here. I should have stayed back in Blackwell Falls, and maybe he would still be alive. Why hadn't I listened to Asher when he asked me not to go? How many people had to die? Gabe should have left me in that prison . . .

"Stop it," Gabe ordered.

I blinked back the tears that had begun to form. For a girl who rarely cried, the waterworks wouldn't stop.

Gabe continued in a neutral tone. "These guys used Asher against you, but how could they know he'd lead them straight to you? For some reason, they were watching him."

"What makes you think they weren't watching me?" I asked. "We met in the forest a couple of times. They could have seen Asher and me together and figured out I cared about him."

Gabe shook his head. "No way. They followed Asher."

"What makes you so sure?"

Gabe threw an arm over the back of the booth, giving every appearance of being relaxed but for the way the tendons stood out in his neck. "If they knew how to find you without him, you'd have been dead and Asher would still be alive."

His words rang with truth. If Gabe meant to cause me more pain, the barbs hit home, heaping shame on top of grief. Asher died because of what I was.

I balled up my napkin and tossed it on my plate. "What does it matter, Gabe? What does this have to do with my family?"

"The Protectors don't exactly hide their whereabouts from each other. Our numbers are small, and we stay connected." He waited for that to sink in. "Those men knew we weren't from around here. Do you know how easy it will be for them to find out where we live?" He snapped his fingers. "A two-minute phone call, and they'll be in Maine by tomorrow, if they aren't there already. And from what those guys told me, you and Asher didn't hide how you felt about each other."

A lightbulb went off. "They'll be looking for me in Blackwell Falls." Another horrible thought followed, and I stared at Gabe helplessly. "Oh God. My family."

He reached across the table and grasped my forearm when I tried to stand. "They're safe. I spoke to Lottie this morning and she checked on them. Your dad is at work, and your mom and Lucy are at home."

I sank back into my seat with a *thud,* and he let me go.

"You can't go home. The second you show up there, your family ends up being collateral."

I tucked my hair behind my ear, thinking. "Won't they attack my family to draw me out?"

"Not if they know you're here. You're going to show yourself just long enough to get their attention. And then you have to go back to your grandfather's."

Gabe sipped his coffee like he hadn't dropped a series of bombs on my head.

"Are you crazy?" I exploded. I wasn't ready to take the Protectors on again. And I refused to chance leading them to my grandfather's doorstep.

"I didn't say you should invite them into your grandfather's home, but you have to admit, the old man has done a good job at keeping his people hidden from our kind. They're better equipped to keep you safe right now."

My grandfather had said the same thing when he tried to persuade me to stay with him. He'd also told me that I would put my friends in danger if I went near them. My family was the only good thing left in my life. Without them, I really was alone. What if I never saw them again? Could I give them up when I'd just found them? The bigger question, though, was whether I would risk getting them killed so I could keep them.

I sagged in defeat. *No.*

"I won't hide forever," I whispered to Gabe, giving in to the inevitable. "I'm going to find those men and make them sorry for what they did to Asher."

"And I'll be at your side when you do," Gabe said. "You have my word."

I can do this. For them, I can do this.

Gabe backed off to give me privacy as I dialed my house on his mobile phone. We'd paused in the park. The sun had come out, and people had crowded onto the green lawns with their blankets and Frisbees and laughter.

I gripped Gabe's phone and prayed Lucy wouldn't pick up. I wasn't sure I could do this if I spoke to her.

After two rings, my father answered. "Hello."

"Dad?" My voice shook, and I touched a finger to my quivering lip.

"Remy? Hey, sweetheart! How are you? Are you having fun out there? We can't wait for you to come home. We're all coming to the airport to pick you up on Sunday."

He sounded so pleased to hear from me. It almost broke my resolve. Then I felt Gabe's bracing hand on my shoulder, and I steeled myself against my grief.

"That's kind of what I'm calling you about. I'm not coming back."

Silence greeted me on the other end of the line, and then my father said, "You're staying longer?"

I ducked my head to hide behind my hair. "No, Dad. I'm not coming back. My grandfather asked me to live with him, and I've decided it's the best thing for everyone."

That was the truth, and I held on to that.

"Remy, why are you doing this? Did I do something wrong? I've made so many mistakes, but I've been try—"

My stomach ached at the worry in his voice, and I cut him off.

"You didn't do anything wrong. It was too much. With everything that's happened with my mom and Dean, there are too many memories. I just need a fresh start. Please don't be mad at me."

"I'm not mad," he answered and he didn't sound mad. He sounded sad and hurt. "I don't really have a right to be mad, do I?"

You do have the right. My father blamed himself for abandoning me to everything that Dean had put my mother and me through. My leaving would make him think I blamed him, too.

"Will you tell Laura and Lucy good-bye for me?"

"You should talk to them. They're going to be hurt if you don't."

"I can't," I choked out.

"Where should I send your things? Are you coming home to get them? What about the Mustang?"

"Keep it. I don't need anything," I said.

More quiet. "You know, I have some vacation time. We could always come visit you. I could bring your things."

"No. I have to go."

"Wait!" he shouted. "Something's wrong, isn't it? What's going on? Talk to me, sweetheart."

He sounded heartbroken and desperate. I'd made my father sound like that. Gabe squeezed my shoulder. I was doing the right thing. My father would tell people I wasn't coming back. Word would get out that I'd left them all, and the Protectors would have no reason to attack my family.

"I love you, Dad," I whispered. "All of you. Thank you for giving me a home. Take care of each other."

Then I hung up, severing the last tie to anything that mattered.

Chapter Twenty-one

*H*anging up on my father had finally flipped off the part of me that wouldn't stop crying. A person could only take so much pain before they shut down, and I'd reached that point. A kind of inability to feel anything settled over me. I embraced it.

Gabe and I took a train to the city. On the way, he called Lottie and told her to hide out in case the Protectors came looking for the Blackwells. He wanted our enemies to believe that the Protectors had left Blackwell Falls, along with the town Healer. After he said good-bye, we stared out opposite windows in silence. I had nothing to say.

In San Francisco, we exited the BART train station, and Gabe hailed us a cab. He ordered the driver to let us out several streets over from my grandfather's house in the Presidio. The cab drove off, and I faced Gabe on the sidewalk.

"You can walk from here?" he asked.

Concern furrowed his brow, and I nodded to reassure him.

"Okay," he said. He seemed to want to say something else, but he stopped. I wrapped my arms around my waist to ward off the chill in the air, and he added, "Remember, I'll be watching from a distance. I promise you'll be safe."

I nodded again. For what it was worth, I believed Gabe thought he was telling the truth. Asher had said the same thing, though. I left Gabe at the curb and walked to the place where my grandfather and I had eaten breakfast several times. Gabe had suggested I call Franc and ask him to come get me. He would be less suspicious if I pretended I'd taken a bus to the café. As it was, I would have a lot of explaining to do.

At the café, I asked if I could call my grandfather. I must have looked pathetic because the waitress who'd served us before immediately handed me the cordless phone.

"Hello?" Franc picked up after the first ring, as if he'd been waiting for my call.

"Franc, I'm at the café by your house. Can you come get me?"

"I'll be right there," he said and the line disconnected.

Outside, I sat on the curb to wait. Less than five minutes passed before my grandfather's truck rattled to a stop in front of me. He rounded the hood and yanked me into his arms in a hug that threatened to crush my ribs. Somewhere nearby, Gabe watched, and if I'd learned anything about my grandfather at all, he had at least one man doing the same.

Franc let me loose and studied me. "Where have you been?" he asked, his brow wrinkled in concern.

"Protectors," I answered simply.

I didn't blink under my grandfather's searching glance. I felt empty as I waited for him to call me a liar.

"Oh Remy," Franc whispered gruffly.

Gabe had said Franc would believe me when I told him I'd escaped from the Protectors. I wasn't sure how Gabe knew this, but he was right. Franc's voice held a wealth of understanding, as if he'd grasped some of what I'd gone through, even though no wounds marred my skin. His arms closed around me, tugging me into another suffocating hug. I didn't fight him, and he didn't let go for a long time, even when I didn't return the embrace.

The inquisition lasted for hours. Dorthea, her husband, and a couple of men I'd never seen before joined us in Franc's living room. They asked question after question. I steered as close to truth as I could, while leaving Asher and Gabe out of my story.

I'd gone for a walk and had been captured. I'd woken up in a prison with no idea how the Protectors had discovered me. They'd tortured me. I'd used my powers on them and run for my life. As soon as I could, I'd made my way back to the city and called my grandfather. I didn't know what had happened to the Protectors. I described Xavier and Mark, and my grandfather knew exactly who they were.

"They live in the city," he said. "We've been watching them for months, and they've shown no indication that they knew we were here."

"I think they killed Yvette." I mentioned how they'd cut me in the same way they had the Healer. Franc's eyes dropped to my exposed skin, and I explained, "I healed myself as soon as I got away."

There was talk of moving me from my grandfather's house. They didn't know if I'd been followed to Inspiration Point. It was possible they'd just been waiting to get me alone. Franc surprised me by insisting we stay put. Gabe and I had been sure he would move me to Pacifica. Instead, my grandfather ordered additional security precautions. That meant more men watching the house and less freedom for me.

"No more going off on your own," he warned me. "I

hope you understand now how dangerous it would be for you to return to New York by yourself. Imagine what would have happened if one of your friends had been with you."

A shadow crossed his face, and I tensed, picturing a gun pointed at Asher.

"I'm staying in San Francisco," I answered flatly.

"Good," he said and nodded with satisfaction. "At least one good thing has come of all of this."

He turned back to the men who were organizing shifts of people to watch the house. I rubbed my arms and wondered if they would notice if I slipped away to bed. I wanted to curl up and sleep for a thousand years so I could forget everything. Except I feared sleep would be impossible. I pictured Lucy and Laura's faces when my father told them I wouldn't return. Would they ever be able to forgive me?

A warm hand brushed a tangled strand of hair from my face. Dorthea sat beside me on the couch. She patted my hand. "I'm glad you're safe, Remy."

That makes one of us.

The days blurred together.

I did as my grandfather asked and didn't go anywhere alone. In fact, I didn't leave my room if I could help it. I'd been wrong about never sleeping again. Sleep had become the thing I was best at. Beyond my closed curtains, night and day slipped back and forth, while I huddled under my covers.

Franc checked on me several times a day. He tried to get me to go to Pacifica to see Erin, and when that failed, he had her try to get me out of my room. I showered and joined them at the kitchen table, but Erin's efforts to involve me in conversation failed. In the end, I went back to bed for a week, and Erin didn't return. Franc's check-ins happened less frequently, and I lost track of time. I could tell my apathy upset him, but someone had pulled the plug on my ability to feel anything.

Then one night I dreamed the Protectors had found Lucy and begun torturing her to force me to heal them. Her screams lingered in the air, and then clear as day, I heard Asher's voice. *I love you,* mo cridhe.

I woke gasping, with his name on my lips. My quiet voice echoed in my empty room. Asher was dead. Why couldn't I believe that?

I tried to go back to sleep, but that escape evaded me. In the distance, a clock ticked. My grandfather had probably gone to bed hours ago. When I couldn't stand the silence anymore, I got up and dressed.

Franc's men were watching the house, but I'd overheard them planning their vantage points. They often talked while I was in the room, treating me like I was invisible. Earlier that day, they'd been discussing Xavier and Mark while they ate in the kitchen. The Protecters had moved their home base, and Franc had ordered his men to find them.

In the kitchen, I flicked the edge of a curtain aside and spotted the silhouette of a man in a truck two doors down. No way could I go out the back door unnoticed. I thought about giving up and going back to my room, but then a noise caught my attention. A trash can had tipped over down the block, and the man had turned to investigate it. I used his distraction to slip out the door and into the forest. There would be hell to pay if my grandfather caught me, but I had to get out.

Once I reached the safety of the trees, I understood why I had really come outside. The scent of pine reminded me of Asher. The salty wind tasted like home as I ran full-tilt. For the first time in days, I was alone without prying eyes. I could simply be and not think. My feet hardly touched the ground as I raced without direction, trusting my instincts to steer me around obstacles.

Feet pounded the ground behind me. I glanced to the right, and green eyes flashed at me from a few feet away. *Gabe.* After I noticed him, he fell back, trailing me from a distance. Giving me space.

I didn't stop running until I reached Fort Point, where Asher had shown me the surfers and the Golden Gate Bridge. My legs ached pleasantly when I jumped the road barrier and sank down on a rock at the edge of the water. I sensed him before I heard him.

"Gabe, it's okay. You can come out."

My voice was quiet, but a moment later, he crouched gracefully on a rock a few feet away. A breeze lifted the hair off of his forehead, and he looked so much like Asher that I wanted to scream. I forced my gaze back to the lights of Sausalito across the bay.

"How are you?" Gabe asked.

"I should be asking you that."

And it was true. His brother had passed, and I'd hardly spared a thought for his grief. Or Lottie's, for that matter.

"I heard your grandfather's friends talking about you. They're worried, Healer."

"I know," I said, retying a shoelace that didn't need retying. "I'm doing the best I can."

"Do better."

The arrogant demand surprised a smile out of me. "You're such a jerk, Gabe."

"I've been called worse."

"By me, even," I agreed.

He snorted, and we fell back into a silence that wasn't uncomfortable.

"What are we doing out here?"

I sighed. "I had a nightmare. I needed some room to breathe."

"Your grandfather giving you a hard time?"

"Not really. Mostly I've kept to myself. I've kind of been out of it," I admitted. "Actually, they act like I'm invisible. They're trying to find Xavier and Mark."

I thought back to the conversation I'd overheard earlier that day. It was probably the reason I'd dreamed up Asher's voice.

I hesitated. "Can I tell you something?"

Gabe nodded.

"Promise you won't laugh?"

"I don't much feel like laughing these days. Spit it out."

"I dreamed I heard Asher's voice tonight." My confession tumbled out in a rush. As soon as I said the words, I wanted to take them back. "I know it's stupid. He's gone."

"What did he say?" Gabe asked in a quiet voice.

"He told me that he loves me."

Gabe's gaze seemed to turn inward, the beauty of the view lost on him. "That sounds exactly like something he would say."

I didn't tell Gabe how much I missed his brother, but I thought maybe he understood. Grief had changed him, too. He'd never been quick to smile, but now his face seemed carved into a permanent frown.

A large wave hit the rocks, and the spray doused my shoes before I could move away. Gabe climbed back to the parking lot above the rocks and then reached out to pull me up beside him. My shoes squelched and left wet marks on the road as I shifted my weight.

"I should get back. Franc checks on me, and I'd rather not have him know I was gone."

With one last glance at the water, I headed back toward the path that would lead me to Franc's. Gabe fell into step beside me.

"Thanks for knocking over the trash can, by the way."

Gabe's expression didn't change. "What makes you think I did that? Maybe it was a cat or a raccoon."

"Or maybe it was a Protector with an ego the size of Texas?"

One corner of his mouth loosened into a half smile.

We reached the cover of the trees, and Gabe said, "I didn't realize how fast you'd gotten. You like the speed, don't you?"

"It's the best."

Almost like a gift that Asher had given to me. A piece of him that would stay with me. Gabe nodded as if he knew what I meant. I started running, and this time he kept pace beside me the whole way back to my grandfather's. He called to me softly to stop about a half mile from Franc's yard.

"I think you should introduce me to your grandfather as a friend from New York."

I rocked back on my heels. "You're kidding, right?" I asked in disbelief.

He acted like I hadn't spoken. "The security around here is too tight. They've almost caught me a couple of times when I was checking on you."

"Then watch me from farther away."

He shook his head. "No way. I wouldn't be able to get to you if you needed help."

I opened my mouth to tell him to go home, and he clamped a hand over my lips.

"Before you say it, Healer, let me make it clear that I'm going nowhere. I'm doing this for Asher. If your grandfather's men find Xavier and Mark, I want to be there. It's the least I can do."

Guilt had sunk its claws into Gabe, too. He blamed himself for not getting there in time to save his brother. Asher had once told me that Gabe could not be made to change directions once he'd decided his course. Right now, his course was set on revenge.

If I was honest, I wanted vengeance, too, even if it put my life at risk. Gabe had a right to want the same. Maybe more of a right. We'd kept Asher a secret because I wasn't sure what we were walking into with my grandfather. Now I knew for sure that the Healers didn't have my ability to sense out Protectors. They relied on intel. So long as Gabe wasn't on their radar and they believed him a normal human, he should be safe.

"It's your neck," I said.

"Thanks for your concern."

He almost sounded sarcastic, and I added, "I meant, it's not up to me to tell you what to do."

"I know what you meant."

His tone put an end to the conversation, and I wondered if I'd hurt his feelings. I frowned, unsure what to do with the concept of Gabe feeling anything for me except condescension and irritation.

I shrugged my unease away when he launched into a matter-of-fact explanation of how we would introduce him to Franc. The situation was weird enough without introducing *feelings* into it.

CHAPTER TWENTY-TWO

*T*he next morning I dressed and went downstairs for breakfast like I had in the first days of my visit. My grandfather looked surprised and acted like I was a deer that could spook at any moment. He cautiously set a mug of coffee in front of me on the table, and I blew on the steaming liquid gratefully.

I waited for him to be seated before I announced, "My friend is coming for a visit today." Franc's eyebrows drew together in quick fury. "Calm down. I didn't tell him where you or any of the Healers live. He already had plans to be in the area, and I mentioned I might be around."

Franc pounded a fist on the table. "What the hell were you thinking inviting someone here?"

With outward calm, I took a gulp of my coffee that burned my throat on the way down. "I'm thinking that I want to see a familiar face and that I need a friend. After everything I've been through, I need someone who knows me."

"How well could this boy know you if you've hidden who you are from him?" He started as a thought occurred to him. "You didn't tell him you're a Healer?"

I scowled. "Of course not." *His brother did.*

Franc settled down a bit, his expression evening out.

"Good. I'm afraid I can't allow this, Remy. I'm sorry, but you'll have to tell this boy you won't meet him."

He rose and took his mug to the sink as if the subject were closed.

"I said I didn't tell him I was a Healer. I didn't say he didn't know I was a Healer." My grandfather spun around, and I shrugged. "I healed him once when we were in junior high. He kept my secret."

"You're just now telling me this?" Franc said slowly.

"When I got here, I didn't know you or how far you would go to keep your secrets. My mother feared you enough to run away and never look back. So why would I immediately trust you with everything about me?"

The accusation hit its target the way Gabe had told me it would when he gave me the ammunition. My grandfather flinched, and his eyelids shuttered. I felt a twinge of shame, but I kept going. "I'm meeting Gabe at the BART station in an hour. I'll see you later."

"I forbid it, Remy."

"Fine. I'll pack my bags and clear out."

I turned to go.

"You're not going anywhere."

I'd been bluffing about leaving, but the quiet rage in my grandfather's voice raised the hair on the back of neck. My stepfather had used that tone, usually right before he hit my mother or me.

I shoved all hints of fear deep down into a corner of me, the way I had with Dean, before I faced Franc. "I understood that I was a guest here. Are you telling me that I'm now a prisoner?"

He'd made a mistake. His eyes had rounded with the realization that he'd crossed a line with me.

"Of course not," he blustered. "You're my granddaughter. I would never treat you like a prisoner." He sighed.

"Forgive me. You are impulsive in a way that reminds me of your mother. To be honest, it scares the shit out of me."

Hearing my white-haired hulk of a grandfather curse shocked a smile out of me. "I'm sorry I sprang this on you. But Franc, please understand that I've lost my home and more these weeks. I haven't asked for much, but I need this. One visit with Gabe. I'll meet him away from here if that's what worries you. And if I think I've been followed, I'll stay away. Please know I would never do anything to put you or the others in danger."

He considered me for a long time. Finally, he said, "I've got a better idea. Why don't you invite him to come here? I'd like to meet the boy who kept your secret."

Damn, Gabe. He'd predicted my grandfather would suggest that very thing. He was going to gloat when I called him, and I would have to suck it up. I hated arrogant men.

Franc immediately loved Gabe Reynolds.

He'd shown up at Franc's with a new last name and wearing a Yankees baseball cap and a backpack. All traces of his British accent had disappeared, and he spoke like a New Yorker through and through. He looked younger and more carefree than I'd ever seen him, joking around with Franc about who was a better team, the Yankees or the Giants. I knew it was an act put on for my grandfather, and still I had to make myself stop staring in confusion at this charming version of Asher's brother.

My grandfather had decided to barbecue on the grill out back. I laid out plates and utensils on the patio table, while Gabe kicked back in a lawn chair, stretching his legs out and resting his joined hands on his belly. When Franc asked me to grab the potato salad and sodas out of the fridge, Gabe volunteered to help. He even threw a companionable arm around my shoulders, which I shrugged off as soon as we entered the kitchen.

"Seriously?" I asked him. "You're capable of turning on that charming act and you choose to be an arrogant ass?"

He grabbed a lemon out of the bowl on the counter and tossed it from hand to hand. "Why else do you think the Sororitoys want me?"

I frowned. "I can't imagine. I figured they were shallow and after your body."

"You noticed my body?"

Gabe flexed the muscles of one arm as I passed, and I shoved him.

"Hey!" he protested. "Does Asher know you're checking me out?"

The air hissed out of the room, and we both froze. Gabe looked stricken.

"God, Remy. I'm so sorry. I forgot for a second. I can't believe I did that."

The funny thing was, I understood. Asher's name was never very far from my lips, either. "Don't worry about it. I forget all the time."

Gabe's expression didn't change, so I pushed him again as I headed outside. "Quit with the drama queen thing already, and grab those napkins, Gabriella."

The insult snapped him out of it. Just before the kitchen door closed behind me, he taunted, "I'm not the drama queen. That would be you, Remington."

A laugh bubbled out me, surprising my grandfather almost as much as it surprised me.

Over dinner, my grandfather's gaze bounced between Gabe and me frequently. I'd trained with Asher's brother for months, but I'd never seen this playful side of him. He teased me, obviously trying to make me smile. To my consternation, it worked. Somehow, it felt wrong to be laughing when Asher was dead. I felt like I'd betrayed him, sharing a joke with his brother.

When Franc turned the conversation to my abilities, Gabe nonchalantly steered the conversation back to more casual topics. By not admitting he knew what I could do, even to my family, Gabe earned a grudging respect from my grandfather. It was scary how well Gabe could read people.

After he left to go wherever he went when he wasn't with me, I headed to my room. Franc rapped on my open door to get my attention as I readied for bed.

"I like your friend, Remy. I can see why you trust him. He mentioned he might be sticking around for a while?"

I nodded. "He's thinking about applying to colleges around here."

Liar, liar, pants on fire.

Franc lingered in the doorway and then suggested, "Why don't you invite him to go to Pacifica with us tomorrow? He might like meeting your other friends, and I know Erin would like to see you."

My mouth had dropped open, and I quickly snapped it shut. I hadn't expected a gesture this big. I hesitated. "Aren't you worried he'll tell people about you?"

Franc shook his head slowly. "He's kept your secret this long. If you trust him, that's good enough for me."

His gesture of faith touched me, and my lip trembled. "Thanks, Franc."

He pushed off of the door frame. "I wouldn't have raised such a fuss if I knew how you felt about him. And I can see he cares about you. You should have told me he was your boyfriend, Remy. 'Night, then."

He disappeared down the hall and into his bedroom. I stumbled backward and collapsed on the bed.

Boyfriend? He thought Gabe was my boyfriend?

What a joke. Why, then, did it feel like I'd betrayed Asher in some way?

★ ★ ★

The longer I lay there, the more unbearable my thoughts became. I needed to move, to run, to exhaust myself until I couldn't think anymore. Gabe had slipped me a new mobile phone that day and said I should text him when I wanted to get out. He'd promised to distract my guards. As much as it killed me to do it, I texted him and waited for his return text some twenty minutes later that signaled I could make a break for the trees.

He waited for me fifty feet into the forest. Leaning against a lumbering pine with his hands in the pockets of his jacket, Gabe appeared relaxed. He'd ditched the baseball cap at some point, but he looked like Asher. Most of the time I could handle that, but at that moment, I felt too raw. Was it too much to have an hour to myself without a constant reminder of what I'd lost?

"I've been thinking," Gabe said. "We should start training again."

No greeting. Just more orders. I'd become a puppet with my grandfather and Gabe taking turns pulling the strings.

"Not tonight," I answered.

"What's wrong?" he demanded, coming to attention.

"Nothing. I need some space. Can you do that?"

His eyes flashed when I walked past him without a word. He caught up with me easily and grabbed my arm to stop me. *Why won't you go away, Gabe? I don't want you here!*

"Space? The walls are closing in around us and you want space?"

He sounded pissed off, but I'd been stewing for hours. I yanked my arm from his hold and lifted my chin.

"What walls are you talking about?" I turned a circle and gestured toward him. "From where I stand, you look free to go at any time. I'm the one locked away here. You want to go? Do it! I never asked you to come here."

I stomped away, shoving a branch out of the way.

"You're a spoiled child," he said to my back.

I froze. "What did you say?"

"You heard me. The one thing you got right is that you didn't ask me to come here. No, you asked *Asher* to come here. And you know what? The longer I'm around you, the more confused I am about what he ever saw in you."

I didn't think. I struck out, wanting to hurt Gabe as badly as I ached. I threw myself at him and landed a solid blow to his jaw before he managed to get both of his arms around my ribs. He lifted me off my feet, pinning my arms to my sides. I kicked out, and Gabe grunted when my boot connected with his shin.

"Stop fighting me! I don't want to hurt you!"

I stilled, and Gabe's breathing sounded loud in the air. He set me on my feet and let me go cautiously. Even as he began to back away, I pulled my arm back and slugged him in the stomach as hard as I could. I doubted I caused him any pain with his stupid Protector inability to feel anything.

"Damn it, Remy! That hurt!" Gabe doubled over, bracing his hands on his thighs.

Oops. Somebody is becoming mortal around me. Too bad!

He glared at me, and I reversed in the opposite direction at the anger darkening his expression. "You want to fight? Fine. Let's get this over with," he said.

Common sense suddenly returned when Gabe's hands closed into fists and he rose to his full height. He looked dangerous.

"Gabe . . ." I said in a halting voice.

I stopped because I refused to beg him for anything. That left one option. I tucked tail and ran. I'd gone three feet before Gabe tackled my back and I sprawled on the ground. He rolled to his feet and dropped into a crouching position. I spit out the dirt I'd inhaled and rolled in the opposite direction. My hands came up in defense when I jumped to my feet and faced him.

"Leave me alone, Gabe."

"Or what? How will you stop me?"

He launched forward in a shadowy blur. When he appeared at my side, he wrapped a hand around my wrist, and his energy struck me with a force that sent me to my knees.

My mental walls, I realized. I hadn't bothered with them around him lately, and I regretted it. The onslaught of his power didn't feel like the times he or Asher had helped me heal myself. Fear sent a drop of sweat trickling down my back, and my galloping heart slowed to a dull, quiet thud as an icy wind blew through me. Frozen shards stabbed me from the inside out, and I gasped and he pulled me closer.

Gabe was stealing my energy. I could feel his power growing by the second.

His voice rumbled low in my ear. "This is what they'll do to you. They'll take everything. The pain will be so great, you'll be begging them to kill you. This isn't a game. You're not like other Healers that they'll toss away. You can cure them, and that makes you very valuable."

Abruptly, his hold on me disappeared and Gabe's energy receded as he fixed his walls into place again. The beat of my heart thundered loud in my ears once more, and the pain faded. I sucked in a breath and raised my mental walls, too.

Asher had used this tactic on me once. I hadn't understood how dangerous he could be. I'd been too trusting and he'd done exactly this to warn me off. It had worked for a time, but I'd loved Asher too much to stay away.

We'd fought to find a way around our abilities so we could be together.

I didn't love Gabe, though. And I was so freaking sick of people hurting me to manipulate me. If Asher had tried this on me again, I would have been furious. With Gabe, white-hot rage quickened inside me, and I fought to shutter my expression.

"You've made your point," I said and I was proud of how calm I sounded.

Gabe relaxed, and I took advantage of that. I wavered and stretched out a hand, pretending weakness. He automatically reacted to help me. I dropped my walls in a rush. He sensed my *humming* instantly, but by then I held his hand and it was too late.

This time it was my energy filling his body and hurting him. The night Dean had shot Asher, we'd discovered that I could steal energy like any Protector could. Except my Healer side gave me an advantage Protectors didn't have. Gabe's kind could only steal from Healers, whereas I could take my pickings from either bloodline. It was why Asher and I had to be so careful with each other. Why we had to keep our guard up so often to ensure this didn't happen.

That wouldn't be a problem again. Asher was gone. And suddenly that knowledge didn't hurt as fiercely with Gabe's energy melding with mine, sparking coils of heat under my skin. The monster inside me roared with pleasure as it fed on Gabe.

"Remy, stop. Please . . ." Gabe begged.

Like coming out of a deep trance, I forced myself to focus on him. His face had lost all color, and lines of pain had appeared. His green eyes—Asher's green eyes—stared at me helplessly.

Horrified, I released Gabe, and he collapsed to the

ground. I choked on a sob and covered my mouth to stifle the sound.

*What have I done? What the hell kind of freak am I becom-
ing?*

The wind bristled the pine needles above us. I didn't
know what to say to him. I wasn't even sure how I felt
about it. Except that the monster inside me roared in fury
at being denied Gabe's energy.

"You don't mess around when you're pissed off, do
you?" Gabe said, forcing humor into his strained voice.

"Are you okay?" I asked.

I didn't dare to go near him, even though we both had
our walls up now.

"Oh, I'm grand," he said. "Never felt better." He tried
to stand and groaned. "Shit, Remington. It's like you ran
me over with a forklift."

I laughed and it sounded more like a sob.

"Come here," Gabe said.

"Are you going to hurt me?" I asked in a small voice.

"No," he answered in a rueful tone. "I think we've done
enough damage to each other for one night. But you look
like you're going to fall and I could use a hand getting up."
I hesitated a moment more and he added, "You can trust
me. I swear it."

I went to him and stooped to put my shoulder under his
arm to help him stand. I muttered, "He said before he
killed her."

"Don't even joke," Gabe said.

"Who's joking?"

We stumbled to a nearby rock, and I lowered him to sit.
I made to step back, but Gabe pulled me down beside
him. He let me loose when I tugged on my hand, but I
didn't move away.

"Franc thinks we're dating," I blurted out.

Gabe did a double take. "He what?"

"Don't make me say it again. It was bad enough the first time."

He swallowed. "Did you correct him?"

I shook my head. "I didn't get a chance. He said all this stuff about how he could tell you cared about me and that you were welcome to go to Pacifica with us and then he left."

"Well . . ." Gabe cleared his throat.

A nearby bush shuddered as a small animal explored. An unseen car's brakes squealed on a road in the distance. And all I could think about was how awkward this was and how even sitting with Gabe now felt like a betrayal of Asher.

I shook myself. *Don't go there, Remy. It's not like you could ever feel anything like that for Gabe.*

Gabe's mouth compressed into a line. Then, he gave a small smile. "You and I both know your grandfather's wrong."

I nodded. "Right. It's not like you would even be here if not for Asher."

He looked up thoughtfully. "You know, we could use this."

My mouth dropped open, and I recoiled from him. "Are you crazy? I'm not going to pretend we're together. No way. Absolutely not."

"Tell me how you really feel, why don't you?"

I shoved his shoulder, realizing he was messing with me. He seemed to have recovered, and I rose. "Shut up, Gabe. Come on. I need to get back."

We walked together in the direction of my grandfather's.

"How long have you been feeling things, Gabe?" I asked, tossing a curious glance at him over my shoulder.

His smile looked sheepish. "Damn. I thought I'd snuck that one by you."

"Uh-huh. You shrieking 'that hurt, Remy' totally fooled me."

"I didn't shriek. I yelled. Like a manly man," he said.

That almost got a smile out of me. "Quit trying to avoid the question. How long?"

I thought he wouldn't answer, but he finally spoke in a serious tone. "Always with the *humming*. More so since I helped you heal yourself."

I frowned. "I'm sorry, Gabe."

Initially, pain had been the only sensation Asher experienced around me. Gabe had never really made it clear what he thought about becoming mortal. He'd been excited that I might be a cure for the Blackwells, but then, he'd known that Asher longed to be human again. Lottie liked being an immortal and hated me for making her feel anything. Gabe . . . Well, he'd kept his thoughts to himself.

"For what?" he asked.

He sounded taken aback, and I added, "For hurting you. For using my ability against you. For making you feel again."

He'd gone out of his way to help me, and I kept fighting him. *Like Asher all over again,* I thought, and the comparison hurt.

Gabe waved a hand. "Are you looking to win the Oscar for Best Drama Queen, Remington? Get over yourself. I'm not that hurt, and I've met five-year-olds that were stronger than you."

I made a sound of derision, and we started arguing about who could beat the other to a pulp first. It didn't escape my notice that Gabe had distracted me on purpose. To my surprise, I didn't dislike Gabe as extremely as I'd thought. In fact, I would almost call Asher's brother a friend if I didn't have a small doubt that he would throw me under a bus in his quest for revenge.

CHAPTER TWENTY-THREE

Gabe settled in with the Healers faster than I had. He'd morphed into an affable guy who put everyone he met at ease. All arrogance had been suppressed. It was shocking how quickly they seemed to accept him coming around. It didn't hurt that Gabe was hot, and the women happily glommed to him. I wanted to smack him more than once when I saw him using that fact to his advantage.

For his part, Gabe gave them no reason to be suspicious. He always had his walls up, unless we were alone. He never asked questions, and he stuck to my side unless my grandfather assigned him some chore around the house. In fact, he spent more time with me than at the Marina hostel he'd checked into. According to him, he was biding his time, waiting for the Healers to locate Xavier and Mark.

A month after I'd introduced Gabe to the group, my grandfather set him to patching a section of the roof that leaked when it rained. Erin, Delia, and I lounged in folding chairs in the backyard, sipping iced tea and enjoying the sun with the dull ring of a hammer in the background.

I'd been reading another book my grandfather had procured from his library. A library I'd yet to find, though I'd searched Delia's, Erin's and Franc's houses. This particular tome went on and on about the Healers pre-War. The author, one Augustus Rue, practically worshiped Healers.

After the third chapter extolling their near sainthood for seeing to the suffering so selflessly, my eyes had begun to close.

"Man, you are lucky, Remy," Erin said.

I shielded my eyes from the sun to follow her gaze. Gabe stood on the roof with his shirt off and his chest glistening with sweat. Even I had to admit that he looked good, although I preferred Asher's leaner body. Gabe noticed me watching and grinned. I flipped him a rude gesture without the others noticing. He just laughed and went back to work.

"What makes me so lucky?" I asked Erin.

"Duh. Gabe. The way he watches over you is so sweet."

"Yes. Sickeningly so," Delia added drily.

I decided to ignore that one. Every time someone made some teasing comment about Gabe, I thought of Asher and ached. To these people Asher had never existed. It killed me a little more each day to pretend I didn't think of him all the time and wish that I had him back. If not for all the practice I'd had lying when I lived with my mother, I wasn't sure I could have kept up the charade.

"Speaking of sick, where's Alcais?" I asked. "I haven't seen him around much lately."

Come to think of it, I hadn't seen him in over a week, and I'd been spending a lot of time with the Healers.

Franc had persuaded me to allow his people to test my skills, though I'd refused to let them draw blood. I didn't offer a reason why, and to my surprise, Franc didn't press me. I'd had visions of men in white coats conducting experiments on me, while they gleefully rubbed their hands at finding out what I could do.

In reality, Juliette and Micheline wore jeans and spent most of their time with me jotting notes onto clipboards that they were rarely without. Both Healers asked probing questions about how my powers worked. For the most part, I answered honestly. Some days, they would make tiny cuts on me or on one of them. Then, they'd observe what happened when I used my abilities. None of the tests really hurt all that much. The worst part was taking care that I didn't lose control and take energy from them. Always, I had to beware of that monster.

Gabe didn't like these experiments, but I didn't see the harm in them so long as I hid my Protector side. Maybe I couldn't help Asher, but someday I dreamed of going home to my family. If that day arrived, I wanted to know everything I could about who I was so that I could keep them safe.

Even more than the experiments, Gabe hated Alcais and had made it his goal to keep the boy away from me at all times. I could tell this incensed Alcais, but I didn't care. I hoped the toad found a mud hole to crawl into.

While Alcais didn't come around as often, Delia had taken to joining Erin and me when we hung out. I'd told Gabe that I thought this had more to do with him than me, but he'd shrugged it off.

Even now, I could see Delia practically salivating as she watched Gabe work. I considered telling her to put her tongue back in her mouth, but we'd been getting along okay and I didn't want to provoke her. Ever since Alcais had hurt Erin, Delia had been spending less time with him.

"Are you sure you two aren't dating?" Delia asked, gesturing to Gabe.

"Yep. I think I'd know it if we were."

"Your grandfather thinks you are," she said.

I shrugged. "I can't control what Franc thinks."

Delia stood suddenly. "You know, Gabe looks thirsty. I think I'll take him some iced tea."

She wandered off, and Erin made a face after her.

I hid a smile behind my book. "She doesn't stand a chance with him."

Erin shot me a wry look. "I know. He's smitten with you, even if you won't admit it."

I dropped my book to my chest and scowled. "No. He's really, really not."

She smiled and settled back in her seat to watch the Delia show. "Whatever you say."

The longer I stayed at my grandfather's, the more I felt like I lost myself. And the more time I spent with Gabe, the more I felt Asher slipping away from me. I would never confuse Gabe with Asher again, but they looked so much alike. The same hair and eyes. Similar facial structure. Then there was the way they carried themselves, always moving with a combination of confidence and arrogance that came from their Protector abilities.

Gabe and I had tolerated each other because of Asher and our love for him. I could hardly describe what we'd become now. Delia and Erin believed he watched me because he cared about me. They imagined we had feelings for each other.

They were wrong. I would never feel that kind of love for Gabe.

I'd begun to wonder what the point of all this was. Revenge for Asher. Would he even want that? I hardly knew anymore. What if I left the Healers and my grandfather? I couldn't go back to my family. I had no money or friends. Really, I had no place to go.

You could always charge for your abilities. As soon as that thought crept in, I rejected it. I refused to be like those greedy Healers who'd healed the highest bidders. Besides, healing people in the open would just make it easier for the Protectors to find me.

I tired of tossing and turning in my bed. The dark room suffocated me, and I rose and made my way to the kitchen to brew a pot of coffee. The hot liquid warmed my hands as I stood over the sink with a mug, sipping and watching the sun rise over the forest. For once I didn't long to be out running away from this place. No, I wanted to be in Blackwell Falls, and I would never reach my home on foot.

The ache for my family had become a physical thing. Some days my insides felt hollowed out by all that had happened these last months. It was the kind of hollow that hurt, like when your stomach cramped with hunger.

"Remy? You okay?"

Franc's voice startled me, and I sniffed. He still wore the sweats and T-shirt he'd worn to bed. He yawned and ran a hand through his hair, making it look wilder than usual.

I gave a weak smile. "Just a little homesick."

He took my mug and set it on the counter, before pulling me into a hug. Taller and broader, he engulfed me. I settled against him and wished that I had the power to forget. That would be a useful ability.

Franc gave me a pat on the back and stepped away. "Hey, what do you say we get the heck out of here today? Maybe head over to Muir Woods? It might do us some good to change things up."

I nodded. "I would love that."

"Come on, then. Let's get dressed and get a move on."

An hour later we drove across the Golden Gate Bridge. The fog hadn't crept in yet. On one side of the bridge, the city rose out of the hilly landscape, surrounded by the blue waters of the bay. On the other side of the bridge, the Pacific Ocean stretched endlessly into the horizon. I couldn't decide which view was more beautiful.

I flicked a finger over the phone I'd hidden in my pocket. Earlier I'd texted Gabe to let him know I would be out for the day, but he hadn't answered. That had never happened before, and it worried me. I tried to tell myself that I needed some time away from him.

Eventually we left the ocean and the bridge behind. My grandfather drove into the hills, winding past homes situated in the woods just off the road. I'd heard about Muir Woods, with its massive redwoods, some large enough for groups of people to stand inside of the hollowed trunks. We reached a crossroads with a sign directing us toward the national park. I frowned when Franc turned the opposite way.

He noticed my confusion. "I have a quick stop to make," he said. "And then we'll be on our way."

Ten minutes later we pulled into a private driveway. The modern two-story home had more windows than walls, giving the owners little privacy. I doubted Healers lived there considering the way they kept to themselves.

Franc hopped out and gestured for me to follow him when I hesitated. A woman in her thirties opened the front door before he could knock, and I stepped back in surprise. Average height with average brown hair of an average length, nothing about the stranger stood out. If you had asked me to pick her out of a crowd tomorrow, I doubted I would have been able to. Something was off about her, though, but I couldn't figure out what.

"Hey! You made good time."

"Melinda, how are you?"

They made small talk about the drive and the weather. All the while, the woman's gaze devoured me. She gestured for us to enter, and Franc walked past her into the living room. I pretended to study the interior of the house beyond her shoulder when my grandfather introduced us and she held out her hand for me to shake. Every instinct I had screamed for me to avoid touching this woman.

Her brow furrowed in confusion when I gave her a wide berth as I followed my grandfather into living room.

Franc sat on the couch, and the woman took a seat next to him. They continued talking about friends they had in common, and I tuned out of the conversation. I paced restlessly to the floor-to-ceiling windows that overlooked the driveway.

Why is this lady freaking me out? She wasn't a Protector. I would have sensed that right away. I'd never met her before. I was sure of it, although she reminded me of someone. Someone from my past in New York.

I snuck a glance at her over my shoulder. That was when it hit me. Mrs. Rosenbaum. She reminded me of Mrs. Rosenbaum, the teacher from my old school. The one I'd told Delia, Alcais, and Erin about. She'd had stomach cancer, an illness that had almost killed me when I'd accidentally knocked into her. Back then I hadn't known how to shield myself. I'd been fourteen and had spent weeks in pain while I healed a little at a time. Since then, I'd avoided healing anything related to the big C or coming into contact with anyone I knew who had it.

Melinda had the same look Mrs. Rosenbaum had. She was sick, and if I had to guess, I'd say it was serious. In the window, my grandfather's reflection studied me with a speculative look on his face that I didn't like. I knew what was coming, and I held my breath waiting.

"Remy," he began hesitantly, and I turned to face them with my head tilted in defiance. He'd tricked me into coming here.

Please don't ask me. My stomach twisted into a double knot.

I hardly listened when Franc began a long-winded explanation of how Melinda had a rare blood disease. It was killing her and none of the other Healers had been able to cure her, but their tests had shown that I could heal things they couldn't. He hated to ask me, but could I . . . would I . . .

He couldn't even get the question out. His chin dropped to his chest as if he felt ashamed of himself for bringing me here. I opened my mouth to refuse. Obviously I couldn't do this. I couldn't risk my life to heal this stranger. Hadn't Asher and Lucy told me to weigh the consequences? Was my life worth less than this woman's?

Melinda reached for my grandfather's hand and gripped it. I bit my lip as I noticed how closely they sat together. They shared a glance, and there was such intimacy in it that I felt like an interloper for witnessing it. Geez, my grandfather loved this woman.

Questions began to form in my mind. Why had he kept her from me? Were they together? Why hadn't he even mentioned her before now? I should have felt angry, but that would have made me a hypocrite. I had a thousand secrets.

Still, bile rose in my throat. My grandfather had to know there was a possibility that curing this woman could kill me. Did he even care?

I shook my head. "I'm sorry," I said to Melinda. "I can't help you. I wish I could, but . . ."

Her smile was sad. "I told him it was too much to ask. It's okay. Really," she added when I bit my lip.

The room grew quiet. They shared another one of those knowing looks that I wasn't part of.

Franc pressed Melinda's hand and spoke to her softly. "We have to tell her."

I frowned. *Tell me what?*

Melinda tried to pull her hands away, protesting, but Franc hushed her. "You listen to me, Mel. I know my granddaughter. She would want to know."

"What are you talking about?" I asked.

My grandfather stood and pulled Melinda up with him. He tugged her forward with a supportive arm around her shoulders. His solemn gaze made the hair on the back of my neck rise. I wasn't going to like what he had to say.

"Don't!" Melinda said, but he ignored her because even I could tell it was a token protest.

"Remy, she's your cousin."

I squeezed my eyes shut, as he explained that he'd first stayed with the Healers in hopes of finding a cure for Melinda's illness. But with the Protectors always on the hunt for Healers, Franc had thought it better to keep my cousin away from the Healers in order to keep her safe. She was the reason he'd chosen to stay in San Francisco.

She's your cousin.

For a second, loathing threatened to choke me, and my fingernails bit into my palms as I grasped for control. Franc had cornered me, knowing I wouldn't refuse to heal *family*. Even family I didn't know well. Not after I'd felt so responsible for how my mother died.

Had my entire time here been building up to this moment? Had he kept me here, treated me with kindness, and sheltered me so that I would do as he asked?

A sudden overwhelming despair snuffed out every other emotion. These people did not love me. They wanted to use me like Dean and the Protectors, and even Gabe in his quest for revenge. I'd wanted a normal life, but I'd been kidding myself. Asher was dead. I could never return to my family. What was the point of hoping for more when I would always be a pawn in somebody's game? What was I fighting for?

Everyone betrays you in the end.

I opened my eyes to find my grandfather and cousin staring at me with desperate yearning in their eyes, and the last hope I had for a life better than this shattered and blew away.

"Fine," I said tonelessly. "I'll do it."

CHAPTER TWENTY-FOUR

*I*t almost killed me. Hours after healing her, the poison of Melinda's blood disease hunkered down inside me like a hibernating beast. My powers had shorted out, and I couldn't heal myself. A brush with Mrs. Rosenbaum had left me sick for weeks. How long would this last? Better yet, would I ever be able to heal myself?

"You son of a bitch! How could you do that to her?"

Gabe yelled at my grandfather, while I pretended to sleep. They'd been going at it ever since we'd arrived home and my grandfather had carried me into the house. I hadn't said two words, and it had been up to Franc to explain why I could hardly lift my head.

Gabe sounded frantic, but I felt nothing. Blissful nothing. The post-healing hypothermia had passed beyond chattering teeth and skipped to sluggish limbs and a slowed pulse. Was this what it felt like in that moment before a person froze to death? I'd read that it was like going to sleep once the pain stopped. Part of me wanted to tell Franc and Gabe to leave me the hell alone. Their shouting voices grated, slicing into the numbness that had taken hold of me. I wanted nothing more than to drift away. But they wouldn't shut up.

"Remy agreed to the healing. Nobody forced her to do it."

"That's bullshit," Gabe insisted. "You manipulated her. Anyone who knows her understands that she takes too many chances to help others. You should have been looking out for her."

"I was!" my grandfather shouted. "She has a gift, and a responsibility to use it. Hell, she cured cancer! Who knows what the limits to her abilities might be? Do you know how many people she could help?"

"You mean *your* people. You intend to use her to help your fight against the Protectors."

A silence followed that accusation. A wisp of a wish formed that my grandfather would deny Gabe's accusation.

Then Franc spoke slowly, "I think it's time you left, young man. I appreciate your concern for my grand-daughter, but we can take care of her."

Wishes were for idiots.

I thought Gabe might fight my grandfather, but a long moment later, the front door slammed. He'd gone. Asher's brother had gone. Now I really was on my own. Perhaps it was better that way. I was so tired of being used by people who pretended to feel something for me.

If I regained my strength, I would leave this place. I would run and hide, and I could do that better on my own. Caring about people just made them marks for those who wanted something from me. Really it was better to live alone.

Even as the thought occurred, I knew it was a lie.

I insisted on staying on the couch when my grandfather went up to bed. I told him it was because I didn't want him to have to carry me up the stairs. Truthfully I didn't want him or anyone else to touch me. My walls were down and my senses wide open. I couldn't protect myself if I wanted to.

"Remy," Gabe whispered, and I jumped.

No floorboards had creaked when he crept into the house. I hadn't even heard a door open and close, but Gabe knelt beside the couch. His eyes shone when a little slant of light hit them. *He came back.* A surge of relief swept through me, but I ignored what that emotion might mean.

"What are you doing here?" I whispered. "Franc will be pissed if he sees you."

"I'm here to help you heal yourself."

"No, Gabe," I answered. I'd never felt so exhausted, and it resonated in my voice. Even my bones seemed made of lead. "Go away, okay? We'll talk tomorrow."

"What did he do to you?"

Gabe's gaze flicked upstairs. The anger I'd heard in his voice earlier still simmered under the surface.

"Nothing," I said. *Nothing that everyone else hasn't done.*

Gabe didn't believe me. Doubt narrowed his eyes.

I faked a smile to reassure him. "I'm okay. I just need some sleep. You can go."

He didn't answer. Instead, he surged to his feet, sweeping me up blanket and all. He lifted me against his chest and carried me through the house to the back door. Somehow he managed to avoid bumping into any furniture.

"Gabe . . ." I protested.

"Shh, Remington. We need to talk. Please."

Gabe saying "please" shut me up. It didn't happen often. He peered out the kitchen window for a moment, and then maneuvered us out the back door. As soon as it closed behind us, he took off running at a speed that sent the sky swirling with the treetops in a whirl of black, dark green, and tiny white pinpoints. My stomach flipped, and I closed my eyes.

Why was Gabe doing this? Did revenge mean so much to him? A longing tumbled through me like a leaf set afloat on a pond. I'd thought I'd set that hopeful part of me aside, and yet . . . I wished that one person would put me first. That one person would be on my side and never disappoint me.

I'd thought that person was Asher, but what had loving me ever gained him aside from pain and ultimately death? My ability would never allow me to be normal. I would hurt people over and over, and if I wasn't the one doing the hurting, then the people chasing me would be. *I deserved to be alone.*

Gabe gripped me tighter. "You're not alone, Remy."

He only said that to be nice. Eventually he would have to go back to what remained of his family. And if he wouldn't go on his own, I would have to find a way to make him go. I would—

I froze. "What did you say?"

Gabe tilted his face away to hide his expression, but not before I glimpsed his resigned expression.

"Gabe?" I insisted.

We reached a hiking trail. To one side of the dirt path, someone had constructed a bench out of fallen logs. Gabe sat down with me still tucked safely in his arms. His hands gripped me too tightly, almost as if he thought I would run away. I waited.

His Adam's apple shifted and then he admitted, "I said you're not alone."

The worst kind of déjà vu crept over me. It couldn't be. It wasn't possible. Not twice. Not after Asher. I . . . No. Just no.

Gabe wouldn't look at me. I would have pulled his chin about so I could see the truth on his face, but the blanket held my arms captive. Frustration and horror mingled, and the screaming protest swelled in my head.

Gabe winced in obvious pain.

I shuddered, finally accepting a new, screwed-up reality. With my weakened powers, I couldn't even raise my mental walls to shut him out. I felt stripped bare, every raw nerve exposed to the night breeze. A moan hitched in my throat, and Gabe pulled me closer as if to comfort me.

"How long?" I choked out. "How long?"

How long have we been bonded? How long have you been reading my mind?

"Since the night at the motel when I helped you heal yourself."

The sobs ripped out of me. I'd thought the bonding had been unique to Asher and me. We weren't the first Healer and Protector to bond, but I had thought it only happened once with one person and my ability to bond had died with Asher. Even Asher had said our bonding was different from any he'd heard about. Like how he could read my thoughts, and I could cure his immortality. I'd hated it that he could read my mind, but I'd dealt with it because I loved him. I'd even accepted that it could be an advantage in a fight, and I'd begun to believe it added to the way we felt about each other. But bonding with Asher's brother? I imagined Asher's face if he knew and cried harder.

How could this happen?

"Talk to me, Remington," Gabe pleaded.

I pressed my lips together. *Don't call me that. Don't act like we have cute names for each other.*

"Hey, this hasn't been a joyride for me over here, you know." Gabe's voice had a hard edge to it. "It's not like I asked for this!"

I managed to get a fist free and swung at him weakly. His head snapped back and I missed him.

"Are you seriously yelling at me?" I shouted. "You've known about this for how long? Maybe you could give me a minute to process the little secret you've been keeping to yourself?"

His mouth turned down. "I'm sorry. You're right."

We sat in silence. I wanted to tell Gabe to get his hands

off of me, but he'd know that I would simply fall over without his support. Mind eavesdropping eclipsed verbal lies every time. A desire to continue weeping nearly overtook me.

Pull yourself together, Remy. What good are tears anyway? I rubbed my forehead. *Oh Asher. How could this happen?*

Gabe swallowed. "Do you know how often you think about him? How often you daydream about him and wish I was him? Geez, Remington, it's like I'm grieving for him twice, hearing your thoughts."

His voice sounded raw with hurt, and I cringed. I thought back over the last weeks. Lost in sadness for Asher and my family, I hadn't been careful with my defenses. Sometimes I'd even left my walls down *because* the humming of my energy hurt Gabe. Like a small, cornered animal, I'd turned on him, wanting to cause him pain so I wouldn't feel so helpless. My petty actions had shamed me more than once. And Gabe had never betrayed that he'd known exactly what I was doing.

Even now he wore that irritating distant expression, and I hadn't a clue what he was thinking.

"Why would you let me hurt you?" I asked, confused. "Why wouldn't you just tell me that we'd bonded?"

The tendons stood out on his neck, and the impersonal mask slipped a little.

"Gabe?"

"Leave it alone, Remy. You might not like the answer."

His eyes finally touched on my face. They burned with a heat that had little to do with anger. Once upon a time Asher had looked at me like that. Usually before he kissed me, he would—

"I'm not Asher, damn it!"

I jolted in Gabe's arms, shocked by the frustration in his voice. For the first time, I looked at him, really looked at him. Not as Asher's brother or as an enemy Protector, or even as someone who had become my friend. Gabe might be angry, but he held me with tenderness and care. He kept his energy in check, even though he could kill me. Over the last weeks, he could have killed me a thousand times. The way I'd kept my defenses down, it had almost been a challenge to him. An invitation to send me to Asher when I'd tired of fighting. He'd never come close to hurting me.

I'd thought he stayed out of loyalty to Asher. Or to avenge Asher's death, but it wasn't a bloodthirsty desire for revenge that made Gabe's heart beat faster under my hand. I shivered. Gabe cared for me.

And that scared the shit out of me.

"Yeah. You and me both," Gabe whispered.

He closed his eyes and took a deep breath. Something about that gesture caught my rapt attention. He looked as if he was savoring a favorite scent, the way I inhaled deeply just before I took my first sip of coffee. I stared. Guilt colored his cheeks.

Oh hell.

"You can smell," I accused.

All of Gabe's senses were returning. His constant nearness to me would make him more and more mortal. More and more vulnerable to attack.

"Help me heal myself," I demanded.

After the evening's revelations, he'd expected me to fight him, rather than let him help me. I'd surprised him, but Gabe shifted into immediate action. His energy swept over me, and I set aside my chaotic emotions. With new eyes, I reached for the tendrils of his power. In the last weeks, it had become easier to use his power. Why hadn't I remembered how the same thing had happened with Asher? The more our bond deepened, the more comfortable I'd been using his power as if it were my own.

It took forever to heal myself. Melinda's disease was

lethal and widespread. I took it one step at a time, focusing on one area of my body at a time. An hour later, beads of sweat dripped down my face, and I wanted to give up. There seemed to be no end to the damaged blood cells. I'd finally met an illness I couldn't recover from.

"You give up, and I swear I'll never let you hear the end of it."

Gabe sounded upset, so I tried for a smile. "You think insulting me is going to help things along?"

"It's always worked before." He wiped my forehead with the edge of the blanket, and I saw how tired he was, too. He added, "You've got this. After fighting Dean and a whole group of Protectors, this is a cakewalk."

"It wasn't a group. Two isn't a group."

"Shut up and concentrate."

I did. I put every bit of effort I had into it. Too much time passed before green sparks lit the air and I could feel myself returning to normal. I was *humming* again.

For all of a minute, I let myself regroup. A cold breeze dried the tears I hadn't known I'd been crying, and I shivered. Gabe swayed in exhaustion, and I put my mental walls back into place to protect him. Then I sat up and pushed myself away from him. He let me go when I stood and the blanket fell to the ground. I walked a few feet and shoved my hands into my jeans pockets. A plan had formed the instant I found out he was becoming mortal because of me. Time to get a move on.

"You have to go, Gabe."

"If this is because of how I feel about . . ." His voice trailed off, leaving the words unspoken. He sighed. "I already feel like I've betrayed Asher. You don't have to worry about me giving you my class ring or asking you to the prom."

The last he'd said with forced humor, mocking himself and our situation. I'd always thought Gabe arrogant and prideful. Obnoxiously so. He was, but he'd had his reasons. He'd purposely held himself apart from me to protect himself. Fat lot of good it had done.

"I want you to leave, Protector," I said in a frigid tone. *Enough. No more pain and death because of me.*

Gabe stilled in the act of picking up the blanket. "What are you talking about?"

"I belong here with my grandfather and his people. My people. I'm going to let them test me. If I'm the answer to everyone's problems, then it would be selfish not to agree. You would only interfere with that if you stay. I don't need you anymore, okay?"

"Stop it, Remy."

Despite Gabe's anger, I kept going, focusing on the bark of a tree above his head. The forest reminded me of Townsend Park and Asher and a day when we had resolved to stay together and face our uncertain future. Would he have made the same decision, knowing he would die such a short time later? The memory firmed my resolve. This was the right thing to do, even if it meant hurting Gabe. Better hurt than dead.

I went for the jugular. "I don't care about you, Gabe. I never will. It's pathetic for you to hang around hoping that changes."

I'd never been so purposely hurtful, and I wanted to scream that I was sorry. My stomach clenched, and I physically ached with the need to take the words back. Instead, I bit my lip and squared my shoulders.

"Hey, Remington?"

Gabe's affectionate tone caught me off guard. I looked down to find him smiling at me, with his arms crossed over his chest.

"Do you remember the night you broke my arm because I threatened Asher?" he asked.

I nodded, confused at why he would bring that up. I'd

been goofing off instead of training, and Gabe had taught me a lesson. He'd shown me quite effectively that my inattention could make Asher vulnerable in a fight. Gabe had guessed that I would take my training more seriously if I'd put Asher in harm's way, and he'd been right. So right that I'd demonstrated a new power. I'd broken Gabe's arm from across the room without laying a hand on him. I'd only been able to do something like that one time since, when Dean had threatened Asher. I was glad because that night I'd hurt Gabe, I'd scared myself.

Gabe continued. "After you hurt me, you and Asher had this one-sided argument. I only heard his side of things, of course, because he was reading your mind. You were so pissed off, you yelled at him to get out of your head. Do you remember what he said?"

I thought back to that night. I'd been furious at Asher. My walls had been up during that argument, but he'd still heard my thoughts. We'd discovered that when I felt something strongly, my ability to block him out didn't always work. My feelings had been crushed when I believed Asher afraid of me after what I'd done to Gabe, so my walls had failed miserably. I'd accused Asher of invading my mind, but he hadn't really been given a choice in the matter that night.

"Asher said it felt like I was shouting my thoughts at him," I answered slowly.

Gabe nodded. "Yep. That sounds about right."

He patiently waited for me to catch on. When I did, I crossed to the bench and sank down beside him, completely deflated. So much for good intentions. Apparently I felt strongly about lying to make him go.

"Damn it, damn it, damn it," I said.

"It was a nice try. Honestly, I appreciate the effort you put into it. My favorite part was when you called me a Protector in your best gloom-and-doom voice."

He imitated me, and I said, "Shut up, Gabe."

"No, really. You're such a badass, Remington."

Somehow he made me want to laugh when I least felt like it. I didn't get it. The day had been one more crappy day on top of dozens of others. Bad news kept piling up until I thought I would never be able to shovel my way out. And still Gabe could cheer me out of a good cry. I couldn't believe I'd once thought him unable to joke. I bumped my shoulder against his, and he put his arm around me. I rested my head against his shoulder.

Gabe? I meant a little of what I said. About what I feel. I don't want to hurt you.

"I know. It doesn't change anything."

He sounded a lot sad and even more resigned.

"How did this happen, Gabe? I thought a bonding only happened once."

"Me, too. It has to be you. That's the only thing I'm sure of."

"What do you mean?" I asked.

He sounded sure, and I could see he'd thought about this. "Everything that's happened is because you're different. You should have bonded with me first, but you didn't. You made that happen. Not Asher. Not me. I don't get the whys, but you are definitely driving this bus."

I tried to imagine how that was possible, but I hadn't wanted the bonding. I hadn't even known what it was when it happened to Asher and me. If I hadn't already cared about him by the time I'd found out, I would have run away.

The whole thing made my head spin. "Are you sure you want to stick around?" I asked.

Gabe shrugged. "It's summer. There's nothing on TV except reruns. I have nothing better to do."

"Jerk."

Despite everything, I selfishly was glad that he wasn't

going to leave me alone, but tonight's discoveries brought on more problems. With Gabe becoming mortal, we couldn't possibly stay. There were too many threats. The Protectors could come back. If my grandfather found out Gabe was a Protector and vulnerable . . . I didn't want to imagine what Franc might be capable of.

"We have to leave here," I said out loud.

Gabe nodded, his chin bumping into my head. "Sooner would be better."

"Let me have tomorrow to say good-bye."

He nodded again and squeezed my shoulder. One more good-bye. One more Band-Aid to rip off. One more day, and I would be completely without family.

"You have me," Gabe said, tugging on a strand of my hair.

I did have him, and I thought maybe that made me a bad person because I almost wished I could love him back.

CHAPTER TWENTY-FIVE

I packed my things before grabbing a few hours of sleep on the couch. I'd decided to pretend to be weak, hoping I wouldn't have to explain how I'd healed so quickly. The plan was to leave as soon as Franc left for Pacifica. Until then I would savor the last of my time with my grandfather. He might have been a bastard for asking me to heal Melinda, but I could understand sacrificing for family, even while I ached, knowing that he didn't love me enough to put me first.

Franc's steps vibrated through the house when he plodded down the stairs in the morning. I rolled to face him and he spied me awake.

"I'm glad you're up," he said, resting both hands on the back of the couch. "After breakfast we're going to Pacifica."

"What?" I rubbed sleep from my eyes, seeing our plan to leave today falling apart. "Why?"

My grandfather leaned over me and eyed me with concern. "I want to see if our Healers can help you."

"But you said—"

He scowled. "I know what I said. They couldn't help Melinda, but maybe they can help you. We have to try. I should never have pushed you this hard."

He shoved off the couch and started for the kitchen. I

hadn't expected this. I couldn't let the other Healers help me. They would know I wasn't sick anymore, and there would be too many questions. I threw off the blanket.

"Hey, there's no need, Franc. I'm already starting to feel better."

My grandfather turned, and I pretended to move slowly.

His forehead wrinkled like he didn't believe me. "Nonetheless, I'll feel better if the others have a look at you."

I stared at his back as he walked out of the room. It looked like I was going to Pacifica.

I texted Gabe from my room before we left. He wanted to come with us, but Franc would never have allowed it. Not after the way they'd left things the day before. I would return to San Francisco later that evening, and until then I would fake my way through their examinations. And tonight, I would sneak out to meet Gabe, and we would leave together. Part of me didn't mind one last trip to Pacifica. I planned to make the most of it and spend time with Erin. It would be more of a good-bye than I'd been allowed with Lucy.

My grandfather followed me tensely as I crept my way from his truck to Erin's front door. He'd wanted to help me, but I refused, wanting to prove that I was feeling better. On the way to Pacifica, we argued.

"I'm fine. I don't know why you're pushing this."

He shot me a disbelieving look. "You cured a fatal disease. You're not fine."

No matter how I insisted that a night of sleep had done wonders, giving me the time I needed to begin healing, he refused to cave and we lapsed into silence.

At Erin's house, Franc entered without knocking and ushered me in. I paused on the threshold of the living room. They'd obviously been expecting us. Five Healers waited in the room. Two of them were the women who'd run tests on me before. The other three I'd only met briefly and didn't know. Delia, Erin, and Erin's mother were conspicuously absent.

A worm of unease slid down my back.

"Come on, Remy. Let's do this. You'll feel better afterward."

Franc pressed a hand between my shoulders to urge me along.

"No," I said.

Something told me I could not allow these women to touch me. One woman studied me with cold speculation, and another bit her fingernails and wouldn't meet my eyes. Franc put a little more force into moving me, and I stumbled a bit.

I tossed him an irritated glance over my shoulder. His smile remained gentle, and I wondered if I was reading something into this because I felt nervous about getting caught out. I glanced around the room again.

No. Whatever was going on, it wasn't just me.

I squared my shoulders and twisted to face my grandfather. I tilted my chin up to meet his eyes.

"I said no, Franc! I don't want this. I'm not a freaking experiment!"

Horror or surprise widened his eyes. "Of course not! God, Remy! I'm so sorry. I didn't mean to make you feel that way."

"Then what's this?" I gestured to the women in the living room.

He shrugged and held his hands out to me in supplication. "I should never have asked you to risk your life for Melinda. I wasn't thinking. After I saw you so sick last night . . ." Franc stopped, his lips pressed together. "You came to me for protection, and I put you in harm's way. I let you down yesterday. This seemed the only way to help you. By no means do I want to force you to do anything you don't want to do. Please forgive me."

He hung his head, and I felt stupid for doubting him. My guilt about running away was warping my perception of everyone and making me think everyone had evil intentions.

I gave him a wry smile. "No, I'm sorry for yelling. But trust me when I say that I really am feeling better. I just need you to give me a little space to rest and get my energy back. Please?"

Franc nodded. He went into the living room to talk to the Healers, and I headed toward the hallway that led to the bedrooms, hoping to find Erin. On the way, I passed an open door and glanced in. Alcais's bedroom. Clean, almost to the point of obsessiveness, every object had its nook or slot. No wrinkles marred the bed's gray bedspread. The leather-bound books on the shelf over his desk had been lined up according to size and color. *Neat freak much, Alcais?* He was one person that I would definitely not miss.

I'd searched the room before and come up empty. I started to walk on, but something stopped me. After a quick look around to ensure I was alone, I entered the room. I glanced around, trying to figure out what was bugging me. *The books,* I realized. *The spines had no titles on them.* I stepped up to the shelf and pulled down the smallest book from the far end. It looked old. At some point, the red binding had fallen apart and someone had repaired it with tape. It smelled ancient, and my nose wrinkled at the musty old-person scent. I cracked it open to a random page and read.

Those Healers and Protectors who have broken the strictures against mating should be punished instantly and publicly. Any offspring created by these unions shall be put to death. Allowing these half-breed abominations to live—

"Remy?"

I swung about guiltily, before I realized Erin was calling me from the kitchen. Quickly, I shoved the book into my bag, hoping Alcais wouldn't notice the gap on the end of his shelf. I shot one last wistful look over my shoulder at the other books, but there was no way to take another without chancing discovery.

It seemed I wasn't the only one who had been seeking out the library. Excitement surged through me. Had I discovered the person responsible for Asher's death?

I was sure I'd been caught. Hanging out with Erin and Delia in the garage, I had to force myself to ignore my bag. I'd never stolen anything, and I now knew why. I didn't feel that thrill of getting away with something. I wasn't riding on a high. No, it felt like someone had erected a sign over my bag that flashed STOLEN OBJECT HERE in bright neon. The sign only existed in my imagination, but that didn't stop me from wanting to cast guilty glances about.

"You still with us, Remy?" Erin asked with a concerned look. "Franc mentioned how awful that healing was. Are you sure you don't want us to take a look at you?"

She reached for my hand where it rested on the table, and I jerked back before she could touch me. Her lips narrowed as if I'd hurt her.

"I'm a bit off still," I said. "I'm sorry."

Please let it drop, Erin.

"She said she doesn't want help. Why can't everyone leave her the hell alone?" Delia said.

My jaw dropped open. *When had Delia become my de-*

fender? She shifted her glare to me, and I snapped my mouth shut. I decided to change the subject.

"Where's Alcais?"

"Running an errand for Franc," Delia said.

I happened to be looking at Erin and noticed how she had suddenly found her fingernails wildly fascinating. Her knuckles whitened. She noticed me watching her, and her unsettled expression brightened in an instant smile.

"What errand?" I asked casually.

Erin remained silent, obviously waiting for Delia to answer. If I hadn't been feeling so guilty about the stolen book, I probably wouldn't have noticed how weird she was acting.

"What are we? His keepers? How the hell should we know?" Delia almost snarled.

Touchy. I decided to ignore that for now. We started playing Texas poker, which I hated. I could never understand why people liked card games. An hour or so later, Delia went off to use the bathroom.

Erin and I sat in silence. Things had never been awkward between us. I wondered if maybe she'd seen me coming out of Alcais's room and really did suspect something. A part of me wanted to confess, but what would happen then? Better to keep my mouth shut.

"Why did you heal Melinda?"

Erin's quiet question sounded loud in the garage. Startled, I considered the question for a moment before answering.

I shrugged. "If I could help her, then it seemed like I had to try."

"But you risked your life!"

"What else could I do? She's family."

Erin sucked in her breath, and I thought she chewed on the inside of her cheek. Shy as she was, the other Healers and their families sometimes spoke over Erin. They didn't always listen when she voiced her opinion, but if one waited patiently, she had a lot to say. I let the silence stretch on until it almost started to breathe.

Finally, she exhaled, sending her bangs flying. "Melinda isn't your family, Remy," she whispered.

I froze. "What do you mean?"

Erin's gaze stayed trained on the kitchen door. "Franc told us all to pretend Melinda was family if you asked about her, but we've never met her. He shouldn't have lied to you like that. It was wrong."

My grandfather had lied to me. And it wasn't a little fib. It was a huge freaking lie that had convinced me to risk my life for a stranger.

"Why? Why would he do that?" I rocked backward in horror. "Did he charge that woman?"

How much had my life been worth to Franc?

"Not that I know of, but he wouldn't exactly tell me." She shook her head, her mouth creased in frustration. "It was a test. He wanted to force you to use your other abilities. To see how powerful you are. You were keeping secrets, and he wanted to force your hand. I overheard my mom saying that he didn't think you'd go through with it. But you did."

And I'd awed her. I could hear it in her words. What abilities did Franc think I hid? Did he know what I was?

Voices sounded in the distance. Delia would return any minute, and Erin had sparked a dozen questions tumbling over each other through my mind. Tonight I would leave and never have the answers.

"Erin, what's going on?"

"He knows more about you than you think. You and your friend."

"Gabe? What does he know about Gabe?"

Erin sent another worried glance toward the door. "I'll be in so much trouble if they find out I'm talking to you like this."

"Erin?" I stretched a hand across the table toward her. "If Gabe is in danger, please tell me," I pleaded.

I thought she wouldn't answer. Then, as the door to the kitchen started to swing open, she whispered, "Gabe's not in danger. At least not yet. It's your other friend. The one who followed you to California."

Asher. She meant Asher.

I shot to my feet, and Erin grabbed for my hand, trying to pull me back down. At her pleading expression, I sank back into my seat. Delia entered, and I struggled to wipe the shock from my face.

Alcais followed Delia into the garage and studiously ignored me. Was he part of this? Had he learned of my grandfather's suspicions? I'd never been so glad to be invisible as they made their way to the dartboard and began a game of Twenty.

My mind had caught on what Erin had said. She'd said that my other friend was in danger. If Asher was in danger, present tense, then . . . My stomach twisted and I pressed a hand to it.

I scooted my chair closer to Erin. Delia tossed us a curious glance over her shoulder, and I slid a magazine across the table toward Erin as if we were looking through the slick pages together. *Nothing to see here, Delia.* I blindly pointed at something on a page, which turned out to be a model's nose, while Erin bent her head over the page.

Alcais began mocking Delia, and their usual bickering began. Under the cover of their loud voices, I whispered, "Just tell me . . . Is he still alive?"

Erin hesitated, ducking her head further so that her chin nearly dug into her breastbone.

"Please, Erin. Please." My throat closed around the words, almost as if it, too, was trying to clamp down on hope.

I flipped a page, nearly ripping it in half because my hand shook so badly. I took a deep breath, every fiber of me concentrating on Erin while I pretended to give a crap about the fashion magazine in front of me. Fear and hope threatened to strangle me.

And then Erin's head tilted in the slightest nod, and I could breathe once more.

CHAPTER TWENTY-SIX

*S*omehow Erin and I had given ourselves away. Alcais and Delia refused to leave me alone with the shy girl the rest of my visit, and I wanted to scream. Alcais watched us with suspicion, and he leveled more than one pointed look at his sister when he thought I wasn't paying attention. I tried to pull answers from Erin's expressions, to gather more information from her smallest gestures, but she had wiped her face clean.

I slipped away to the bathroom. I prayed they hadn't noticed that I'd slid my phone into my pocket. It wasn't until I had locked myself in the bathroom that I remembered the stolen book in my bag in the garage. I began to sweat as I paced back and forth in the small space.

Asher is alive.

What should I do? Where could he be? And how had the Healers learned he was alive? Tears clogged the back of my throat, and I ruthlessly stuck my fingernails into my arm until they retreated. I couldn't cry. Not now. It would be a dead giveaway that I knew something.

I ran my fingers through my hair, trying to keep it together. If the Healers knew Asher lived, then it followed that they might know where he was. Franc must know, but he would never tell me. He'd betrayed me. He'd lied to me and used me. I . . .

Those tears rose again, and I shoved them back again. *Think, Remy.* Okay. Franc had scarcely left my side in these last visits to Pacifica. I doubted he would lead us to Asher. He was too careful. Too on guard. There had to be another way.

Someone knocked on the door, and I bashed my elbow on a towel rack. I bit off a curse and rubbed the skin.

"What are you doing in there?" Alcais asked. "You've been gone forever."

I shuddered. He'd definitely guessed something was up to follow me to the bathroom. I swallowed and tried to project my usual animosity toward him.

"Piss off, Alcais. I wanted a minute alone, okay?"

The door shuddered as if he'd slapped a hand against it. "Excuse me for checking on you." He muttered something I was glad I couldn't hear, and then said, "Well, hurry up. You're not the only one who needs to get in there."

His footsteps retreated, and I leaned against the sink. He was such a prick. He'd been an ass to me ever since I arrived. He'd . . . I paused. He'd been disappearing a lot lately. I'd thought that was because he disliked Gabe or was afraid of him, but maybe I'd been wrong.

And then tonight they'd all begun acting weird. What kind of errand would Franc send him on that Delia hadn't wanted me to know about? Franc had no idea how Alcais hurt and used Erin and Delia. Sometimes it had seemed that he almost hated his own people, or at least how powerless he was in comparison to the Healers and Protectors. How far would he go with his hatred? And then there was the book I'd found in his room. A book about "half breeds" like me. All the pieces fit in a jumbled way.

Probably because I was forcing them to fit. I hated Alcais. Was I simply seeing what I wanted to see because I couldn't stand him?

Maybe I was off base, but it wasn't like I had any other

guesses. Alcais might know something. I took a chance and texted Gabe.

ASHER ALIVE. NEED YOU NOW @ ERINS.
FOLLOW ALCAIS. BE CAREFUL.

Then I left the bathroom and prayed that Alcais would lead us to Asher.

It was more difficult than I'd thought it would be to say good-bye to Erin. I wouldn't miss the others—especially Alcais—but Erin was different. I'd come to care about her. I surprised her with a hug and squeezed her a little too tightly. She made a *squawk* and then giggled. I whispered, "Thank you," into her ear, and she squeezed me back. Delia rolled her eyes when I waved, and I ignored Alcais entirely.

I followed Franc to the truck, stung by real regret that I would never see Erin again and feeling helpless because I couldn't force Alcais to tell me what he knew. Somewhere in the dark, Gabe waited to follow Alcais. If that boy left the house again, Gabe would follow. His limbs could be half torn off, but he would still be there because Asher might be alive. My pulse leapt at the thought, and I had to shove the anxiety away again.

On the way back to San Francisco, I stared at the lights reflected on the passenger window and sat on my hands to hide how they trembled. Uncertainty howled through me. Had my grandfather's affection been playacting—a staged game to keep me pacified? How had I forgotten that my mother had once run from him?

I gritted my teeth, anger crackling under my skin. How much did he know about what Alcais was up to? That thought nagged at me, and it killed me that I couldn't come right out and ask without giving away what I knew.

Back in Blackwell Falls, I had hoped that my grandfather would know what I was and maybe have a way to "fix" me. Or perhaps know a way for me to be with Asher without killing him. Now, I just wished that I could go home and undo everything that had happened here. I had risked everyone I cared about for nothing. I'd thought I'd gained more family, but I'd gained nothing. This community, these people—they were not mine. I did not belong.

Out of the corner of my eye, I spied Franc tapping his fingers on the steering wheel in time to a song on the radio. He appeared carefree. Cheerful even. Except his gaze cut toward me with an assessing glance, as if he was considering new ways to test me and push me, while keeping me in line. Was that what tonight would have been about if I'd consented? Another test? I'd wanted him to love me and had ignored the signs that I was being manipulated. It was my mother all over again.

Poor Remy. So desperate for love, she'll do anything for a family.

That bitter voice in my head mocked me. Rightly so. I had led us all to this point. Either my grandmother's death had screwed up Franc more than I'd realized, or his time leading the Healers had done it. I studied his wrinkled skin, searching for answers and wishing I was wrong.

"What?" he asked when he caught me staring.

I paused. "Nothing. I was thinking that I was glad that my mother sent me here. Thank you for taking me in, Franc." I lied through my teeth without an ounce of guilt.

He reached over to squeeze my hand. "That's what family does." His hand returned to the wheel, and I fought not to wipe my fingers on the seat. "You're pretty amazing, Remy. I don't think I've done right by you since you arrived. I should never have asked you to help heal your cousin." He shook his head in regret. "I'm really hoping you believe in second chances."

The sincerity in his voice sent me spiraling again. Perhaps I was reading everything wrong. What did I really know? Erin had said that Franc had lied about Melinda being family. That he knew more about me than I realized. She'd implied that I was in danger because of it. When I replayed our conversation, though, she hadn't actually said Asher's name or said my grandfather was guilty of anything except testing my abilities. Acid frothed and churned in my stomach. It would kill Gabe if I'd sent him on a wild goose chase to find his brother. It would kill me, too.

I wanted to press Franc for answers, but now wasn't the time. If I asked him the wrong question, he might become suspicious, and I needed him to believe things were the same as ever. If Asher was alive, my grandfather had hidden that fact from me, along with everything else he'd learned. That made him a very dangerous man.

So I bared my teeth in a smile and told my grandfather, "Of course I believe in second chances. That's what family does."

My suitcase stood sentinel at the door, packed and ready to go. I sat cross-legged on my bed, chewing on my fingernails and imagining myself as the crazy woman doing loops along the walls in *The Yellow Wallpaper*. I hated being stuck here, unable to help. I'd texted Gabe, but he hadn't responded. Franc had gone to bed hours ago, and I could feel my chance to slip away tonight disappearing with every tick of the wall clock's hands. Much worse than that, though, I worried that Gabe hadn't texted me because he'd been captured. I refused to imagine anything beyond that, but my stomach churned at the possibilities.

By 3:00 A.M., I'd bitten my right thumb bloody and had to fight the urge to pace across the squeaky floorboards. The stupid clock was driving me mad. It had begun to sound like it ticked "Asher is dead. Gabe is dead. Asher is dead. Gabe is dead." Finally, I gave in to the urge to yank it off the wall and stripped the batteries out of the back.

That was when I discovered that the silence was far worse than the *ticking*.

I couldn't take it anymore. I smothered my face with a pillow and shrieked into it. The muffled yelling didn't help, and my imagination bounded out of its confines. *Freaking Gabe.* When he showed up, I was going to—

A pebble hit my window. I dropped the pillow and ran to open it. Outside on the lawn, Gabe stood out in the open where my grandfather's men could see him. I stage-whispered, "Are you crazy? Hide—"

He shook his head. "No need. I took care of the guys watching the house. Get down here, and bring your things."

He didn't have to tell me twice. I grabbed my purse, bag, and suitcase and tiptoed down the stairs. Gabe met me at the back door and took my bags.

"What did you do to my grandfather's men?"

Gabe tipped his head toward a truck parked down the street. It looked empty. "They're tied up in the truck bed. I knocked them out."

I didn't say anything.

"You're not going to ask me why?"

"No. I assume you had a good reason."

"I did. Get in, and we'll talk."

I followed him to a black sedan that he'd left running at the curb. He threw my things in the trunk, and we both climbed in. He'd probably stolen the car, but I didn't care enough to ask. That was how far I'd fallen. It should have worried me, but all I cared about was finding Asher. What had Gabe discovered that we were no longer hiding our escape?

I spared one last glance for my grandfather's house, until I couldn't see it anymore. Regret rose up, but I shoved it down. There were other matters to deal with.

"Gabe, what's going on? Did you learn anything?"

His quick glance only lasted a second, but in that second, I saw a flood of emotions. Hope, fear, happiness.

I clutched his arm. "You found Asher?"

"Yes," he said in a tense voice.

A sob escaped out of me, and I shoved a fist to my mouth. I gasped, and Gabe's fingers clutched my other hand so tightly I could feel his bones smashed against mine. I didn't care. I gripped his hand back, and I didn't have to say anything. He knew exactly what I felt.

"Tell me," I demanded.

He kept his eyes to the road as he spoke. "I followed Alcais like you said. He left his house about ten minutes after you did."

"Did you steal this to follow him?"

"Didn't have to. He walked." I stared and he continued, "Asher's been just blocks from their house this whole time."

Had I walked right by Asher's prison? I felt sick and rolled the window down to get some air. Another thing to set aside to process later.

"You saw him?"

"Through a window. He didn't look good."

Gabe swallowed, and I looked away for a second. If Gabe said he didn't look good, then Asher must be in terrible shape.

"So my grandfather's men have him," I said bluntly when I could speak.

Gabe shook his head again and turned the car onto the highway. "No. That's the weird thing. Alcais went to this small cottage, and I hid nearby to watch the place. There were a few guys hanging about, coming and going as if they were on shifts. He definitely knew them, but they weren't part of your grandfather's community."

Okay. I didn't know what to make of that, except that Alcais was dead. He'd known about Asher all this time. I was going to hurt him in such a way that no Healer could fix him. He would be sorry he'd ever messed with me. The only good thing I could see about this was that Gabe and I could easily manage rescuing Asher from a few men.

"Remy, they were Protectors."

I stared at Gabe's profile. "No. You have to be mistaken."

"I'm not. I knew a couple of them. At least the ones I saw. I told you. Protectors tend to know of each other."

Why would Alcais be with Protectors? That made no sense. Unless . . . Unless he'd been working with the Protectors all along. We'd thought that the Protectors had captured Asher and me because they'd been following Asher, planning to use him as bait to catch me. But why had they kept one of their kind hostage? And how had they discovered his connection to me in the first place?

Franc. My mind latched on to a memory. My grandfather had seen me with Asher that one time. He'd seemed suspicious, but I'd thought I'd convinced him that Asher was a stranger. But what if Franc hadn't been convinced? And what if he'd sent the Protectors after Asher, knowing that only a Protector could capture him?

But why would my grandfather have let them take me, too? Unless that had been an accident. I'd snuck out that night. We'd thought Asher was bait, but maybe he'd been the target all along. My grandfather might not have meant for me to be taken, too. If he had allowed me to be taken, that would make him a sadistic bastard because then he purposely let them torture me. I thought about my return to his house, and how he'd used my fear to convince me to stay. Horror squeezed my heart. That couldn't have been his plan.

Things that hadn't made sense before crystallized, forming an ugly truth. He pretended to hate them, but my grandfather was working with the Protectors somehow. He'd sent them after Asher. And he'd continued to have my boyfriend held hostage. Franc had known that I was dating a Protector and never said a word. And he probably knew what I was, too. What Gabe was. He'd truly duped me.

Each new realization fanned breath on the smoke inside me until it blazed into a raging fire. *I could kill him,* I thought. *If my grandfather were here, I could kill him.*

"Take a deep breath," Gabe told me. "There's more."

"What?" I bit off.

"I counted at least five bodies guarding Asher. I didn't see all their faces, but at least some of them are Protectors. I'm not sure how we're going to get Asher out. We need a plan. A very good plan."

Our plan was half-assed at best. It was entirely possible that we were all going to end up dead. Gabe and I had come up with our idea during the twenty-minute drive to Pacifica. He boldly parked the car (which did turn out to be stolen) in front of the house where Asher was being held.

"Here?" I asked, shocked.

Gabe frowned. "You know this place?"

"Sort of."

I left it at that. There wasn't time to explain about Yvette or how the last time I'd been inside the house, it had been to see the body of a dead Healer. I wondered if Franc had betrayed her, too. Or maybe the whole thing had been more lies. Maybe Yvette wasn't even a Healer, and Franc had been manipulating me again. Hadn't that night threatened my relationship with Asher when I saw firsthand what a Protector could do to a Healer? Protectors would only work with Healers if they were getting something out of it in return. I thought of Yvette again. Had my grandfather used her life as a bargaining chip? I could hardly tell what the truth was anymore.

I reached for the door, but Gabe stopped me.

"If we do this, I need to know you're going to be calm."

"I'm calm," I snapped.

He said nothing, and I turned away for a second. All right, I was the opposite of calm. A maelstrom of emotions torpedoed through me, ricocheting off every new realization of how I'd been betrayed and the sharp tug of fear at what we would find inside the house. But I had to focus. I thought back to living with Dean. He'd fed off my emotions, and I'd learned to hide them away. To shove them down until I could be alone to sort them out. Time to find that place again. I took several deep breaths and reinforced my walls so no stray bits of my energy could escape to clue anyone in on what I was. Then I met Gabe's eyes.

"I'm calm," I repeated, and this time it sounded true.

He nodded and passed me one of the handguns from the backseat. Gabe had lifted the weapons from the men parked in front of Franc's house. I had never held a gun before, and I tested the weight in my palm. It felt heavy.

Gabe took the safety off. "Point and pull the trigger if anyone even breathes in your direction. Understand?"

"Yes. And if you go down, I run."

I didn't know if I could really do that, but I didn't want to argue with Gabe. There wasn't time. We didn't have long before my grandfather would realize I was gone. This was our only chance to take them by surprise.

We climbed out of the car, and I tucked the gun into the waistband of my jeans at my back. Yvette's house sat in darkness, but as we approached a light in the living room flipped on. Of course, the Protectors had heard our car pull up with their supernatural hearing. The door opened before we could knock on it. As we'd planned, Gabe and I launched forward in a display of Protector-speed and shoved past the man who stood in our way. Gabe bore the brunt of using his strength to knock the man aside, both of us wanting to hide that I was weaker. It worked. Within seconds, we were in the living room and the man had fallen to the floor.

"Where is our brother?" I shouted.

Everything hinged on these Protectors not knowing what Lottie Blackwell looked like, which would have been easier if these people didn't bump into each other across the decades.

A man and a woman appeared from the hallway, and I whipped the gun from behind my back. We'd woken the Protectors from their beds if their clothing was any indication, but they didn't appear sleepy in the least. On the drive here, I'd suggested sneaking in, but Gabe had tossed that idea out. He'd been right, too, considering how alert the Protectors were. They'd have heard our approach even if we tiptoed.

"Who the hell are you?" the woman demanded.

I thought she might be in her late twenties. Everything about her seemed delicate, from her tiny bones to her short stature and pale eyes. I stamped down a bit of fear. This delicate woman could break every bone in my body and steal my energy. I reinforced my walls, and she sent me an odd look.

"Lottie Blackwell," I said, doing my best to project Lottie's attitude. "You have my brother." I took three steps toward her, pointing the gun at her heart. "Since when do we hold our kind prisoner?"

One of the men twitched as if to attack me and found Gabe holding a gun to his temple. The man didn't look worried, and a wisp of fear swirled through me as I re-

membered how easily Gabe had once taken down Asher
in a fight. I prayed Gabe hadn't become too mortal being
near me. Now more than ever we needed his Protector
strength to make our story believable.

"Lay a finger on my sister, and I'll put a bullet in your
head. Even you won't get back up from that," Gabe
threatened in a soft voice that made the hair on my arms
stand up. He gestured to the man he'd knocked over in the
entryway. "You! Get Asher. Now!"

The Protector launched to his feet. He shared one look
with the man that Gabe held at gunpoint, and then disappeared down the hall. Sweat pooled under my arms, and I
checked my defenses. The woman stared at me unblink-
ing, and I met her gaze with false bravado. This wasn't like
facing Dean at all. To her, I would be a thing to torture
and use and feed upon. She would kill me so easily, and I
could do very little to stop her. The only thing holding
her back was her belief that I was like her, so I wouldn't
give in to my terror. I had to be strong for Asher. He
would need me.

The woman's muscles bunched and her gaze slid sideways, giving me warning.

"Please do it," I told her in a flat voice that made me
proud. She froze. "Do you understand how much I hate
you? You're a traitor to our kind, working with the Healers the way you are."

The man made a noise of surprise, and Gabe laughed.
"That's right. We know all about you. And we're not the
only ones. You actually thought you could keep your
arrangement secret?" He made a *tsking* noise. "There are
more of us coming. A lot more. You'll have to learn to
share."

Deflect and confuse, Gabe had said when he came up with
this plan. *Make them think about something besides us.*

"How did you find out?" the man asked. He sounded enraged, and the woman actually flinched, her dark brows lowering in worry.

"Now that's a question I'd ask your friends," I tossed out.

"What are you—"

The Protector's sputtering was interrupted by the return of the first man. My entire body yearned to see if he had Asher, but I couldn't take my eyes off of the woman.

"What did you do to him?"

The horror in Gabe's voice almost broke my control. The gun in my hand wavered for a second, but a cunning light shifted across the woman's face. One second of inattention and she would be on me. I leveled the gun again, and she scowled.

"You're going to carry him to our car," Gabe directed someone. Then he said, "Lottie, back up toward me."

Without turning around, I took several steps backward until I stood beside Gabe. He passed me the keys to the car.

"You follow her out," he told the man holding Asher. "I'm right behind you, Lottie."

Torn between leaving with Asher and leaving Gabe alone with two Protectors, I wavered. And while I wasted time, a man appeared in the kitchen doorway. My heart stuttered, and then began to tap out a million beats per second. Fear slithered over me, and sweat trickled down my back.

"Where do you think you're going, darlin'?" Mark said. "I've been looking forward to seeing you again."

Xavier stood slightly behind him. His face looked scary calm. "She's not one of us," he told the others. To me, he simply said, "Hello, Remy."

The two Protectors had healed since I'd last seen them.

Maybe they'd had help from the Healers. Gabe was probably kicking himself that he hadn't spotted them at the
house. These men hated me, and our odds were now five
Protectors to one slightly mortal Protector, one unconscious even more mortal Protector, and one half breed.

We're so dead.

"You've figured things out, have you?" Xavier said.
"Good girl. I'm surprised it took so long, though. Marche
must be a better liar than I realized."

He meant Franc. Any lingering doubts about my grandfather's involvement faded. From out of nowhere, a new
calm settled over me. Dean had taught me this. When
death was certain, you had nothing to lose by fighting it.

Nobody in the room breathed. They waited for us to
move so they could attack. I could sense them assessing us,
looking for our weaknesses. Gabe, they knew about. One
Protector against five would never stand a chance. It was
me. I was the unknown, the reason they hesitated.

"Go!" Gabe shouted.

I ignored him, tucked the keys in my pocket, and spoke
to Xavier, who watched me without blinking. "So he ordered you to take Asher and me. He paid you to test me
and see what I could do."

I'd refused my grandfather's tests, but he'd found another
way.

Xavier smiled. "If by paid, you mean he gave us the lady
of this house, then yes."

And they'd killed her right away. No hesitation like
they'd shown with me. Which meant Franc hadn't let
them kill me. Part of me wondered why they hadn't dis-
obeyed his orders once he told them what I was. And then
the lightbulb went off.

"You have no idea what I am, do you? Even now."

It was a guess, but it hit home. Xavier's mouth tightened. I continued. "Franc kept that from you. But you know enough to understand that I'm not like other Healers. And I'm certainly not like you."

Xavier pushed past Mark. The others watched him as if he was their leader. "Tell me then. What are you?" he asked.

I smiled with all the confidence I didn't feel. "I'm the one who can make you mortal again for as little or as long as you desire." I took a step toward the man carrying Asher. "But you can't force me to use my powers. And the way I see it, you have two choices."

"What's that?" Xavier said softly, his eyes measuring my every movement like a cat about to pounce.

"One . . . You let us walk out of here. You get to keep your sweet setup with the Healers, and you forget all about us."

"Or?"

I hovered my free hand over Asher's back and dropped my mental walls enough that the Protectors could sense it. They stared at me with hunger, and I had to hold back a shudder.

"Two . . . I transfer every one of Asher's injuries on to each of you. But first, I make you mortal enough to feel it." I let more of my energy swirl in the air. The *humming* began, and I could see how the pain of it surprised them. I hoped it made them yearn for more sensation. Otherwise, this would never work. I let the threat hang in my words as I met Xavier's gaze. "Trust me when I tell you that I can do it."

He studied me. At last, he said, "Option three. They can go, but you stay."

He gestured toward Gabe and Asher.

"No!" Gabe yelled.

"Done," I said.

"Give me your gun," Xavier demanded.

I shook my head. "Not until they're outside and in the car."

Gabe gripped my arm. "You don't honestly think I'm leaving you here."

"I do."

No way was he backing out now when we'd already jumped in with both feet. Everything was going as we'd planned. Sort of. They hadn't believed I was Lottie, but we'd known they wouldn't willingly let me leave. *This is a stupid plan, but it's all we've got.* Gabe looked like he would argue, and I thought, *This is our only option. Besides, it was your idea. Get on with it.*

Gabe's mouth tightened. He held my hand for a second when I passed him the keys and whispered, "Stay safe." He looked like he wanted to add more, but he couldn't chance it when the others might hear him. He stepped toward the man who held Asher and gestured at him with the gun. "You carry him out to the car. Let's go."

Xavier gestured for the man to do as Gabe said, and then they left. The door closed behind them. Gabe had told me to give him thirty seconds to get away. Thirty seconds to get his brother in the car before he came back for me. Only we hadn't counted on a Protector carrying Asher. Now Gabe would have to take out the Protector and save Asher. Thirty seconds seemed inadequate, but I figured that was all the time I had. I didn't dare take my eyes from the others in the room with me. Everyone had that alert, ready-to-attack stance. I couldn't blink. In my head I began to count down. *30 . . . 29 . . . 28 . . .*

"Remy," Xavier said, taking a step toward me. "The gun."

I lifted the gun to my head. *27 . . . 26 . . . 25 . . .*

Xavier raised his hands, his expression changing to one of surprise. "You don't have to do that."

"You tortured me. I won't go through that again." The fear in my voice was very real.

The woman took an aggressive step toward me. My finger tightened on the trigger, and I prepared to squeeze it the rest of the way.

"Back off!" Xavier shouted at her before turning back to me. "Come on, Remy. We didn't know what you could do. It doesn't have to be like before."

They need you alive, Gabe had said on our way here. If they knew what I could do, they would keep me alive long enough to take what they wanted. Sure, they would kill me, but on their terms. So I threatened to take what they wanted, and kept counting. *21 . . . 20 . . . 19 . . . Come on, Gabe.*

"You're lying!" I shrieked. "You just want to use me!"

I did my best impression of someone coming unhinged. The fact that I trembled in real terror helped. I sensed time running out. *16 . . . 15 . . . 14 . . .*

I took several steps back away from the big front window. "Stay away from me!"

Mark appeared to Xavier's left. "I'm tired of this. Let's end this already."

"Not yet." Xavier smiled at me. "You're not going to shoot yourself, are you? You think your friends will come back for you. You think they're different from us, but it's a lie. They're only pretending to care about you. They think if they're patient, you'll give them what they want." A telltale emotion must have shown on my face because he smirked. "That's the truth, isn't it? I've spent some time with Gabe. How far do you think he'd go to feel again? Something tells me he would go pretty far."

8 . . . 7 . . . 6 . . .

"Did he tell you he'd come back to save you? Is that why you're stalling?"

The hand holding the gun wavered. *5 . . . 4 . . . 3 . . .*

"Enough. Give me the gun."

Xavier's harsh demand reminded me of the things they had done to me before. I could almost feel the slice of his knife into my skin.

2 . . . 1 . . . Time had run out.

"He's not coming for you," Xavier said.

The old doubts flickered through me. Almost everyone in my life had abandoned me, including my mother. I had no reason to think Gabe would risk his life now that he had his brother safe. The Blackwells could leave and go back to their lives without anyone knowing the difference. Then I imagined Gabe's fierce promise earlier. *I'll come back for you. No matter what.* The worry puffed out, and I pointed the gun at Xavier with a steady hand. His eyes widened and then narrowed in rage.

"You're wrong," I said. "Come on then. Do your worst."

Xavier launched forward. There was a blur of motion coming toward me. A hand covered mine on the gun, and I stumbled, trying to keep my grip. The blur came to sudden, startling focus a mere foot in front of me. Xavier jerked the weapon away from me, and I let go as a blast sounded in the room. He stared down at me, his eyes huge. I gathered my energy in case I needed it. Then he dropped his gaze to the dark stain spreading across his chest. He'd been shot him in the heart when he grabbed the gun, I realized. Asher had once told me that there were some wounds even a Protector couldn't recover from. Was this one of them?

Xavier collapsed at my feet, and I didn't pity him. He'd hurt Asher and murdered Yvette. He could die for all I cared. I sensed movement to one side and raised my head in time to see Mark appear next to me. He grabbed my shirt with both fists and lifted me off my feet. I kicked him as hard as I could, and he threw me sideways. Cathedral bells rang in my skull when I hit the wall headfirst. I crumpled to the floor, too confused to avoid the next blow.

Mark stood over me, but somehow I saw Dean's face. The world froze in remembered agony as he pulled back his leg to deliver a vicious kick.

That was when a truck drove through the living room wall and burst into flames.

The corner of the bumper smashed into the back of Mark's legs, and I heard a *snapping* sound. He fell forward, and I forced myself to roll out of his reach. A broken leg— or even two—wouldn't stop a Protector who couldn't feel anything.

Three down, I thought. *Two to go.*

The male Protector ran for the driver's door and ripped it open. "Nobody's in the truck!"

He threw an arm up to shield his face. The fire blazed in the cabin, I realized. The gas tank hadn't exploded: someone had set a fire in the truck before sending it into the house. *Gabe.*

I slid my back against the wall, using it to steady myself as I stood. The bells had reduced to whistles. Irritating whistles that made my head ache. The woman rushed toward me and yanked on my arm, jerking me after her as she ran for the kitchen. I stumbled and tried throwing my weight in the opposite direction. That didn't slow her down, so I dropped to the floor, forcing her to drag me.

She cursed and almost yanked my arm out of the socket. She stopped short when Gabe appeared in the kitchen doorway. Before she could make a sound, he'd punched her in the face. The sleeve of my shirt ripped as she flew backward, stumbling over me.

"You okay?" Gabe said, reaching for me.

The male Protector appeared behind him. He had a

knife in his hand and swung it in an arc toward Gabe's back. I opened my mouth to shriek a warning, but I was too late.

Gabe's eyes widened, but it was the male Protector who fell over, blood oozing from a gaping wound in his head. He groaned. Asher stood over him with a broken lamp hanging from his limp fingers.

CHAPTER TWENTY-SEVEN

"Remy," Asher said, with a disbelieving look at me. Then he passed out.

Gabe and I rushed toward him. Gabe lifted him and threw him over his shoulder.

"Grab the guns," he ordered.

I did, and then ran after him to the car he'd left parked at the curb. I couldn't see Asher's face. All I could make out in the poor lighting was how limply he hung over Gabe's shoulder. A belt tightened around my heart.

I glanced away and gulped. Neighbors were approaching from both sides of the street. If the gunfire hadn't woken them, the crashing truck had. We were going to be surrounded in about ten seconds. I ran ahead of Gabe and got in the backseat. He placed Asher on the backseat beside me. Then we were all in, the car doors slammed, and we pulled away from the curb with a screech of tires.

I glanced back at Yvette's street and saw her house lit up in flames, big plumes of black-gray smoke billowing into the night air above. Even the Protectors wouldn't survive that blaze. I had an insane sense of déjà vu, as I wondered if this was anything like what my mother had seen when Franc drove her away from their burning home. Except somehow it seemed like poetic justice this time after what the Protectors had done to Asher.

Beside me on the seat, he lay unmoving and twisted. I pulled on his shoulder to roll him on his back and sucked in a breath when I got my first good look at him in a passing streetlight. His hair had been chopped off as if a child had taken blunt scissors to it. One side of his scalp had scabbed over, and I realized that was where the bullet had grazed him when I'd seen him shot in the head. His captors had beaten him brutally. Bruises and cuts crisscrossed his heavily whiskered face. His nose and one cheekbone appeared to be broken. Dried blood had crusted under his jaw. And the smell. Oh God. The smell coming from him. Infection and grime. They'd left him to rot, and the stench made me gag.

I'm so sorry, Asher. You're safe now.

I wanted to hold him, but I couldn't find a place that wouldn't cause him pain. I touched his hand, the fingernails smeared with dirt. His chest lifted in steady breaths and his heart beat steady, if a little slower than usual. I scanned him quickly before pulling away to stop my body from healing him. I wanted to cry. He had at least a halfdozen broken bones, and the bruises on his face were only a sampling of what covered him. Some of the cuts looked fresh and still bled. His eyelids didn't even flicker when I pressed the corner of his T-shirt to one cut.

"How is he?" Gabe asked. He tossed me a glance over his shoulder and wiped blood off of his lip. His face looked battered now, too, and I winced. I wondered what had happened to the Protector who had carried Asher out of the house.

I smoothed a hand over Asher's mangled hair. "He's in bad shape, but he'll live. We need to get somewhere where I can heal him."

"First we have to get rid of this car. Too many people back there could have seen the plates. As soon as we can, we'll get rid of the guns, too. I don't want anything left behind with our prints."

"Right." I was a criminal now. I'd shot someone. I set that aside for the moment. "Gabe?"

Our eyes met in the rearview mirror. *Thank you. For getting us out of there.*

Gabe laid a hand over his heart in a gesture that could have meant *you're welcome* or even *I love you.*

Gabe found us a new car. I didn't ask questions as we transferred an unmoving Asher from one car to the next. During the switch, I laid a finger against Gabe's wrist to see how bad his injuries were. I'd scanned a deep tissue bruise on his shoulder and a cut on his lower back before he pulled away from me with a reprimanding scowl. I wasn't sorry for checking up on him. He would suffer in pain before he'd tell me he'd been hurt.

"I'm fine," he said. "Let's just focus on getting my brother safe. How's your head?"

He must have seen me pressing a hand against it. "Fine," I said. He gave me a doubtful look, and I frowned. "I have a headache, okay? I'll live."

I settled in the backseat with Asher again. I couldn't stop touching him and staring at him. Morning light crept over the horizon, revealing more injuries. I wanted to begin healing him, but I could be incapacitated and I didn't want to leave Gabe taking care of both of us until we were all safe. Gabe drove north for almost two hours, determined to get us out of the city. At one point, we drove through the Presidio, so close to my grandfather's I almost could have spit on his house. Then we were farther up Highway 101, crossing the Golden Gate Bridge as the sun fully rose, its rays rippling over the bay. In a weird way, that sunrise felt like a promise. A promise that things would get better.

I blinked back tears. It wasn't time to cry yet.

Eventually, we arrived at an inn in Guerneville, a small town on the edge of the Russian River. Surrounded by redwood forests and wineries, the land offered a quiet place to lick our wounds. Since I was the least damaged looking, I checked in using Gabe's credit card. Gabe carried Asher into the room, and I followed with our bags and the deluxe first aid kit we'd picked up from a store along the way.

Gabe took Asher straight through to the bathroom and climbed into the shower stall with his brother. Then we worked together in silence, removing Asher's clothes. Each discarded piece of clothing revealed another mile of damages. Gabe set his jaw, and I swallowed around the ache in my throat. What had they done to him?

"I'll kill them," Gabe whispered fiercely.

You're going to be okay, Asher. I swear it.

Gabe shot me a weird look, and I realized we were down to Asher's boxer briefs. My cheeks heated, but I nodded for him to go ahead. Modesty had no place in this moment. Once Asher stood nude, I stepped back and Gabe turned on the shower as hot as he could stand it. He placed Asher directly under the steaming water. Dirt, blood, and grime mixed in trailing rivulets down Asher's body and swirled down the drain. He'd lost weight these weeks, his muscles not as thick as they once were. Had they even fed him?

"Why don't you find something in my bag for him to wear?" Gabe asked. "I have this handled now."

I almost ran out of the bathroom to do as he asked, but once I was alone I gave in to the urge to sit on one of the beds and cry. They'd tortured Asher. They'd held him for weeks, hurting him over and over, and I'd made him mortal enough to feel it all. How could I even ask him to forgive me? I wouldn't blame him if he wanted me out of his life.

From the bathroom I could hear the soothing murmur of Gabe talking to Asher, though I couldn't make out the words. Asher's voice didn't respond, and I wondered what Gabe said to him. I made myself get up and set out clean clothing for both Asher and Gabe on the bathroom counter and closed the door on my way out. It felt intimate and uncomfortable to do this for both brothers. Afterward I sank down one of the queen-sized beds to wait.

At last, the water shut off and I heard Gabe maneuvering Asher about. I jumped to my feet when the door finally opened and Gabe hefted his brother over to the closest bed. Hauling Asher around had obviously worn Gabe out. Dark circles had formed under his eyes, and his skin looked pale.

"You look tired, Gabe," I told him. "Why don't you rest and let me see what I can do?"

He gave me a weak smile and shook his head. "No rest until we're all seen to."

He would wait to help me heal whatever injury I took on from Asher.

Are you sure?

"Do your thing already, Remington."

I shifted my attention to Asher. Gabe had dressed him in shorts and left him bare-chested, and I winced at seeing the condition of his body again. Even with the filth and blood gone, he looked awful. I breathed through my nose and inhaled the scent of soap. The stench that had clung to him before was gone. Then, I laid my hands over Asher's heart.

This time when I scanned him, I took my time, searching out each and every injury. A couple of dozen bruises.

Just as many abrasions or cuts. The scab on his head from where the bullet had missed his brain by a millimeter. A busted lip and black eye that had swelled shut. A broken nose and cheekbone. Two broken ribs, along with a bruise in the shape of a boot. Broken right ankle and left wrist. A dislocated kneecap. And to top it off, a ruptured eardrum. I couldn't even imagine what kind of pain he'd been in.

Gabe hissed a curse as he heard the list of injuries in my thoughts. I wanted to curse, too, but I was afraid I'd lose it. If I started crying again, I wouldn't be able to stop. I gulped, thinking of the pain to come. I would take it, though. I would take every wound and a hundred more to have Asher safe and alive beside me. I leaned over, pressing my lips to his.

I love you, Asher. It's time to come back to me. I need you.

Gabe laid a hand over mine until I glanced up. His mouth had turned down, and I knew he'd heard my thoughts. I opened my mouth, unsure what to say, but Gabe spoke first.

"We do this slowly. An injury or two at a time, and then we heal you and rest a bit. Grand gestures won't do him any good."

I wanted to protest, but I couldn't. "You're right," I admitted. "Of course, you're right."

I nodded and Gabe released me.

Setting aside my fears, I picked an injury—the ruptured eardrum—and sent my energy winding toward Asher.

"We have to stop now," I told Gabe through chattering teeth.

Thirteen hours. It had taken thirteen hours to heal the worst of Asher's injuries. Some of the cuts and bruises remained, but I couldn't keep going. Pain came and went in waves as I absorbed wounds and then healed them. Exhaustion threatened to melt my bones until I became a heap of nothing. And Gabe . . .

He'd almost fallen over at one point, wasted from loaning me his energy to heal myself. Now, when I called a halt to the healing, Gabe didn't even protest. That told me more than his words could have. We probably should have stopped an hour before I'd insisted.

Asher still hadn't woken up, but I couldn't find any brain injury or trauma that would keep him knocked out. I sensed his sleep had more to do with exhaustion and thought we should let him rest.

"Gabe?" He swayed and his eyes drooped. "That's enough for now. Why don't you get some sleep?"

He nodded and dropped onto the opposite bed. He was out almost before his head touched the pillow. Both brothers snored, I observed, and for some reason that made me feel too much.

I grabbed Gabe's phone and snuck into the bathroom, shutting the door behind me. There was one thing I had to do, and it couldn't wait any longer. I dialed, and a muffled voice answered.

"Erin, is that you? It's Remy."

She didn't respond, but I could hear her breathing.

"I don't know what they told you, but you need to be careful. Franc and Alcais are working with the Protectors. They—"

"You really believe that? That I would work with the people who murdered my wife?"

I almost dropped the phone when my grandfather's agonized voice came over the line. He'd guessed that I would call to warn Erin. If he thought he could trick me with more lies, he was seriously delusional. I started to hang up, but something kept the phone glued to my ear.

"If you hate them, why give them Yvette?"

My grandfather sighed. "The truth? When you're a leader, you have to make choices. Difficult, awful choices. A small group of Protectors discovered us last year, and I did what needed to be done to keep my people safe."

Erin had once said that a few Healers had died in the area, and I shuddered, realizing Franc had been behind it all. "You sacrificed those Healers."

"A few to save the many. It's better this way. We stay in one place, our numbers grow, and soon we'll be able to overpower the Protectors. One day we're going to kill every last one of them."

My legs gave out, and I sank down to perch on the edge of the bathtub. My view of the room blurred. This was stupid. I had to hang up soon. I didn't think he could track the call, but I couldn't chance it.

"Remy?"

"Why are you telling me this?" I choked out.

"We need you," he implored. "You're not like the other Healers. Somehow you've adapted, and we've seen how you affect Protectors. That one boy had experienced the return of his senses."

He meant Asher, except Asher wouldn't have willingly admitted that information. What had they done to get it out of him? I smothered a sob with my fist.

My grandfather heard me. "Don't cry, kiddo. I understand you were alone and scared after your mother died. He and his brother tricked you so they could use you." He offered comfort like he had before in these last weeks. All lies. "I've already forgiven you for bringing them here. Just come home. Everything will be okay."

I dropped my fist. "I'm not coming back. You won't see me again, Franc."

"Don't do this," he said, his voice brittle with anger. "If you choose them, I—"

"I am them." I exhaled. No more lies. "Don't you get it? Mom hid me for a reason. Let me go," I pleaded.

I hung up before he could answer. Maybe he wouldn't come looking for me now that he knew what I was. Nothing else had convinced him that I didn't want to be his pawn. I scrubbed my eyes. I couldn't deal with this now. Later. Much later, when I didn't feel so battered.

Right this minute, everyone I cared about was safe. I didn't have to be afraid or sad or hurt. I could let myself feel peaceful, even if only for a moment. The danger would return. Pain always returned. But for now . . .

I shivered, powered off the phone completely, and left the bathroom. I lay down next to Asher, and finally let myself rest.

A door closed in the distance, waking me from a deep sleep. *Gabe,* I thought. *He's gone to check our surroundings.* I curved toward Asher, sliding back into dreams.

Warm lips pressed a kiss to the corner of my mouth, and whiskers tickled my skin. Half-asleep, I smiled.

Asher.

At some point in the night, we'd rolled onto our sides facing each other. My hand pressed against his heart, and the rapid beat of it made me dizzy with relief. I didn't have to scan him to see that he would be okay. I opened my eyes to Asher's solemn gaze.

We stared at each other.

The sun had risen, and the soft light painted Asher's skin. For weeks I had thought about him and dreamed about him. I'd wished for him to be alive so hard that the wishing had become a constant ache, a gaping wound that I dragged around with me. The impossibility of ever seeing him again had changed me.

Now, with him lying beside me, I could feel myself changing again.

Asher brushed the hair from my cheek and laid his palm over my neck.

"They told me you were dead," he said, his voice rough like sandpaper. I realized he was feeling for my heartbeat, too, to convince himself that I wasn't a ghost or a dream.

"They shot you in the head," I said. "I saw you die."

We fell silent again, each of us absorbing what that had done to the other. We'd both been tortured, but nothing had come close to the agony of losing each other. Asher's eyes traced my face, and it felt like a touch, the way they lingered over each feature. Soon, his fingers followed, skimming over my skin in a barely there sensation. The quiet relief of having him beside me slid into something heated as my heart sped up.

I missed you.

I worried for a moment that he couldn't hear my thoughts. With everything that had happened, had our bonding remained? It seemed too much to hope for.

Asher smiled. "You have no idea how good it is to hear you again."

He rolled onto his back, and I propped myself up to see his face. A cut remained across his cheekbone. I laid a finger against it and closed my eyes. The *humming* began, and Asher stilled as I healed the last of his injuries. I wished the memories would fade as easily, but I knew that wouldn't happen.

I opened my eyes again. Asher watched me with a worried expression as his injuries formed on my skin.

"You healed me?" he said.

He hated the idea. His eyes swept over me looking for evidence of his other injuries.

I nodded. "Gabe helped."

Asher smiled ruefully. "I don't know how I'll ever repay him. What he did last night . . . And you . . ." He shook me a little. "Walking into a house with five Protectors. What were you thinking?"

I settled against his chest and let my finger trail up to the scar on his eyebrow. "Well, Gabe and I had a plan."

Asher wrapped both arms around me. Heat whipped through me. I'd missed that. Missed his touch and how alive it made me feel.

"You had a plan?" Asher asked doubtfully. "Did it involve getting dead? Because that seemed to be where you were heading."

I couldn't resist pressing a kiss to his bare chest. "I didn't say it was a good plan. But hey, it worked. You can't argue with results."

"No, I guess I can't."

His hand swept from my shoulder blade to my waist, and my breath skipped.

Fierce love for him had me squeezing my eyes closed on a new crop of tears. In that instant, I decided I would savor every moment with him. Every second I'd thought him dead had been lonely and terrifying. Getting him back was a gift. I would not let fear hold me back any longer.

"Hey," Asher whispered. I lifted my head. "I love you. I don't want to be afraid anymore, either." My hair fell forward and brushed his face. He turned his nose into it and breathed. "I dreamed of you all the time, but every time I tried to remember your scent, my imagination fell short. I longed for this."

His forest green eyes burned, and I said, "Asher?"

The hand on my back moved lower. "Hm?"

"Kiss me already."

He did, and it felt like I'd come home at last.

By the time Gabe returned to our room, Asher and I had taken turns in the bathroom and dressed. We sat on

the small sofa, talking about nothing, avoiding heavy topics. Neither of us felt ready to face what was ahead, or to
discuss what had happened in the weeks we were apart. I'd
put my guard up to have a little privacy, and Asher hadn't
mentioned it. Gabe's gaze paused on both of our faces and
then fell to our joined hands. He turned away quickly, but
not before I saw pain flicker across his features. I was suddenly glad that Asher couldn't read my mind at the moment.

Gabe pulled a chair over and sat, propping his legs on
the coffee table and his hands on his stomach. He'd wiped
all emotion from his face.

"So," Gabe said. "What do we do now?"

They both looked at me.

"What? Why do I have to decide?"

"It's your grandfather. We can stay and fight him."

Asher picked up where Gabe had left off. "Or we can
go home and get on with our lives."

Home. I hadn't thought we could ever return to Blackwell Falls or see my family again. The Protectors knew
where the Blackwells lived, and they knew I'd helped
Asher escape. But they'd all died at Yvette's house. I'd
watched the house burn. Everything had changed.

"Your grandfather was behind it all," Gabe said. "There's
no reason now why you can't go home."

"What if the Protectors told him?" I asked.

"No," Asher said. "I heard them talking about Franc
sometimes. Trust me. They didn't tell him anything."

Shadows crossed his face, as if he couldn't escape the
memory of what had been happening to him while he'd
overheard those conversations. I squeezed his hand, and he
seemed to shake himself back to the present.

I pictured Lucy, Laura, and my father. Would they want
me back after everything? What could I even say to earn
their forgiveness for leaving the way I had? Maybe I

should stay away to make things easier for them. Yet, I couldn't deny a yearning to be with them again. It was selfish, but I wanted to put me first. I needed my family, and I wouldn't give them up if I could help it.

And Asher . . . I looked up at him, clutching his hand. He needed this, too.

"I want to go home."

Chapter Twenty-eight

I didn't call ahead. What would I have said? *Gee, Dad, so sorry I broke your heart and cut you off. Hey, Lucy, you're the best sister I could have asked for, and I hope you forgive me for not even bothering to say good-bye when I ditched you.* No, a call wouldn't have fixed anything. Some apologies had to be made in person.

We grabbed the first flight to Maine, which meant we'd cleared out of the motel and hit the airport within a few hours. I thought the worry would eat me alive during the six-hour flight, but I had plenty to distract me. Due to the last-minute booking, we couldn't get three seats together. Asher, Gabe, and I found ourselves spread out across the plane, to my relief.

I longed to sit with Asher, but I didn't know how long I could keep the truth from him. I had bonded with each brother. They could both read my mind. Except Asher didn't know that, and I didn't know how to tell him. How did you blurt out something like that? I had to say something soon, though. The way Gabe watched us made it too obvious that it hurt him to see Asher and me together. Soon Asher would notice it, too. I'd kept my guard up on the way to the airport, not ready to face what I'd soon have to confess.

If what Gabe said was true, I had caused this mess, but I had no idea how to undo it. I didn't understand how I could bond with two men, so how could I make it stop?

In Portland, Maine, Gabe had arranged for a car to be waiting. We skipped the taxi lines and were on the road within a half hour of landing. Gabe drove, and I took the backseat, forcing Asher to sit in the front with his brother.

As we got closer to Blackwell Falls, giant beasts beat their wings against my insides. My family hated me. I'd made sure of that with that last call to my father. I imagined scenario after scenario of how they would react when they saw me. In every one, they rejected me. I couldn't tell the truth about my grandfather or what had happened to me. In place of the truth, every useless lie would make things worse.

Then we arrived in town. Blackwell Falls had become part of me when I lived here. Seeing it again eased another bit of the ache that leaving my home had created. I'd thought never to see the forests and sea cliffs again. I opened a window and inhaled. The salty air had never tasted so good on my tongue.

It smelled like home. I'd been loved in Blackwell Falls. I'd met Asher here. I'd had a family and a place where I belonged, but I'd thrown those away. To keep them safe, yes, but how could that matter when they'd never know it?

The plan was to leave me at my house, while Asher and Gabe went home to Lottie. They would drop off my luggage tomorrow. I didn't think my family would appreciate the Blackwells being there when we first saw each other. And Asher looked exhausted again after the flight. Those shadows wouldn't let him loose long enough for him to rest.

At last we pulled up to my father's house, and I stared at the cottage. I'd lived here. I wanted to run up to the front door, let myself in, and shout to everyone that I was home. *Would they want me?*

"Remy?" Asher said.

I met his gaze in the rearview mirror.

"They'll be angry and hurt, but don't ever doubt they want you."

Gabe was less gentle. "Get out of the damn car. The fear of the thing is worse than the thing."

I snorted. Then I took a deep breath and got out of the damn car.

I knocked on the front door, but nobody answered. If I'd been paying attention, I would have noticed that there were no cars in the driveway. It was the middle of the day, which meant my dad was most likely at work. Laura and Lucy could be anywhere. I stood on the porch for a minute feeling stupid and regretting that I'd waved Asher and Gabe on their way. Now what?

I shrugged and used my house key.

"Hello?"

My voice echoed without response. I was alone. I wandered from room to room, an interloper in this place that I belonged to and yet didn't. I'd changed since my father had brought me here. I wasn't even the girl that had fought Dean to save Lucy. Maybe I no longer fit here.

I climbed the stairs and immediately faced my bedroom. I dreaded opening the door. Had they packed up my things and turned it into an office? A guest room? My steps faltered, and I pushed the door open.

Nothing had been moved. Papers, makeup, clothes . . . They were scattered about exactly where I'd tossed them the day they drove me to the airport.

My family had left my room untouched, ready and waiting for me to return.

I walked to the bed. It still smelled of the lavender that Laura washed into the sheets, and I couldn't resist kicking off my shoes and sliding between them. My head hit the pillow, and my eyes grew heavy. The sun was setting outside my window, and orange light bathed everything in a familiar glow that hypnotized me.

I was home.

I woke in complete darkness, curled up on my side. Instantly, I was back in the room where I'd watched Asher die, and then waited to die myself. Something touched me, and I froze in terror when I heard light breathing. Someone lay in the bed with me. A hand touched my hair.

"Shh, Remy."

My fight-or-flight response had kicked in, and I barely missed punching Lucy in the face. I flopped onto my back, trying to catch my breath as adrenaline flooded through me.

Lucy touched my hair again, this time more tentatively. "I didn't mean to scare you. You were having a nightmare."

"What time is it?"

My eyes adjusted to the dark, but I couldn't make out her features. She dropped something on the bed between us and I heard a *click*. The screen of her phone lit up, and I could see her at last.

"Three twenty-four," she said.

I rolled to face her, and she touched a button that turned her phone into a night-light. She pulled the covers over our heads, creating a cocoon where only the two of us existed.

"Hey, sis," she said. "I missed you."

And that was all it took to open the floodgates. I cried in silence, and we stared at each other.

"I didn't think I'd see you again," I confessed. "I'm so sorry, Luce. You must hate me."

"Can I ask you one thing?"

I nodded and swiped my runny nose with my sleeve like a kid.

"Did you leave to keep us safe?"

I nodded again. I opened my mouth to tell her about it, but thinking about everything that had happened stole my ability to speak.

"Was it awful?" she asked, and she didn't sound as calm.

"The worst."

My voice cracked. Lucy used her own sleeve to wipe my cheeks. It didn't escape me that our roles had reversed, and she'd become the one doing the comforting. I wasn't the only one who had changed in these last months.

"Then we'll talk about it when you're ready. For now . . . how about I tell you what you missed this summer?"

I nodded eagerly, and she began whispering. She didn't talk about what my leaving had done to her or our parents. If she blamed me, she hid it well. Instead, my sister told me about our friends and our town and Laura's new hobby (learning to play the flute) and Dad's old hobby (working on cars in the garage in an effort to escape beginner's flute). The phone battery died, the sun rose, and eventually we heard our parents waking and heading downstairs.

"Do they know I'm here?" I asked.

Lucy shook her head. "Nah. Gabe called, or I wouldn't have known you were home. Are you and Gabe friends now? He sounded worried."

"It's complicated."

Her eyes gleamed. "I'm going to let that go because we

need to tell our parents you're here, but don't think I'm going to forget you said that. I know a good story when I hear it."

I hissed a laugh because that sounded like the sister I knew, intent on prying gossip out of me. "Understood."

We took turns using the bathroom, and then I followed her down the stairs to the kitchen, trying to control my nerves. Lucy hadn't given me any clues about what to expect. I didn't see my father, but Laura stood in front of the coffeemaker in her robe and slippers, seemingly willing it to brew faster like she had many weekends before. My eyes welled up again. She'd taken me in as if I were her own daughter despite everything. Did she feel like I'd tossed that back in her face?

"Mom," I said.

"Good morning. Coffee's ready." She didn't look up as she poured herself a cup of coffee. "What are you doing up so early?" she asked as she rounded with her mug in hand. She froze when she spotted me, and the hot liquid sloshed dangerously when she shrieked.

Lucy plucked the cup from her before she spilled it, and I found myself crushed against Laura. She hugged me tight enough to suffocate me, but I didn't care. Her welcome went far beyond anything I'd dreamed of. She pulled away to look at me, crying and smiling all at once. I smiled back, feeling wanted.

Then the smile faded, and she scowled. "Remy O'Malley, where the hell have you been? Do you have any idea what you put us through?" She lifted my hand and stared at it. "So your fingers aren't broken. There goes that excuse for not bothering to call a single time to tell us you were alive."

I'd never seen my stepmom so enraged. She launched into a tirade that blistered the air. She threatened to ground me and take away every privilege and belonging I owned, including my car. The fact that I'd gone over three months without these things didn't faze her. She didn't stop to let me speak, and I didn't care. Because through all her recriminations and anger, she assumed I was home to stay.

And that felt better than heaven.

She had just begun to wind down when my father appeared in the doorway.

The world stopped spinning as he stared at me with hollow eyes. He didn't come forward to hug me like Laura had, or tell me he'd missed me like Lucy had. I didn't know what to do. His arms crossed over his chest; he looked unforgiving and unapproachable.

"Donuts," Laura blurted out. We all turned to stare at her, and she said, "I want donuts for breakfast. Ben, why don't you take Remy with you to get them?"

The Queen of Subtlety, that was my stepmom.

Nobody moved, and she glared at us and bellowed, "Get me some freaking donuts. Move!"

And we did.

We could have walked to the donut shop, but my father chose to drive. I wondered if that was so he could get the trip over with more quickly. We arrived at the bakery in minutes, ordered donuts and two coffees, and were on our way home without having said a word to each other. Laura's plan to throw us together had crashed and burned.

But at the house, he pulled into the driveway and honked the horn. The front door opened and Lucy appeared. Ben waved to her and handed her the box of donuts when she ran over.

"We're going for a drive," he told her. "Let your mom know, okay?"

She nodded and sent me a worried glance.

Ben pulled back onto the road and headed for the shore. He stopped in the parking lot at the beach I'd found myself on that first morning I'd decided to stay in Blackwell Falls. It had also been the morning I'd met Asher. So much had happened since then.

My father shut off the engine, grabbed the coffees, and left the car. I followed more slowly, planting my feet into his vacated footprints in the sand as we plodded toward the water's edge. He plunked down on the ground and handed me a coffee when I sat beside him. I couldn't read him. Was he angry? Disappointed? Hateful? All of the above?

I waited.

Ben sipped his coffee in silence, watching a sailboat cut through the water.

I fiddled with my cup.

"I love you," he said at last. "You are my daughter. I don't understand why you left the way did because I'd thought we'd gone beyond that. But you are my daughter, and you are not deliberately cruel. So I believe that you're keeping secrets about your mom and Dean and your grandfather, and I also believe that you're protecting me by not telling me those secrets. You don't trust me, and that hurts. And I'm angry at you. That good-bye you telephoned in was bullshit. I've been worried that Dean found you, or that something else happened to you, and you left me with no way to find you. And we've all missed you because you left a hole in our family when you didn't come home. And I know better than to expect explanations from you. But I love you, and now I'm asking you to promise me that you won't ever do that to us again."

He stopped talking, and I realized it wasn't so he could take a breath. He faced me with grim expectation for a moment. Waiting for me to answer. Duh.

"I promise," I said.

His mouth pursed thoughtfully and he gave one stiff nod. Then he said, "Drink your coffee, Remy."

I did, even though it tasted awful.

"I love you, too, Dad."

He didn't answer, but a moment later he put an arm around my shoulders and we watched the sailboat until it disappeared over the horizon.

CHAPTER TWENTY-NINE

I ran straight for the Edge of the World, passing land-marks so familiar I ached. The cement barricade I'd struck with my car the night Dean tried to kill me still stood sentry at the viewpoint, and I jumped over it easily.

Two days had passed with no word from Gabe. I'd spoken to Asher, and he'd even come to my house yesterday. I hadn't told him about bonding with Gabe, and it never seemed like the right time. But Asher could sense something was wrong. I'd spent most of our time together blocking him from my thoughts, and that wasn't normal for us.

Weather had eroded the cliff, and yet nobody had fenced it in yet. A few locals liked to stroll down the dirt path, but hardly anyone came here. I walked right up to the edge, and loose dirt and rocks tumbled down, down, down to the rocky shore below. Stretching as far as I could see, water and sky melded, the blue monotony broken by orange clouds lit on fire by a setting sun. The last time I'd stood here, Dean had tried to kill me, threatening to toss me to the rocks below like so much trash washed ashore. Since then, I'd been tortured, used, and nearly killed. Asher had been tortured. I'd been betrayed by family, and I'd betrayed my family.

Everything had changed irrevocably. Things weren't

perfect at home, though I'd apologized. I told them I'd made a mistake by deciding to live with Franc, but I didn't go in to the reasons. I'd lost my family's trust, and it would take time to earn it back. They were worth the effort, though. I'd never been as happy as I had been here, and I'd given it all up for nothing.

Suddenly, rage yawned out of me. All the emotion I'd been stuffing down for the last two days exploded as if I were a bottle of soda and a Mentos had been dropped down my throat. I threw back my head and yelled as loud as I could into the wind. My voice broke on a sob, and I braced my hands on my thighs, breathing hard. Deflated, I fell to my knees.

My grandfather. Asher. Gabe. My family. My mother. Dean. Erin. Alcais. Yvette. The Protector I'd killed. Names and faces flashed through my mind without order or reason. Too much had happened, and I couldn't get my bearings.

I knew one thing to be true: I didn't want to hurt anymore.

The air cooled once the sun had set. I didn't hear him approach, but a warm hand pushed my hair aside and settled on my neck.

"Remington."

Gabe sat down beside me in the moonlight. The wind whipped my hair about, and he gathered it in his hands, pulling the strands through his fingers tenderly. He seemed to realize what he was doing, or maybe he saw himself through my eyes because he stopped suddenly and dropped his hands.

He sighed. After a moment, he looped an arm around me and tugged me into his side. It was a position that had become familiar over the weeks we'd spent together, I realized, but one that was more intimate than I had considered. We'd grown used to taking care of each other. Somehow, the thing that had helped me survive felt wrong. What were we supposed to do with that now that Asher had returned?

"I don't know," Gabe said. "I don't know."

An owl hooted from a nearby tree. I wished the moonlight wasn't so bright so I could hide my expression.

"Where's Asher?" I asked.

"Looking for you. We thought it was time to talk. He thought you might go to Townsend Park. I volunteered to check here." He shrugged and dropped his arm. "You can't run away from this."

"I know. I'm sorry." *We have to tell him, Gabe.*

"We will, Remington."

This sucks.

"We'll do it together."

I thought of several ways to start that conversation, but nothing worked.

"We just say it."

For all his bravado, Gabe sounded nervous, too. My stomach did a little flip.

I nodded with more confidence than I felt. "Sure. It's not like it's a big deal, right?"

Hey, Asher. I accidentally bonded to your brother while we thought you were dead, and now you can both read my mind. Please pass the sugar.

"That could work," a voice said behind us. "Or I could just overhear it in your thoughts."

I jumped. Asher stood behind us. Gabe didn't move, and I guessed he'd heard his brother coming toward us. I knew he had when he looked guilty. That was probably why he'd dropped his arm.

Asher stared at Gabe. "You knew she'd come here."

It wasn't a question. Gabe lifted a shoulder in a shrug. "I guessed."

"No, Gabe," Asher insisted, a new awareness settling over him. "You knew. The labyrinth was our place, Remy's and mine, but you knew she'd come here instead."

Asher's angry voice sent a chill skating down my back. His uneven hair stood on end and his half-grown beard gave him a dangerous appearance. I hadn't consciously avoided Townsend Park, but it made sense. I was scared of Asher finding out about Gabe.

"Asher?" I whispered.

I took a step back at the ravaged look in his eyes. He stared at me like I'd betrayed him. I'd never seen that expression on his face, and I shoved a fist into my stomach.

"You bonded to my brother."

The flat statement made me feel guilty.

I raised my hands, helpless to defend myself, and Asher said, "Every damn day, they tortured me in that house. They tried to get me to tell them everything about you, and I kept my mouth shut. And the whole time, the two of you were . . ." His voice faded off, and he shook his head, gesturing to where Gabe and I sat together. "I don't even know what you are."

"It's not what you think," I said.

Under his breath, Gabe added, "Speak for yourself, Remy." Louder, he told Asher, "It's exactly what you think. At least for me."

Shocked, I shoved Gabe in the chest. "Why would you say that?"

"Because it's true. You may not like it, but I have feelings for you."

I pulled away from him. *Shut up, Gabe! You're making it worse.*

"Too bad, Remington. It's time we get this all out in the open."

Asher laughed, but there was no humor in the sound.

"This just gets better. Are you reading her mind?" Gabe didn't answer, and Asher accused, "You are, aren't you?"

"Yes," I finally said, rising to my feet. "It started weeks ago."

"Shit!"

Asher's shout echoed off the cliffs like mine had earlier.

"Are you kidding me?" he yelled at the sky. He turned away from us, running a frustrated hand over his head. He'd gone a few steps toward the barricade as if to leave, but just as suddenly he shot back toward us. "How the hell did this happen? How could you let this happen, Gabe?"

Gabe stood, crossing his arms over his chest. "It's not like I planned it, man."

Asher froze, his eyes widening. "No, you didn't plan it. You hoped for it, though, didn't you?"

I almost missed the guilty expression on Gabe's face. Confused, I asked, "Gabe? What is he talking about?" He wouldn't look at me. "Asher?"

Neither of them responded, and I threw my hands in the air. "Somebody tell me what the hell is going on!"

"He's been pissed at me since the day I bonded to you, Remy," Asher said in a harsh voice. "The eldest son bonds with the Healer, remember? It should have been Gabe, not me. And he never let me forget it."

I'd known that, but my bonding with Asher had always been one more way that I was different from other Healers. I hadn't really questioned the why of it. It didn't matter, anyway. The night I'd bonded with Gabe, neither of us had been capable of thinking past surviving.

"You're wrong, Asher. He couldn't have known it would happen," I argued. "You don't understand."

Asher ignored me. He strode up to Gabe until they were almost touching. "She may not believe it, but I do.

How long did you wait after you left me to rot in that place? How long before you moved on her?"

"You really don't know what you're talking about," Gabe told him, a pulse beating at his neck. "Shut up before you say something you don't mean."

"Family means everything, you said. Do you even care what they did to me, brother?"

This was exactly what I'd feared. The two of them looked ready to tear each other apart.

I stepped between them, placing a hand on Asher's chest. "It wasn't like that."

He stared at my hand and then looked at Gabe over my shoulder. "I won't forgive you for this."

Asher stepped back with an air of finality, forcing my hand to drop from him. In defending Gabe, I'd lost Asher. How could I make him understand what had happened when I couldn't understand it myself? I'd missed him so desperately, I'd wished I'd died in his place. How could Asher not know that?

Gabe placed a hand on my shoulder, either in comfort or to stop me from reaching for Asher. Touching me was a mistake. Asher's eyes lit on that hand and his sadness morphed into rage.

"We're finished, Gabe."

I opened my mouth to argue, but Gabe picked me up and set me to one side, his eyes narrowed in fury.

"You're pissed at me?" Gabe asked, his voice filled with scorn. "You think I wanted to be here? That I wanted to be forced to protect her when you couldn't? Does that even sound like me?"

That stung, and I protested, "Hey! Nobody asked you—"

Gabe rode right over my words. "You did this, Asher. I told you to stay away from her. You didn't. I told you she would destroy our family, but you wouldn't listen. Have you even given a thought to what this did to Lottie?"

Gabe shoved Asher. He looked shocked by what he'd done. The violence appeared to take his brother by surprise, too.

Gabe continued, his voice getting louder with each word. "No, you kept bringing her around. And then you ran after her to San Francisco. You got captured because you weren't careful, and you let them capture Remy. Hell, you practically invited them to take her. You don't deserve her."

He gripped Asher's T-shirt in both fists by the time he finished.

Asher shook him off and straightened. "You think you deserve her, Gabe? If it was up to you, you would've let Dean kill her months ago."

Gabe's hands clenched into fists. "Screw you."

Asher crouched in readiness.

"Don't do this. Please don't do this," I begged.

They didn't listen. They hit each other with such force that it echoed off the cliffs. Asher swung a fist at Gabe, and bone crunched into bone. Gabe's head jerked back, but he retaliated by planting his fist in Asher's stomach. Their supernatural strength made everything far more brutal. Blood spurted out of Gabe's nose from one blow, and Asher's lip split open on another. They pummeled each other like they would kill each other, and I could do nothing to stop them.

Paralyzed by the violence, I shrank into myself. This wasn't like training, or even my skirmishes with Gabe. This wasn't self-defense. Every sound came straight from the soundtrack of my childhood, and I could almost taste the iron on my tongue. I covered my ears and squeezed my eyes shut, shrieking *STOP, STOP, STOP,* except my throat had closed and I couldn't get the words out because I was drowning.

Coward. You're such a coward, Remy. Are you really going to fall apart and let them kill each other?

The thought centered me. Somehow, like all those times with Dean, I fought my way back to shore. With my eyes closed, I dropped my mental walls. I filled my mind with an image of me snapping a bone in my arm. Something small, but painful enough that it would get their attention. And then I let the *humming* begin.

"Stop!" Asher shouted at the same time Gabe said, "Remy, no!"

Arm intact, I opened my eyes and let the *humming* fade. They staggered a few feet in front of me, barely able to stay on their feet. Gabe lifted the hem of his T-shirt to wipe his bloodied nose. One of his eyes had already begun to swell shut. As for Asher, his torso would be covered in bruises from Gabe's fists. He had a fat lip, and two of his knuckles had split open and bled.

It was so senseless. So stupid and reckless.

I vibrated with rage. All of those hours spent healing Asher, all those injuries I'd taken from him, and he'd done this to his body without a thought. Why had I bothered? If they cared so little for their bodies, why should I give a damn?

"No more," I said. "I won't come between you more than I already have."

I started to walk away. I had to.

I'd hardly gone two steps when Asher asked in a bleak voice, "Are you in love with him?"

The bit of calm I'd found snapped off and blew into the wind.

"You idiot!" I shouted. I stalked up to him and shoved him as hard as I could. He hadn't expected it, and he sprawled on his backside. I stood over him. "Why would you do this? Why would you think . . ."

My voice tapered off, and I bit down on my tongue. Nothing had been resolved. These two had been best friends before Asher had met me. Everything was screwed up now because somehow I'd bonded to both of them. And Gabe thought it was my fault, that I'd been "driving the bus" even though I had no idea how. I ran my hands through my hair. I would fix this, even if it meant saying good-bye to both of them.

"Just answer me," Asher shouted. "Do you love him?"

"No!" Gabe winced, and I wanted to scream. Everything about this sucked. I took a deep breath. "I'm sorry, Gabe. You know I care about you. I just—"

He shook his head, cutting me off. "Don't lie to make me feel better. Please, don't. It makes it worse." He grimaced in pain and clutched his stomach.

"I'm not healing you," I told him. "You deserve whatever pain you're in. You were trying to provoke him into hitting you."

He gave me a half smile. "You have a mean streak, Remington." He shrugged, completely unrepentant. "What can I say? I'm pissed. He gets the girl." He turned to Asher and threw a handful of dirt at him. "You get the girl, asshole."

"You're in love with her."

Asher didn't sound angry anymore, and Gabe nodded in defeat. "Yeah."

Don't, Gabe.

He gave me a funny half smile. "I love you, Remy."

He hadn't said the words before. He'd known how I felt about Asher, and he'd been careful to avoid the words. Now they were out there in the world. There were no take-backs on "I love you." What was I supposed to say?

"Don't say anything. Please."

His grim expression made me ache for him. *I'm sorry if I made you think . . .*

"Stop. You were pretty clear about your feelings." Gabe struggled to his feet and waved me off when I tried to help him. "I think you need some time alone. Tell him I didn't do this on purpose. Make him understand. Do that for me?"

I nodded.

Gabe turned to Asher. "She should have bonded to me first, but she chose you. Over and over again, with every thought, she chose you."

With a sad smile, Gabe limped off.

"Remy?" Asher asked, confused.

"Oh Asher. You misjudged him." I sank down beside him and held out my hand. After a moment, he placed his palm over mine. "I think you need to know what happened after I saw you die."

CHAPTER THIRTY

*A*t some point, Asher lay back and I curled into his side. I told him everything, sometimes letting the images flood my mind when I couldn't find the words. One scene after another, I showed Asher what had happened while he'd been held hostage. The Protectors torturing me. Gabe arriving to break me out. How destroyed Gabe had been to find out his brother was dead. Our bonding happened when Gabe helped me heal myself. Later, my grandfather betrayed me, and Gabe stayed, even when I fought him every step of the way.

The sun had risen by the time I finished.

"You care about him," Asher said. "I can hear it in your thoughts."

I hesitated, unsure how to answer. Honesty, I decided. After everything that had happened, I owed him that.

"I do care for him," I confessed. Asher pulled away, putting more than physical distance between us. I rushed on. "He was there for me, Asher. I tried to make him go away. I was mean to him." I shook my head, remembering. "Geez, I intentionally hurt him. But he wouldn't go. Instead, he grieved with me. He was the only one who understood how I missed you. He kept me going when I thought about giving up."

"I get it," Asher said softly.

He stood, and I rose with him, placing both hands on his chest. He didn't pull away again, and I took that as a good sign.

"No, you really don't. I care about Gabe, but not like you think. When I thought you died, a part of me died, too." I smoothed a hand across Asher's shoulder, the warmth of his skin through his shirt reminding me that once upon a time we dreamed of a future together. That hadn't changed for me.

"When we found you, and I saw you that first time, I felt . . . whole. Like a missing piece of me had been found." Frustrated, I tossed about for the right words. "It sounds so lame to say I'm in love with you, but there it is. I wish I had more origin—"

Asher tipped my chin up and kissed me. My breath caught at the zing his touch sent through me. We would talk. There was more to be said, but at that moment I didn't care. I'd missed him and his lips and the way his kisses overwhelmed me. The weeks apart hadn't changed that, but we had changed. Could we get past the differences?

"There's one more thing. Gabe said . . . He thought that somehow I'm behind us bonding."

Asher ran a finger over his scar in thought, but didn't say anything.

I shrugged and shoved my hair behind my ear. "I don't know how or why, but I think I made this happen. I caused this mess, and I don't know how to make it stop."

What if he didn't believe me? What if that answer wasn't good enough?

He tugged on my hand, and I realized I was still pulling on my hair. I let go, and he took over curving the loose strands behind my ear. "Always worrying and taking the responsibility for everything," Asher said, with a smile in his voice. His breath tickled the hair near my ear, and I shivered. "You haven't changed that much."

Eavesdropping, as usual. You haven't changed that much, either.

He laughed, but sobered again a moment later. "Forgive me?" he asked, and I knew he didn't mean for listening to my thoughts.

"Maybe." I kissed his chin, and he tilted his head as I trailed my mouth to his neck and brushed my fingers across his whiskers. "If you promise to shave."

I squealed when he lifted me off my feet in a hug.

His smile was gentle. "We'll figure it out, *mo cridhe.*"

Asher wouldn't let me heal him.

"I'm not going to let you do it. You were right. We shouldn't have fought."

I gave up on arguing with him. I placed my shoulder under his arm so he could use me as a crutch, and we started walking back to his house. "What happened to you, Asher? You were so quick to believe Gabe and I abandoned you. What did they do to you?"

He didn't speak for a long time. "They screwed with my head. They would tell me you were dead one day, and then the next they would say they were torturing you somewhere else. They described the things they were doing to you. They said . . ." He stopped and cleared his throat. "Well, I didn't know what to believe. Then, a couple of weeks ago, this guy Alcais started coming around. He knew things about you, Remy. Things about your grandfather."

I scowled at the mention of Alcais's name. "He's how we found you. Gabe followed him to where they were keeping you. What did he say to you?"

"At first, he talked about how your powers worked and

tried to get me to tell him more. He said your grandfather had plans for you, that they were testing you. And then last week, he suddenly began to talk about your boyfriend, Gabe. About how the two of you couldn't keep your hands off of each other and how you were always texting each other."

That creep! Alcais had known Gabe wasn't my boyfriend, and he'd tortured Asher with those lies, probably his only way to get back at me. "He lied, Asher. My grandfather must have known that Gabe was your brother all this time."

"I know that now. I swear I didn't believe him until I overheard you and Gabe. Then it seemed like a confirmation of what I'd heard. That maybe I'd fooled myself into believing what I wanted. What reason could Alcais have had for lying about that? I feel stupid."

I couldn't read his expression, but his voice gave away his distress. I hesitated a moment, and then went with my gut, running my fingers through Asher's chopped hair. *This is why Alcais said those things.* I pictured how cruel he'd been, hurting Erin to get me to use my powers. Then I showed Alcais writhing on the ground after I'd taught him a lesson about using people to get at me. *He hated me, Asher.*

Asher's chin dropped to his chest. "I owe Gabe an apology, don't I?"

"I don't know. He's your brother. I think he gets it."

These last weeks we'd all blamed ourselves for things beyond our control. Wished we'd done things differently or been more than who we were. Me, Gabe, Asher. We could keep torturing ourselves, but in the end, we'd done the best we could.

I walked Asher back to his house, acting as his crutch. He wouldn't let me heal him, so I helped him to his room and tucked him into his ginormous bed. I stayed with him until he slept, and then I wandered downstairs.

I heard the sink running in the kitchen and followed the noise, expecting to find Lottie. Surprisingly, she was one of the few people not angry at me. She was so happy to have her brothers home that she'd forgiven all. I entered the kitchen and stumbled upon Gabe instead. He was drinking water from the tap. Bright moonlight spilled through the window, highlighting the bruised planes and shadows of his face.

"Ever heard of a glass?" I whispered.

Of course he'd heard me coming.

He smiled, unsurprised to see me leaning against the counter. "If I use a glass I have to wash it."

Despite his words, he filled a glass, drank from it, and then passed it to me. I took a sip and then hitched myself up to sit on the counter. I patted the spot next to me, and Gabe hopped up to sit beside me. I noticed that he took care not to touch me.

"You're leaving, aren't you?" I guessed.

Since we'd returned to Blackwell Falls, Gabe had distanced himself from me. Tonight, he'd confessed his feelings, knowing there was no going back to being just friends. He rarely did anything by accident.

"Can't get anything past you, Remington," he teased, but the humor sounded forced.

"Don't," I said. "Don't joke. It matters too much."

"Forgive me," he said in a hard voice. "My heart is breaking over here. I'm doing the best I can."

He started to hop off the counter, but I touched his arm. "Don't go."

I wasn't sure if I meant now or tomorrow. Maybe both.

"I have to. If I stay, I'll fight for you. He needs you more than ever now, but I'd fight dirty to win you, and it wouldn't matter that he's my brother."

I couldn't look away from the intensity of his gaze. "I'm not worth that, Gabe."

"Yes, you are, and it kills me that you don't see that."

Silence lapsed between us. I couldn't think of anything to say that I hadn't already said. I loved Asher. I'd made my choice. And he was right. Asher did need me now.

"Can I ask you something?"

I nodded.

"Do you think that if we'd met first, you would have chosen me?"

I sighed. "How am I supposed to answer that?"

I jumped off the counter, but Gabe grabbed my hand. He used it to tug me toward him until I pressed against his knees. He curled his fingers into my hair.

"Please, Remington. Give me this."

He wanted me to say that I would have chosen him, but I couldn't know that. If I lied, he would know. I felt trapped. His eyes took on that bleak look and his grip loosened. I couldn't bear it. I held his hand to my cheek and closed my eyes.

I pictured us meeting. It took ages for Gabe to get over his suspicions about me. When he did, we started dating. We held hands and did normal couple things, walking on the beach and going to the movies. But gradually, Gabe's rose-colored glasses fell away. He tired of my need to heal everyone in sight and having to defend me from every Protector or Healer that showed up in town. His senses began to return. One day he realized that I wasn't that special at all, and I understood that I'd become another of his toss away Sororitoys. He missed his freedom, and we fought all the time until one of us walked away.

Everything I showed him was exactly what I imagined would have happened if we'd met first. I told him our story without saying a word, and he gazed at me sadly when I opened my eyes.

It would never have worked. You forget that you never wanted me here.

"And you forget that you'd already picked Asher by the time we met."

"I wish you wouldn't go."

But he would. I knew that. It hurt, but I understood. I don't think I could have stood by and watched Asher love Lucy.

Gabe smiled, looking like the shark I remembered calling him once. "And you should go home. I'm about to do something that I wouldn't be able to forgive myself for tomorrow."

I scurried to the doorway.

"Remington."

I glanced over my shoulder.

Gabe's eyes flashed. "You're wrong about us. If you were mine, I would never have let you walk away without a fight. Good night."

I ran all the way home. It was a long time before I fell asleep.

The next morning Asher called to say that Gabe had left in the middle of the night. They'd talked. Gabe wasn't angry at Asher, but he needed time to get past this. To get over me. And he couldn't see us together and do that. So he'd left with the promise to call when he'd landed somewhere.

I missed him already, and I thought Asher knew. Maybe that was why he'd chosen to give me the news over the phone, where he couldn't read my mind and feel how sad I was that his brother had gone.

CHAPTER THIRTY-ONE

*M*y family sat around the living room watching a movie. My dad had talked us into putting on the *Rocky Horror Picture Show*. He and Laura had gone to live screenings of the movie when they'd been dating. They described shadowcasts where amateur performers acted out the film on a stage below the screen, and the whole audience had interacted, throwing objects and screaming things on cue. He and Laura demonstrated the audience participation parts while Lucy and I threw popcorn at them. Then they started doing the Time Warp dance, and I howled with laughter.

It was a perfect night, the first I'd had since Gabe had left three days ago. He hadn't called Asher yet, and I tried not to worry about him.

The movie credits were rolling when my phone rang.

"Whoa. Sounds like you're having fun over there."

My stepmom was demonstrating the Time Warp again and had talked Lucy into trying it. They had no idea my dad filmed the whole thing on his phone. I laughed, and he pressed a finger to his lips.

"We just finished watching a movie. Want to come over?"

"I have a better idea. Meet me in the labyrinth?" Asher asked.

We'd hardly had two minutes alone since we'd been back. Neither of us had wanted to stray too far from our families, but that meant that our time without them had been cut short. Some small part of me wondered if he blamed me for bonding with Gabe, even though we hadn't spoken of it again. Eventually, we'd have to talk about it, but for now . . . I just wanted to be with Asher.

"Ten minutes?"

"Last one there has to keep their walls up," he challenged.

"Oh, you're on!" I said. That meant there would be kissing. I grinned.

I hung up a second later to find my dad filming me, while Lucy and Laura watched.

"What do you think, guys? Does she have a date with Asher?"

My sister and stepmom answered my dad with catcalls, and I flushed. I couldn't help laughing, too. I went up to my bedroom to change into something besides sweats, while they decided to break out the Monopoly game. Then I waited by my window, watching for Asher as he entered the labyrinth at Townsend Park. The sun set late in September, and I could see everything below. A blur swept through the trees, and I raced down the stairs to go after him.

Exhilarated, I hit the tree line and zipped along my favorite trail. It led straight to the center of the labyrinth, and I laughed as I reached the clearing, anticipating being in Asher's arms.

The laughter froze in my throat. Xavier and another man had pinned Asher on his stomach. Xavier had a fist in Asher's hair and shoved his cheek into the dirt. Desperation and fear lit his face as he tried to fight back. Xavier and the other man simply laughed.

"Remy."

The voice stopped me when I would have gone to Asher. I glanced around and found my grandfather seated on a bench. A stone dropped and landed on my chest.

It had been too easy, I realized. I should have known we hadn't really gotten away. I would never be free of this nightmare. I'd tried to think of my ability to heal as a gift, but it just brought tragedy on me and my family. On Asher.

I stared into his eyes. They were bleak and I understood that he saw no way out of this.

My grandfather called to me again and patted the seat beside his leg. "Come here."

It wasn't a request, and I had no choice but to obey. Maybe he didn't know about my family. Maybe he'd followed Asher. I had to believe that and do what I could to keep them safe. Seconds later, I perched on the bench as far from Franc as I could get. I wished I'd never met the bastard.

"What are you doing here, Franc?" I whispered.

"I've been watching you," he answered, bracing his elbows on his thighs. "You and your family. It wasn't what I expected." He paused, studying my features. "A father. A sister. And a Protector boyfriend. Was anything you said true?"

I bowed my head in defeat for a moment. He knew. "What do you want me to say? Mom warned me not to tell you about me or my father. She didn't trust you." My voice broke as Xavier did something to hurt Asher. "She wasn't wrong, was she?"

My grandfather made a gesture at Xavier, and the Protector eased up slightly with a dark scowl in my direction. I should have made sure he died in that fire. Why hadn't I gone back to check? *Stupid, Remy!*

"Why are you here, Franc?" I asked again.

"I'm here for you," he said simply.

"You're going to kill me."

"That's entirely up to you." He sighed. "We need you. Our people need you. You're going to come back and submit to the testing. You'll do everything we ask so we figure out how to beat the Protectors."

A dull throb pounded in my head. He meant to make me a lab rat after all. "And them?" I glanced at Xavier and the other Protector. "They're going to go along with your plan and betray their own kind. Why would they do that?"

Xavier didn't look upset at my accusation. He smiled.

"Because they get you," Franc said. My eyes rounded in horror, and he rushed to continue. "It's not what you think. I'm not a monster. You're my granddaughter, after all. I would never let them kill you."

"Then what?" I choked out.

"All the other Healers die when the Protectors steal their energy. But not you. You're able to heal yourself. If you submit to them, and do what they ask, nobody else has to die. You'll be doing this for the Healers, Remy, not for me. Girls like Erin will be able to go out and do amazing things. Who knows how many lives you'll save? And it won't cost you much. After what you did for Melinda, I know you can do this. Sure, you might take a few days to heal in between Protectors, but I promise to take care of you. You can do this. Think of the good you'll be doing."

He believed what he was saying. His face shone with it, his lips tilted in a gentle, encouraging smile. In his mind, he'd found a simple solution to an ugly problem. I would be a savior to the Healers but for one snag: the future he described for me sounded brutal and soul-shattering. My grandfather would make me into something far worse than a lab rat. My throat ached with unshed tears. This was my mother's last gift. She'd sent me to him to be "safe." Had she understood what his idea of safe would be?

My mind raced, but I couldn't think of a way out. Maybe it was time to stop fighting this. Hadn't I been hurtling toward this future all along? At least if I left with them now, my family might be safe.

Asher choked and screamed, "Remy, no! Run!" He groaned when Xavier struck him in the back of the head.

Franc sent Asher a probing glance, as if he were a thing to be studied. "I can't let him live. You know that, right?"

I sucked in a breath and begged. "*Please.* I'll go with you. I'll do whatever you want. The tests, the Healers . . . I won't fight any of it. Please just let him go."

Asher began to fight in earnest, and Xavier and the other man took turns kicking him until he lay there, inhaling dirt with every breath. I gripped the edge of the stone bench to keep myself still when everything in me wanted to go to him. Franc would never allow it, though.

He placed a hand over mine, and I fought not to shove him away. "I know you're angry now, but you'll see this is the right way. These Protectors have tricked you into thinking they're the good guys, but we both know they're not. Protectors are incapable of good."

"You know what I am," I said in a flat tone.

He nodded. "I do. I'm so sorry, child, that it's come to this. Before you can come back to us, we need a show of loyalty. I need to know that you'll never call yourself an ally to another Protector again. You must choose sides."

He sounded so right and sure that a shiver slithered down my spine. "I have Protector blood in my veins, Franc. How am I supposed to un-choose that? Kill myself?"

Calm and sure, Franc yanked me to my feet. "No, you're going to kill your father."

My grandfather refused to listen to my pleas. He calmly explained that my father and the Blackwells were the enemy. My mother had been sick, and she hadn't trained me to know the difference.

"I blame myself for leaving her vulnerable and prey for your father."

"She loved him," I answered, my throat hoarse. "She said so. If not for me, she would have stayed with him."

His muscles bunched, and I thought he would slap me for that. He gathered himself and laid a hand on my cheek. "Lies. They've tricked you, Remy. You have to leave these people behind before they destroy you. Choose."

Choose what? A life of tortured servitude? A life without Asher or my family? A life in which I'd murdered my father?

"No," I whispered. "I kill Ben. You kill Asher. I lose no matter what."

Franc's hand moved, and he grasped my chin in his fingers, squeezing until I grimaced. "You forget about your sister." A tear trickled down my cheek, and he wiped it away. "I'm not cruel, Remy. Your sister and her mother can live in ignorant bliss when we're gone. We've watched her. She's a powerless child, and I don't want to hurt her. But I would if it meant keeping you. So choose."

Somebody would die today no matter what I did. I closed my eyes and said nothing. I didn't have to tell my grandfather that I was caving. He knew.

He ordered me to text Ben and ask him to come to the center of the labyrinth. Then he took my phone away, and we waited. I couldn't look at Asher and do what had to be done, so I averted my face and stared at the sky. Minutes later footsteps crunched in dirt and brushed past leaves. My father called my name.

Everything in me wanted to scream, to warn him to run.

Franc squeezed my arm until I thought the bone would

break. I bit my lip until Xavier pressed a foot to Asher's neck.

"Here!" I choked out.

I stood, listening to the steps coming ever closer. "How do you want me to do this?" I asked my grandfather bitterly. "I can't exactly take him with my bare hands."

He reached into a pocket and pulled out a knife. He'd thought of everything. He handed the blade to me and threatened, "We can make Asher's death short or we can draw it out until he begs us to die. Remember that."

Then he touched my chin, as if to encourage me, and my stomach heaved.

I gave a choppy nod and cradled the knife in my palm. Using it on my grandfather wouldn't save Asher, and I would never be able to take out two Protectors on my own. Franc knew that, had counted on it.

Too soon, Ben appeared at the same opening I'd come through. He smiled when he saw me, and then the look faded as he took in the scene and the gun that my grandfather now trained on him.

"What the hell?" he asked.

I shuffled a few halting steps toward him, hiding the knife in my hand.

"Remy?"

Sobbing, I stood in front of my father, close enough to do as Franc demanded. My father trusted me, and I could kill him. He would never see it coming. Would never imagine I was capable. He would do anything to keep Lucy safe, though. I knew that. He would forgive me for this betrayal if he understood the reason behind it.

I stared into my father's navy eyes, and he gazed back.

"Are you okay, sweetheart?" he asked. "Did they hurt you?"

Hurt me? What a stupid joke.

"Kill him!" my grandfather shouted, and I jumped.

"Choose, or watch as every member of your family dies, beginning with Lucy."

Understanding lit my father's face when he glanced down at the knife. He didn't panic, yell at me, or try to fight me off. He reached for my hand and held it in his, but he didn't take the knife from me.

"It's okay, Remy. You do what you have to. I trust you."

He grasped enough to know that Franc was forcing me to do this against my will. That other lives were at stake. I gripped the hilt of the knife. I turned to face Asher where he lay on the ground, bruised and bloody. I willed him to read my mind, to give me his blessing for what I would do.

And he answered with the slightest nod.

I flipped the knife over and handed it to my father. He took it with a bewildered expression.

"I won't do it, Franc. I am a Healer *and* a Protector. You can't cut that side of me away by killing the people I love. So do what you're going to do to me. I don't care anymore. I won't let you make me a monster."

Betrayal twisted Franc's features, and he raised the gun.

"Dad? Are you out there? Mom needs your help getting the game out of the closet."

The forest froze. Lucy shouted to my father from one of the trails, heading right toward us. I couldn't hide my terror, and Franc saw it all.

He would use her against me.

Panicked, I swung about to face my father. The light glinted on the knife in his hand, and an awful idea popped into my head. Without me, this could all end. Without me, this would all go away, and my grandfather would have no need to kill my sister. My father might never forgive me, but I couldn't see another way.

Sacrifice one for the many. Maybe I was like Franc after all.

"I'm so sorry, Dad," I whispered.

I grabbed his outstretched hand and jerked the knife toward me, plunging it into my belly. It sliced through my skin with less resistance than I expected. Warm blood gushed out, and my stomach burned.

"No!" Franc shrieked behind me.

My father stared down at our hands. Shock gave way to horror, and his mouth opened in a silent shout. He dropped his hand and stumbled back. The knife remained, blood welling around the hilt.

It felt like long minutes had passed since I'd heard Lucy, but mere seconds had ticked by. I shoved my father aside, and he fell to the ground. I could do this. I could stop my grandfather if it was the last thing I did. I had to for my father and Lucy and Asher. Franc saw the knife. He hesitated a moment, lowering the gun, and that was all I needed. I gathered my energy, praying my power would work without touch. I imagined my injury becoming Franc's, and sent my energy flashing toward him.

The air crackled and hissed, and red sparks shot through the air. Franc cried out and blood spread across his shirt in a brilliant red stain. He pressed a hand to his side. In the distance, Lucy screamed and called out for help, her voice fading as she ran away from us.

Xavier and the other Protector readied to attack me. I held out a bloody hand in invitation and leveled a dare at Xavier. He knew I could transfer my injuries by touch. Would he chance coming near me?

I gathered what energy I had left and let it swirl in the air.

Xavier wheeled about and ran. The other man stared at Franc for two seconds and then took off after him.

All my bravado crumpled, and I collapsed to my knees, holding a hand to my stomach and trying to remember how to breathe. Franc took a few stumbling steps back-

ward and almost tripped over the bench before sinking
down onto it. The gun fell to the ground.

"Asher!"

He rolled to his side, but didn't lift his head. "I'm okay,
Remy. You?"

"Stabbed," I said.

"Ah, the usual, then."

I snorted and immediately regretted it when my stomach muscles burned like an unholy fire.

My father rose to his feet beside me, slowly approached
Franc, and took the gun. "Who the hell are you?" he
asked.

Ben's eyes narrowed, and I thought he might be considering shooting Franc.

I said, "Dad, meet my grandfather. Granddad, meet my
father."

"Stop it!" my father shouted.

I jerked and grimaced.

"Just don't. Don't joke," he said in a softer voice. "I
stabbed you, and you're acting like . . ." He swallowed and
gathered himself. "I'm going to get an ambulance, and
when I get back somebody had better tell me what the hell
is going on."

He handed me the gun. "Will you be okay?"

I nodded. He smoothed the hair off my forehead and
then was gone, crashing through the trees. His expression
lingered in my mind. I'd freaked him out. Fear and shock
had drained the color from his face, and his hand shook.
When I couldn't hear him anymore, I shrieked in frustration. He would hate me now that he knew what I was.

"He didn't know about you," Franc said in wonder.

"Why couldn't you leave me alone?" I despaired.

He didn't answer. Tires squealed in the distance. Too
soon to be an ambulance. I gripped the gun tighter. Xavier
appeared and helped Franc up. They disappeared into the

forest in seconds, heading back toward the road with Xavier helping my grandfather along.

I flattened on the ground, my energy reserves depleted.

"Remy?" That was Lucy's voice shouting from the edge of the forest. "Is Dad with you?"

"No! He ran back to the house to get help!"

It sounded like Lucy was at the house. She should have bumped into Ben.

An engine started on the road and a car pulled away. I listened with half an ear.

Except the Protectors had run off before Ben.

"Ben!" That was Laura yelling. I pulled myself up and saw Asher doing the same. Something was very wrong.

A crash thundered and echoed through the forest, followed by the squeal of those tires. The Protectors had hit something when making their getaway. I stared at Asher, and his eyes filled with equal dread.

And then Lucy's screams exploded into the evening air, shattering what was left of my world.

CHAPTER THIRTY-TWO

"*L*ucy, we have to go."

We lived at the hospital the first week.

Machines and tubes kept Laura alive, and we were terrified to leave her. Lucy and I watched over her, but she wouldn't wake up. *Head-induced trauma that had led to a coma,* the doctors said. I'd tried to heal her, but nothing happened. Head wounds had always been my nemesis. I hadn't been able to heal my mother, either.

As soon as the doctors in Blackwell Falls had stabilized Laura, we'd made arrangements to move her to a hospital in Chicago under a new name. The better to hide her from the Protectors. I'm not sure how Asher had moved that mountain, but I would forever be grateful. Who knew how many Protectors were crawling all over our hometown by now?

They had taken Ben. The Protectors had forced him into their car and driven off. And then—by accident or on purpose?—they'd struck Laura as she'd run after them. Lucy had watched the whole thing and spent too much time rocking silently in her seat, lost in her thoughts.

A week had passed, though, and we couldn't chance staying put any longer. The Protectors or my grandfather would come after us, and we needed to find a safer place to hide. Lottie had surprised me by volunteering to stay with our mother. When I questioned Asher, he simply said, "You and Lucy can't stay. Your mom can't be moved. Either I stay or she does. She wants to stay."

Rather, she didn't want to be stuck with me. I couldn't blame her. So Lottie and our mom would stay in Chicago, while Lucy and Asher ran with me.

I touched my sister's shoulder, wishing I could make that shell-shocked look disappear from her face.

Lucy glanced up with bruised eyes. "I can't leave her. What if she wakes up and she's alone? What if—"

"Lottie promised to check on her. You know we can't stay."

They would use her against me. My friends and family would be little more than collateral to control me. We had to run and figure out our next steps.

"When we find somewhere safe to hide, we'll bring her to us if we need to. But she'll be awake by then. You'll see."

I put an arm around Lucy's waist when she stood. We took turns saying good-bye to Laura, but our only answer was the beeping of the machines.

Lucy's steps dragged as we left the room, and she tucked her head down. Outside the hospital, Asher and Lottie waited, saying their good-byes. She shook her head at my asking look. Still no word from Gabe. He had no idea what had happened. At least he hadn't been in danger.

Lottie helped Lucy into the backseat of the car, and Asher stopped in front of me.

I kept wondering what I could have done differently in the forest. Had there been a way to avoid all of this? Asher rested his forehead against mine. We'd healed our injuries, but it hardly seemed to matter anymore.

Would we ever see Laura or my father again?

"Ready?" Asher said.

I nodded, and he took my hand. We climbed in the car.

Within minutes, the hospital and then the city disappeared behind us, and I stared out the back window long after there was nothing to see.

Lucy's shoulders shook as she hunched down and cried.

I stroked her hair. "Everything will be okay, Lucy. I promise."

And I prayed I wasn't lying as we left everything we knew behind.

FOOD FOR THOUGHT

1. At the beginning of the novel, Remy is determined to seek out her grandfather despite the protests of her friends. Why is it so important to her to find him? Are her actions brave or rash?

2. In *Touched,* Remy was dealing with the trauma of the physical and emotional abuse her stepfather Dean and her mother inflicted on her. How has she changed with Dean and her mother out of the picture? Are there ways in which she hasn't changed? How does her past abuse affect her relationship with Asher, her family, and the Healer community?

3. Remy often makes decisions based on pure instinct, while Asher and Lucy challenge her to think before she acts. Who do you agree with? How has the habit of going with her instincts helped her or harmed her?

4. Remy believes in healing people she can help, even when it causes her harm. Is her ability a gift or a curse? If you had her ability, how would you decide who to heal or what injuries to take on?

5. Remy and Gabe start out as enemies in *Touched.* How does their relationship change in Pushed? What reasons would Gabe have for helping Remy?

6. The Healers have formed a community after years of running from the Protectors. What advantages are there to sticking together? What are the dangers? If you were

Remy, would you prefer to be a part of the community or to live outside of it?

7. Remy keeps her abilities a secret from her father and stepmother. How does this decision impact their relationships? Is she making the right choice? How do you think her parents would respond if they found out the truth?

8. Asher and Gabe bring out different sides of Remy's character. What are these differences? How does each character become a stronger or better person when they begin to change? Are any of the changes negative?

9. Remy realizes that people have been able to manipulate her because of her desire to belong to a family. Where does her desire come from? Have your emotions ever been manipulated by someone because you wanted to belong?

10. Remy's grandfather believes that he's doing the right thing for the Healer community. Should an individual be sacrificed for the greater good of the many?

SOUNDTRACKS

When I begin a book, I create a playlist. The songs I pick fit the mood of the novel, or the lyrics may reflect a certain moment or character. As I write, I listen to these songs over and over. By the time I finish a book I've listened to each song upwards of 100 times each. They become so much a part of my process that they feel like the backbone of the story. Below is a partial list of songs that I listened to while writing *Touched* and *Pushed*. A lot of these bands may be new to you, but I hope you check them out

Touched

Song (Artist)
Because of You (Kelly Clarkson)
Waiting on an Angel (Ben Harper)
Daughters (John Mayer)
Breakable (Ingrid Michaelson)
Yes I'm Cold (Chris Bathgate)
Trouble Is a Friend (Lenka)
You're Not Sorry (CSI Remix / Taylor Swift)
Hangin' by a Thread (Jann Arden)
Falling (Tyrone Wells)
Inside My Head (Clare Reynolds)
Come Down to Me (Saving Jane)
The Death of Us (The New Amsterdams)
Hero/Heroine (Boys Like Us)
Falling (Keri Noble)
Next to You (Tim Easton)

Closer (Kings of Leon)
Hang On (Isobel Campbell & Mark Lanegan)
So Long Sweet Misery (Brett Dennen)
Winter Song (Sara Bareilles & Ingrid Michaelson)
Arrivals (Aqualung)
I Would Die for You (Jann Arden & Sarah
   McLachlan)
That'll Be the Plan (Daniel Martin Moore)
The Night Will Go As Follows (The Spill Canvas)
All I Can Do (Tyrone Wells)
Don't Give Up (Clare Reynolds)

Pushed

The Light Song (The Homes)
Come Over Here (Sarah Bettens)
Someone to Fall Back On (Aly Michalka & I Can't
   Go On, I'll Go On)
The Fear You Won't Fall (Joshua Radin)
The Road Knows (The Homes)
Stay Over (The Rescues)
Youthless (Beck)
Into Dust (Mazzy Star)
Safe & Sound (Taylor Swift)
Sit with Me Tonight (Garrison Star)
Jungle (Emma Louise)
The Trapeze Swinger (Iron & Wine)
The Only One (The Black Keys)
Lonely Hands (Angus & Julia Stone)
Fever (Adam Freeland & Sarah Vaughan—Verve
   Remixed 3)
Run (Katherine McPhee & *Smash* Cast)
Firefly (Ed Sheeran)
Call It Off (Tegan and Sara)
The House That Built Me (Miranda Lambert)

Somebody That I Used to Know (Gotye)
Free (Graffiti6)
If Not Now, When? (Incubus)
Falling Awake (Gary Jules)
Live Forever (Drew Holcomb & The Neighbors)
Sail (AWOLNATION)

The Sense Thieves series continues in

IGNITED

Turn the page for a special sneak peek!

A KTeen trade paperback in June 2014

CHAPTER ONE

I hid in the alley, painted in shadows and praying that I hadn't stepped in whatever caused the putrid scent burning my nose. Across the street, a lone pay phone—the first one I'd seen in the last hundred miles—stood under the glaring spotlight of a street lamp. *Two more minutes, Remy,* I promised myself. *Two more minutes of cowering, and then I run for the phone.*

Warm fingers pressed into my back, seeking comfort and offering it at the same time. My half sister, Lucy, waited behind me, and I could feel how she shook. Talk of fear rarely entered our conversations these days, but after four months of living like hunted animals, I knew what horrible thoughts might be running through her mind. I had to remind myself that she was only seventeen. I was only a year older, but my experiences had aged me compared to her. My fingers trembled, too, around the knife I gripped, and I used a cloth to wipe my warm blood from the blade. I lifted my thin T-shirt to tuck the weapon into the back of my jeans' waistband and pressed a hand to my stomach when the torn muscles protested. The part of the plan where I had to be injured sucked.

"Well? See anything?" Lucy whispered into my ear, peering around me with wide brown eyes. Her heart-shaped face glowed white against her curly black hair, and she looked small and scared.

I shook my head and tucked a loose blond strand back under my ski cap. My bones had frozen some time ago in the frigid January air, and I shoved my fingers into my bulky coat pockets to thaw them. Then I dug deep for courage like it was buried treasure. "It's time. Wait here. If anything happens or Asher signals, you run. You hear me?"

My husky voice sounded harsher than normal as I tried to swallow my emotions.

"Got it, Buffy."

She stumbled over the joke, her voice flat, but it didn't matter. That my sister could attempt to joke about me being a heroine nearly killed me. I could be brave for her. I lifted my chin, imagining my spine made of iron rebar, and looked down at her one last time before I stepped out of the shadows and onto the sidewalk where anyone could see me. Nothing happened. No Healers or Protectors jumped out at me. Maybe we really had given them the slip two days ago. Encouraged, I looked both ways down the deserted street.

Maple, Alabama, could be called many things, but nobody would call it a party town. Home to a whopping population of 863 people, the town had one stoplight, a gas station, a diner, and a few small businesses lining the main street where we stood. Everything had shut down around six, as people went home to their families. As far as I could tell, Lucy and I were the only ones out on the street. Well, the two of us, and Asher who hid somewhere nearby.

Earlier today, the three of us had crashed for a few hours at a tiny motel sixty miles down the highway. Then we had packed our few belongings into the car, knowing that we might have to run in a hurry after I made this call. There was a very good possibility that our enemies were hidden, waiting for me to come out into the open. I shivered again, and then rolled my shoulders back.

Now or never, Remy.

I marched into the street, walking straight though it sent spikes of pain to my stomach. My steps echoed, and the sound encouraged me. That meant I would hear others approaching if they tried to sneak up on me. I cast another glance around when I reached the phone. Then I picked up the receiver, dropped some coins in the slot, and dialed the number that I knew by heart.

I counted three rings before a male voice answered. "Hello."

Memories crashed and tumbled into each other at the sound of my grandfather's deep voice. I once thought we could be family, but François Marche was incapable of loving anyone.

"Hello?" he repeated.

I swallowed, suddenly mute.

"Remy." He almost purred my name, the confident bastard. "I wondered how long it would take you to call. You lasted longer than I thought you would."

Four months. It had been four months since I'd seen him, heard his voice, watched him threaten my family. My nails formed half-moon circles in my palms when my hands tightened into fists.

"Franc," I choked out.

"How are you, sweetheart?"

The fake concern reminded me of how naïve I'd been, taken in by this huge hulk of a man towering over six and a half feet tall with crazy white hair and a booming laugh. My grandfather called me "sweetheart" in his old voice, the charming voice, as if he hadn't destroyed my life.

I buried my rage, keeping my voice light. "I'm a little tired from ditching your guys so often, but I can't complain. How about you? Sacrificed any Healers to your friends recently?"

God, if the Healer community he led knew how he'd betrayed them to the Protectors, they might rise up against him. Franc rationalized that sacrificing a few of his Healers to the Protectors would save the larger community.

Franc sighed. "I do what I have to. It doesn't have to be like this, Remy. You could stop it all."

Take their place, he meant. Unlike full-blooded Healers, I wouldn't die from the things the Protectors would do to me. Bile swam up the back of my throat as I pictured Asher as he'd been when we rescued him from my grandfather. Tortured, broken, hopeless. That would be my life if I caved to my grandfather's demands.

"Never," I whispered with revulsion.

"Think about it. Nobody else has to die."

Disgust and fury sharpened my words. "I have thought about it. I've had nightmares about it since the day you suggested it. You remember that day, right? Because I do. By the way, how's your stomach?"

Franc had tried to force me to kill my father, but I'd escaped using the only weapon I had against them—transferring my injuries to those who hurt me. The last time I'd seen my grandfather and his Protector allies, they'd been bleeding out from a stomach wound I'd inflicted on myself.

"Healed," he bit off when I wondered if I'd gone too far. "You're more powerful than I gave you credit for. You caused me a lot of pain."

Smug satisfaction curved my mouth.

"You're lucky I'm not a man who believes in petty revenge. I don't think your father would survive what I'd do to him."

I gripped the cold metal ledge beneath the phone to stay upright. I had to try twice before I got the words past the golf ball wedged in my throat. "He's . . . He's alive?"